Praise for
Rooftops of Tehran

"*Rooftops of Tehran* is a richly rendered first novel about courage, sacrifice, and the bonds of friendship and love. In clear, vivid detail, Mahbod Seraji opens the door to the fascinating world of Iran and provides a revealing glimpse into the life and customs of a country on the verge of a revolution. A captivating read."

> —Gail Tsukiyama, author of *The Street of a Thousand Blossoms* and *The Samurai's Garden*

"In his haunting debut novel, Mahbod Seraji brings humor and humanity to a story of secret love in the brutal last days of the Shah. Set against the background of repression that launched the Iranian revolution, Pasha and Zari's story shows that love and hope among the young thrive even in the most oppressive of times. Seraji is a striking new talent." —Sandra Dallas, author of *Tallgrass*

"*Rooftops of Tehran* combines a coming-of-age love story with a compelling tale of struggle against dictatorship. You learn a lot about Iranian culture while coming to understand characters with universal appeal. This would make a great movie."

> —Reese Erlich, author of *The Iran Agenda: The Real Story of U.S. Policy and the Middle East Crisis*

"*Rooftops of Tehran* evoked many memories, along with tears and smiles, of starry nights on rooftops, long-lost loves, and intense, passionate feelings of anger at the injustices and the absurd excesses of the Pahlavi regime."

> —Nahid Mozaffari, editor of *Strange Times, My Dear: The PEN Anthology of Contemporary Iranian Literature*

continued...

"*Rooftops of Tehran* takes an uncommon and refreshing view of Iran and reveals how an American immigrant is born out of a young foreigner's desperation for self-determination and social freedom."

—Susanne Pari, author of *The Fortune Catcher*

"What a profound pleasure to discover such solid storytelling and splendid prose in a debut novel. With the voice of a poet, Seraji has told a universal tale of love, loss, and ultimately of hope. It is this hope, most of all, that will linger long after the last page is turned. Thank God for authors like Seraji, who show us that no matter how distant apart our worlds may be, in the humanness of our hearts, we are all united."

—William Kent Krueger, author of *Red Knife* and the Cork O'Connor series

"A stirring story about the loss of innocence, *Rooftops of Tehran* reveals a side of Iran understood by few Westerners. An ambitious first novel—full of humor, originality, and meaning."

—John Shors, author of *Beneath a Marble Sky* and *Beside A Burning Sea*

Rooftops of Tehran

Mahbod Seraji

To Mahsa, Tiana & Shahriar—
I love you guys!
Mahb.

NEW AMERICAN LIBRARY

New American Library
Published by New American Library, a division of
Penguin Group (USA) Inc., 375 Hudson Street,
New York, New York 10014, USA
Penguin Group (Canada), 90 Eglinton Avenue East, Suite 700, Toronto,
Ontario M4P 2Y3, Canada (a division of Pearson Penguin Canada Inc.)
Penguin Books Ltd., 80 Strand, London WC2R 0RL, England
Penguin Ireland, 25 St. Stephen's Green, Dublin 2,
Ireland (a division of Penguin Books Ltd.)
Penguin Group (Australia), 250 Camberwell Road, Camberwell, Victoria 3124,
Australia (a division of Pearson Australia Group Pty. Ltd.)
Penguin Books India Pvt. Ltd., 11 Community Centre, Panchsheel Park,
New Delhi - 110 017, India
Penguin Group (NZ), 67 Apollo Drive, Rosedale, North Shore 0632,
New Zealand (a division of Pearson New Zealand Ltd.)
Penguin Books (South Africa) (Pty.) Ltd., 24 Sturdee Avenue,
Rosebank, Johannesburg 2196, South Africa

Penguin Books Ltd., Registered Offices:
80 Strand, London WC2R 0RL, England

First published by New American Library,
a division of Penguin Group (USA) Inc.

First Printing, May 2009
10   9   8   7   6   5   4   3   2   1

 REGISTERED TRADEMARK—MARCA REGISTRADA

LIBRARY OF CONGRESS CATALOGING-IN-PUBLICATION DATA

Seraji, Mahbod.
Rooftops of Tehran/Mahbod Seraji.
p. cm.
ISBN 978-0-451-22681-5
1. Tehran (Iran)—Fiction.   I. Title.
PS3619.E7356R66   2009
813'.6—dc22   2008031902

Set in Warnock Pro • Designed by Alissa Amell
Printed in the United States of America

PUBLISHER'S NOTE

This is a work of fiction. Names, characters, places, and incidents either are the product of the author's imagination or are used fictitiously, and any resemblance to actual persons, living or dead, business establishments, events, or locales is entirely coincidental.

The publisher does not have any control over and does not assume any responsibility for author or third-party Web sites or their content.

Acknowledgments

Thank you to Marian Clark, Tim and Sue Ellen Kane, Sudi Rafian, Kevin Daniels, Kim Levin, Nancee McVey, Laura Hubber, Mojgan Seraji, Mehri Safari, Kamran Heydarpour, Donnell Green, Debbie Shotwell, Nancy Fallah, and Mauni Seraji for your enthusiastic cheers during the course of my writing this book. Each of you, in your own unique way, made me believe that I had a story worth sharing.

Stephanie Howse: my heartfelt gratitude for your keen perspectives and insights, and for the ways in which you keep helping.

My dear Sepi: Your insight helped me unravel Pasha better than I ever could by myself. And thanks for cheering me on all the away to the end.

Thank you to my agents, Danielle Egan-Miller and Joanna Mac-Kenzie of Browne & Miller Literary Associates, for your faithful determination, for never giving up, and for being the catalysts for a life-changing experience. Thanks, too, to Alec McDonald for your editorial help and to Mariana Fisher for your early enthusiasm.

And finally, to Ellen Edwards, my gifted and diligent editor: Thank you for taking a chance on me, and for taking on the responsibility of sharing my book with the rest of the world. Working with you has been the ultimate learning experience.

I hear someone's voice chanting, and the repetitive verses lap like water at the edge of my consciousness.

> *If I had a book, I would read it.*
> *If I had a song, I would sing it.*

I look around until I see an old man standing a few meters away chanting in a steady, empty tone. The place does not look familiar to me. The blue robe that covers my body, the wheelchair I am sitting in, the sunlight creeping between the shades that warms me—all feel strange.

> *If I knew a dance, I would dance it.*
> *If I knew a rhyme, I would chant it.*
> *If I had a life, I would risk it.*
> *If I could be free, I would chance it.*

Outside in the yard, men of all shapes and ages shuffle around in blue robes. There is something peculiar about each of them. They look lost.

Suddenly a surge of emotions fills my chest and rushes into my throat. A little nurse with a kind, full face that resembles an apple runs up to me and plants her hands on my shoulders and screams, "Help me out here, help me out!" A man in a white uniform runs over and tries to hold me down.

"Stay in your chair, honey. Stay in your chair," Apple Face shouts, which means I must be moving. I focus on sitting still, and look toward the old man on the far side of the room. He is gazing at me as he frantically repeats his mantra:

If I had a horse, I would ride it.
If I had a horse, I would ride it.
If I had a horse . . .

I am taken to a room with a bed, and Apple Face says, "I'm going to give you a sedative to make you feel better, darling."

I feel a pinch in my arm, and suddenly my head and arms become unbearably heavy and my eyes slide shut.

1

My Friends, My Family, and My Alley

Sleeping on the roof in the summer is customary in Tehran. The dry heat of the day cools after midnight, and those of us who sleep on the rooftops wake with the early sun on our faces and fresh air in our lungs. My mother is strictly against it, and reminds me each evening, "Hundreds of people fall off the roofs every year." My best friend, Ahmed, and I trade hidden smiles with each warning, then climb the stairs to spend our nights under stars that seem close enough to touch. The alley below settles into a patchwork of streetlight, shadow, and sound. A car hums slowly down the deserted street, cautious not to wake anyone, as a stray dog in the distance releases a string of officious barks.

"I hear your mother calling," Ahmed mumbles in the dark. I smile, aiming a good-natured kick that he easily rolls away from.

Our house is the tallest in the neighborhood, which makes our roof an ideal spot for stargazing. In fact, naming stars for our friends and the people we love is one of our favorite pastimes.

"Does everyone have a star?" Ahmed asks.

"Only good people."

"And the better you are the bigger your star, right?"

"Bigger and brighter," I say, as I do every time he asks the same question.

"And your star guides you when you're in trouble, right?"

"Your star and the stars of the people you love."

Ahmed closes one eye and lifts his thumb to block out one of the brighter stars. "I'm tired of looking at your big fat face."

"Shut up and go to sleep then," I say, laughing, letting my gaze relax into the velvety emptiness between each pinprick of light. My eyes travel down the sky until they rest on the familiar rise and fall of the Alborz Mountains, which serpentine between the desert and the blue-green Caspian Sea. I get distracted for a moment trying to decide if the darkness is black or so deeply blue that it just appears inky in comparison.

"I wonder why people are so unabashedly afraid of the dark," I ponder, and Ahmed chuckles. I know without asking that he is amused by my eccentric vocabulary, the product of a lifetime of heavy reading. My father pulled Ahmed and me aside one day and asked me, in front of family friends and relatives, what I thought life was about. I promptly said that life was a random series of beautifully composed vignettes, loosely tied together by a string of characters and time. My father's friends actually applauded, much to my embarrassment. Ahmed leaned over and whispered that I would soon be inaugurated as the oldest seventeen-year-old in the world, especially if I kept saying things like "unabashedly" and "beautifully composed vignettes."

Ahmed and I have just finished the eleventh grade and will be entering our last year of high school in the fall. I look forward to the end of preparatory school as much as the next seventeen-year-old, but this lively anticipation is tempered by my father's plans to send me to the United States to study civil engineering. Long ago, my father worked as a ranger, protecting the nationalized forests from poachers who cut down the trees illegally for personal profit. He now works in an office, managing an entire region with an army of rangers reporting to him.

"Iran is in dire need of engineers," Dad reminds me whenever he gets the chance. "We're on the verge of transforming ourselves from a traditional agricultural country to an industrial one. A person with an engineering degree from an American university secures a great future for himself and his family, in addition to enjoying the prestige of being called 'Mr. Engineer' for the rest of his life." I love my father, and I would never disobey him, but I hate math, I hate the idea of becoming an engineer, and I would hate being called Mr. Engineer. In my dreams I major in literature and study the philosophy of the ancient Greeks, evolution, Marxism, psychoanalysis, Erfan, and Buddhism. Or, I major in film and become a writer or a director, someone who has something worthwhile to say.

For now I live with my parents in a middle-class neighborhood. We have a typical Iranian house with a modest yard, a large guest room, and a *hose*—a small pool in the front yard. In our neighborhood, just like any other in Tehran, tall walls separate houses that have been built connected to each other. Our home has two full levels, and my room occupies a small section of the third floor, where a huge terrace is connected to the roof by a bulky mass of steel steps. Ours is the tallest house in the neighborhood, and has a southern exposure.

"I wouldn't live in a home with a northern exposure if it were given to me for free," my mother states repeatedly. "They never get any sun. They're a breeding ground for germs." My mother never finished high school, yet she speaks about health issues with the authority of a Harvard graduate. She has a remedy for every ailment: herbal tea to cure depression, liquidated camel thorns to smash kidney stones, powdered flowers to annihilate sinus infections, dried leaves that destroy acne, and pills for growing as tall as a tree—despite the fact that she stands an impressive five feet tall in stocking feet.

The peace of each summer night fades with the noises of families starting their day, and our alley bustles with kids of all ages. Boys shout and scuffle as they chase cheap plastic soccer balls, while girls go from house to house, doing what girls do together. Women congregate in different parts of the alley, making it easy to tell who likes whom by the way they assemble. Ahmed has divided these gatherings into three groups: the east, west, and central gossip committees.

Ahmed is a tall skinny kid with dark features and a brilliant smile. His strong but slender body, bold, broad jaw, and bright hazel eyes make him the picture of health, according to my mother's expert opinion. He's well liked in the neighborhood, and funny. I tell him he could become a great comedian if he took his God-given talent more seriously.

"Yes, more seriously," he replies. "I can become the most serious clown in the country!"

I've known Ahmed since I was twelve years old, when my family first moved to the neighborhood. We met for the first time at school when three bullies were beating me up. All the other kids stood by and watched, but Ahmed rushed to my aid. The boys were tall, big, and ugly, and despite our heroic attempts we both took a beating.

"I'm Pasha," I introduced myself after the fight.

Ahmed smiled and reached over for a handshake. "What was the fight about?" he asked.

I laughed. "You didn't know? Why did you help me?"

"Three to one! I have a problem with that. Of course, I knew they'd still take us, but at least it wasn't as unfair as three guys thrashing one."

I knew right then that Ahmed was going to be my best friend forever. His gallantry and upbeat attitude won me over instantly. The experience bound us together and prompted my father, an ex–heavyweight boxing champion, to start teaching us how to box—much to my mother's dismay.

"You're going to make them violent," she would complain to my unsympathetic father. To make things right, every night after dinner she would hold out a glass of amber liquid that smelled like horse urine on a hot summer day. "This will reverse what your father is doing to your temper," she assured me, while forcing me to drink the nauseating brew.

I loved boxing, but my mother's remedy nearly drove me to quit.

After a few months of training, as our punches became crisp—short and quick, but heavy when they needed to be—I began to ache for a rematch with the three bullies at school. My father overheard our plans for revenge and intervened.

"Sit down, Mr. Pasha," he said one day after practice. Then he pointed to Ahmed. "Would you join us, please?"

"Of course, Mr. Shahed," Ahmed responded, and as he was sitting next to me, he whispered, "I think we're in trouble, Mr. Pasha!"

"When one learns how to box," Dad started thoughtfully, "he joins the fraternity of athletes who never raise a hand against people weaker than themselves."

My mother stopped what she had been doing and walked up to stand sternly next to my father.

"But, Dad, if we don't beat up people weaker than ourselves, who do we beat up?" I asked, stunned. "And wouldn't it be dumb to pick on people stronger than ourselves anyway?"

Dad was doing his best not to look at Mom, who was staring at him like a tiger checking out a deer right before the final, fateful dash.

"I taught you how to box so you could defend yourself," he mumbled. "I don't want you to go looking for a fight."

Ahmed and I couldn't believe what we were hearing.

"I want you to promise me that you will always respect the code of our fraternity," my father insisted.

We must have been slow to react.

"I want you to promise," he repeated, his voice rising.

And so Ahmed and I grudgingly joined the fraternity of athletes who never beat up bullies who break the faces of kids weaker than

themselves. At the time, of course, we had no idea that such a fraternity never existed.

"Iraj is lucky your dad made us promise," Ahmed says later, making
us both laugh.

Iraj is a small, scruffy kid with a long pointed nose whose sunburned
features make him look Indian. He's smart, has the best grades in our
school, and loves physics and mathematics, the two subjects I hate
most.

I am convinced Iraj likes Ahmed's oldest sister, because he can't
keep his eyes off her when she is in the alley. Everyone knows you
don't fancy a friend's sister, as if she were a girl from another neighborhood. If I were Ahmed and caught Iraj checking out my sister, I'd
kick the shit out of him. But I'm not Ahmed. "Hey," he'll shout, trying
hard not to smile when he startles Iraj, "stop looking at her or I'll
break my pledge to the sacred brotherhood of the boxing fraternity."

"Sacred brotherhood of the boxing fraternity?" I whisper under
my breath with a smile. "Brotherhood and fraternity mean the same
thing. You shouldn't use them in the same sentence."

"Oh, you shut up." Ahmed laughs.

Iraj is the chess champion of our neighborhood. He is so good that no
one is willing to play against him anymore. When we play soccer in
the alley, Iraj plays chess against himself.

"Who's winning?" Ahmed asks with a smirk. Iraj ignores him.
"Have you ever beaten yourself?" Ahmed asks. "You could, you know—if
you weren't so fucking preoccupied with my sister."

"I'm not preoccupied with your sister," Iraj mumbles, rolling his
eyes.

"Right," Ahmed replies, nodding. "If you have any trouble beating
yourself, let me know and I'll be happy to do it for you."

"You know," I tease, "I used to get mad at him for looking at your sister, but it might not be so bad to have a chess champion as a brother-in-law."

"Bite your tongue," Ahmed growls, "or I'll raid your mother's pantry to mix you a special brew that will grow hair on your tongue."

The threat has some weight, considering the way my mother has applied her unique brand of knowledge and listened to her gut to diagnose me as an extreme introvert.

"Do you know what happens to people who keep everything to themselves?" she asks, not waiting for my answer. "They get sick." When I object that I'm not an introvert, she reminds me of the time I was four years old and fell down the steps. My two aunts, two uncles, and grandparents were visiting us that day, and my mother estimated that watching me tumble down two flights of stairs nearly caused two heart attacks, three strokes, and a handful of small ulcers.

"You broke your shin in three places!" she chides. "The doctor said he'd seen grown men cry after a break like that, but not you. Do you know what that kind of stress does to your body?"

"No," I say.

"It causes cancer."

Then she spits three times to atone for the thought.

In order to cure my introversion, she insists I drink a dusky concoction that looks and smells like used motor oil. I complain that her remedy tastes horrible, and she tells me to be quiet and stop whining.

"I thought this potion was to bring me out of my shell," I remind her.

"Hush," she orders, "whining doesn't count. If you want to be successful in life you must force yourself to be an extrovert," she explains. "Introverts end up as lonely poets or destitute writers."

"So," Ahmed ponders one day, "the engine oil makes you an extrovert, and the horse urine helps you crawl back into your shell." He shakes his head in empathy. "You are going to be one fucked-up person by the time your mother gets done with you."

2

Faheemeh's Tears and Zari's Wet Hair

Our summer nights on the roof are spent basking in the wide-open safety of our bird's-eye view. There are no walls around what we say, or fears shaping what we think. I spend hours listening to stories of Ahmed's silent encounters with Faheemeh, the girl he loves. His voice softens and his face quiets as he describes how she threw back her long black hair while looking at him—and how that must mean she loves him. Why else would she strain her neck to communicate with him? My father says that Persians believe in silent communication; a look or a gesture imparts far more than a book full of words. My father is a great silent communicator. When I behave badly, he just gives me a dirty look that hurts more than a thousand slaps in the face.

I listen while Ahmed's voice chatters on about Faheemeh, but my gaze usually wanders into our neighbors' yard, where a girl named Zari lives with her parents and her little brother, Keivan. I've never seen Faheemeh up close, so when Ahmed talks about her I picture Zari in my mind: her delicate cheekbones, her smiling eyes, and her pale, soft skin. Most summer evenings Zari sits at the edge of her family's little *hose* under a cherry tree, dangling her shapely feet in the cool water as she reads. I'm careful not to let my eyes linger too long because she is engaged to my friend and mentor, Ramin Sobhi, a third-year political science major at the University of Tehran whom everyone, including his parents, calls Doctor. It's low to fancy a friend's girl, and I shove all thoughts of Zari from my head every time I think of Doctor, but Ahmed's lovesick ramblings make it hard for me to keep my mind clear.

Every day Ahmed bikes ten minutes to Faheemeh's neighborhood in the hope of getting a glimpse of her. He says she has two older brothers who protect her like hawks, and that everyone in the neighborhood knows that messing with their sister means getting a broken nose, a dislocated jaw, and a big black eggplant under at least one eye. Ahmed says that if Faheemeh's brothers learned that he fancied their sister, they'd make his ears the biggest parts of his body—meaning that they would cut him into little pieces.

Not one to be thwarted, Ahmed picks a day when Faheemeh's brothers are in the alley and intentionally rides his bike into a wall. He moans and groans with pain, and Faheemeh's brothers take him inside their home and give him a couple of aspirin, then immobilize his injured wrist by wrapping a piece of fabric around it. Faheemeh is only a few steps away, and knows full well what the handsome stranger is up to.

Ahmed now rides his bike to Faheemeh's alley without a worry in the world, spending hours with Faheemeh's brothers and talking about everything from the members of this year's Iranian national soccer team to next year's potential honorees. He says he doesn't mind that her brothers bore him to death as long as he is close to her. They play soccer all afternoon in the alley and Ahmed insists on playing goalie, even though he stinks in that position. While the other kids chase the ball in the scorching heat of Tehran's afternoons, Ahmed stands still. Supposedly he's defending his team's goal, but really he's watching Faheemeh, who watches him from the roof of her house.

After only a few games, Ahmed is forced to abdicate his post as the goalie. He is so preoccupied with Faheemeh that he is never prepared for the opponent's attackers and his team always loses by at least five or six points. When Ahmed begins to play forward his team starts to win again, but now he has to run after the ball, which means he can no longer exchange silent looks with Faheemeh.

So Ahmed comes to me with a plan. I am to accompany him to Faheemeh's alley the next day. He will introduce me to his new friends and will make sure that I end up on the opposite team. I will aim at his knee during a crucial play and he'll fake a bad fall and a serious injury. Then he will have no choice but to play as goalie again. He will be a goalie in agony, playing despite his pain, and that will undoubtedly impress Faheemeh.

I agree to go along but worry deep down about what Faheemeh might think of me after I knock Ahmed down. I feel better when I imagine the day we tell her the whole thing was a setup to get Ahmed back in the goalie position.

"Don't hurt me for real, now," Ahmed warns with a smile on his face.

"Make sure the orthopedic surgeon is on call, pal," I respond, getting into the spirit.

"Oh, come on. You know I have fragile bones. Just touch me lightly and I'll do the rest."

The plan is carried out masterfully. Ahmed deserves an Oscar for his portrayal of a boy in pain, and a gold medal for playing goalie after his dreadful injury. Looking at his face, which glows with the knowledge that Faheemeh is watching, I worry that he might really hurt himself with his courageous dives to the left, to the right, and under the feet of our attackers—all of this on asphalt. We can't score on him. He scrapes his hands and elbows, and tears his pants at the knees. Each time he stops us he grimaces with pain, releases the ball,

and looks up toward the roof where Faheemeh is watching attentively. I even see her smile at him once.

One of Faheemeh's brothers notices that I'm looking toward the
roof, and I know from that moment on he doesn't like me anymore, just
as I don't like Iraj for staring at Ahmed's sister. He doesn't shake my
hand when I say good-bye to everyone. I size him up surreptitiously.
He's taller and bigger than I am. I leave with the comfort of knowing
that I would not be letting down the sacred brotherhood of the boxing
fraternity if he ever decided to be an asshole to me or to Ahmed.

A couple of weeks pass, and I'm sitting on our roof in the dark, my
ears and eyes filled with the rush and sway of the light wind that bends
the treetops, when I hear the door to Zari's yard open, then shut.

Don't look, I think resolutely, but my body resorts to quick, shal-
low breaths as soon as it recognizes the sound. *It could just be Keivan*,
I reason. I decide to close my eyes, but my heart races as I realize that
doing so has only sharpened my hearing. Bare feet pad across the yard,
then the water in the *hose* begins to murmur with the slow churning of
her legs as the pages of her book turn with the soft, rhythmic hiss so
familiar from my own hours spent reading. She's read four pages by
the time Ahmed arrives on my roof. He sits silently on the short wall
that runs between our rooftops and lights a cigarette with shaking
hands. The momentary illumination from the match reveals tears in
his eyes.

"Is something wrong?" I ask, my chest growing tight at the expression on his face.

He shakes his head no, but I don't believe him. We Persians as a
people are too deeply immersed in misery to resist despair when it
knocks on our door.

"Are you sure?" I insist, and he nods his head yes.

I decide to leave him alone because that's what I wish people
would do for me when I don't feel like talking.

He sits as still as stone for a few minutes as the cigarette's glowing coal creeps toward his fingers, then whispers, "She has a suitor."

"Who has a suitor?" I ask, glancing below at Zari; her ivory feet stir the moon's reflection on the water's surface so that it shimmers like liquid gold.

"Faheemeh. A guy who lives a couple of doors down from them is sending his parents to her house tomorrow night."

It feels like someone knocked the wind out of me. I don't know what to say. People who insist on sticking their noses into other people's business seldom know what to say or do. I wonder why they ask in the first place. I pretend to study the blinking city lights that sprawl across the shadowy distance.

"When did you find out?" I finally ask.

"After you left this afternoon, her brothers and I went into her yard to get some cool water and that's when they told me."

"Was she around?"

"Yes," he says, looking up hard at the sky to keep the tears from falling down his face. "She was pouring water from a pitcher into my glass when they told me." He remembers his cigarette and takes a big puff. "I was sitting in a chair and she was standing over me, actually bending over me. She looked at my eyes the whole time, never blinked." Ahmed shakes his head as his lips twist into the ghost of a smile. "She was so close I could feel her breath on my face, and her skin smelled clean—like soap, but sweeter. One of her brothers asked if I was going to congratulate their little sister, but I couldn't make my voice come out of my throat." Ahmed lets his face and his tears fall as he drops the spent cigarette and steps on it.

"She's too young," I whisper. "For crying out loud, how old is she, seventeen? How can they marry off a seventeen-year-old kid?"

Ahmed shakes his head again, mute.

"Maybe her parents will reject him," I say, to plant hope in his heart.

"Her family loves him," he says with a short bitter laugh as he pulls another cigarette from the pack. "He's a twenty-six-year-old college graduate who works for the Agriculture Ministry, owns a car, and will soon be buying his own home in Tehran Pars. They won't say no to him." He lights the cigarette, then holds the pack out in my direction. I picture my father appearing unexpectedly and pinning me down with one of his dirty looks, the ones that hurt more than a thousand slaps in the face. I shake my head no.

I look at Ahmed's sad face and wish I could do something to help him out. This is a historic night for both of us. We're experiencing the first major personal crisis of our young lives. It's sad, but I must admit, on some level it's also exciting. It makes me feel grown-up.

"Do you know how bad this feels?" Ahmed asks between puffs.

"Well," I begin, wanting desperately to carry his pain, "I've only read about it in books," I confess, somewhat embarrassed. Then I look toward Zari's yard, and add, "But I think I can imagine."

Late the next afternoon, Ahmed asks me to go to Faheemeh's alley with him. I do, despite my apprehension about seeing Faheemeh's brothers again, especially the one who hates me for being like Iraj. The sun has just set, and the lights in the alley are springing on one by one. Some people have just watered their trees and hosed their sidewalks, as is customary in Tehran, and the scent of wet dust makes the dry heat of the evening feel more tolerable. A group of kids is playing soccer and making a lot of noise. I figure it must be the final game of the evening. The ladies stand close to each other trading talk while the younger girls run arm in arm, giggling.

I have never seen Ahmed so consumed by grief. We walk up and down the alley, and he slows every time we reach Faheemeh's house. "I can feel her on the other side of these walls," he says, resting his forehead against the stone and closing his eyes. "She knows I'm here," he whispers. "We're breathing the same air." Some kids walk by and recognize Ahmed. They want to chat, but neither Ahmed nor I is in a mood to talk, and we continue to pace. When we reach Faheemeh's house again he stops and presses both fists to the stone, like a tired warrior at the base of a fortress.

Inside, a bunch of adults are discussing a lifetime's commitment between two young people. The mother of the bride-to-be is usually happy and proud, unless the suitor is a real loser. The mother of the groom-to-be is civilized and calm; she makes mental notes to use later if a deal cannot be consummated, details that will stay fixed in her mind until the couple is happily married off. Who knows what will happen between two strangers? Good information can always tilt the balance in her favor if the union should fail. Everything is fair game, from the color of the wallpaper in the living room to the size of the future mother-in-law's bottom. The fathers are agreeable and more concerned about drinking, eating, and bragging about the stuff fathers brag about: people they know in high places, the bargain they got on a prime piece of land by the Caspian Sea. Then there is the cast of aunts and uncles, best friends and family members, all happy to be there because they have nothing better to do with their time.

Most of the discussions will focus on money. What does the groom have? Does he own a house? Does he drive a car? What model and year is it? Hopefully it's an American car, a Buick or a Ford. How much is the dowry? How much does the family of the groom pay the family of the bride for this auspicious occasion? What would be the alimony if there were a divorce in the future?

The bride- and groom-to-be normally sit far apart and don't speak. They even avoid looking at each other. I know Ahmed is wondering what Faheemeh is thinking, sitting quietly in that crowded room. That's what I would be worried about if, for example, I loved Zari and she were being married off to someone other than Doctor. I would wonder if Zari were thinking of me. I would wonder if she had made herself pretty, and if she had, I would be questioning why. Doesn't she want my rival to think that she is ugly, and not worthy of marriage? I would be so jealous of the man who would be looking into her beautiful blue eyes, thinking of embracing her, touching her face, feeling her warm body against his. *God, I'm so glad I don't love Zari; poor Ahmed must be going through hell.*

We wait until ten o'clock, but no one comes out of Faheemeh's house. We ride our bikes back to our neighborhood, have a quick dinner, then retreat to the roof. Hours crawl by in heavy silence. The outline of Mount Alborz, usually uplifting, seems to huddle in the growing dark like a lonesome dog. The heat has been unusually persistent all day, and we sit and sweat without speaking for what feels like days. What do you say to a seventeen-year-old boy who has fallen in love with a seventeen-year-old girl who is about to be auctioned off for a few thousand Persian toomans of dowry and the dubious promise of happiness?

"I think you should tell her that you love her," I blurt, suddenly.

Ahmed exhales with a derisive snort. "What good will that do? Besides, don't you think she already knows?"

"*Maybe* she knows . . . *maybe* she thinks that *maybe* you love her—but she doesn't know for sure, does she? You haven't told her how you feel, and you certainly haven't done anything to show her."

"I communicate in silence with her every day," he mumbles.

His answer makes me smile. "Ahmed, she's the only one who can stop this wedding. Her parents may still force her to marry him, so there's no guarantee that your actions would change anything, but you have to give her a reason to fight."

"You think she might?" Ahmed asks, genuine wonder trembling in his voice.

"I think she might if you intervened, and if she doesn't, what have you lost?"

The light above Zari's door blinks on, and she comes into her yard and kneels gracefully at the edge of the *hose*. The night has been slow to cool, and she leans down and to the side to wet her hair, dipping it in the water, then twisting it artfully and pinning it to her head so that the water slides in drops down her neck and back. I'm not sure how long I've been looking into Zari's yard when I feel Ahmed staring at me.

"So," he says, scratching the top of his head thoughtfully, "you think if someone walked up to Zari and told her he loved her, she would reconsider marrying Doctor?"

"That's not . . . that's different," I stutter. "Zari wants to marry Doctor, so that's not a fair question, and this is not about Zari and me. I mean, this is about you and Faheemeh."

Ahmed bites his lower lip to mask his smile, then asks, "You think she would go against her parents' wishes?"

"I said Zari's situation is different!" I bark back.

"I didn't mean Zari. I was talking about Faheemeh." This time Ahmed doesn't bother to hide his smile. "So you think she would go against her parents' wishes?" he repeats.

I shake my head slightly to dislodge any more thoughts of Zari, then fix my friend with a confident stare and answer, "People do amazing things for love. Books are full of wonderful stories about this kind of stuff, and stories aren't just fantasies, you know. They're so much a part of the people who write them that they practically teach their readers invaluable lessons about life."

Ahmed notes the gleam in my eye, shakes his head and chuckles. "I know, I should read more."

I wake the next day alone, squinting at the hot sun hanging dead center in the sky, and realize I must have slept late. My waking fog clears sharply as I notice that Ahmed is already gone. I run downstairs, pull my shoes on, and mumble a hello to my mother, who is heading up the hallway with a large glass of her special engine oil for me. I grimace, then sprint past her into the yard to my bike.

My mother yells, "Where're you going? You haven't eaten breakfast!"

"No time!" I shout as I'm jumping on my bike, and hear the familiar muttering of my mother cursing under her breath.

I pedal as fast as I can to Faheemeh's alley, and my heart sinks as I round the corner. A bunch of kids are holding back Faheemeh's two brothers, and Ahmed's face is covered with blood. There's lots of screaming and yelling, and Faheemeh's oldest brother is telling Ahmed to get lost. Ahmed is standing quietly, with no one holding him back. I jump off my bike and run up to him.

"What's going on?" I ask, anxiously. When Ahmed doesn't speak, I assume the worst and whirl to face our attackers. I will my body to become loose and ready, bouncing lightly on the balls of my feet and shaking my hands briefly to warm them before I curl them into fists.

Ahmed smiles gently and grabs my arm. "I followed your advice. I was trying to tell Faheemeh I love her," he explains, pointing up to the weeping girl on the roof, "but I think the whole world heard."

Faheemeh is watching us, knowing full well that a seventeen-year-old boy has taken his first step toward becoming a man, and in the process has made her feel more like a woman than all the aunts, uncles, and formalities of the night before. If she must marry a man her parents have chosen for her, at least she knows that she is loved by someone with enough courage to defy tradition.

I can only hope that she will summon her own courage to defy her parents, for Ahmed's sake.

A few nights later, at dinner, my mother mentions a rumor she's heard about a sweet young girl in a nearby neighborhood who is being forced to marry a man she doesn't love. "I don't know her," Mom says, "but I feel horrible for her." I listen hard, but keep my face still. "I hear that she has locked herself in a room and refuses to come out, eat, or speak to anyone," Mom reports.

My father shakes his head. "It's time for the parents in this country to learn that the souls of their children are more important than tradition," he says. "You young people need to assume responsibility for your own futures," he tells me. "If someone's old enough to be married off, then they're sure as hell old enough to decide who they should marry." My mother nods in agreement.

Sitting out on the roof after dinner that night, I smell Ahmed's cigarette and hear his steps on the stairs long before he settles down beside me.

"Do I have a star up there?" he asks. I know he isn't expecting an answer, so I remain silent. "I see yours," he claims, pointing at a brilliant star far from the horizon. "It's blinding!"

"That's not me," I argue, my face warming imperceptibly. "Too bright. Must be Faheemeh. The light is stronger because she's thinking of you."

Ahmed sighs as he stretches out on his back and closes his eyes. I follow suit, knowing that the hushed symphony of night noises won't be nearly loud enough to rescue us from our worries. I breathe in the scent of wet asphalt, enjoying the way the night breeze brushes my closed eyes.

Winter of 1974
Roozbeh Psychiatric Hospital, Tehran

I wake just enough to turn over beneath the covers, missing the heat my body leaves behind as soon as my skin hits the cool, unused sheets on the other side of the bed. I lie still with my eyes closed because my mind feels too weary to process anything I might see. Sounds draw my attention—the hollow click of a cane followed closely by the drag of slippers on linoleum, the muted ticking of a wristwatch in the drawer of the bedside table—but the relative silence wakes me. I am alone in the room, feeling lost without the old man's rhythmic chanting. I turn to my other side, only to find the sheets already chilled, and wonder if I'll ever open my eyes again.

It is either a few minutes or several days later the next time I am conscious. I notice pink patches of healed skin on my hands and forearms. The new skin looks tender, but doesn't hurt. *Was I burned? Why? How? Did someone try to kill me?* Not that I care. The back of my skull aches to the dull beat of my pulse, while each slow breath I draw between my sore ribs feels as if it is struggling to lift a weight.

My days and nights begin to be plagued by dreams. Dark clouds roll over the roof of our house near enough to touch, and lightning strikes so close that the thunder knocks me off my feet. I open my eyes to see the wheelchair on the other side of the room. *Can I walk?*

Am I paralyzed? Maybe I fell off the roof, as my mother always feared. Or did someone push me off? Why? More shivers, more hours of unconsciousness.

The next time I'm awake the clouds are even darker. I am still on the roof. I see a man dressed in a black suit looking up at me from the alley. His predatory eyes glint. His face is bloated. He howls into a radio clutched in his hand. A muffled sound fills the air, more like an angry roar matching the thunder in its ferocity. A cold wind blows through the alley, whirling up dust and debris as the color of everything turns into winterish gray. I can't tell if it is the man down below or the dark clouds overhead that send a chill down my spine.

3

Summer of 1973
Tehran

The Red Rose

It's difficult not to like Doctor. His thick round glasses slightly magnify his smiling brown eyes and his tidy appearance makes him look like a young professor. His calm demeanor and strong, gentle voice tend to disarm even his worst enemies. He lives nearby with his parents, Mr. and Mrs. Sobhi, and comes over often to see Zari.

When we play soccer in the alley, Doctor cheers us on like a true fan, jumping up and down, encouraging both sides, and admiring unselfish plays. We sometimes invite him to join the game, but he always laughs and says something like, "Oh, no, no. I'm too old." Then he turns to Zari, who smiles and shrugs her shoulders, as if to say he should do what he likes. In the end he never joins us, and I don't blame him. What would the neighbors think if they saw the young scholar, engaged to the prettiest girl in the alley, running after a plastic ball with a bunch of kids?

I admire Doctor, but I can't stop myself from thinking about Zari. This, of course, is something I would never admit to, especially given how we pester Iraj about looking at Ahmed's sister. My thoughts about Zari are pure and innocent, most of the time. The most shameful fantasy I've indulged in was to think that if I ever got married I would want my wife to be exactly like her: smart, beautiful, delicate, proper, and polite—everything a man should want in a woman, or so I thought. Reviewing Zari's qualities, however, quickly led to imagining our first kiss on the night of our marriage, which felt as if someone had poured boiling water through my veins: her bright eyes closing as our faces came together, breathing in her delicious scent as our lips met in a silent flood of softness. I forced my mind to empty at that point, and haven't had thoughts like that about her since, at least not consciously.

Doctor is always reading, even while he's walking. Ahmed swears he's seen him walk right into a light post a couple of times. That's how he became my friend and mentor, as one of the only people who liked the same books I did. He admires the philosophies of Karl Marx, Friedrich Engels, Jean-Paul Sartre, and Bertrand Russell. He owns every play by Bertolt Brecht and George Bernard Shaw, as well as the works of great American storytellers like Jack London, John Steinbeck, and Howard Fast.

I met Doctor through Ahmed. "He is the smartest guy in our neighborhood," Ahmed said. "Much smarter than you," he teased, before looking around and whispering, "I think he's one of those guys who doesn't like the Shah."

"That makes sense," I mumbled, knowing that most university students violently opposed the tyranny of the regime. "What makes him so smart?" I asked.

"They don't call him Doctor for nothing," Ahmed responded in a smart-ass tone. "He's not a physician—you know that, right?"

I smiled and nodded yes.

"He's read everything. He knows everything. He's like an encyclopedica."

"What's an encyclopedica?" I asked, laughing at his slip.

He ignored me and continued. "I think he may be the only person who uses bigger words than you! And he is always arguing politics;

thank God you don't do that." He showed me the back of his right hand, as if he was about to smack me.

I laughed again.

In time I really got to know Doctor. His Marxist language became a welcome part of my days. He discussed dialectical materialism, determinism, and the centralization and concentration of capital, praising and quoting scholars like Louis Althusser, Erich Fromm, and Antonio Gramsci—Marxists scholars whose publications were banned in Iran.

Doctor asked about my interests, my hobbies, and my school experiences. His eyes lit up when he learned that I was a fellow reader.

"Who's your favorite author?" he asked eagerly.

"I love Gorky's work," I said hesitantly, a bit intimidated by the guy who was supposedly an encyclopedica. "I like all the Russian writers I've read, Dostoyevsky, Sholokhov, Pushkin."

"Really?" Doctor shouted, grinning. "Where have you been, my friend? That is so great."

After a long discussion of Russian literature and its impact on the 1917 Bolshevik Revolution, Doctor asked, "What do you think about the condition of the people in our villages?" His question did not surprise me, given my conversation with Ahmed earlier. Before I had a chance to respond, he said, "Their living conditions are deplorable. Have you ever been on a farm?"

I nodded yes.

"You know, some people think I'm too idealistic, but I wish for a day when no one goes to bed on an empty stomach. I want to find a way to educate every human being so that they can achieve their fullest potential. I want equality and justice for all regardless of social status and class."

I sensed the heat of Doctor's enthusiasm along with his sincerity. Soon I was overtaken by a startling surge of goodwill toward him.

"I don't know about you," he continued, "but I can see myself as a missionary in the villages helping people dig wells, teaching them new irrigation techniques, harvesting crops and filtering drinking water. Do you know how many people die annually from drinking polluted water?" I shook my head no. He shook his head, too, naked sorrow in his expression, before continuing. "I want to help them take control of their lives instead of waiting for some God to deliver them from their troubles. Do you understand?"

"Of course," I said with a smile, deciding right then and there that I wanted to be just like him when I grew up: kind, smart, visionary, and yes, idealistic, too. At that moment Zari walked up to us with a tray of cool drinks. "You must be thirsty," she said to me, her voice a sweet sound that hummed in my ears. "I've been watching you. You haven't had anything since you walked in the door."

She has been watching me? Wow! Then I heard Doctor's voice telling me to drink up. It seemed as if his words suffered a delay between his lips and my ears because my heart had stumbled and was caught so completely by the sound of Zari's voice. Looking at Doctor, I wondered how I could so faithfully and simultaneously admire and envy him.

Doctor has had to work to help support his family since he was twelve years old, when his father suffered a debilitating accident in the machine shop where he was in charge of heating metal for processing purposes.

"One day, at the end of a double shift, my father was so tired that he fell asleep for a few seconds," Doctor told me once, his eyes filling. "His right hand was burned so severely that it had to be amputated the second he arrived at the hospital. Years before that day, when I was just a kid, he used to get severe migraines. When I'd ask him what I could do to make his pain go away, he'd smile and ask me to kiss his forehead. As soon as my kiss had landed, he'd jump up and down and say that the headache had disappeared." Doctor shook his head with a sad smile. "He'd thank me and give me a coin. That's when he started calling me Doctor. For a long time I thought my kisses could cure him, so every night he was in the hospital after the amputation I sat by his bed and kissed his heavily bandaged arm while he slept." Doctor massaged his forehead, as if to work the worry from his skin, then added, "They fired him for being careless, after twenty-five years of loyal labor. That's capitalism for you."

Watching Doctor argue politics and religion—the only two topics he gets passionate about—is like imagining the majestic and serene Mount Damavand belching smoke into the sky. He hates the Shah and the *mullahs*, the educated religious officials. "The Shah is a dictator and a puppet of the West," he says, "and I'd rather kiss a rattlesnake on the lips than shake hands with a mullah."

Doctor's hatred for the mullahs is so deep that he was reluctant to summon our local clergyman to carry out his grandfather's funeral ceremonies. "Why do we need him?" he kept arguing with his father. Eventually, however, he had to give in to his parents' desire for a traditional funeral. At the time, Doctor was a freshman at the university and I was in the tenth grade. Seeing how distraught he appeared over his mission, I offered to go along with him, and he eagerly accepted. The mullah was a middle-aged fat man with a big belly and a thick salt-and-pepper beard. He had a white turban wrapped around his shaved head, and wore a white shirt and black pants under a chestnut brown robe. He seemed genuinely sympathetic to Doctor's loss, and wanted to know how old the deceased was, how he died, who was mourning the death of the poor man, and so on. I had heard such horror stories of the wicked ways of the mullahs from Doctor that the friendly vibes coming from this gentle, good-natured man left me pleasantly surprised. As he was collecting information about the deceased, he suddenly dropped his gaze and asked Doctor, "Now, how old did you say your grandma is?"

"Sixty-two," Doctor answered, hesitantly.

"Not very old," the mullah noted, trying to appear casual. "Who will take care of her now? She has so many years ahead of her, the poor, lonely lady." He put his right hand on Doctor's shoulder and, with one of those looks that adults give kids when teaching them a lesson, said, "You know, my son, when God closes one door he always opens another! Now, where did you say your grandma lives?"

Doctor's face stiffened with rage. He batted the mullah's hand from his shoulder and turned on his heel to march out of the mosque. I hurried to follow, and heard Doctor cursing under his breath. "Fucking prick!" he spat. "He's trying to pick up my grandma. If he even *thinks* about her, I'll rip the turban from his ugly head and strangle him with it."

Doctor could be sentenced to many years in prison if the SAVAK—the Shah's secret police force—catches him with his collection of government-banned books. One day, we are walking home from a bookstore when I tell him about how my father used to keep banned books in a little vault he had built in the closet.

"When I was six years old, the SAVAK raided our house," I say. "My mother tried to stop them from entering the yard, but they pushed her out of the way. My dad was reading in his study, but when he heard the commotion he dropped the book on the floor and ran from the room. Instinctively, I picked up the book, walked into the vault and shut the door behind me. I have no idea why, except maybe because my father used to call the vault 'our secret' and made me promise not to tell anyone about it."

The bright smile on Doctor's face encourages me to finish the story.

"The agents searched the house for a couple of hours, but didn't find anything. They left empty-handed, and since then my father doesn't keep banned books in the house."

"I'm glad you didn't run out of air in there," Doctor says in a worried tone.

"I don't remember it getting bad at all," I say.

Doctor takes his glasses off and puts a gentle hand on my shoulder, speaking softly. "Has anyone ever told you that you have *That*?" I must look thoroughly confused. "You've never heard of *That*?" he asks, surprised.

I shake my head no.

"It's a priceless quality that's impossible to define, really," he explains, "but you recognize it in the actions of great people."

Showering friends and strangers with inflated but disingenuous compliments is a customary tradition in Iran called *taarof*, but looking into Doctor's eyes, I don't think he's *taarof*-ing.

Some great person I am, I think, as the heat of embarrassment is joined by the heat of shame climbing up my chest and neck, *secretly desiring my friend's fiancée and itching to use my new boxing skills to break the face of some bully*.

Sensing my unease, Doctor changes the topic. "You know how they caught the gang, don't you?" he says, referring to the group of young men and women who have been arrested by the SAVAK for plotting to kill the Shah. "They were looking for illegal books in the home of one of the members and found the plans."

I nod, aware that for weeks now the media has been promising that a sensational trial will be broadcast live on television, the first time in our history that an event like this is being shown on TV. Most of the time the fact that the opposition even exists—the Toodeh party, the Communists, the Islamist Marxists—is denied, or those groups are referred to as *kharab-kars*—subversive activists, terrorists, and people who commit appalling acts in the name of politics. According to the media, Iran is a unified nation in the service of the King of the Kings: the Shahanshah Mohammed Reza Pahlavi. Acknowledging the existence of political opposition is considered blasphemous by the SAVAK. One may as well deny the existence of God. So despite the arrests, the tortures, and the incessant suppression of the opposition groups, adulation of the Shah continues as if the country is a model state for democracy.

"People say that the gang members will cry and beg for forgiveness on live television," I add, "and then the Shah will pardon them in an orchestrated attempt to make him look like a benevolent, merciful leader."

I see a strange expression spring to life on Doctor's face, almost a sneer. He shakes his head and says, "But the circus and its ringmaster may be in for a surprise."

In the alley, Doctor and I find Ahmed's grandmother wandering around as if lost.

"Have you seen my husband?" she asks, peering sweetly at us.

Doctor and I exchange a look, knowing that her husband died two years ago.

"No, I haven't seen him for a while, Grandma," Doctor says. "Is there anything we can do for you?"

Grandma pauses to think. "It's very strange," she muses. "No one has seen him since we buried him a couple of years ago. Have I ever told you how my husband and I met?" Both Doctor and I have heard this story a million times, but we smile and shake our heads no. Grandma describes again how she met her husband at a party in the American embassy, and even though he was married to forty-three other women at the time, he fell in love with her and divorced all of his wives to marry her. She says he remained faithful to her until the day he died trying to save a cat from a burning house.

"What a beautiful story, Grandma," Doctor says. "He must really have loved you, and he certainly was a brave, compassionate man."

"Yes, he was a brave man," Grandma echoes, as she shuffles away. "He was a compassionate man."

Doctor and I tip our chins to our chests, both aware that Ahmed's grandfather never visited the American embassy, didn't have forty-three wives, and definitely would not have risked his life to save a cat because he hated them passionately.

That night a number of our family and friends come over for dinner to watch the trials with my parents and me. The house buzzes with excitement and anticipation. The alley has emptied by the time the judge's gavel announces the start of the proceedings.

The accused take the podium one by one, most of them confessing and begging for the Shah's pardon. They read their testimonies from prepared documents whose words are carefully chosen to ensure that any mention of the royal family is respectful. Some of the gang members weep openly, appealing to the queen as the mother of the nation. "Help your unruly children to be forgiven," one woman cries out. "You're a mother, have mercy on my children."

I roll up my sleeves with quick, efficient jerks, then press my clenched fists to my mouth as I watch their faces on television. Each accused manages an expression of polite distress; most are clearly terrified, while others seem to have already left their bodies and the whole situation behind.

Golesorkhi, the group's leader, is the last to stand and testify. His name means "the red rose." His likeable face, medium height and build, square jaw and thick mustache make him look like a young Maxim Gorky. He takes his jacket off, rolls up his sleeves with slow, deliberate thrusts, and walks to the podium.

"This court is an illegal institution," he yells, his fist crashing down on the podium with such force that we all jump in our seats. "The Shah is a tyrant, a servant of the Americans, and a puppet of the West."

My breath has caught in my throat, making it hard for me to swallow. I sit up straight and busy my hands with turning my sleeves back down, but the very air in the room seems to be carrying an electric current.

"Is he not afraid of dying?" one of my dad's friends murmurs. "They'll torture him to death tonight, pull his nails from their beds with a pair of pliers, then cut off his fingers and toes one at a time." He stops when my father fixes him with a warning look, suddenly aware that the women in the room are in tears. The judge orders Golesorkhi to be quiet, but he will not be silenced.

"You, sir, may go to hell," Golesorkhi says, chin high and eyes unblinking. "People, take note of what he looks like," he shouts, addressing the whole room. "Make sure he is identified everywhere as a crony of the greatest dictator alive."

"It's about time someone stood up to these bastards," Dad whispers, careful not to look over at me. Not that he has to, because the space between his beating heart and mine feels taut, as if they've been tied together with a string.

My mother is crying. "He's so young," she wails, "not a day over thirty. His poor parents, his poor wife!"

Golesorkhi's testimony is stopped abruptly by the judge and the broadcast is terminated. The screen goes black, and then crackles back to life with a repeat episode of an American soap opera called *Peyton Place*.

I retreat to the roof without bidding our guests good night, knowing that Ahmed will spend the evening trying to soothe his family, probably making jokes and doing impressions that will soon have everyone clutching their sides with laughter.

The night is well into morning when I finally close my book and stand up with a sigh. I had hoped that reading would take my mind off Golesorkhi's explosive tirade, but the words on the page look foreign and I have to read every line twice to drown out his voice booming in my head. Most of the windows are dark, but I can feel that I'm not the only one who is too agitated to sleep.

I decide a walk might calm my mind, and make my way out into the alley. I am stepping slowly and methodically, hands in my pockets, willing my thoughts to slow when the silhouette of a man crosses swiftly through the pool of yellow light cast by a streetlight ahead of me. His head is covered with a hat, and he is working quickly to glue something to the wall. He dips a brush into a small pail, then strokes a large X on the wall and slaps a large piece of paper up, moving quickly up the alley. I creep forward to look, and see a poster with a red rose at its center.

"Golesorkhi," I say out loud, clapping my hands over my mouth when I hear how my voice rings out.

The man turns, startled; his face is painted black, his round glasses glittering.

"Doctor?" I whisper, squinting.

He freezes, and I know we've both stopped breathing. Reactions flash in his eyes—fear, regret, conviction, anger? After a moment that feels like a month, he runs away without answering, and I'm left with a pounding heart to add to my racing mind.

The next morning the neighborhood wakes up to walls papered in red roses.

"Who put these up?" everyone wants to know.

"What does it mean?" another person asks.

"Oh, the Red Rose," some people say, understanding.

"Red is the color of love," one person tells another.

It's also the color of blood, I think, my heart sinking to meet a rising stomach when I consider the risk my friend has taken. If the SAVAK ever finds out that he's responsible for this, he'll be finished.

Five days pass before Doctor finally comes to see me on the roof.

"Listen, I'm going away," he says, his eyes anxiously scanning the horizon. "I'll be away for some time."

"Where're you going?" I ask, my voice flat with frustration.

"To a village up north by the Caspian Sea with a bunch of my college buddies." Doctor continues quickly, "It's no big deal, we do this every year."

I think back to the previous summer and know he didn't go away then. The fact that he's lying makes me furious. He must sense my anger because he can't seem to get the words out of his mouth fast enough.

"People in the villages need to be educated," he says passionately. "We'll be teaching the adults how to read and write. We'll teach them about health issues. We'll help them dig wells and show them more efficient irrigation techniques."

"Really?" I snap. "The government suspects people who engage in those kinds of activities."

His shock is plain, both at my words and the fever behind them.

"When I come back, I plan to marry Zari," he says, more calmly, really looking at me for the first time since he arrived. "I need to settle down. I love her so dearly."

The sound of Zari's name and the poised way in which he declares his love for her jolts me. Suddenly, all my anger about his thoughtless bravery evaporates into the vast warmth of his gentle brown eyes.

"Does she know?" I ask.

"No," Doctor says. "This will be our secret, okay?"

"Okay," I say, ignoring the sharp pain at the center of my heart.

"After what we all saw on TV a few nights ago," Doctor adds, referring to Golesorkhi's trial, "I need Zari in my life." Doctor's eyes fill with tears. "Golesorkhi is the most compassionate man I've ever known, and he'll be placed against a wall and shot to death like a common criminal." He roughly wipes the tears from his face. "It's time . . . ," he begins fiercely, then stops.

"Time for what?" I ask.

Doctor draws in a deep breath, then smiles and asks, "What's the most precious human commodity?"

"Life," I answer, without the slightest hesitation.

He laughs good-naturedly and shakes his head. "Time," he says. "Time is the most precious thing we possess." He touches my shoulder and says, "It's time to understand that we can't waste any more time. 'It is not the consciousness of men that determines their social being; it's their social being that determines their consciousness.' Do you know who said that?"

I say Karl Marx, and he smiles again but doesn't confirm the answer. His quote reminds me of my grandmothers, who attribute everything to God—including the most dreadful calamities—and are then unable to explain the reason behind God's inexplicably unmerciful actions. I quickly check the blasphemous thoughts and discreetly bite the skin between my index finger and thumb. This is the gesture you're supposed to use when you say or think something sacrilegious, so that God will forgive you rather than causing the roof to collapse on your head.

Doctor reaches into his side pocket and takes out a book called *The Gadfly*. "This is for you," he says. "It carries a sentence of at least six months, so be very careful."

I take the book and quickly shove it in the side pocket of my jacket. "This will become my most prized possession," I vow, trying to hide my shame over my secret feelings for Zari, though I am sure they must be stamped on my face.

"About the posters—" Doctor begins with his head down.

I interrupt him. "Don't know who put them up, but it was a nice touch."

He lifts his head and looks at me from the top of his round glasses. A thoughtful expression covers his face.

"And that's *That*," he says.

4

Suvashun

For reasons the adults don't understand, kids ringing the bell and running away has become a widespread problem in our neighborhood. It happens with more frequency in the early parts of the afternoon when no one is out. Ahmed and I think that the kids are from our own alley. My mom, of course, thinks the kids in our alley are too polite to do that.

One afternoon when my father is walking home, he sees Ahmed's five-year-old brother standing by the door to Iraj's house. "Hi, Aboli," my father says with a big smile. "What're you doing?"

"Can you help me ring the bell to Iraj's house?" Aboli asks innocently. "I can't reach it."

My father says sure and rings the bell. The second the bell sounds, Aboli grabs my father's hand and says, "Okay, now run!" My poor father suddenly realizes what he's done. He lifts Aboli off his feet and starts running toward our house. Ahmed and I are sitting in my yard when Dad rushes in and shuts the door behind him, leaning back against it to catch his breath.

"What's the matter?" I ask, surprised by his condition.

He looks at Aboli and begins to laugh. Then he tells us the story, which makes all of us join in the laughter. When we've finally stopped chuckling, my dad lifts Aboli off the ground and says, "You're lucky you're so cute, little buddy."

The next day, Iraj invents what he calls an "ingenious" device to catch the bell ringers. His gadget is comprised of a little tube connected to a small water pump. The device squirts water at the person ringing the bell. The tube is placed over the door so that it's hidden from view. He activates the device in the early part of the afternoon in the hope of catching the culprits who ring his family's bell at least two or three times a week. Of course, his invention never works and everyone remains dry.

Some days I wish I had the courage to tell Ahmed about Zari. God, if Zari were only a few years younger and not engaged to Doctor, I'd tell Ahmed about her deep blue eyes, her crooked smile, and her beautiful chin and cheekbones. I'd tell him how her walk makes me crazy, that when she talks I can't breathe and that I can't stop thinking about her. As nauseating as the thought is, I'd drink an entire pitcher of my mother's engine oil if I knew it would give me the courage to spill my guts to my best friend.

I can hardly listen to Ahmed's stories about Faheemeh anymore because I'm always thinking about Zari. I never think anything sexual about her; she's too pure for that and I would go crazy with guilt and shame. I imagine Doctor and Zari as a happily married couple with many children, and I accept my role as a good friend in their lives. Instigating Ahmed's revolt against Faheemeh's family has soured the daydream for me, though. I know I can't do what he did. First of all, Zari loves Doctor. Second, I don't have Ahmed's courage. Third, I just couldn't pull something like that on a great guy like Doctor. Sometimes, however, I wonder what my relationship with Zari would be like if Doctor were not in our lives, and each time, I involuntarily and swiftly bite the skin between my thumb and index finger.

In my mind, I live the rest of my life with a sweet secret that no one will ever know. But one evening on the roof while Ahmed is talking and I'm staring at the star-studded skies of an early summer night, I find myself interrupting him. "I want to tell you a secret," I say.

"Is it about you and Zari?" he asks immediately.

"When did you first know?"

"When did I know my best friend was in love?" He grins. "I guess every time he got restless when a certain individual walked by, or when he couldn't look her in the eyes even when she was talking directly to him. Like the time she brought us cold *sherbet* after soccer, and your hands were shaking when she offered you a glass, remember? Oh, and this one is my favorite. She asked you what time it was and you looked at your watch and said five minutes to lunch."

I look down at my feet as Ahmed laughs.

"You know one other thing you always do?" he asks. "You've named the biggest and the brightest stars after her, night after night."

"Really?"

"And didn't you ever notice how I always name the star next to her after you?"

I shake my head.

So, it's my turn to tell Ahmed everything, and his turn to listen all night. I tell him about her walk, her chin and her cheekbones. I tell him about her eyes and about my dreams, my guilt and my constant efforts not to imagine her in inappropriate ways. But I don't tell him about Doctor's plans to marry her when he returns. After all, a promise to a friend must always be kept.

Ahmed smokes a cigarette as he listens, offering me one. I could smoke the whole pack, but I decide not to risk my father's dirty look.

"When did you first know that you love Zari?" Ahmed asks.

"For as long as I can remember," I say, my head down. "I think maybe your situation with Faheemeh forced me into accepting it."

We're quiet for a while. The look on Ahmed's face is serious as he thinks. Being insecure about the appropriateness of my decision to confess my feelings for Zari, I ask nervously if he thinks I'm evil.

"What in the name of God—" Ahmed laughs.

"Well, you know, because of Doctor and all," I stutter. "He's . . . he's our friend and . . . and we're sitting here talking about his fiancée. I mean, not you but me. It's horrible."

Ahmed laughs some more and shakes his head.

The next day, Ahmed tells me that Zari's six-year-old brother, Keivan, is building a little doghouse.

"Why? Is he getting a puppy?" I ask.

"Nah. It's just a summer school project." His stare makes me self-conscious.

"Why're you looking at me like that?" I ask.

"How's your carpentry?"

I laugh since I'm not handy at all. Ahmed rings the bell of Zari's house anyway, and before I know it we're in the yard helping Keivan. Zari's parents are at work, as they are every day, jointly managing a small restaurant they have owned for over twenty years in a nearby neighborhood.

Every time Zari comes out to the yard, she steals all my attention. I burn with shame and tell Ahmed that this is getting too complicated for me. Not only am I betraying Doctor, I'm pretending to be the friend of a six-year-old in order to be around his sister. Ahmed tells me to relax.

Zari is dressed in a tight blue T-shirt and a long black skirt covered in a flower pattern. Her damp hair is neatly combed back and she has a touch of makeup on. I'm too nervous and shy to look her in the eye, so every time she comes out to talk to us I clumsily busy myself with unfamiliar wood scraps and tools. When her back is to me, I look at the curve of her bicep and her delicate wrist. I notice the tiny

blond hairs on her arm that shine under the sun, and I get so excited
I want to jump out of my skin. There's a soothing tranquility in her
gaze, in the smiling eyes of a woman I would love to love. Her tiny
waist makes me wish I could wrap my arms around her. I have to look
the other way and squint a couple of times to wipe the image from my
mind.

She brings us cool drinks and thanks us for helping her little
brother. I'm so unsettled in her presence that I pour most of the drink
on myself as I nervously attempt to sip.

"Your chest's thirsty, too?" Ahmed asks in a smart-ass tone.

I give him a dirty look, which he ignores. Zari laughs at Ahmed's
comment and says, "Leave him alone, the poor guy is hot and thirsty."

When Zari goes back inside the house, Ahmed says, "She can't
keep her eyes off you."

"She hasn't even looked at me!"

"You don't know women. You think they're not looking at you, but
they watch your every move. Their brains work like radar. They see
you, but you have no idea you're on their screen. Don't be so bashful!
Talk to her when she comes back out."

A few minutes later Zari comes back into the yard. She sits at the
edge of the *hose*. She dips her pretty white feet in the cold water and
begins to read a book.

"Go talk to her," Ahmed whispers.

"No," I say abruptly.

"Go."

"No."

"You're hopeless," he says to me. "What're you reading?" he calls
to Zari.

"*Suvashun* by Simin Daneshvar."

Ahmed turns to me in mock amazement. "Your favorite book,
wow!" He tells Zari, "He loves that book."

I want to kill him. I haven't even read *Suvashun*.

"What do you think of it?" Zari asks.

"Well, Daneshvar is one of the best writers," I mumble nervously, as I try not to look her directly in the eyes for fear I might stop breathing altogether. "She's so good. Actually much better than good, she's very good."

From the corner of my eye I see Ahmed shaking his head. Zari listens attentively.

"And her husband," I continue. "Jalal Al-Ahmed is just as good or even gooder."

"Oh, much, much gooder," Ahmed confirms.

"I . . . I mean, maybe a better writer. I'd read anything by the two of them." I realize that I'm babbling, and I shut up.

"Yes," Zari says. "I would read a story by Daneshvar and Al-Ahmed, too." Her eyes wander back to the book. I let Ahmed know with my eyes that I'm going to kick his ass as soon as we're alone, and he winks at me.

By that afternoon, the doghouse is finished. We are about to leave when I hear Zari tell Ahmed, "Of course, anything for you. I'd love to."

"What was that about?" I ask him angrily when we are in the alley.

"I asked her if she wanted to kiss you, and she said she would love to."

"You son of a bitch," I say, and attack him. He starts running toward his house.

"Well, is it my fault you're so cute that she wants to kiss you?"

"Shut up!" I shout as I'm chasing him. "You made me look like a fool."

"How was I supposed to know you haven't read *Suvashun*? You've read every other fucking book in the world," he says, looking back to make sure I'm not closing in on him.

"You son of a bitch," I curse again, kicking my feet out at him. "I'll kick your ass for what you did to me."

"What happened to your pledge to the sacred brotherhood of the boxing fraternity?" Ahmed teases as he disappears into his house, shutting the door behind him. I stand there for a few minutes, breathing hard, sweating and angry. Then I hear him from the other side of the wall. "Is Al-Ahmed really a gooder writer than his wife?"

Furious though I am, I collapse with hysterical laughter.

Winter of 1974
Roozbeh Psychiatric Hospital, Tehran

I know I am dreaming, even though I'm not sure where my body sleeps. In my mind, I'm in a pasture with Zari, Faheemeh, and Ahmed. We are running aimlessly, sometimes toward, sometimes away from one another. Zari stops and tilts her head to one side, smiling at me. The wind blows her long hair and it bends in the same direction as the tall green grass brushing our knees. I walk up to her and pull her body to mine. She fills my arms. I lift her in the air and we spin for what seems like an eternity. I can see Ahmed doing the same to Faheemeh. Lines from a poem by Rumi unfurl in the air around us, spoken in Doctor's voice on the wind.

Happy the moment, when together, you and I.
In two forms, but one spirit, you and I.
Parrots of love in heaven they sing
And we'll laugh cheerfully, you and I.

I see Doctor walking away from us in the distance. Zari looks at me, leans in slowly, and kisses me on the lips. Then she and Ahmed stand up and follow Doctor. Faheemeh and I begin to weep inconsolably.

Humming through the white noise of my dream, the verses of the
Rumi poem are replaced by a blank, rhythmic chanting.

If I had a gun, I would aim it.
If I had a mask, I would wear it.
If I had a pain, I would hide it.
If I had a heart, I would share it.

I concentrate on opening my eyes, and find myself in the wheelchair again. Apple Face is sitting next to me, her face turned toward
the old man on the other side of the room. I know I was just dreaming,
but my mind can't hold on to the details; trying is like gripping silk.

"Water?" I whisper.

She turns toward me calmly, but the brightness in her eyes be-
trays her excitement. "What did you say?" she asks.

"I'm thirsty," I croak.

Her eyes scan my face from left to right, then right to left. She whispers that she'll be right back, and disappears behind me. She comes
back a few seconds later with a pitcher of water and a glass.

"How thirsty are you?" she asks.

"Very thirsty."

She fills the glass with water, and looks at my body slumped in the
wheelchair.

"Take it," she says, bringing the glass close to me.

I reach out, take the glass, and empty it in one continuous gulp.
Her face breaks into a warm smile, and I think I see tears in her eyes,
but I have no idea why she is crying.

"Where am I?" I ask.

"You're here," she says, in a smart but gentle tone.

"Who're you?"

"Don't you know me?" she teases. "Everyone knows me, including
me."

"You're Apple Face," I say, and laugh weakly. She laughs hard.

"My ribs hurt," I say.

"I know. Nothing's broken, don't worry."

I look at my arms.

"Why do I have burned spots on my arms and hands?"

Apple Face doesn't respond.

"And I have nightmares, all the time. I see a man with wicked eyes. Who is he?" And as I talk about my dreams, something snaps inside me, pulling a swell of emotion up from the depths of my stomach, and I begin to cry. Apple Face sits in the chair next to me and puts her arms around me.

"Cry, my darling. Cry."

"Why am I crying?" I ask, pulling back to search her streaming eyes.

"Don't you remember anything?" she asks, startled.

"Remember what?"

She leans back, rocking slightly. "Never mind," she soothes, "just close your eyes. No one needs a reason to cry."

5

Summer of 1973
Tehran

Under the Cherry Tree

Ahmed and I are in the alley watching Iraj demonstrate one of his newest inventions to a group of semi-interested kids when Faheemeh walks past us. She looks at me with a smile and winks, then rings the bell to Zari's house. When Zari opens the door they hug and kiss as if they have been friends for a million years, and Zari pulls Faheemeh into the house. I ask Ahmed if they know each other.

"Are you kidding? They're like sisters."

"Since when?"

"Since today," he answers, grinning. He explains that Faheemeh will be coming to Zari's house every day for the rest of the summer. "We are going to sit around Zari's *hose* and chitchat about life. Are you ready?"

"Ready for what?"

"Just follow me."

He runs inside his house and I follow him up the steps toward the roof.

"Where're we going?" I ask, anxiously.

"We can't let the neighbors see we're getting together at Zari's house. They talk, you know. It wouldn't be good for the girls."

"How did you get Zari to agree to this?"

"I promised to bring you along."

My heart skips as I say, "You're lying."

"Yes, I am," he says, laughing.

We run the rest of the way up to Ahmed's roof and cross over mine and then to Zari's, where she is waiting to let us in. I can feel my heart thumping a rhythm in the pit of my stomach from excitement. Zari smiles and says hello to both of us as she lets us in the house.

Down in the yard, the four of us sit on a red blanket in the shadow of the cherry tree by the *hose*. Ahmed, Faheemeh, and Zari exchange small talk, and I watch them silently. Guilt, shame, and excitement crowd my heart, making it impossible for me to focus on anything that's being said or think of anything to say myself. Even in my private thoughts, Zari was never anything more than the object of a timid and cautious desire; to explore possibilities with her would have been beyond anything I ever dared to imagine.

On the other hand, I console myself that nothing will ever come of this. So what's the harm in a little bit of fun, especially since she's getting married to Doctor in a couple of months anyway? The summer stands open like a doorway between adolescence and adulthood with the four of us on the threshold. After this year I'll go to the United States, Zari and Doctor will start their life together, and Ahmed will marry Faheemeh. Things will be very different for all of us. So why can't I enjoy the company of a beautiful girl in a completely harmless way?

Ahmed and Faheemeh sit next to each other and Zari is directly across from me. She brings us iced drinks in the early parts of the afternoon, and then later, as the weather cools, hot, sweet Lahijan tea— the best black tea in the world.

Ahmed and Faheemeh look great together. Faheemeh is a beautiful woman, although I would never compliment her on her looks because it's not polite to tell a friend's girlfriend that she is pretty. She has long black hair, which she habitually tosses back over her left shoulder with a graceful movement of her head. She almost always ends her comments with a question and an inquisitive look. The personal way she addresses you makes you feel like an old and trusted friend. Her black bell-bottomed pants and white silk shirt fit her perfectly. I know I'm going to like Faheemeh a lot.

Zari and I are not in tune with each other. She talks about Doctor, a sure sign that she misses him dearly. "He's gone away on a university project," she tells us.

A university project? I ponder. *He told me he was going to work with the peasants.*

"Doctor and I have been together since birth," Zari says. "Our parents vowed that their children would marry each other. This was their way of ensuring that their friendship would be preserved for as long as they lived."

"Wow, I didn't know that," Ahmed says, genuinely surprised.

"I feel lucky that Doctor has turned out to be a great guy, or I would have had a difficult time agreeing to it."

Arranged marriage? I think cynically. *Doctor is one of the most progressive thinkers in our neighborhood. How could he go along with such an absurd and outdated tradition?*

Ahmed winks at me, raises his eyebrows, and nods a couple of times as if he's reading and confirming my thoughts.

As Zari talks, I look at her tiny ears, her rosy lips, her silky, fresh skin, and my face burns with desire. She has a soft, low voice that sounds confident, even a little too mature for her face, but perfect in my ears. When she leans forward I can see some of her chest through the opening of her shirt. Then I remember that she is Doctor's girl and I am once more seared by guilt. She looks mostly at me when she speaks, but she seems to have a restrained attitude toward me.

"I don't think she wants me here," I tell Ahmed and Faheemeh when Zari goes inside to check on Keivan.

Ahmed's thoughts are preoccupied. "Arranged marriage?" he

mumbles, irritated. He looks at Faheemeh. "What is it with you girls? Why're your parents always trying to ditch you?"

"Oh, be quiet," Faheemeh says, smiling.

When Zari comes back, she pours tea for us in small teacups she brought from the kitchen. Then she asks Faheemeh and Ahmed how they met.

"I used to follow her home from school every day," Ahmed explains.

"Did you know he was following you?" Zari asks Faheemeh.

"The whole world knew." She tells Zari about Ahmed's public display of affection, after she was set up for an arranged marriage.

Zari laughs. "Good for you." She taps Ahmed on the back. "I'm proud of you." Then she asks Faheemeh, "How do your parents feel about what he did?"

"They aren't happy. They're embarrassed. The groom's parents don't talk to them anymore."

Ahmed sits straighter at the comment, puffing his chest out as if proud of his accomplishment, and Faheemeh swats his arm playfully.

"Would your parents ever agree to you two . . . ?" Zari doesn't finish the sentence, unsure where their relationship is heading.

"Well, they've forbidden me to see him," Faheemeh says with a sad look. Then she suddenly cheers up. "But once they get to know him, they will fall madly in love with him. I'm certain of it." She reaches over and grabs Ahmed's chin in her hand. "Look at this face, can you blame them?"

Ahmed turns red as Zari and I laugh.

"When he was following you, did you want him to talk to you?" Zari asks after a few seconds.

Faheemeh thinks for a while, and says no.

"No? Really?" Ahmed asks, surprised. "You didn't want me to talk to you?"

"I was scared. I didn't want you to get in trouble," Faheemeh says quietly. "I felt as if someone was pulling my heart out when my brothers were beating you up." Tears fill her eyes.

I look at Zari. She bites her lower lip and smiles. Ahmed blushes again. Then he points to me while talking to Zari and says, "They were lucky my buddy here didn't go after them. Did you know he's a boxer?"

Zari shakes her head no.

A boxer? Punching a bag makes me a boxer?

"Oh, he's a marvelous boxer," Ahmed says. "He's faster than anyone I've ever seen."

Uncomfortable with Ahmed's undeserved compliments, I try to change the topic, but Ahmed continues. "Well, he's the son of an ex–heavyweight boxing champion. He's got good fighting genes."

I finally break in. "So, you and Doctor have known each other forever, huh?"

"Yes," Zari says as she sets the full teacups in front of us. Then she turns to Ahmed and Faheemeh. "I admire people like you. I have always been intrigued by how strangers fall for each other. For as long as I can remember, I was supposed to be in love with Doctor."

Supposed to be in love? I wonder, bitterly.

Zari puts a sugar cube in her mouth and starts to drink her tea while looking at Faheemeh. "I always wondered how it happens," she says. "I mean, what makes two perfect strangers fall in love? How do you know you're making the right decision?"

Faheemeh looks at Ahmed, and he shrugs his shoulders.

"You don't," I say, as though I'm some kind of an expert on love. "In an arranged marriage, you rely on the wisdom of the elders; in cases like theirs, on the intuition of your own heart."

I wish Mom were here to see that I'm not as introverted as she thinks I am. I have no doubt, however, that she would claim her engine oil is working.

Ahmed gives me a smile and a little wink.

"Intuition of the heart," Zari repeats with a spark in her eyes. "I like that: intuition of your own heart."

"He's got a way with words, doesn't he?" Ahmed boasts. Then he looks at me with an expression that tells me he's about to inflict some serious pain.

"His words are like beautifully composed vignettes strung together unabashedly by characters and time."

I know at that very moment that Ahmed will not live long enough to marry Faheemeh.

Zari looks at Ahmed for a while. I think she's trying to figure out what he just said. Then she turns to Faheemeh. "Giving in to the intuition of your heart must've been a lot more exciting than going along with the wisdom of your elders, huh?" she says, obviously thinking of Faheemeh's narrow escape from her arranged marriage.

"It was," Faheemeh confirms joyfully.

"It's like what you see in Hollywood movies," Zari says. "Letting someone new into your life, sharing your secrets with him, learning new things about him, all of it sounds so romantic to me. It also sounds risky and dangerous. I never had to deal with any of that with Doctor."

"You didn't?" Faheemeh asks.

"No. He and I were playmates as children," Zari explains. "Of course now I only get to see him a couple of times a week. He's much too busy. And he only comes over when my parents are home. He doesn't want people to talk; you know what I mean? He's very traditional in that sense. I suppose there is a lot of good in our relationship, but your story is the kind of stuff people write books about."

I can tell from Zari's restless body language that she is not comfortable talking about Doctor's visits to her house. Is her discomfort due to wanting to see Doctor more, or because she's not excited about her arranged marriage?

Faheemeh smiles as Ahmed winks at me again. I know exactly

what is going through his head. The next time we are alone, he will say that Zari is not really in love with Doctor and that theirs would be a marriage of convenience. This, Ahmed will argue, is a custom an educated guy like Doctor has a moral obligation to resist. What would everyone say? The promising young scholar marrying a girl his parents picked out for him before he was even born? Ahmed will try to convince me to do something stupid, like shouting from the rooftop that I'm in love with Zari, and that Doctor should step aside as her intended husband and devote his life to emancipating our country from the grip of backwardness.

Later in the day, Zari tells us about her relatives and parents. Her mother was raised in an extremely religious family in Qum, one of Iran's holiest cities. Most of the women on her mother's side cover themselves with *chadors*. She has a cousin who could be a movie star if she lived in the United States or in Europe, but she wears a *burqa* that covers her from head to toe, like the women in Saudi Arabia. Zari calls her the "Masked Angel."

"The Masked Angel?" I ask. "Sounds like a great title for a movie."

Ahmed uses this opportunity to promote me again. "He's seen every classic American movie ever made," he says. "He's like a movie encyclopedia. He knows all the actors, all the directors, and all the producers. He'll be a great filmmaker himself someday."

Zari looks at me and says, "You want to be a filmmaker?"

"I do," I respond.

"That's very exciting."

Ahmed grins in triumph.

"I like the American movies, too," Zari says. "But Doctor believes Hollywood is dominated by the Jews promoting Zionism." She adds that she doesn't know what Zionism means but knows that it's not good to be a Zionist.

Faheemeh says her father is a columnist for *Keyhan*—the largest newspaper in Iran—and his childhood dream was to interview Walt Disney, but someone at *Keyhan* told him that Disney is an agent of Zionism. She admits that she doesn't know what Zionism is either, but from the sound of it, it must be awful to be a Zionist!

Ahmed turns his head toward me to coach me, mouthing, "Talk about Zionism! Talk about Zionism!"

"A lot of the kingpins of the Hollywood studio system were actually Jews," I say, taking the bait. "Zucker, Meyer, Selznick—they were all Jews, but I'm not sure they made any movies that promoted the creation of the state of Israel, which is what Zionism is about."

"Wow," Ahmed says, in mock amazement. "How do you know all this? I'm always learning something new from you."

"May I have some water?" I ask Zari, hoping to interrupt Ahmed.

Every time Zari goes inside the house to bring food and beverages, I wish I were somewhere else so that Faheemeh and Ahmed could be alone, but I don't know where to go. Finally, Zari comes to my rescue. She calls me from inside the house. It is the first time she has called me by my name, and it sounds distinctive when she says it. Hearing my name on her lips makes me a more important person, somehow. I walk into the house and see her peeling an orange with her back to the kitchen door.

"I wanted you to come in so they could have a little time together," she says, as she turns to smile at me.

"I know. What can I do to help?"

"Nothing. Just keep me company." She turns back and continues peeling the orange.

The pressure is on. This is the first time I've been alone with her and I have no idea what to say. Keivan walks into the kitchen, gets a glass of water, and leaves immediately. *Maybe Iraj isn't such a bad guy after all*, I tell myself as I think of how he looks at Ahmed's sister.

Zari says, "They look lovely together."

I agree. "It's nice of you to do this for them."

"Oh, I would do anything for Ahmed. He's a great guy."

"He is," I concur, and realize that I'm out of things to say.

A long, awkward pause ensues.

"Are you always so quiet?" she asks, flashing me a smile over her shoulder.

"No, not usually," I say, struggling to think of something profound to say about the way I interact with people, but failing miserably and slinking back to my silence.

"Is there anyone special in your life?"

I don't know what to say. She notices my pause and turns around to see if I'm still there. She grins when she notices that I'm blushing.

"Don't be shy. I'm only a couple of years older than you are. You can tell me anything. That is, if you want to."

"Yes, there's someone special." I think this is the best answer because it gives me something to talk to her about.

"Ah, I thought so. I see you and Ahmed up on the roof every night. I figured you two must talk about girls." She pauses for a little while. "So now I know he talks to you about Faheemeh. Who's the queen of your stories?"

I feel tremendously excited to have her attention focused on me. I look around a little bit, throw my arms up, shift my weight from one leg to the other a couple of times and say, as she is intently watching me, "I can't tell you who she is."

A smile springs up to her face. "You're so cute," she says. After a few seconds, she walks up to the refrigerator and takes out some apples. "Now, why not? Why can't you tell me?"

I don't reply.

"Quiet *and* shy!" she teases. "Girls love shy and quiet guys, the mysterious kind, did you know that?"

I shake my head no, while wishing my mother could hear that some people think being introverted is immensely attractive.

"Now you must tell me," Zari insists. "You know how people become good friends? By sharing secrets. So tell me, who is she?" She walks back to her original spot. "Is she pretty? Do I know her? Does she live in our alley? Come on, who is she?"

"You know her," I whisper.

"Oh, good. So she must live in the alley. This is good, we're getting somewhere now."

I keep quiet.

"Does she go to school?" she asks.

"She just graduated from high school."

"An older woman! That's always exciting. Is she pretty?"

"She's the most beautiful woman on the planet," I blurt out. "She has blue eyes, a lovely chin and great cheekbones."

I notice that she stops peeling for a few seconds, and fear that I've gone too far. After all, she's the only girl in our alley with blue eyes.

"She sounds great. Where does she live?" she asks, keeping her back to me.

"Close by," I say, hesitantly.

"What do you like about her, besides her looks of course?" she continues, her tone a bit more serious.

"Everything," I admit. "She reminds me of snow, pure and clean; of rivers, calm and flowing; of rain, revitalizing and refreshing; of a mountain, strong and majestic; and of flowers, delicate and soft."

Zari turns around and stares right at me with a puzzled but thoughtful, crooked smile. Her gaze is loaded with questions, the kind that strike the mind like a flash of lightning, momentarily illuminating your surroundings then leaving you wondering, in the ensuing darkness, what you actually saw.

"Does Ahmed know who she is?" she finally asks.

"Yes."

"I'm going to ask him—you know that, don't you?"

She begins to laugh, and we carry the food and beverages out to the yard. I feel so weak that I have to use every ounce of energy in my body not to drop the fruit bowl. When we get back to the yard, Zari brings out her father's camera and teaches Keivan to take a picture of the four of us sitting around the *hose*. She says she will make a copy of the picture for each of us, so that we can remember this summer when we became the best of friends.

That night in bed, I relive every moment of the day, including the part when I made an ass out of myself by comparing her to rivers and flowers. "What do you like about her, besides her looks?" she had asked. I wish I had not babbled on like a romantic idiot. I should have talked about her favorite colors, her favorite food, the kinds of movies she likes, and the books she enjoys reading.

I suddenly realize that I don't know much about Zari. In fact, I don't really know anything about her. I don't know how she chooses friends, what her hobbies are, or what kinds of people she likes. All I know is that I love her. Is this how everyone falls in love? I wonder how much Ahmed knows about Faheemeh—probably not much. I know that my father first saw my mother on her way home from school and followed her every day for a month before finding the courage to say something to her. A month after their first conversation, he sent his parents to her house to ask for her hand.

God, I'm thoroughly confused. Love is an all-consuming affair; it brings life to a standstill. I can't think of anything but Zari anymore. How do grown-ups fall in love and work at the same time?

I look toward Ahmed's roof. He's fast asleep, and I can hear him snoring. I walk over to his bed and wake him up.

"What's going on?" he asks.

"Zari asked me what I liked about the woman I love, and I couldn't think of anything to tell her," I say in a desperate voice.

Ahmed stares at me with a confused look on his face

"I read somewhere that people in the West, like in the U.S. and

Europe, date for a long time before falling in love," I say, restless with anxiety. "Did you know that?"

Ahmed shakes his head no.

"It's true. I've seen it in the movies, too. They date for a long, long time. Sometimes for ten or even twenty years!"

"Wow," Ahmed whispers.

"But here in Iran, we look at someone, and we fall in love. All the girl has to do is smile, and we're swept off our feet. No dating, no getting to know each other, no real opportunity to get acquainted, do you know what I mean? Like, do you really know what Faheemeh is like? Do you know her favorite colors, favorite food, hobbies?"

"No."

"Aren't you worried?"

Ahmed nods with a troubled look on his face.

"What if she's not the girl you think she is? What if Zari is incompatible with me? What if I married her and had kids with her and she turned out to be totally different from me? What could I do then?"

Ahmed puts his hands on his mouth and gasps.

"Don't you worry about that?" I ask.

"Yes, yes, I do now that you've mentioned it." He lights a cigarette. "My God, this is a real problem." He scratches the top of his head. "Let me think about it. I think you're onto something really big. I can finally see how all that reading is making you smarter."

I begin to elaborate on my point, but he tells me to be quiet because he's thinking. I sit there on the edge of his bed as he rocks back and forth and makes strange facial expressions, as if he's concentrating, looking at things from different angles, forming hypotheses and then rejecting them as implausible. He mumbles to himself, emitting strange sounds, lifting his eyebrows, moving his hands, and covering his upper lip with his lower one while looking toward the sky. He puffs on his cigarette and then blows the smoke out while sighing, as if genuinely disappointed by his inability to solve a simple puzzle.

When he finally finishes his cigarette, he walks up to the edge of the roof, puts it out, and throws the butt on the neighbor's roof to make sure that his father doesn't see it. Then he goes back under his covers and whispers, "I think I know what you should do. Why don't you go to the West, date somebody for a while, get to know her really well, and then come back and marry Zari." And with that, he turns over and begins to snore.

I sit there watching him for a few seconds. Then I get up, kick him in the ass, and return to my bed.

6

Vignettes of Love

Ahmed, Faheemeh, and I spend almost every day at Zari's house. I complain to Ahmed that all we do is sit around and talk, and that as wonderful as being with Faheemeh and Zari is, we should be doing other things, or the girls will soon get bored with us.

"Doing what else?" Ahmed asks.

"Take them out, go to the movies, go out to dinner," I say. "You know, exciting stuff."

"Really?" Ahmed asks sarcastically. "Now, would we tap into your checking account or my savings for that?"

I frown and shrug.

"And where the hell do you think we live, in America? This is Iran, and we're in our neighborhood—"

"Okay, okay, forget I said anything," I interrupt, knowing never to broach the topic again.

As the summer passes, it's evident that we're becoming better friends because we easily share our most intimate and personal experiences with one another. It's hard to say good-bye in the evenings. No one wants to leave, and we joke about it endlessly.

"It's time to go," one of us will say.

"Yeah, definitely time to go," someone else confirms, but no one moves and we all laugh. "Okay, maybe just a few more minutes, but then we really ought to go."

"Oh, yeah, definitely. Just a few more minutes."

It's easy to see that Ahmed and Faheemeh are in love. A special softening and sense of contentment take over Ahmed when he's around Faheemeh. He says he feels almost religious in her presence. "It's like I'm not me anymore. I can even tolerate being around Iraj," he says.

"It's so exciting to watch their relationship evolve," Zari says one time when we're alone. "They look more like a couple every time we see them, don't they?"

"They do."

"Their relationship is so different than mine with Doctor."

Every time she mentions Doctor, I involuntarily begin rolling up my shirtsleeves.

"Theirs is exciting and new," Zari continues dreamily. "Ours feels sort of dull in comparison, you know what I mean? Like we've already been married forever."

Then, as if she suddenly realizes that she is talking negatively about Doctor, she giggles and says, "Don't get me wrong. I adore Doctor. He's a wonderful human being. He's so smart, so compassionate. I feel so lucky to have him. Can you imagine a girl like me getting a guy like Doctor?"

She's trying too hard. Doctor is a great guy, but Zari cannot be entirely happy with their arranged marriage and with the lack of opportunity to experience love on her own. Does Doctor know how she feels? What would he do if he knew? Does he really love Zari, or is he just relying on the wisdom of his elders instead of the intuition of his own heart?

Every once in a while, Zari makes up an excuse to go inside the house to do a chore, and she always asks me to go along.

"Let's leave them alone for a little bit," she whispers as soon as we are a couple of steps away from them.

"Yes, let's," I respond, exploding inside with excitement.

One day when we're in the living room, she shows me a notebook and asks me if I can keep a secret.

"Of course," I say, relishing the thought of being promoted to the status of a trusted companion. She opens the book and shows me pencil drawings of our alley.

She doesn't want anyone to know that she draws and I assure her that I will keep her secret. Then she points to one of the pictures and says, "You guys playing soccer! Can you tell which one is you?"

"Which one?"

"You weren't there that day!" she teases with a smart-aleck smile on her face. I grin back. She says people and places are her favorite things to draw, and shows me a picture of Ahmed's grandma and her late husband. Grandma is standing still under a tree while he is walking toward her with a warm expression on his face. She seems oblivious to the fact that he's only a few meters away from her.

"He was a good man," Zari says. "He used to give me candies when I was Keivan's age. I really miss him."

There's a caricature of Iraj surrounded by girls. His eyes are wide open, as if he's trying to devour each girl with his gaze.

"You're an observant woman," I say.

"It's hard not to be observant when you feel his eyes burning a hole through you!" she says, and laughs loudly. I laugh, too, but inside, I wish I could get my hands on that horny little prick and pluck his beady, shameless eyes from their sockets.

Then Zari takes out a family album and shows me a picture of the Masked Angel.

"She's beautiful, isn't she?"

I glance at the picture. The Masked Angel is about the same height as Zari. Her long straight hair covers her shoulders and comes all the way down to her waist.

"Her eyes are blue, too. Just like yours," I say.

"It's our Russian background. Most girls in my family have blue eyes. By the way, this is the only time she has ever taken her burqa off in front of a camera."

"Your face lights up when you talk about her."

"She's my best friend," Zari says. "Her real name is Soraya. She's a brilliant girl. She's memorized all of Hafiz's poetry, can you believe that?"

"That's incredible," I say, as I think how grueling a mental practice it must be to memorize so much. "By the way, have you ever taken a *fahll* with Hafiz?" This is a customary tradition in Iran that involves closing your eyes, making a wish, and opening the book to a random page to find the answer to your dilemma.

"Yeah," Zari says. "That's one of my favorite things to do, but Doctor says it's an insult to Hafiz. He says Hafiz never intended to write a horoscope."

I laugh. I want to say that Doctor should relax, but I don't. Instead I say, "One of these days, I'll bring my Hafiz book here and we'll take a couple of *fahlls* together. And we won't tell Doctor. That'll be our other little secret."

A radiant smile covers her face. "I would love that."

One day I'm standing next to her as she is washing dishes in the kitchen. "Are you nervous about going to America?" she asks.

"Nervous?"

"You know, being so far away, alone, in a foreign country. And then your father's expectations; I hear he has big dreams for you. Doesn't it all get to you?" She stops washing dishes and turns to face me. She apologizes quickly. "Sorry if I sound like I'm prying."

"No, you're not," I say, as I hear my mother's voice in the back of my head: *People are dying from hunger in Africa and you want me to worry about your father sending you to the States? Would Bangladesh be a more suitable place for you?*

Then I remember the time I was frustrated with Dad's insistence that I go to America, and said to my mother, who knew how I felt about his plans, "See? Your engine oil is not bringing me out of my shell. I still can't discuss any of this with him. So, would you please stop pouring it down my throat?"

"You're right, my medicine isn't working," she conceded. "What a pity!" And with that she doubled my daily dose. "This should do the trick."

A smile creeps across my lips.

"Why are you smiling?" Zari asks.

I tell her the engine oil story, and she laughs heartily and says that I do a great imitation of my mother.

To answer her original question, I explain how a few days earlier my father came home with a magazine that was sent to him by a friend living in Europe. "It was the last three years depicted in pictures with a brief explanation of each photograph," I explain. "People starving in Biafra, a Chilean mother running to an ambulance outside a morgue to see if her jailed kid was among the ones executed that day, and many more. One picture in particular deeply troubled me. A little twelve-year-old girl had been repeatedly raped by the Nigerian soldiers in Biafra and left in a ditch to die. The picture was taken after she was transferred to a hospital. She had a smile on her face because she was told her mommy was on her way to visit."

"Oh, my God." Zari puts her hand on her mouth.

"Stuff like that helps put things in perspective, doesn't it?" I say.

She seems extremely sad now. Then a wistful smile appears on her beautiful face. She taps me on the shoulder and says, "You're so together. I love that in you."

A wonderful sensation rambles through me as she uses the words "I," "love," and "you." God, if she had only dropped those other two words from her sentence.

On the last Saturday of August, almost a month before the end of the summer, Ahmed and I take two roses to Zari's house and present them to the girls. The rose Ahmed gives to Faheemeh is red, meaning that he loves her. The one I give to Zari is white, meaning that she and I are good friends. The girls are genuinely touched by the gesture. Faheemeh hugs Ahmed and kisses him on the cheek. Zari shakes my hand and tells me that I am really sweet. Then she puts the rose in her hair, looks me right in the eye, and smiles. I'm so nervous that I immediately drop my gaze and blush. From that day on, I notice that Zari seems to dress nicer when we go over to her house.

"She's trying to look pretty for you," Faheemeh whispers. "Why don't you tell her you appreciate that?"

I vigorously shake my head no, and she and Ahmed laugh. The thought of complimenting Zari, however, feels extremely tempting. So one afternoon, when Zari and I are in the kitchen and she's washing the teacups, I muster up enough courage to tell her that her hair looks nice. I mumble my compliment in such an incomprehensible way that she turns around and asks, "What?"

I nervously try to repeat what I said, but my voice gets caught in my throat.

"Did you just say my hair looks nice?" she asks.

I nod yes. She smiles, turns around and continues to wash the dishes. I'm not sure what to do or say next.

"You like it better this way?" she asks.

I struggle to respond. "No, yes," I manage to stammer. "I mean, I like it both ways, but this way is very good. Of course this way or like before, I like them both. Both are nice, very nice." My jaw moves involuntarily and I have no way of stopping it.

"Okay, this is how it'll be from now on," she says quietly, without looking at me.

A special tenderness fills my heart, the likes of which I have never experienced before.

When I tell this story to Ahmed, he pats me on the back and says, "Excellent, excellent. Your plan is working."

"What plan?" I ask.

"The plan to make her wonder if you love her. Nothing makes a woman more curious than the suspicion that she's loved by someone. She'll do anything to confirm it now, you'll see. She'll go out of her way to find out if you really do. That's just human nature. Who doesn't want to be loved?" Then he scratches his head and continues. "Trust me. A storm is brewing inside this cool cat now. She'll gradually break down and you'll see what's behind the clouds."

7

One More Story, Please

It's Keivan's seventh birthday and the four of us are assigned to chaperone the party. Most of the small kids in the alley are invited to Zari's house, and Ahmed and I are there to help. Or, at least that's how Faheemeh and Zari explain our presence. We spend all day decorating the house with red, white, and yellow ribbons and balloons, which we hang from the ceilings and the walls. Faheemeh and Zari prepare sandwiches as I set out paper plates and cups and plastic knives and spoons. Ahmed has volunteered to be in charge of music. He has borrowed a small, inexpensive stereo-cassette player from a friend and has been working on setting it up all day.

"Preparing the right music for a party is the most critical part of the whole thing," Ahmed says. "You realize that, don't you? The whole party can be ruined if I don't come up with the right assortment of songs."

Faheemeh says, "Yes, honey, we do," as Zari laughs at Ahmed's clowning.

"Do you really realize it, or are you just agreeing because I'm so good-looking?" he taunts.

"Both, honey. You're right, and very good-looking," Faheemeh responds.

Ahmed begins to play his favorite songs as he dances in the middle of the room.

"You're a good dancer," Faheemeh compliments him.

"I had dance lessons from Tennessee Williams himself."

"Tennessee Williams was not a dancer," I argue.

"I tried to tell Tennessee that, but he wouldn't hear of it."

It seems as if all the kids show up at the same time. Ahmed says they must have been waiting outside the door, planning their invasion. His arrangement of songs is messed up within five minutes. Keivan is thrilled to be the center of attention. He wants to play horsey, and would like Ahmed to be his horse. Ahmed bends over and spends the rest of the day giving everyone horsey rides. I try to get on him once, but he kicks me away and mumbles profanities under his breath. Faheemeh and Zari laugh and applaud my attempt.

Kids run in the yard, up and down the steps, and from room to room. They yell, scream, push each other, and fight constantly. At one point, Keivan falls down and scratches his knee. Zari and Faheemeh and I sit down beside him to try and soothe him, but he keeps on crying.

"You know, I once broke my shin in three places and never cried," I say.

"How come, didn't it hurt?" Keivan pouts.

"Oh, yes, it sure did," I say. "But I figured crying wouldn't make the pain go away."

"Really?" Keivan asks.

I lift my arms in the air, doing my best to look puzzled. "My mom thought that was pretty weird, too. She said, 'How can you break your shin in three places and not cry?'" My imitation of her makes Ahmed chuckle in the background. "So now she gives me a tablespoon of syrup that's supposed to help me cry when I need to."

"Do you?" Keivan asks hesitantly.

"Only when I'm taking her syrup." I twitch my face as if I'm drinking my mother's horse urine potion.

Everyone laughs as I gently touch Keivan's knee. "It doesn't hurt anymore now, does it?"

"No." Keivan shakes his head.

"See, the pain goes away when you laugh."

Keivan jumps up and the games resume. Zari whispers thank you. Her gentle gaze makes my heart go wild.

Late in the afternoon we decide to play a game called Who Am I? All the kids gather in a circle, and Ahmed mimes a character while we guess who he is. The kids love the game, and so do Faheemeh, Zari, and I because it gives us a chance to sit down and relax. As we watch Ahmed assume different characters, Zari leans toward me and says, "You know, the question for you is not who am 'I' but who is 'she'?"

"Who is she?"

"Yeah, the one who's as soft as flowers and majestic as mountains? What else did you say?"

"Oh, forget that. That was stupid," I say, bashfully.

"I thought it was beautiful. She's a lucky girl to have you. You know that, don't you?"

I want to melt. I want to scream. I want Ahmed to hear this.

"Thank you," I say.

"I hope she's not jealous that you're helping me today."

"She's not the jealous type."

"No? All girls are jealous, don't you know that?"

I want to ask if she is jealous, but that might be rude.

"Well, how does she describe you?" she asks with a curious look on her face.

"I don't know. We haven't had that kind of talk yet."

"No? You haven't told her you love her yet?"

"I think she knows," I say hesitantly.

"But you haven't told her?"

"Not in so many words."

"Have you consulted Hafiz yet?" she asks. "Taken a *fahll*?"

I shake my head no.

"Well, you should and you'd better tell her soon. A girl wants to know she's loved, you know. Now, what did you say her name was?" she asks abruptly, hoping to trick me into revealing my secret.

I smile. "I can't tell you yet."

"You can't tell me because . . . ?"

"I . . . I don't know."

Zari keeps smiling. I'm shaking, and I think she knows it because she slowly slides away from me and we continue watching Ahmed miming different characters. A few minutes later, Zari goes to the kitchen and comes back with a plate full of different kinds of sandwiches. "I knew you wouldn't get a chance to eat, so I set these aside for you," she says.

The knowledge that she was thinking of me spirals around in my head like a song.

"I hope you like cold sandwiches," she continues.

How could I not when they were made by her?

After the kids leave, Ahmed, Zari, Faheemeh, and I sit around a small dining table completely exhausted. I stare at a bowl of ice cream that has been in front of me for at least twenty minutes. The girls look at the mess created by the kids and can't believe that we still have to clean up.

"My back is killing me," Ahmed says. "You know, my parents are going away for a few days. Why don't you come over and we'll have a party for the four of us to celebrate surviving these kids? We'll play slow songs and dance all night long."

My heart sinks as I think of Zari in my arms. I look at her and she smiles and drops her gaze.

"Are we going to have any kids?" Ahmed asks Faheemeh.

Faheemeh shows him four fingers and winks. Ahmed grabs his head.

"You two would make beautiful babies," Zari says, looking lovingly at the two of them.

Ahmed points to me and says, "He and his honey would make beautiful kids, too."

"Oh, yes. Beautiful, beautiful kids," Faheemeh agrees.

"He should've invited her to the party," Zari says. She waits for Ahmed and Faheemeh to respond, but they don't say anything. Then she turns to me. "This would've been a perfect opportunity for you to tell her how you feel."

Ahmed immediately snaps into his scholarly pose and says, "Well, I don't know about that. You see, he believes he has to get to know her before telling her that he loves her."

I know where Ahmed is heading, and I want to reach across the table and strangle him.

"What do you mean?" Zari asks.

"You see," Ahmed lectures, "most people in Iran fall in love without knowing much about each other. In the U.S. and Europe people date for a long time and get to know each other before falling in love." He points to me and continues, "He has a very intelligent theory about this. He told me all about it a few nights ago on the roof." Facing me he says, "Tell them."

I kick him as hard as I can under the table.

Zari and Faheemeh look at me, waiting for me to talk. I cough, mumble, and eat a spoonful of my melted ice cream to buy a little time. Finally I say, "Yes, in Europe and the United States people do spend a lot more time getting to know each other before declaring their love," and then I don't have anything else to say. After an awkward pause, I add, "In the West, relationships between men and women are readily accepted. In countries like ours, we're more concerned about God's will and destiny. Anthropologists should study the correlation between the advancement of technology and the forms of relationships between couples in these different kinds of societies."

I feel like a complete ass as I look at Ahmed's grinning face. *Why do I let him do this to me?*

Zari thinks for a while and says, "Interesting."

Ahmed puffs out his chest again and I kick him so hard that he stiffens up, trying his best not to groan in pain.

Zari looks at me and says, "When will you tell me who she is?"

"Probably not until the anthropologists publish their findings," Ahmed says, as he throws me a wink.

I will kill him! I swear I will!

We start cleaning the house. In the living room I see a picture of Doctor and Zari on the shelf. Doctor is smiling and has his arm around her shoulders. She has her patented crooked smile on, and her head is resting on Doctor's left arm.

"That's a horrible picture of me, but my mom likes it," she says, walking up behind me. "I keep hiding it away, but she finds it and puts it back on the shelf. One day I'm going to burn that picture."

"Why? It's a nice picture."

"Doctor looks nice, but not me," she says, avoiding my gaze.

I look down at the picture, and whisper, "I don't know about that. You have that smile."

"What smile?"

"Your crooked smile—your trademark," I whisper.

"My trademark," she says, as if it were a statement and not a question.

"Yeah, no one else smiles like that. I like it."

"You do?" she asks, head still down.

"Yeah. I also like the way you have your head tilted to one side."

"Yeah?"

"I like your eyes, too. They're smiling, like they do most of the time."

"They don't always?"

"They always smile when you're happy."

She looks up at me. "Are they smiling now?"

"Yes, they are."

We look at each other for a while. We're standing so close I can feel her breath on my face. My knees feel weak. In one split second, everything I've learned about her flashes in my head. Her favorite color is blue. She says that blue is associated with vastness; the skies are blue, the oceans are blue. I wonder why she always omits the fact that her eyes are blue, too. She is a storyteller. She and Keivan lie on a red blanket under the cherry tree in the yard every day after lunch. Zari always lies down on her side with her face toward the roof. I can tell she watches me by the way she follows my movements. I hear Keivan begging, "One more story, please, just one more." I wish she would whisper tales of our future into my ears, and then I, too, would beg for just one more. She wakes up early every morning and walks to the bakery at the end of the alley to buy hot fresh *lavash* for breakfast. I watch her all the way there and back from my position on the roof. She knows that I'm watching her because she looks up often.

Intoxicated with my knowledge of her ways, I feel her breathing deeply, her chest rising and falling just a few centimeters from my own. I am in love with her beyond the point of going back. I could bring our lips together with the smallest gesture, and we've both begun to lean in when Keivan walks into the room.

"Where's my blue shirt?" he asks.

Zari and I stand there motionless, staring into each other's eyes for a few more seconds.

"The one Doctor sent for my birthday," he clarifies.

Zari slowly turns her head and looks at Keivan. Then she turns toward me. "Doctor sent him a beautiful shirt," she whispers. "You should see it, very thoughtful of him." Then she walks toward the closet. "He's a very thoughtful man," she says, sounding choked up. "A very good man."

When I get home, my father wants me to watch *Casablanca* with him. He says that this is one of the greatest classics of all time. I want to tell him that I know because I'm a movie encyclopedia, according to Ahmed, but I don't. As we watch the movie, I listen carefully to the dialogue between Humphrey Bogart and Ingrid Bergman. Maybe I can learn how lovers talk. I think of what I said about the anthropologists and forms and patterns of relationships, and I want to die of embarrassment. Will Zari, Doctor, and I end up like the three main characters in *Casablanca*? I can see Doctor as the revolutionary who fought the Nazis, and I am the lonely bar owner who thinks he has the woman until the other man comes back. Would I have the strength to let her go as Bogart does? Would I find a getaway plane for Doctor to escape with my love from the Nazis? Would I sacrifice myself for the sake of their happiness?

After watching *Casablanca*, I go to the roof. I look toward Zari's room. Her lights are off. Suddenly, I notice a piece of paper on the wall between our houses with a little rock resting on it to prevent it from being blown away by the wind.

I pick up the paper. Zari has drawn a picture of me. I'm standing in the alley, in the rain, leaning against a tree. I'm looking to my right at a girl who is walking away toward a river in the background. Actually, she's floating away—a faceless angel. She has a white rose, like the one I gave Zari, in her long hair. A mountain is visible in the distance, its summit covered with snow. Zari has captured it all, pure, majestic, calm, and flowing. An inscription at the bottom of the page reads, "When you tell me who she is, I will complete your angel's face."

Winter of 1974
Roozbeh Psychiatric Hospital, Tehran

I'm standing on the roof, watching the swaying figure of a woman as she comes up the steps to join me. I can't make out her features, but the flowing walk and the full-blown, snowy rose in her hair intrigues me, and reminds me of Zari. Is it her? I hope so. The wind is both gentle and strong, rolling over my skin and carrying the rose's simple scent across the distance. I try to wait, but my legs betray me and I find myself running toward her, arms spread wide to gather her in. I see her arms reach out, I think I grab her, but she slips and falls off the edge. My voice trapped in my throat, I sit up in my sweat-drenched bed, gasping and choking, while my mother's mantra about people falling off roofs echoes in my ears.

I am alone in the room, a dull shaft of light falling from the small square window in the door. I squeeze my cold fingers then shake them, hard, as if I can fling the night terror from me like so much dark water. The sounds of the other patients who aren't sleeping drift up and down the hallway outside my room, and I find them strangely comforting. The lids of my eyes get heavy, but I don't dare fall back to sleep. Instead, I strip the soaked sheets from my bed and lie on the bare mattress, counting each of the nurse's steps along the corridor as they make their endless rounds.

A series of questions assaults my mind again: *Why am I here? Why can't I remember certain things, including recent events? Sometimes I don't recognize my parents when they enter the room. Why? Why can't I be free of the nightmares that have plagued my nights and days?*

It is excruciatingly painful for my sedated mind to actively search for answers. So I exercise my only option: ignoring them and letting the fog of unconsciousness roll in to obscure my surroundings. The mental haze is like a tent that I crawl into to remain safe from what seems baffling and threatening to me. And that is how I get through the night.

The next time I see Apple Face I tell her that I need something to stop the dreams. She asks me to describe them and I tell her that I can't remember most of them.

She assures me that my condition is normal and probably temporary.

8

End of Summer 1973
Tehran

Doctor's Night

Soraya, the Masked Angel, is visiting Zari. Faheemeh and her parents have gone to the Caspian Sea for the last few days of the summer, and Ahmed and I are bored to death. Without Faheemeh, it wouldn't be acceptable for us to go to Zari's house.

Iraj tries to show us his new inventions every chance he gets, but we don't pay any attention to him. In fact, most of the time we can't even tell what he's trying to make; his inventions seem like stupid gadgets that have no practical function.

My mother has discovered that powdered sorb prevents liver diseases. She has bought a brand-new pestle that she uses to crush the brownish plant. She intends to place the powdered substance on a board in the sun to dry for a few days before storing it in a small glass jar she has purchased specifically for that purpose. Ahmed and I wonder how she's going to make us eat it.

"She'll pour it in our tea," Ahmed says. "I'm not drinking tea at your house anymore."

"I'm not either," I say, and we both laugh.

From the roof of my house we see Soraya and Zari in her yard, sitting by the *hose* under the cherry tree. Soraya is always wearing her burqa, even when she's in Zari's yard. I guess she knows we can see her from the roof. She has mesmerized everyone in the alley. Iraj's mother, her biggest fan, tells everyone that Soraya is the most beautiful creature on earth.

"She has the face of an angel, and the body of a mermaid. The look in her large blue eyes takes your breath away! Her skin is soft, and her hair is like a calm sea. Her words are like poetry, delicate and tender. Her voice is like the chanting of an angel, magical and soothing."

I tell Ahmed that Soraya's burqa reminds me of our religion teacher, Mr. Gorji, telling us last year that every woman in his family wore the chador. He said unveiled women commodify their sexuality, that everyone knows that men are programmed to desire women who show off their faces and bodies, and that in a moral society you can't have horny men desiring other people's wives, mothers, and sisters!

"He really said all that?" Ahmed asks. "Must have been on one of the days he threw me out of class."

I say that as sad as this story sounds, it's all true. Then I tell him how Mr. Gorji said it is against the tenants of Islam for women to seek the same rights as men. Mr. Gorji called January 8, 1936, the day Reza Shah unveiled women, the darkest day in Iran's history. He said that in a just society, the government creates an atmosphere in which women can compete against one another in meaningful and appropriate roles specifically designed for them, such as raising children, teaching little girls, and cooking.

Ahmed laughs and says he will run all this by Faheemeh to ensure she knows where she stands in the family.

Ahmed and I have noticed that Iraj spends a lot of time in the alley these days. An anxious expression steals over his face every time the Masked Angel and Zari are there. He becomes clumsy and awkward, speaking with a stutter, as he follows the Masked Angel with his eyes everywhere she goes. He told me once that if he were a couple of years older, his mother would want him to marry Soraya. He really wishes he knew what she looked like.

I recall Mr. Gorji's lecture about desire and morality, and begin to laugh. The burqa is protecting Soraya from Iraj's lustful eyes, but it's obviously not preventing him from desiring her.

Early one evening, I'm sitting under the wall that separates my roof from Zari's, reading a book, when I hear her voice from the other side of the wall. She's speaking to the Masked Angel. I'm about to stand up to say hello when I realize that Zari is crying. I remain seated, not wanting to cause her any embarrassment.

"Be strong," the Masked Angel says. "Take heart because God takes care to guide things in the best interest of all parties involved. As long as you're well intentioned and live life with a pure heart, God's grace will turn your goodness into good fortune."

"I'm afraid God may punish me for my disloyalty," Zari cries out quietly. The Masked Angel recites a poem by Hafiz. I can hardly hear the verses, but they are something like:

The long-drawn-out cruelty of sorrow shall end.
Prayers dart to all directions I send.
Perhaps one hits the target I intend.

Zari keeps on crying without saying anything.

"Does anyone know?" Soraya asks.

"No," Zari responds, "just you. You're the only one who knows."

Zari's mother calls them for supper, and they hurry away. I wonder what it all means. Were they talking about me? Was she crying because she doesn't know what to do? My head is filled with questions, and I can't read anymore. I close the book and set it aside. Loving is a laborious and complex business.

There are only two weeks left before school starts, and Doctor should be coming back any day now. Despite being madly in love with Zari,

I still deeply respect and admire Doctor. I think it ironic that he
would be the person with the most constructive insight and advice
about my ordeal, if I ever had the courage to tell him about Zari.

The Masked Angel leaves for Qum, and Ahmed and his father
take their annual trip to Ghamsar, the town where Ahmed's relatives
live. I have never been to Ghamsar, but Ahmed says it's so small he
runs out of people to tease in less than twenty-four hours.

Late that afternoon, I begin to notice strange activities around
Zari's house. Doctor's parents come and go, hurriedly and quietly.
Zari hasn't been to the yard for hours. I think I hear Doctor's mother
crying for a few seconds, but then total silence fills the house again. I
wish I knew what was going on.

Thoughts of the mysterious activities at Zari's house keep me
awake. The night is hot and close, and I'm in my bed on the roof when
my solitude is suddenly interrupted by the heavy footfalls of a man
running down the alley. I look down, and instantly recognize Doctor.
He's running fast, breathing hard, moaning in fear, as if a hungry tiger is chasing him.

He stops at Zari's door, rings the bell, and looks back down the
alley as if expecting to see his pursuers close behind him. Doctor
doesn't wait for anyone to open the door. He climbs over the wall and
drops softly inside the front yard. He sits with his back pressed to the
wall and waits. Three men turn the corner and enter the alley. One of
them looks toward me up on the roof. He is vile and wretched, I can
tell even from this distance. He's tall and dark, about thirty-five or
forty years old. He has long wavy hair that is pulled back tight. I can
see his eyes searching, absorbing every detail of everything that goes
on around him.

A paralyzing numbness rushes through my joints and muscles. I
want to lower my body behind the short wall that edges the roof, but
I can't move. The man curses into a two-way radio that the hunt has
gone cold.

I don't understand the muffled reply, but the three men begin to run again. They run right past Zari's house, and relief calms my horror-stricken heart.

This must be the SAVAK. "They're nasty," I remember my father saying after they raided our house in search of his books. "They look like normal people. They live among us, work with us, come to our homes for dinner, participate in our happiness, mourn our losses, and then someday you find out that they have a second job working for the most loathed agency ever created in this country, thanks to the Americans and their CIA."

Doctor is sitting down, his head between his knees, shaking with fear and occasionally jerking and twitching like a man gripped by an unstoppable, uncontrollable fit of emotions. I see Zari run out of the house into the yard, followed by her parents. Doctor springs up quickly and puts his finger on his lips to let them know that they should be quiet. He doesn't need to. They are as silent as ghosts when they come out of the house. They know exactly what's happening to Doctor. People from the SAVAK must have been calling all day. I wonder what Doctor was doing all summer long. This explains the strange afternoon activities. The neighbors know, too, at least the ones who have heard the commotion and are watching this drama unfold from behind their pulled curtains. Their silhouettes are a stark reminder of how real the fear of the SAVAK is.

Zari puts her arms around Doctor and begins to weep, quietly. Her mother is praying, moving her lips rapidly without uttering a single audible sound as Zari's father, Mr. Naderi, an ex–Olympic wrestling champion, circles around his family like an old, wounded lion. Nobody says a word. Nobody needs to.

I know what fate would await Doctor in jail. My father has told me numerous stories of what they do to *kharab-kars*, subversive activists, like Doctor. They would put him in a cell for a few days to increase his anxiety in anticipation of his interrogation. Then they

would take him to a room and beat him up. They would ask him a
bunch of questions, and then beat him up some more. They would
threaten him with heart-wrenching descriptions of their newest
torturing techniques, and make casual comparisons to some of the traditional favorites: pulling out fingernails, breaking fingers, and sub-
merging the prisoner's testicles in boiling water. They might talk
about bringing his closest female relative to the prison, where she'd
be gang-raped while he watched. They could carry out the threats,
but often don't have to. Doctor is too young and too small a fish in the
ocean of political opposition to face a punishment so severe. They'd
keep him in jail for a while, beat him up occasionally, then one day
they would simply let him go, hoping they had scared him enough
that he would never try anything foolish again.

I can see that more and more neighbors are watching from their
darkened rooms. No one wants to be seen, but everyone wants to
know how this will end. I think of how helpless Doctor must be feeling at this moment. My father once said that nothing leaves you feeling
as unprotected as facing the government's secret police. There's no
authority to appeal to, and no one who can save you from the abyss of
pain and misery you're about to be thrown into. I remember telling
Doctor about the day the SAVAK agents raided our house. That was
when he told me I had *That*.

In prison, the agents will take away Doctor's most valuable possession, his time. They will lock him up in a small cell away from his
beloved books. To infuriate him, they may even give him a couple of
trashy novels to read, the kind with a picture of a seminude woman
and a handsome man on the cover. The kind he considers garbage.

I can't take my eyes off the scene that has frozen in time in Zari's
yard. A sound suddenly diverts my attention to the end of the alley.
The man with the radio is looking at me. I quickly sit down behind
the short wall, but it's too late. He must have been watching me for a

while, and from the direction of my gaze he has pinpointed the house in which Doctor has taken sanctuary.

I look up briefly and see him. He smiles wickedly, and slowly begins his walk toward Zari's house. The other two guys show up quickly, and a car pulls up in front of the house. The man with the radio knocks on Zari's door. Doctor lets go of Zari. Zari's mother begins to drive her head into the wall. I will never forget the dull sound of her skull thudding against the brick. Zari's father looks like a helpless warrior. He moves around aimlessly, as if facing an enemy he shouldn't fight. Zari is weeping.

Doctor opens the door and walks out, with Zari holding tightly on to him. His head is up, his shoulders square; he will not allow anyone to take away his dignity. One of the agents punches Doctor in the face. Zari shrieks as if a harpoon has pierced her heart. I feel my blood rising, slamming in my ears. The other two agents are watching, and a fourth is sitting behind the wheel of an agency sedan, smoking a cigarette.

Doctor is on the ground now. The man with the radio kicks him in the face. Blood spurts all over the sidewalk. Zari's cries reach a new peak. Zari's mother begins to chant while hitting herself in the head and pulling her own hair. Mr. Naderi is looking at the agents, perhaps thinking that he could kill these detestable, repulsive creatures with his bare hands—but these are secret government agents, and his interference would only make things worse.

Some of the neighboring families—including my parents, who were asleep until Zari's screams woke them—have rushed out into the alley. The agents detest crowds witnessing the inhumane treatment of their captives. They quickly push Doctor into the car and take off. The agent with the radio looks toward the roof and blows me a kiss as the car is pulling out of the alley. I swear to myself that someday I will find him, and kill him. Never in my life have I felt as much anger, not even when those bullies were beating me up at school, or when Faheemeh's brothers bloodied Ahmed's face.

Zari runs after the car, and the neighbors run after her. Zari's mom faints on the sidewalk, and some of the women, including my own mother, try to revitalize her by spooning hot water and sugar into her slackened mouth. Mr. Naderi is leaning against a tree. He rocks back and forth, whispering incomprehensible words. The alley is now crawling with people. I wonder if anyone saw the agent thank me before disappearing into the night.

I rush downstairs, my body still shaking, my knees weak, and my nerves raw. In the alley I hear a little girl asking her mother what is going on. She bends over and lifts her daughter up, holding her tight against her chest. Zari is crying hysterically as the neighbors try to restrain her. I run up to her and grab her and take her face in my hands and call her name a few times. She recognizes me, throws herself into my arms, and weeps. The sweetness of her embrace could not have come at a more bitter time.

I can see my father consoling Mr. Naderi, when suddenly I hear a loud cry from the end of the alley. Doctor's parents, Mr. and Mrs. Sobhi, are rushing toward the rest of us. Doctor's mother beats herself in the head and scratches her face with her fingernails as she howls her anguish. His father limps toward us with a tormented look on his face. A number of women, including Iraj's mother, are trying to stop Doctor's mom from hurting herself. Her cries are agonizingly painful to hear. Doctor once told me that his mother used to follow him to school from a distance every day until he was in the tenth grade. I can't imagine her suffering.

I see my own mother standing close to Mrs. Naderi. She's looking in my direction. Somehow, I know what she's thinking, even though I'm too young to know what parents think. She's thanking God that I wasn't the one taken away.

Doctor's father sees his son's blood on the sidewalk and collapses at the spot with a cry that could break the devil's heart. He dips his left hand, the only hand he has left, in the blood, brings it up to his face, and kisses it as he wails in despair. I want to run over to hug him, to kiss his hand, to ask for his forgiveness, but I can't. I don't even want to admit to myself that it was my carelessness that gave Doctor away. I wish I could clench my fist, shake it in God's face, and howl defiantly. But that would reveal my disgraceful secret. So instead I take my head in my hands and bite my lower lip so hard that a stream of blood flows down my chin.

9

The Anarchist

Life goes on, and nights like the Doctor's night end, but the impact lingers. We Persians are not sophisticated when it comes to dealing with pain. I've heard that people in the West, especially in the United States, seek therapy when they experience emotional traumas. Our therapist is time. We trust that time heals everything, and that there is no need to dwell on pain. We don't seek psychological treatment because we're not as fragile as the Westerners, or so we claim. Psychological interventions are designed to cure the mind, not the spirit. We bring solace to our hearts by displaying our emotions. When grief strikes, we do whatever it takes to our bodies to wring relief from our wounded souls, without apology or regret. We may beat ourselves, tear our clothes and scream our sorrows, and there is always company, as those around us share in our suffering by doing the same.

I was once watching a Hollywood film and noticed the restraint Americans exercise during funerals. I asked my father why we were so demonstrative and mournful as a people when dealing with death.

"This is a topic deserving of scholarly attention," my dad said. "But you're right. We are different. The intensity of our mourning has historic roots. A recurring theme in our history has been the massacre of our people, in what are now forgotten genocides at the hands of invaders like Alexander of Macedonia, the barbarian who burned down Persepolis; the Arabs, who brutalized our nation for hundreds of years; and Genghis Khan, who in the thirteenth century slaughtered nearly three million of our citizens. Mourning has become a very important aspect of our culture." Then he put his hand on my shoulder. "When our child is butchered in front of our eyes, we bawl as if our soul wants to escape our body. When we're violently wronged, we shriek. That's the gift of history to us, son." He shook his head and rubbed his temples. "Our only recourse in the face of unpardonable evil has been to wail inconsolably. I think, even now, we unconsciously identify death with oppression."

So life goes on in our alley, but at a slower pace. Or at least, that's how it seems. Time may be the most precious commodity humans possess, but it's a real drag when it crawls by. I think what makes time precious is the speed with which it passes.

Zari doesn't come into the yard anymore, Ahmed is still in Ghamsar, and I can't stand being around Iraj, who's forever babbling on about his stupid inventions. My father makes several attempts to talk to me about Doctor, but I avoid him in any way I can. I don't know what I might say if I start talking about the events of that night. I close my eyes and imagine those last few moments on the roof again and again, and each time I duck before the agent sees me. But then I open my eyes and want to scream with pain. I decide that I need to start reading again. Reading is the best diversion for me. I read a lot of Darwin and Freud. I realize that there is more to these thinkers than Mr. Gorji, our religion teacher, talked about last year. I can't remember how he got on the subject, but he told us that Freud was a pervert and Darwin was an atheist, and we should never read their work. The next day I started my search for books with the pervert's and the atheist's names on them.

The works are great, but I have a hard time staying focused. I wish I could see Zari, but I feel guilty even thinking about her now. I obsess about Doctor instead, and wonder if he knows that my carelessness gave him away. If I could write him a letter, I would tell him that I'm sorry, not just about the night he was arrested but for falling in love with his fiancée. I'm sorry I couldn't be like Humphrey Bogart in *Casablanca*. I didn't know he was wanted by the SAVAK. Of course, I knew that he was a Marxist, and I had prayed after the night of the roses that he would never get caught. If I knew he was coming home, I would have waited for the agents in the alley, and acted as his decoy, running in a different direction to make the agents chase me instead of him.

Oh, God, I hate myself. I hate myself more than I hate the bastard whose evil smile keeps me awake at nights. Again I close my eyes. Again I try to relive the moment when the man with the radio spotted me on the roof. Again I duck before he sees me—but reality remains unchanged. God, if only I could go back! I hate the finality of time.

I go to the roof for a few minutes, and when I look at the alley, I realize that the energy has been drained from our neighborhood. I study the shadow of the tree that my father planted in the yard the first day we moved in, and it doesn't seem to move. Most of the kids just sit around and talk. No one plays soccer anymore. Parents don't want the SAVAK back in the alley. They've told their children not to talk to anyone about what happened on Doctor's night, but kids don't understand enough to be scared. "Rebellion is sometimes a beautiful thing," I heard Doctor say, once. I wonder if dictatorial regimes could survive if adults were more like children. Would anyone dare to take someone's kid away in the middle of the night if we all rebelled against authority and control? I remember Doctor saying that anarchy is the precursor to order, and realize that I have no idea what anarchy means. I decide to go to the library and look for a book on the subject. Books are always a great diversion for me.

When I return, I see Iraj and a couple of other kids debriefing Ahmed on the events of Doctor's night. He's obviously upset. When

the two of us are alone, he asks me how I'm feeling. To my embarrassment, tears run down my face.

"Why're you crying?" Ahmed seems shocked. He has heard many
times the story of how I didn't cry when I broke my shin in three
places.

"I gave him away," I say. "I didn't duck in time. The son of a bitch
blew me a kiss. I'll find him and kill him someday."

Ahmed tries to calm me down. He wants to know everything that
happened the night Doctor was arrested. I go through it all, just as I
have many times in my thoughts in the last five days. I can't stop crying as I tell him the story.

"Didn't they tell you?" I beg him. "Didn't they tell you that I gave
him away? Who knows? Please, tell me."

Ahmed swears that no one has even mentioned my name in relation to that evening.

"That doesn't change the fact that I gave him away." I hide my face
in my hands.

"And did you make them chase him, too?" he asks forcefully. "Look,
the clock didn't start ticking at the moment the agent saw you on the
roof. They were already looking for him. We don't know where he was
all summer, what he was doing, who was watching him. What do you
think, they just showed up here, waited for you to look into Zari's
yard, and then jumped him? The search for him must've been going
on for some time."

I wipe my tears off, sniff a couple of times and say, "I just feel so
bad."

"Don't," Ahmed orders stoutly. "Doctor's ordeal has nothing to do
with you. You can't be held responsible for his education and upbringing and what has gotten him to the point of being a Marxist and
on the hunt list of the SAVAK." Then he lights two cigarettes and
gives me one. We sit quietly for a while.

"Why're you reading this?" he asks when he notices my book on anarchism. I tell him about Mr. Gorji's characterization of Darwin and Freud, my contempt for authority, my desire for everyone to defy dictatorship and my lack of familiarity with a political theory known as anarchism. Ahmed looks at me like I'm drunk. He obviously doesn't have a clue what I'm talking about. He reminds me that our religion teacher also warned us about the evils of masturbation, and wonders if I've been shining my little pickle in defiance. I laugh my head off. It's the first time I've laughed since they took Doctor away.

School starts in less than ten days, and I'm not looking forward to it. No one knows where Doctor is, or what is happening to him. Faheemeh visits Zari every day. They have become the best of friends. Ahmed stays away. He knows this is not the time for romance. Faheemeh comes to the roof to talk to us for a few minutes. She says that Zari cries all the time because she is worried about Doctor's physical and emotional endurance under torture. Then Faheemeh puts her arm around my shoulder and says, "Don't worry, sweetheart. Everything is going to work out okay."

Deep down, I'm dying to find out if Zari ever asks about me, but I suppress the need with all my determination. Like Ahmed, I too know it's best to stay away. The neighbors say that Doctor's mother has aged a thousand years since his arrest. Her hair has turned gray, her face looks wrinkled, and her hands tremble all the time. She can't open her mouth without crying. She spends most of her time outside the Evin Prison, begging the guards to tell her if her son is okay. Doctor's father keeps quiet. Two agents showed up at their home one day and told him that the worst thing he could do for his son was to attract attention to his family. "Just wait this out," he was told, "or you'll never see your son again." Doctor's father has a desk job with the city now. He has learned how to write with his left hand. So he goes to work every day and pretends that nothing has happened to the son he loves more than life itself.

Ahmed asks me to define anarchism for him. I do but not in great detail and not enthusiastically.

"Do the world a favor, okay?" Ahmed mocks.

"What?"

"Don't ever become a teacher. You suck at it."

Then he tells me that he has a brilliant idea that will blow life and energy back into the alley. It's about anarchy, he says, and when I insist on knowing more, he adds he still has no idea what anarchism is so how can I expect him to explain it?

I laugh and leave him alone.

We organize a get-together in the basement of my house. About fifteen boys our age show up from all over the alley. Iraj walks in carrying a circuit board that's attached to a wheel, which turns every time he flips on a switch. He says he's experimenting with power efficiency. "If we conserve energy, we won't have these frequent blackouts in Tehran," he says. As usual, everyone ignores him.

Suddenly, Ahmed makes his grand entrance. He is dressed as a professor, wearing his grandmother's spectacles and his late grandfather's black robe. He's carrying a long ruler behind his back. Everyone begins to laugh. He shakes his ruler in our faces and orders us to shut up. We laugh louder as he gets more and more animated. He begins his lesson by informing us of today's topic: masturbation. He tells us that he has a doctoral degree in masturbation from a university in Paris, and that he has published numerous articles and books on the subject. The laughter gets louder every time he says the word "masturbation."

He silently looks from the left to the right of the room from underneath his round spectacles with his arms folded, then demands to know who masturbated last night. No one raises his hand. He walks up to me, hits me with the ruler for being a liar, and demands to see the palm of my right hand. I oblige, and he grabs my hand and shows it to everyone in the room.

"Look how soft the palm of his hand is. You know why? Olive oil, that's why he has soft skin. Isn't that right?" he asks as he looks at me from over his spectacles. Laughing, I say yes, and he hits me again with the ruler. He peers around the room as everyone waits to find out who his next victim will be. He spots Iraj.

"Show me your hand!" he screams.

Iraj shows the back of his hand as he doubles over with laughter. Ahmed hits him in the head with the ruler.

"The palm of your hand, you moron."

Iraj shows him the palm of his hand.

"Soap?" He feels Iraj's hand. "Too dry to be soap. This idiot is using laundry detergent." He hits Iraj again. "Can you imagine how dry the skin on his penis is? Take your pants off, we want to see."

Iraj holds on to his belt and shakes his head no.

"Do you want to see?" Ahmed asks the class.

"Yes! Yes! Yes!" everyone screams.

Ahmed pauses briefly, and then adds, "What's wrong with a dried-up penis, you ask? What happens to leaves when they dry up?" He bends over and stares into Iraj's eyes.

"They fall off, sir," Iraj replies.

Ahmed starts hitting Iraj over and over with the ruler, uttering the warning one word at a time.

"That's . . . what's . . . going . . . to . . . happen . . . to . . . your . . . little . . . penis . . . if . . . you . . . keep . . . masturbating . . . with . . . laundry . . . detergent . . . you understand?"

Iraj shakes his head yes. He's laughing so hard he can't utter a word.

"I can't hear you!" Ahmed screams.

"Yes, sir!" Iraj finally gasps.

Ahmed is a master performer. He keeps quiet while pacing away to give everyone time to laugh this out. As everyone settles down Iraj asks, "Would dishwashing detergent be better, sir?"

Ahmed flies toward him, the ruler flashing. I'm laughing so hard I can't see through my tears. Ahmed hits Iraj over and over. He finally walks away from him and positions himself at the head of the room.

Then he shares with us his "state of the art" masturbation technique. He takes a banana out of his pocket, peals it, and carefully cuts the skin into little pieces. Then he takes one piece, places it between his thumb and his index finger, and pretends he's masturbating. He tells everyone that banana is a nutritious food excellent for counteracting blindness that results from masturbation. I laugh so much I think I might puke.

When everyone leaves and Ahmed and I are alone, I tell him that he was brilliant and that the kids in the alley really appreciated his attempt to lift their spirits. We laugh at the idea that mothers up and down the alley will find it strange that their sons have such a craving for bananas that evening.

"When Doctor gets out," I say, "I'll tell him what you did, and how much it helped cheer everyone up."

"You do that," he says with a smile.

I study him for a while. I want to ask him why he thought his lesson was about anarchism, but I think I know, so I keep quiet.

10

My School and My Teachers

The first day of fall is the first day of school in Iran. That first day always feels different than all the other days of the year. The streets are crowded with boys and girls of all ages. Everyone seems purposeful and preoccupied with the thought of spending all day in class. Kids look more disciplined and more intent, even cleaner than usual, as if their mothers took the utmost care in preparing them for the day.

Iraj, Ahmed, and I walk to school together. Iraj blows his nose loudly into a white handkerchief and tells us his father thinks that Americans should be held responsible for the fate of all the revolutionaries arrested, tortured, and murdered by the government of Iran. Then he stops and looks inside his handkerchief, raising his eyebrows as if he's impressed with what came out of his nose. He folds the handkerchief and puts it in his pocket.

Ahmed shakes his head and says, "You're disgusting. You know that? My sister wouldn't look at you if you were the Son of God!"

Iraj ignores him as usual and continues. "My father was a colonel in the army. He has firsthand knowledge of Americans' spying activities in Iran. He told me once about a gigantic aircraft carrier with sophisticated radar equipment that the Americans have parked in the Persian Gulf to keep track of anti-American Iranian political groups. He said that Americans have such high-tech machinery that they can see through walls, and that's why he always keeps his genitals covered when he's taking a shower."

Ahmed and I are trying to keep straight faces, but it's hard.

"They see everything, and hear everything. They've been watching all of us, all the time," Iraj whispers.

"Hush," Ahmed whispers back. "Don't talk so loud—they may hear us."

"I'm not kidding," Iraj protests.

"Well, you should have told me all this before I shared my masturbation techniques with the world. You know those opportunistic capitalists will steal my ideas now, publish a book, and make millions of dollars." Then he turns to me and asks, "Do you think it's too late to get a patent on those techniques?"

I shrug my shoulders as I laugh.

Iraj says, "If I was living in the United States I'd be an inventor by now because Americans love new gadgets and support people like me who have brilliant ideas about making people's lives easier."

Ahmed interrupts. "Let's organize a fund-raising event to raise money for his one-way ticket to the States."

Iraj ignores Ahmed again. "Americans have invented sophisticated technologies that enable them to spy on anyone, anytime, anywhere."

"See what your fucking Thomas Edison started?" Ahmed chides.

Iraj whispers as if he's sharing a top national security secret with us. "The Americans knew Doctor well, and were scared of him becoming knowledgeable of worldly affairs. They radioed someone inside Iran to get him."

Ahmed looks at me and says, "See, the man with the radio was talking to the crew of the American ship in the Persian Gulf!" I give Ahmed a dirty look for joking at Doctor's expense. "Oh, for God's sake," he says. "He'll be out soon. Mark my words; he'll be out in no time."

Iraj says that Americans spied on another guy in the 1950s, someone much bigger and more important than our Doctor.

Iraj is talking about Mosaddegh, the only democratically elected prime minister in the history of Iran. In 1953 the American CIA overthrew him for a trifling fee of $60,000. He was placed under house arrest after the Shah's return until his death in March of 1967 at the age of eighty-four. Doctor used to say that Mosaddegh's overthrow was the biggest American foreign policy blunder in history. "No one in the Middle East will ever again trust the Americans and their phony guardianship of democracy," he declared angrily.

"This guy," Iraj continues, "was too popular, and killing him would've caused a revolution in Iran. Americans don't want us to be strong because the balance of power in the area will be disrupted. They don't want us to advance technologically, so that they can sell their technology to us."

"I'm only interested in the cameras that allow you to see through the walls," Ahmed says. "I want to see how our neighbors make love to their wives."

Iraj looks around to make sure no one is close by, and whispers, "My father thinks the Shah is a puppet of the United States. They can kick his ass out anytime they want."

A street vendor is selling boiled beets, and Ahmed and I stop to buy some.

"That stuff is going to kill you guys," Iraj says. "Look at the guy who's selling them. When do you think he last washed his hands?"

I laugh. "Yeah, the newspapers are full of reports about people dying after eating boiled beets bought from street vendors."

"And he knows," Ahmed says. "He's read everything, including *Suvashun*."

I slap Ahmed in the chest with the back of my hand and continue eating my sweet delicious treat.

Iraj blows his nose again, but this time doesn't look in his handkerchief. "My uncle is a general in the army," he says, as he puts his handkerchief back in his pocket. "My father could have been a general, too, but he purposely retired early because he knew that if things changed in Iran, the new regime would go after the generals before anyone else."

I nod, agreeing with him.

"My uncle has already bought a house somewhere in New York, which is America's largest city by the Atlantic Ocean," he continues, a scornful look on his face. "He has a huge savings account in Switzerland. Everyone knows that my uncle would be the first one out of the country if there were a revolution. My father, however, is a true Iranian and will never leave the country he defended throughout his professional army career. I will never leave Iran either!"

"What a shame," Ahmed whispers. "The American ship in the Persian Gulf is probably wiring the news to the American papers right now. I can see the headlines: The next Thomas Edison has decided to stay in Iran!"

Our all-boys school looks like a fortress. Tall cement walls surround the three-story brick building. The huge gate is guarded by our *farrash*, a custodian who makes sure nonstudents don't enter the school premises. The school yard is crowded with kids. You can immediately spot the newcomers by the nervous way they watch the kids around them. There are always one or two fistfights on the first day of school. The fights are normally broken up before our discipline teacher, Mr. Moradi, shows up with the long thick ruler that he uses to beat those who engage in violent activities.

"You imbeciles, don't you know that violence can get you in a whole lot of trouble?" he screams as he beats the troublemakers with his ruler. Mr. Moradi is also our gym teacher, despite the fact that we don't have a gym in our school. He makes us line up in the yard once a week and takes us through his favorite warm-up drill in our street clothes.

"One, two, three, four!" he shouts at the top of his lungs. "Jump now, higher, higher, you lazy fools!"

When we are all sweaty and breathing hard, he divides us into groups of four and makes us run from one side of the yard to the other and back. The last ones back out of each group then compete against each other until the "laziest ass in class" is identified. I often wonder if Mr. Moradi knows the difference between lazy and slow. Being that today is the first day of school, Mr. Moradi decides to give us a lecture on discipline instead of making us run up and down the school yard.

"The world would be a much better place if everyone was disciplined. Why is America such a powerful country? Because Americans are a disciplined nation. People in the United States respect rules," he barks, a sparkle in his eyes. He says he once went to America to participate in an international wrestling competition, and was amazed at how people obeyed traffic rules.

"Everyone stops at stop signs, even when there is no car coming from the opposite direction. That's discipline for you. Discipline means respecting the rules regardless of the circumstances. We don't even stop at red lights in this country. We feel that rules are made to be broken, and we feel justified breaking them because we are an undisciplined nation of rule breakers."

He shakes his head in disappointment and continues. "The British are a disciplined nation, too. Have you seen pictures of the guards at Buckingham Palace? Those guards don't blink, even when there is no one around." He points at Ahmed and adds, "Can you imagine Ahmed as a guard at Buckingham Palace?" Everyone laughs. I pray that Ahmed doesn't strike back, and he doesn't, at least not yet. Instead, he laughs, too, and shrugs his shoulders.

"The government of America has installed trash cans every few meters on every street, and everyone uses them to discard their garbage," Mr. Moradi lectures. "The streets of America are so clean, you can eat off of them. That is discipline for you."

He says that people line up and wait their turn in American stores. He shakes his head and says that in our country, we climb over one another to get to the front of the line. "Cheat, push, disregard others, get to the front of the line at any cost. It's disgusting how undisciplined we are," he says, raising his ruler in the air. "That's why I chose to be a discipline teacher." He huffs and puffs, looks around the room, and spots Iraj. "Your father was an army man. Tell me, what's the most important characteristic of the best army in the world?"

"Discipline, sir."

Mr. Moradi nods in agreement. Ahmed raises his hand. My heart sinks. I nervously begin to roll up my sleeves. Looking at Ahmed's face and his patented smart-alecky smile, I know he's about to ask a question that will infuriate Mr. Moradi. I think Mr. Moradi suspects the same because he ignores Ahmed long enough for me to roll my sleeves down again.

"Yes?" Mr. Moradi finally acknowledges Ahmed.

Ahmed's thoughtful pose nearly cracks me up as my anxiety level heightens simultaneously. He asks, "Is it true, sir, that the most disciplined army in the world has a ship equipped with the most advanced spying technology docked in the Persian Gulf?"

Mr. Moradi looks confused.

Ahmed continues, now wagging his finger, as if he is interrogating Mr. Moradi, "And is it also true, sir, that the sailors on that ship listen to every conversation in Iran?"

Mr. Moradi stares blankly at Ahmed.

"And what about the technology that enables them to see through the walls? Because if this is all true, sir, I'm not taking a shower ever again."

Mr. Moradi is trying to hold back his smile. "Where did you hear that?" he asks.

I see Iraj trying to hide behind the student sitting in front of him.

"I heard it from Iraj, sir," he says. "But I'm not sure I can trust him because he is a very undisciplined kid, and has no respect for rules—including the one that prohibits friends from checking out their friends' sisters."

The class explodes with laugher. Even Mr. Moradi's smile rushes to his face.

Mr. Moradi is a strange man, but we like him better than Mr. Bana, our geometry teacher, who is about forty years old and has been teaching since the day he came out of his mother's womb. "Geometry is the mother of all sciences," he says. Ahmed once asked who the father was, and ended up spending the day in Mr. Moradi's office, where he was lectured about the virtue of discipline in the classroom.

When Mr. Bana enters the room, we stand up, as we do for all the teachers. Mr. Bana positions himself at the head of the class and stares at everyone. He says he can identify those who haven't done their homework by the frightened look in their eyes. He always calls on someone from the back of the room because that's where—in his opinion—the lazy students sit. As a result, there is always a fight over who sits in the front rows for Mr. Bana's classes. Mr. Bana particularly loves to call on you with questions he knows no one can solve.

"Euclid gave five postulates. The fifth postulate reads: 'Given a line and a point not on the line, it is possible to draw exactly one line through the given point parallel to the line.' What do you think about that?"

A heavy silence always follows his questions.

"If stupidity was the measure for greatness, you'd all be the greatest people in the world," he mocks.

At the end of each session, Mr. Bana asks if anyone has any questions. If you ask one, he shakes his ruler in your face and tells you that you are stupid for asking a stupid question. "The answer is on page eighty-eight. Look it up, you idiot!" he yells. If you don't ask a question, Mr. Bana says something like, "So, you all know everything there is to know, ha? Well, we'll see about that." Then he points to an unfortunate soul and asks a hard question, which is normally followed by a good thrashing.

I know what it's like to be on Mr. Bana's bad side. During our first trimester exam last year, I solved one of the problems using two different methods. Mr. Bana didn't give me credit for either one, even though both my solutions were correct. He accused me of cheating, and eventually gave me a zero for the whole test. I went to Mr. Yazdi, our principal, and asked for his assistance.

"What do you want me to do?" Mr. Yazdi asked.

"I want to know why I'm being punished for solving a problem using two equally correct techniques."

"Mr. Bana is your teacher. If he says you cheated, then you must have cheated. There isn't anything I can do about that."

"But where's the proof?" I asked.

"Mr. Bana is a teacher. He doesn't need proof. His suspicion alone is good enough for me."

I ended up with a zero on my first exam. I told my dad the whole story. He said that I must prove Mr. Bana and Mr. Yazdi wrong by acing my next two exams. Then he would go to school to convince them to change my first trimester's grade. I felt violated, and wronged. "Everything about this goddamn country stinks," I complained to Ahmed. "I'm so glad I'll be on my way to the United States soon, where the most disciplined people in the world understand logic and don't accuse innocent people of an offense they didn't commit."

I look at Mr. Bana now and thank God for not making any of my relatives teachers.

Unlike Mr. Moradi, our religion teacher, Mr. Gorji—who also teaches dictation—has a strong disdain for the West, especially the

United States. Mr. Gorji is a big fat man whose blustering boorish behavior irritates me a great deal. His face looks dirty thanks to a beard that he never shaves, but never grows beyond a few centimeters. He always wears a light brown suit that matches his unpolished, tattered shoes. His white shirt, always buttoned up to the top, is yellow around the collar. He never smiles, but when he talks, you can always see his yellow teeth. Ahmed says that every time Mr. Gorji looks at him, he feels guilty, as if he'd been caught peeling a banana. Then he winks at me to ensure I get the joke. Ahmed also says that he has heard rumors that Mr. Gorji is rich from lending money to the poor, and then charging them a fortune in interest. "He's a fraud," Ahmed says. "Practicing his brand of Islam will get you a one-way ticket to hell."

Sometimes Mr. Gorji gives us unannounced quizzes. "Any day can be a quiz day," he says. "I do this for your own good because as a student you should always be ready to take a quiz." I wonder, however, if Mr. Gorji is just too lazy to plan things. After all, as my father always says, we are a spontaneous nation; we do everything at the spur of the moment without much advanced planning.

Mr. Gorji chooses the hardest words in the book, and reads each one aloud three times. "Ghostantanieh, Ghostantanieh, Ghostantanieh." I guess he thinks we don't hear the word the first couple of times. "Maghlateh, Maghlateh, Maghlateh." It's easy to misspell these words because letters like *gh*, *s*, and *t* can be written a couple of different ways. Most of the words in the quizzes are covered in previous lessons. However, to differentiate the good students from the mediocre ones, words not already covered could also be on the quiz. And getting a word correct does not necessarily guarantee you credit. Mr. Gorji also grades your handwriting. You can spell everything perfectly, but if he doesn't like the way you write, you could lose two or more points. Mr. Gorji wouldn't reward you with a twenty, a perfect score, even when you don't misspell a word and have the best handwriting in the world. "Nineteen is the highest you can get. Twenty is

God's grade. He is the only perfect entity in the world," he says, while kissing his rosary.

If we get a word wrong, he makes us write it four hundred times in our notebooks. Sometimes he calls our names individually and asks us to go to the board to take a quiz as everyone else watches. He reads each word three times, and then moves on to the next word regardless of whether we are finished with our spelling. Each quiz is worth twenty points, and the passing grade is ten. Even a passing grade of ten to fourteen can get you a couple of slaps in the face and a good verbal thrashing: "You stupid jackass, you lazy cow, you temperamental dog—you will never amount to anything! If I asked you to spell the hardest female name you'd do it in your sleep, but you can't spell words that make you a better person. That's because all you think about is girls, girls, girls. You can't wait for the hour to be over so that you can rush out to the nearest girls' school and act like you're cool. Go sit your fat ass down and write each word four hundred times. I'm warning you, you'd better watch your handwriting."

Mr. Gorji loves to insult us by calling us animal names. Our last year's composition teacher, a young university student assigned to our school by the government, said it was impolite to call a person a "cow" to insult them. He said millions of people in India worship cows, and we should respect everyone's religious beliefs, no matter how stupid they are! Every week, he would give us a new topic to write about, and then he would collect all the papers and read them carefully. No one ever got more than a fourteen in his class because he prided himself on being a hard grader. One time, he asked us to write a paper on the "Benefits of Technology." He called on Ahmed to read his composition in front of the class. Ahmed read that contrary to Mr. Bana's claim, he believed that technology and not geometry was the mother of all sciences, and that he wanted to put his mouth on mother technology's large tits and drink until they were completely empty of the milk of knowledge.

Our composition teacher yelled, "Stop, stop!" He then called Ahmed every animal name except a cow before throwing him out of the class. Last year, our composition teacher was caught in the bathroom with his pants down and a fifteen-year-old kid bent over in front of him. He was immediately reassigned to a school in another district. That day, Mr. Gorji told us that homosexuality is born of a lack of faith.

"If you believe in God, you don't desire anal sex."

Mr. Moradi said that homosexuality results from a lack of discipline, and respect for the rule that prohibits men from seeking other men. He was certain that there were no homosexuals in America because Americans were the most disciplined people in the universe.

Our principal, Mr. Yazdi, said that we would have to be careful not to fall prey to the trap of homosexuals. "They are evil and psychotic," he said. Then he told us the story of Asghar Ghatel, a man accused of molesting and murdering over one hundred teenage boys. I was dying to find out how Mr. Bana and his mother of all sciences would explain homosexuality in the next hour, but to my disappointment, he completely ignored the issue.

11

In the SAVAK's Prisons

No one has heard anything about Doctor since the night he was taken away, a little over two weeks ago. It's as if he's vanished from the face of the earth. His mother's serious illness prevents her from going to the gates of Evin Prison anymore. Zari hasn't been to the yard since Doctor's arrest. When Faheemeh visits her, they spend most of their time in Zari's room.

Ahmed continues to assure me that Doctor will soon be freed, and things will return to the way they were. After one such conversation, he turns to me and asks how I am doing. I want to say that I am frustrated about not seeing Zari, and that I miss her terribly; that although I feel guilty for falling in love with her, I can't stop thinking about her. Instead, I say that I need a diversion from our current predicament, that our teachers make me sick, that the thought of going to America makes me sick, and that sometimes I feel like the whole world makes me sick. I wish I could shoot the man with the radio, after I had a chance to break his nose and spill his blood on our sidewalk. Ahmed puts his hand on my shoulder and shakes his head in understanding. Then he says that we should go see an Iranian movie—the best cure for depression because they all have happy endings.

We decide to take Iraj with us because we don't want to leave him unsupervised in the alley, where he could have a field day looking at Ahmed's sister.

Most of the theaters in our neighborhood only show Persian movies, which don't look anything like their American counterparts. Doctor told me once that Persian movies are made to legitimize class differences in our country. He also said that all Persian movies follow the same generic plot in which the conflict is always between the poor and the rich, with the rich winning the battles, but losing the war. The rich are always portrayed as powerful, but not evil, and certainly not the type against whom you should organize a violent uprising. In fact, Iranian movies go out of their way to establish an emotional link between the hero and the rich villain—a lost son, a displaced relative, or the victim of bizarre circumstances. These movies discourage the masses from confronting the rich, and encourage the poor to stick to their high principles, according to Doctor.

"This is why a revolution in this country would be against the Shah, and not the rich," Doctor told me once, a philosophical ring to his voice. Doctor believes we might rebel for cultural, religious, or political reasons, but never to destroy the wealthy.

God, I miss Doctor.

The best-known actor of this genre is a man called Fardeen. Most critics don't think that he is a very good actor, but I like him a lot, although I would never admit it.

Before getting to the theater, Iraj says that he wants to sit between Ahmed and me. He explains that a couple of weeks earlier he came to see a movie by himself and ended up sitting next to a child molester. A few minutes after the movie started, he noticed that the man was looking at him. He didn't think much of it until he felt the man's hand on his knee. He got up and ran away. He was so traumatized that he ran all the way home without ever looking back to see if the man was following him.

Ahmed says his sister runs home the same way every time she sees Iraj in the alley. I bend over, laughing.

The movie theater is packed with people of all ages eating sunflower seeds, a customary snack in Iranian theaters. In one of the scenes halfway through the movie, a group of hoodlums attack Fardeen and start beating him up. Suddenly, we hear an old woman in the audience scream, "Stop beating him up, you bastards! What's he done to you? Leave him alone! If my husband were here, he would kick the teeth out of your filthy mouths."

Ahmed looks at me with panic in his face. "It's my grandma!" he says.

"They're killing him! Help, help!" his grandma yells as Fardeen falls on the ground and his enemies start to kick his body and face. People start yelling profanities at her.

"Shut your babbling mouth, lady."

"Throw this fool out."

Within seconds, the usher, flashlight in hand, runs into the theater looking for the rowdy old lady. Iraj points to the first row and says, "There she is."

We see Ahmed's grandma waving her hands and shaking her fist, yelling, "Somebody call my husband. He's a good friend of Fardeen. Help! Somebody get my husband!" Ahmed, Iraj, and I run to the front of the theater. Grandma sees us and screams, "Thank God you're here. Help him out! Help him out!"

We try to coax her out of her seat, but she refuses to leave. The usher shouts that we'd better take Grandma out, or he's going to have to do it himself. People whistle and laugh. Iraj grabs Grandma's left arm and Ahmed grabs hold of her right arm. They start to pull, but Grandma starts to kick and throw her body back at the same time. The usher and I try to grab her legs, but Grandma gets a good one in and kicks the flashlight out of the usher's hand, while screaming for her husband.

They stop the movie and turn the lights on in the theater. The whistles and boos get louder, and so do Grandma's screams. Grandma escapes from Iraj's grip, takes her shoes off, picks them up, and starts beating on anything within her reach. Some people encourage her to hit harder. The usher is furious, but doesn't dare get too close to her. Finally, Ahmed and I rush her, pulling her to the ground. With the help of Iraj and three other people, we carry Grandma out of the theater. The fresh air calms her down immediately.

Ahmed is quiet on the way home. He and Grandma walk a couple of steps in front of Iraj and me. "Those guys were lucky that your grandpa wasn't around, or they would've gotten the worst beating of their lives," Grandma explains to Ahmed. "Grandpa was a wrestler, and everyone in Tehran was scared to death of him."

Ahmed's grandpa was a tiny, peaceful man who was never in a fistfight in his life.

I'm on the roof that night when Ahmed comes up. "She says Grandpa took her to the movie," he says. "I wonder how she got in. She never has any money."

"Her devotion to your grandpa is really touching," I say, not sure what else to say. "He must've been the biggest star in her life."

Ahmed doesn't respond.

"Can you believe how she was fighting us?" I marvel. "What is she, sixty-five?"

Ahmed thinks for a while, and then he grins. "Hey, do you think my grandma could beat up Fardeen in a real fight?"

My mother tells me to clean up because we have special guests coming to our house. She mentions a name that I don't recognize. "He used to be your dad's best friend," Mom says.

As I'm taking a shower, I remember Iraj's story about Americans and their sophisticated radar equipment, and wonder if they can really see through the walls. I look down and momentarily cover myself, then shake my head and laugh.

The special guests are Mr. and Mrs. Mehrbaan. When I open the door, Mr. Mehrbaan hugs me as if he has known me all his life, although we've never met. My father runs up to him and they embrace for a long time, as they whisper in each other's ears. I can't see their faces, but I can tell that they're crying. Mrs. Mehrbaan and my mother look at their husbands with teary eyes. They finally come in and sit in the living room. My father and Mr. Mehrbaan look at each other, and continue to cry. They occasionally caress each other's faces and hair. Mr. Mehrbaan says, "It's been eighteen years."

My father says, "Eighteen years, four months, and three days."

I'm curious to know why they let so much time pass without seeing each other. "I hope it's not eighteen years before I see Doctor," I whisper to my mother.

"I hope not, too," she says as she bites the space between her thumb and index finger.

Mr. Mehrbaan is a tall, dark man who walks with a slight limp. His thick black mustache makes his face look manly and harsh. His wife is tall, thin, and pretty. "Mehrbaan" means "kind" in Persian, and both the husband and wife are very *mehrbaan*.

My father and Mr. Mehrbaan drink vodka with a mixture of yogurt, cucumber, raisin, salt, and pepper as the chaser. They talk about the old days when my father was a heavyweight boxing champion and Mr. Mehrbaan was a wrestling star. They talk about old opponents and friends. A couple of their mutual friends have died in freak accidents, while another is disgustingly rich and lives in Europe. Someone else was discovered to be an agent of the secret police—a filthy dog. Mrs. Mehrbaan and my mother look at old pictures and talk about the time they were in high school together.

My father quietly tells Mr. Mehrbaan of another old childhood friend, Mr. Kasravi, who is now a very rich man up in the Caspian Sea area.

"I heard about it in prison," he says. "He always had a good mind for money."

Mr. Mehrbaan has gotten my attention now. Was he in prison for eighteen years? I wonder what for. Does he know Doctor? I think about asking him, but my parents have taught me that it's not polite to get engaged in the conversation of adults, especially when the discussion is very serious.

They drink more vodka, and Mr. Mehrbaan smiles at me. He wants to know my age, what grade I'm in, and whether I read as much as my father did when he was seventeen. My father tells him that I'm a great student, am majoring in math, and plan to be an engineer like my uncle Mehrbaan; in Iran, your father's good friends are referred to as uncles. I feel as if I'm four years old. I want to say that I'm an average student, I hate math, and I don't want to be an engineer, but I don't. I look at Mom, remembering the number of times I have complained about this issue to her. She ignores my piercing glance and looks the other way.

At dinner, Mr. Mehrbaan confirms that he was a prisoner for eighteen years. He talks about his experiences there with a great sense of dignity and pride. I'm fascinated by the effortless way in which he expresses himself. Almost two decades of imprisonment have taught him to be patient with himself, his thoughts, and the articulation of his memories. They broke his right leg several times, which is why he limps. They burned him with cigarettes, and poured salt on his wounds. They beat him every day for information about men and women he never knew.

Mr. Mehrbaan talks about the night they took him away. It was his wedding night, and the guests had just left when the SAVAK raided his house. Mrs. Mehrbaan cried and begged for mercy. This was their wedding night. Could they not wait one day? What had he done to deserve such a cruel punishment?

The crime, she was told, was too serious to be discussed.

It was revealed later, however, that Mr. Mehrbaan was correspond-
ing with some of his comrades in the Bolshevik party in Russia. He was
also accused of distributing Marxist literature among university students in Tehran. Mr. Mehrbaan asked the judge at the trial to show him
the law that prohibited communication with the Russians. He also
asked for evidence that his distribution of the literature in question had
caused anyone any harm. The military judge denied both requests and
sentenced him to life in prison. His sentence was later reduced to eighteen years. No reason was ever given for the decision.

No one knew where he was or what was happening to him for
three years. Everyone was convinced that he was dead, except his
mother and his bride. Then one day they were granted permission to
visit him in prison. He looked weak, tired, and subdued. He had not
shaved in ages, his long hair looked dirty, as if he hadn't showered for
months, and he had lost at least fifteen kilos. He begged his wife to
divorce him because he was never going to get out of prison. She cried
and said that she was going to wait.

"Love is more faithful than an old dog," says Mr. Mehrbaan.

His story, and the dignity with which he speaks while recalling
the darkest moments of his life, touch me. He talks about a period
of time when they injected him with drugs, such as morphine, three
times a day, then stopped to watch him suffer the withdrawal. He
wished he were dead.

The night goes on. The men talk and the women are in the kitchen.
I go to the other room with my head full of thoughts about Mr.
Mehrbaan. I turn on the TV and watch *Bewitched*. Is life in America
really the way it's portrayed on these television shows? Are people so
superficial? Do men really walk around in their suits at home? Are
there men like Doctor and Mr. Mehrbaan in the United States, men
who sacrifice their lives for the cause they believe in? *I Dream of Jeannie* and *The Six Million Dollar Man* follow *Bewitched*. I think of the

character of Jeannie, a woman from the Middle East played by Barbara Eden. I look at Mrs. Mehrbaan, also a woman from the Middle East, and wonder why Americans don't make movies about Middle Eastern women like her. Eighteen years is a long time to wait for someone, especially when there's no hope of his release. Of course, Jeannie waited in a bottle for two thousand years before Larry Hagman found her. Why do Middle Eastern women have to wait so long for their men? I wonder if I'll be able to live in the United States. Doctor used to say that these shows are designed to keep people preoccupied with "the irrelevant." Their ability to entertain keeps their viewers from questioning anything, slowly but surely eroding their intelligence. He complained that these shows have caused the Americans to slip into a political coma. "They are tragically uninformed of their government's unfair and oppressive behavior in other countries," he always disapproved bitterly.

12

The Devils That Broke the Windows

It's been over two weeks since I've seen Zari, and I'm beginning to feel antsy. Something inside weighs me down, something I can't control. Up until now, I used to think I was in command of my fate, but loving Zari has changed all that. She's captured my heart like a ruthless invader, and I'm a slave to thoughts and feelings that don't originate from my conscious self. My mind wanders to where I don't direct it, and I have anxiety attacks that don't seem to have an origin. I'm dying to see Zari, to talk to her, to stare into her eyes, to sit with her under the cherry tree, to hear her talk about *Suvashun*, and to watch her soak her feet in the *hose*. I'm desperately in love, and I feel desperately guilty about it.

A few nights after the Mehrbaans' visit to our house, my father gets a call from Mrs. Mehrbaan. She informs him that Mr. Mehrbaan has been arrested again. Four SAVAK agents showed up at three in the morning and searched their home for hours. They didn't say what they were looking for, but they kept telling Mr. Mehrbaan that he'd be finished if they found it. She is certain that Mr. Mehrbaan did not make any contact with his old friends since his release. "Why, why must it be like this?" she wants to know. She isn't sure she can handle the pain of separation from her husband this time. Have they not already paid for whatever mistake Mehrbaan made as a young man?

"You should have seen the look on his face," Mrs. Mehrbaan cries out. "He was so sad, so angry, desperate, helpless. Oh, God." She begins to bawl.

My mother talks to Mrs. Mehrbaan, too. She cries on the phone while telling her old friend to stay calm. "This must be a mistake, or maybe they are trying to scare him. He'll be released soon. You'll see, they'll let him go."

My father looks utterly frustrated. Mr. Mehrbaan has been suffering from a heart condition, and the stress of jail could be dangerous to his health. Only yesterday Dad took Mr. Mehrbaan to the hospital for an angiogram. The doctor said that Mr. Mehrbaan needed to change his diet, start regular exercise, and stop smoking. "Of course, you can forget about all that when you're in prison," my father says bitterly.

Dad lights a cigarette and starts to think. I sit down next to him. "I wonder if he met Doctor while in prison," I say quietly.

Dad looks up and stares at me for a little while. I think he suddenly realizes that we're suffering the same pain. "You should have asked him," he says, gently.

"I didn't want to take away from the time you had together."

Dad puts his arm around my shoulder and pulls me toward him. "You aren't a child anymore. You can engage in adults' discussions. You should've asked him about Doctor."

I begin to roll my sleeves up and then down. Dad reaches over and stops me. "What's wrong?" he asks.

"I'm sorry about Mr. Mehrbaan, Dad," I say. "It must've been tough being away from him all those years. I know that not seeing Ahmed or Doctor for eighteen years would probably kill me."

"It was tough," Dad admits.

"How did you and Mr. Mehrbaan meet?" And before he has a chance to respond I add, "And, Dad, how come all these years you never said anything about him?"

Dad shakes his head. "I don't know if I've got good answers for your questions. He just disappeared from our lives. He was supposed to be locked up forever, you know. Sometimes it's easier not to think about things you can't do anything about."

Dad smokes his cigarette like it's his last one. It makes me wish I could have one, too.

"Your friendship with Ahmed reminds me so much of what Mehrbaan and I meant to each other," Dad says. "He was my best friend for a long time." He takes a big puff on his cigarette. "He took a big risk for me once. You know, the kind of thing I suspect you and Ahmed would do for each other."

I'm all ears and I think Dad can tell. He says that he and Mr. Mehrbaan have been friends since high school. Their families lived in a small town called Hashtpar in northwestern Iran. After high school, the two of them were drafted into the army and served two years together in a cold, mountainous area close to the Iraqi border. At the time, my father was in love with my mother, and the idea of being separated from her for two years did not suit him well. He craved her, dreamed about her, and wished they were together. Thank God Mehrbaan was there, or he would have lost his mind. Some days, he would go through the motions of living without remembering how the day had passed. Some nights, he would wake up to find himself sweating, angry and annoyed. Of course, all of this was unbeknownst to those around him, including Mr. Mehrbaan, who knew of his situation, but didn't know the extent of his suffering.

They were housed in a huge barracks where the men slept in two-story dormitories. There were at least ten buildings in the barracks and a total of two hundred and fifty to three hundred soldiers. Once the soldiers were in bed, they were not allowed to leave the buildings until dawn. Each soldier had night duty at least twice a month, guarding the area from nameless "intruders" who, in the forty-year history of the barracks, had never bothered to show up. The guards normally slept while on night duty, except on the nights when they knew their old corporal, a serious military man, might be around to check up on them. The punishment for those in violation of the barracks rules, whether sleeping on duty or walking around after lights out, was severe, and involved spending days, if not weeks, in the slammer.

My father's sleepless nights, combined with the frustration of being confined to his bed in those old damp buildings where he could hear the mice eating the columns supporting the roof, became too much for him. In addition, he didn't have much in common with the men in his squad. One soldier used to carry a piece of green cloth in his pocket that his mother had rubbed against the grave of a religious figure to keep the demons away. This soldier knew a great deal about common superstitious beliefs, and spent considerable time teaching his comrades about them. "If you accidentally point a knife at someone, stab the earth three times, or that person's blood may drip from the tip of that knife someday," he would say. "If you ever pour water on a cat, wash your hands three times at the same time each day for three days, or you may get a cyst on the tip of your nose."

One night, my father decided to take a walk around the campground. He needed to be out in the open and temporarily free of the rules and regulations that seemed so absurd to him. The superstitious soldier was on guard duty that night. Without Dad knowing, the old corporal was also awake. As my father was walking, the old corporal, hiding in the dark, blew his whistle. Dad started to run, followed by the corporal and a couple of soldiers nearby. Soon other guards were coming from all directions, running with their guns and whistles and relying on flashlights that weakly illuminated the ground half a meter in front of them. The old corporal began to cuss loudly, shaking his fists in the air, brandishing his gun, and ordering the guards to capture the intruder alive because death without torture would be an unsuitably gentle punishment for a coward like him.

They formed a big circle to ensure that the intruder did not escape. "Watch the gaps between you!" the corporal screamed, over and over. "Keep your eyes open and arrest this trespasser."

Not in their wildest dreams had the guards thought an intruder might actually invade their campground. Their serious, bent postures, nervous strides, the ambivalence with which they held their guns, and the frequency with which they looked to the left, to the right, and back again all conveyed their excitement.

The soldiers in the dormitories were up now, too; everyone was pushing for a spot at the windows.

The guards were closing in on my father. He didn't care if he was arrested and imprisoned, but he didn't like the idea of losing to the old corporal. In a desperate effort to buy more time, he ran up to a jeep that was parked nearby and crawled under it. Then he crawled back out just long enough to pick up a large stone and throw it through the window of a dormitory a few meters away in order to divert the soldiers' attention.

A couple of the guards ran toward the dormitory, but the majority stayed their course and continued zeroing in on my father's location. All hope was lost, and my father was about to crawl out from under the jeep and give himself up when a man in the distance screamed, "I'm over here, you bastards! You are a bunch of stupid fucking morons!" And with that came the sound of a window breaking a few meters behind where the corporal was standing. My father recognized Mr. Mehrbaan's voice. His old pal had come to his rescue, and he broke into a smile as he watched the soldiers run confusedly toward the sound of Mr. Mehrbaan's voice.

"He's over there, you jackasses!" the old corporal screamed. "How did you let him break through the circle? You pack of idiots. You should have been exempted from serving in this man's army! Run, run! Close in on him, don't let him get away!"

The soldiers ran from my father's hiding place. One even walked right by the jeep, but didn't bother to look under it. My father could see the shadow of Mr. Mehrbaan running in the dark. He stopped as a number of soldiers began to close in on him from the other side. He ran to his left, back to his right, then disappeared. My father crawled out from underneath the jeep, picked up a stone, and aimed it at the window of a building close to him. A group of soldiers was standing by the window in their undergarments, watching what was definitely the most exciting event of the year so far. My father gestured at them to move away from the window, and they scattered. He threw the stone, and the sound of shattering glass sent a jolt through the bodies of the guards, who were sure they had the intruder trapped this time.

"Come and get me, you stupid fucking morons!" my father echoed Mr. Mehrbaan. "Didn't you see me walking right by you? You are a bunch of blind bats! God help the country you're trying to defend."

The old corporal went berserk. He aimed his gun at my father's voice and fired a shot. Everyone ducked, including the guards who were standing next to the old corporal. The bullet shattered a window on the second floor of one of the dormitories. Someone from inside the building cried out, "I've been shot! Blood's running down my legs, look!"

Someone else said, "That's not blood, you idiot. You just peed in your pants." The sound of soldiers laughing and cursing brought a smile to my father's face. He ran around the building, making sure he was out of sight in the darkest areas of the campground. The old corporal screamed, yelled, and kicked at the guards who were glued to the ground, fearing that a flying bullet might catch them in the belly. They got up, brushed the dust off themselves, and began to run after my father. They hadn't gone three steps before they heard the sound of shattering windows behind them. They turned around, confused and exasperated, uncertain which way to go, and unsure how anyone could be here one second and on the opposite end of the camp the next. At that moment, another window was shattered on the opposite side of the camp, and still another at a third location.

The superstitious soldier threw his gun down and started to run toward the gate of the barracks, screaming, "It's a *Jen*, it's a *Jen!*" which means an evil spirit or devil. The other guards threw their guns down and began to run away, too, biting the space between their thumbs and index fingers.

"Stop, you fucking imbeciles!" screamed the corporal.

Windows began to bust on both sides of the camp simultaneously. My father and Mr. Mehrbaan had started an all-out stone-throwing assault on every window in the campground. People in the dormitories were screaming and whistling, encouraging this outburst against a system that had taken them from their loved ones for two years to teach them how to salute, and not much else. My father and Mr. Mehrbaan ended up making it back to their dorms without the corporal discovering their identities.

My father takes a deep breath. A tiny smile appears on his face. "The next day, everyone was talking about the devils that had broken the windows in the barracks," he says. He lights another cigarette.

I can tell from the look on his face that the recollection of his younger years with Mr. Mehrbaan has filled him with sorrow.

"He's the best friend I've ever had," he says. "He's the most generous person I've ever known. I thought I had him back after eighteen years. Now I wonder if I'll ever see him again."

13

The Cost of the Bullet

I'm depressed, and Ahmed knows it. He spends even more time with me these days than he used to. I can tell from his never-ending attempts to cheer me up that he's concerned about my emotional well-being.

Ahmed is the pillar I lean on. My father always says that there are two kinds of people in the world: ordinary and great. I have no doubt that Ahmed belongs to the latter category.

I tell Ahmed about Mr. Mehrbaan's arrest as we're doing our geometry homework in my room. Ahmed looks mournful and says that someday, this country will see the bloodiest revolution in the history of mankind. I once heard Doctor say that a revolution in Iran would change the world. Iran is crucial to the stability and balance of power in this vital region.

As soon as I mention Doctor's name, Ahmed changes the subject. He begins to sing, "Nothing makes you a better person than the love of a woman!"

"Did you just make that up?" I ask. "I've never heard that song. And how can you sing and still concentrate on geometry?"

"Who says I'm concentrating on geometry? And yes, I'm a poet, didn't you know that?" he replies.

I laugh and shake my head.

"I'm tired of school because school is for kids, and homework is for nerds," he says. "School and love are two diametrically opposed phenomena."

"Diametrically opposed phenomena?" I tease. "Who's using big words now?"

Ahmed ignores me. "Once you fall in love, academic knowledge becomes irrelevant," he claims. "I'm going to ask Mr. Bana how geometry, the motherfucker of all sciences, distinguishes between the shape of a virgin heart and a heart tormented by love."

"Have you been smoking hashish?"

"No, why? Do you have some?" he teases. "You know what I think we should do?" he asks, a serious look on his face for once.

"What?"

"We should kidnap Faheemeh and Zari and take them on a trip around the world."

"Oh, sure," I say sarcastically, remembering the time he scolded me for suggesting we take the girls out to a movie. "Would we tap into your checking account or my savings?"

"Well, Americans, the most disciplined people in the world, do it all the time. They hitchhike and find work wherever they go to make enough money to get them to the next town. I've seen it in the movies. That's what I think we should do."

"You're nuts."

"You know what's wrong with you?" he asks.

"What?"

"You take life too seriously."

"And what exactly is wrong with that, Professor?"

"Don't take life too seriously; you'll never get out of it alive!"

Then he picks up the phone and calls Faheemeh. Her brother answers the phone. Ahmed changes the tone of his voice and asks if this is Mr. Rezai's residence. Faheemeh's brother says no, and hangs up.

Ahmed waits a few minutes, then calls again. And again Faheemeh's brother answers.

"May I speak to Mr. Rezai?" Ahmed asks politely.

"You have the wrong number," Faheemeh's brother responds flatly.

"Is this 346585?"

"Yes."

"Then I don't have the wrong number. Would you please get Mr. Rezai?"

I start to laugh. Harassing people on the phone is a fashionable thing to do among young Iranians. Although I think such pranks are childish, I admit that I enjoy watching Ahmed torturing Faheemeh's brother, who lets loose with a stream of profanity and hangs up the phone. I tell Ahmed to quit fooling around as I laugh my head off. "You're going to get us into a major fight with those two boys," I chide.

He says, "Watch this, watch this." He calls Faheemeh's house again, and when her brother answers the phone Ahmed says, "Hi. This is Mr. Rezai. Has anyone called for me today?" He holds the phone away from his ear, and I can hear Faheemeh's brother exploding into a rage.

We hear my mother coming up the steps. Ahmed hangs up the phone and pretends to be studying. Mom walks in with a tray of tea and some dates, mumbling something about being proud of her two boys. She loves Ahmed like she loves me, and is very happy that I have such a great friend. She tells us to drink the tea before it gets too cold. It is Lahijan tea, the best tea in the world, and the only way to drink it is hot. She also gives us a brief lecture on the benefits of dates, and how the Arabs eat them to avoid dehydration in the scorching heat of the Sahara, and how the Buddhist monks survive on a single date a day.

When my mother leaves, and as Ahmed and I are checking the

tea for traces of powdered sorb, Ahmed says, "That's funny. I thought monks were celibate and didn't have any dates at all."

I have a hard time falling asleep that night. Around midnight I hear a noise from Zari's house. I run out on the terrace, and see Zari and her mother walk into the yard. Zari looks up and sees me. She puts her head down and disappears quickly into the house. I feel helpless, as if I can't get enough oxygen into my lungs. Does she not like me anymore? Will she ever come back into the yard like she used to? Oh, what great times we had before Doctor's arrest.

I'm still on the terrace when she joins me. The weather is unusually cold for this time of year. She is wearing a heavy dark brown turtleneck sweater. She has pulled the sleeves down and into her fists to keep her hands warm. She doesn't pretend she's up there for any reason but to talk to me. I've always admired her directness and lack of pretense.

She says a soft hello, and approaches the wall that separates our homes. This is the first time we've talked since they took Doctor away.

"How are you?" I ask. She shakes her head. Her eyes are red, and I can tell that she's been crying. She looks pale and devoid of the energy that always characterized her presence. She scratches the top of her head, and I notice that her hands are shaking. Then, as she looks at me, her eyes fill with tears. Her smooth brow lifts into a bed of wrinkles and she bites her lips, trying not to break into a sob. I jump over the wall and put my arm around her shoulders. I think she can tell that this is only a gesture of friendship and sympathy because she doesn't pull back.

"I'm okay," she says. Then she cries some more as I tap gently on her hand to calm her down.

"What am I going to do?" she finally asks.

"There isn't much we can do, except wait and pray."

She crouches with her back to the wall, and I sit next to her. She starts to sob. "No one knows where Doctor is," she says. "Both of Doctor's parents have been hospitalized. His mother is about to lose her mind, and everyone is concerned about his father's heart condition."

"Isn't that strange?" I ask. "Doctor's parents used to say that he was their heart and mind."

"I didn't know Doctor was so involved. All I knew was that he read banned books, and I never saw any harm in that." She sniffs a couple of times and wipes off her tears as she gets more emotional. "I can't believe they can take someone away and not say a word to his family. What kind of savages are these people? Have they no decency at all, no regard for a mother's pain? I won't be surprised if Doctor's mom has a stroke one of these days. Don't these people have any respect for the sanctity of human life?" She sobs bitterly.

We don't say anything for a long time. Finally, she turns to me and asks, "So, how have you been?"

"All right," I lie. "I'm fine."

"Good."

"I'm glad you came up," I offer tentatively.

"I wanted to talk to you earlier, but never got the chance."

"I was worried. I thought maybe you were mad at me," I admit.

"Why would I be mad at you?"

I wonder if I should tell her the truth about the night they took Doctor away. What if she hates me afterward? What if she never talks to me again?

"I was up here the night they came to get him." The words come out involuntarily. "The agent with the radio saw me. I think that's how he figured out where Doctor was."

Zari stares at me silently, surprise in her gaze. I'm instantly sorry for opening my mouth, but it's too late to stop now. "Everything happened so quickly that I didn't have time to duck. For a while, I didn't even know what was happening. I simply froze, couldn't move. I'm so sorry. If you ever see him, please tell him that I love him and I didn't mean for this to happen."

Zari puts her finger on my lips and hushes me. "You should never say that again," she says. "No one would ever think you could intentionally do anything like that to Doctor. Besides, everyone knows how much you love him. Trust me, you're not doing anyone any favors by driving yourself crazy over something like that. They knew Doctor was engaged to me, and they had the entire neighborhood under surveillance for a long time."

I lower my head and stare at my feet. She takes my chin in her hands and turns my face toward her. "Look at me. Look me in the eye."

I look into those pretty eyes and feel a shame I can't control.

"Promise me that you won't ever blame yourself for this again," she demands.

I nod my head yes, although I already know that I can't keep my promise.

She slowly pulls her hand away from my face, and leans against the wall. "They're going to let him go soon. I know it. I just know it," she whispers.

I lean against the wall, too. "I hope so."

After a little while she says, "You know, I miss the days when we used to get together in my yard."

I nod and whisper, "Me too."

She calls them the worry-free days of summer, and I agree and tell her that I wanted it to be the best summer of our lives, the last hurrah of our adolescent years. How sweetly it all began and how bitterly it ended!

"I wonder if this is a payback for our carefree summer," she muses painfully. "Life is a game of balancing acts, you know? No one is supposed to have too much of anything. I just wonder why poor Doctor had to pay for my mistakes." She begins to cry again.

I wonder what exactly she means by her mistakes, but I don't say anything.

"I'm planning to go to Evin Prison next week to see if I can get any information on his whereabouts."

"I'll go, too," I say. At first she says no because they may associate me with Doctor, but eventually she agrees.

Knowing that she is not mad at me helps lift the anxiety I've been feeling since Doctor's night.

"The stars are beautiful tonight," I say softly.

"They are," she answers. "Do you think we each have a star up there?"

"Not everyone," I clarify, "just good people."

"Really?"

"Yeah. And we can only see the stars of the people in our own lives."

"What do you mean?"

"Like I see Ahmed up there."

"Which one's he?" she asks, peering into the night sky.

"That one." I point to one of the biggest stars. She leans over and her face touches my arm as she aligns her gaze with the direction of my index finger. I look at the back of her head and her shoulders. I can smell her hair, and I feel intoxicated with love and desire.

"Oh, yeah, I see him. His star is big, isn't it?"

"It sure is. One of the biggest."

"And let's see, which one's Pasha's star?" she asks.

"Oh, I'm not up there," I say, but I'm hoping she'll insist that I am.

"No?" She turns around and looks at me.

I shrug my shoulders.

"Well, keep looking. You're hard to miss."

I look for a while, then turn back toward her without saying anything. We stare at each other, and then she gets up and heads toward her house. She stops in the doorway to turn around and ask, "Did you ever give her the picture?"

I don't say anything.

"Have you told her yet?"

I shake my head no.

She smiles and disappears inside the house.

It's Friday and Ahmed and I are in the alley because school is closed. Faheemeh is visiting Zari at her house. We hear a story in the alley that a group of terrorists were planning to blow up a dam in the northern part of Iran during the summer. If they had succeeded, thousands of people would have died in the cities that lay downstream. Doctor and his group were allegedly spotted a few hundred meters from the dam, and were chased all the way back to Tehran. I immediately dismiss the rumor as nothing but a lie concocted by the government to justify Doctor's arrest. Doctor is a pacifist. He believes in advancing his political ideologies by educating people, not murdering them.

A few hours after the rumor starts, Ahmed and I are sitting in the shadow of a tree outside my house when an army-style jeep pulls up at Zari's house. Two men get out of the vehicle, and I recognize one of them as the agent with the radio. While I sit frozen, they enter Zari's house without knocking. A few minutes later we hear a scream—Zari. Ahmed and I run toward her house. We force our way inside as the two men are walking out. The man with the radio looks at me and winks. I swear to God that I will kill the son of a bitch someday.

Zari is sitting on the floor, and Faheemeh is hovering over her in concern. Zari seems to be in a state of shock, her face frozen in an expression of despair and disbelief. I run up to her. "What's the matter? What's happening?" She turns toward me and the grief in her eyes sends a chill through my body. Ahmed rushes toward Zari's mother, who has fainted a few meters away. I hear the jeep leave the alley, and soon after, the neighbors rush into the house. The older people start to attend to Zari and her mother. I look at Faheemeh.

"They want them to pay for the bullet," she says, bleakly.

"What bullet?" I ask, going cold.

"Doctor's bullet." She looks at me through tear-glazed eyes. "That's how they can get his body back."

"Did I kill you, Doctor?"

"Did you want to kill me?"

"No."

"Then why are you worried?"

"People may think that I did."

"Why?"

"Well, have you ever loved someone you weren't supposed to?"

"Yes," says Doctor.

"Really? Did Zari know?"

"It wasn't like that."

"What do you mean?"

"It just wasn't like that."

"Please, tell me how it was, then. I really would like to know. Would you have killed for her?"

"Maybe."

"Given your life?"

"Oh, for sure."

"Oh, my God. Then you were in love, Doctor. What happened?"

"I got killed."

"I'm so sorry, but I don't understand."

"I fell in love with ideas, dreams, visions. I fell in love with think-ers I wasn't supposed to admire or even know."

"Forbidden ideas?"

"Forbidden love, forbidden ideas, what's the difference?"

"Well, forbidden ideas are in your head, forbidden love in your heart."

"Let me tell you something. There isn't anything in your heart. It's all in your head. Love, hate, thoughts, emotions, all of it is up there in your head. The heart is just a mechanical organ pumping blood to the rest of your body. Now enough of the biology lesson! Tell me why people might think that you killed me."

"Because I love . . ."

I wake up in a sweat, cold and shivering. I sit up in bed and look around. I try hard to remember what I have dreamed about, but my mind fights back. I think I was trying to tell Doctor that I loved Zari. I hope not. No one should ever know, not even Ahmed. It's forbidden to share forbidden love, even with your best friend.

14

Autumn of 1973
Tehran

Brothers for Life

Doctor's father suffers a heart attack the day he hears the news of his son's death. Most people believe he will not survive. Doctor's mother is in no shape to attend a funeral. With no one in Doctor's immediate family to claim his body, instructions for meeting the agents at the cemetery are sent to Zari's house. The instructions indicate that only Zari or her parents and one or two friends may attend the funeral. The notice also indicates that Doctor was "destroyed" near the end of *Sharivar*—mid-September, exactly a week before school started.

Ahmed and I hear through Faheemeh that Zari wants us to accompany her to Doctor's funeral, since we were closer to him than anyone else in the alley. Faheemeh says that Zari is the most thoughtful person in the world because she refuses to send a message to her cousin and best friend, the Masked Angel, requesting that she come to Tehran. Soraya would be a great source of support to Zari, but her parents are sick and Zari doesn't want her to be distracted with someone else's problems. "Can you believe how sweet this girl is?" Faheemeh says, as she wipes tears from her face. We accept the invitation to go along to the cemetery, knowing that we should keep the plan from our parents. I know my father would worry that the agency would take note of my presence. Fortunately for me, my parents are visiting our relatives in the northern part of the country, and are unaware of anything that's going on in the alley.

It's the evening before the funeral, and Ahmed and I are sitting on the roof of my house. The night is gray, still in its silence and pregnant with grief. I'm wearing a thick brown turtleneck, but the weather still feels brisk and uncomfortable. I watch the sky at the horizon and feel a chill course down my spine. This is a massive world, I think, and in each centimeter of it, a different drama unfolds every second of every day. But we live on as if the next moment in our lives will be no different than the last. How foolish we all are.

I'm not sure how events will unfold tomorrow. Will they let us see his body? Who will carry his coffin? Will they let us say a couple of prayers before they put him in the ground?

I shudder involuntarily. Finally, Ahmed breaks the silence. He points to a big, shiny star in the sky and says, "That's him, I know it."

My eyes fill with tears. "He was a great guy."

"The best."

"Do you think he's mad at me for falling in love with Zari?"

Ahmed turns and looks at me. I lower my head to hide my tears.

"No," he says with certainty.

"I think he is," I mumble. "You're supposed to think of a friend's fiancée as your own sister. How could he not be angry?"

"But you didn't do anything to disgrace him," Ahmed argues. "No one else even knows how you feel."

"I shouldn't have fallen in love with her."

"You think you had a choice? How do you know this wasn't the way it was meant to be? Maybe God knew what was going to happen to Doctor. Is Zari supposed to mourn his death for the rest of her life? Should she never experience love again?"

"And God chose me?" I ask bitterly.

"Well, Iraj would've been an okay choice, too, I suppose," Ahmed says sarcastically.

I smile despite myself.

"Look at that." Ahmed points to the skies. "Do you realize the immensity of creation? Do you see the prescribed order of the universe? God has imposed his rules and laws on everything. What makes you think he exempted you from that?" He puts his arm around me. "Right now, Doctor is looking down at us from the heavens, thanking God for putting you on earth so that you can take care of Zari. Who would have been a better choice than you? Tell me, who?"

I wipe my tears. "I'm not going to cry at the cemetery because I'm sure the man with the radio will be watching. Promise me something."

"What?" he asks.

"We're not going to cry."

He looks at me. I think he realizes that I mean business. "Okay," he says resolutely, and turns his face once more to Doctor's star. "We won't cry."

Anticipation of the next day's events keeps me up all night. The next morning we're standing outside Zari's house and I'm playing with my sleeves when Iraj comes over and asks where we're going. We don't respond.

"Are you guys going to the cemetery?" he persists.

"Yes," I say.

"You shouldn't. The whole thing will be under surveillance. They'll come after you."

"We don't care," Ahmed says.

"No, please, don't go. They won't like that."

"We don't care," I repeat.

"This is a trap. They find the sympathizers this way. You guys really shouldn't go."

Zari and Faheemeh come out of the house. Their eyes are red, and they're both wearing black chadors. Neighbors emerge from their homes as we walk through the alley toward the main street. They look at us quietly with tears in their sad eyes, silently offering us their condolences for the death of Doctor, and their apologies for not attending his funeral. They have families to care for, and the SAVAK cannot be taken lightly. I can hear Zari moaning. She sighs and bites her lips and shakes under her chador. Faheemeh puts her arms around Zari and whispers in her ear to calm her down. I see Iraj following behind us. His worried eyes beg us not to go.

We get a cab, and I sit in the front seat as Ahmed, Faheemeh, and Zari get in the back. I give the directions to the driver, and as he takes off I look in the side mirror and see Iraj running behind us, waving his arms. I can tell he's yelling something, probably still begging us not to go. He stops after a few minutes, bending over and grabbing his knees.

The driver wants to know if the deceased—God bless his soul— was a relative. I say that he was. I turn around and see Zari banging her head against the back window. Faheemeh puts her left hand between Zari's head and the glass. The driver asks if he was young. I nod yes.

"God bless his soul. Destiny, it's destiny, and there isn't anything we can do about it," he says, looking at Zari in his rearview mirror. "I had a younger brother who passed away a couple of years ago. Cancer took him. Never smoked a single cigarette in his life . . . a healthy guy, a real athlete. The pain of losing him is killing my mom, but what can you do? God gives and God takes. It's as simple as that. I have been driving for almost twenty years now. I've taken a lot of families to the cemetery. I know how bad it hurts. I know it from experience, and I know it from observing people. God bless everyone's souls."

He says he's not going to charge us for the trip because it's not right to take money from grieving people. Then he wants to know who the deceased was, who he was related to, how old he was, and what caused his death. I patiently answer all his questions, but instead of saying that Doctor was killed by the SAVAK, I say that he died in an accident. You never know who may be an agent. The driver whispers a prayer but doesn't ask any more questions about the cause of Doctor's death.

Every time I turn around to look in the backseat my eyes meet Zari's. She shakes her head and looks away. I wish I could do something to ease her pain.

I look at Faheemeh and for the first time I realize that she has become an integral part of our lives. She is taking an enormous risk by going to Doctor's funeral with us. I want to reach over and hug her. I love her as much as I love Ahmed. Today would have been much more difficult without her, and I'm glad she's here.

Remembering my promise to Ahmed, I turn to face the road ahead. I look in the side mirror and think of Iraj running after the car. I picture his face, the worried look in his eyes, and the concern in his voice. Maybe Iraj isn't such a bad guy after all.

We get out of the car at the gates to the cemetery. Despite our insistence, the driver won't accept our money. The instructions say that someone will meet us at the gate. There are lots of people dressed in black standing in and around the cemetery.

Inside the gates, we see a woman throwing herself on a grave. She cries out a name in a strangled rhythm and beats herself on the chest as her relatives try to restrain her. Everyone talks at the same time, while many in the crowd cry. I can tell that the scene has disturbed Zari. She weeps bitterly, but quietly. Faheemeh cries, too, as she watches the woman inside the gates throw her body back on the grave, hugging the earth, kissing it and filling her fists with dirt.

"It's her brother," Faheemeh whispers to Ahmed. "Poor woman."

Seeing the rows and rows of graves gives me a strange feeling. Everything is bathed in a lifeless light the color of dust, except the people, who are like shadows dressed in black. There are living people all around, but the eerie presence of death is hard to ignore. The air feels stale and dry, even though the weather is cold. The skies are covered with dark clouds. A few drops of rain make me wonder if a storm is on its way.

On one of the main roads of the cemetery, a coffin is being carried over the shoulders of a few weeping men as a large crowd follows. A man in the front yells, "There isn't a God but the almighty God!" and the procession chants the same in unison after him. "Say it loud. There isn't a God but the almighty God!" shouts the man walking in front of the group again.

"There isn't a God but the almighty God," the crowd repeats.

The procession leaves the road and stops at a grave that has already been dug. They put the coffin down and the crowd gathers around it. A mullah sings verses into a megaphone.

"He was graced with the eternal youth, entering the blissful and glorious kingdom of heaven. Don't weep, for all that live on earth are doomed to die. Only God will live forever. Welcome to heaven, the eternal home of the Muslims. In life, there may be inequalities, but in death everyone is treated the same!"

The cries of the people around the coffin swell louder as a group of men lift the body, wrapped in a white sheet, and place it in the hole. I'm standing next to Zari, and her knees buckle as she lets out a desperate cry. I reach over and grab her. I can tell from the weight of her body that she has lost all strength in her legs. Ahmed and Faheemeh help me hold her up.

Back by the grave, a young woman throws herself into the hole, shouting that she wants to be buried with her beloved husband. From the direction of Zari's gaze, I can tell that she's watching. I turn her around to make sure she doesn't see any more of the burial.

A couple of men are on the other side of the street watching us. I hear Ahmed curse, "Motherfuckers."

We all turn and look. These must be our contacts, the SAVAK agents.

The two men are wearing black suits and shirts. One of them is tall, and the other one is short and stocky. I feel like throwing up just thinking of their dirty profession. There is a sharp pain in my heart, and anger boils inside me.

Faheemeh grabs Ahmed's hand. "Honey, please. Don't say anything, I beg you. You promised me, sweetheart." She tries to hold Ahmed's face in her hands, to pull his eyes from the two men to her own face. "Look at me. I love you. I love you. I will kill myself if they take you away. You promised me, please."

Ahmed can't take his eyes off the guys on the other side of the street. Faheemeh turns to me and says, "Please, tell him to take it easy. I beg you. They'll take the two of you away and that will kill us. Please, I beg you!"

Zari whispers to me, "Please, stop him."

As I look at the two men, my body begins to shake. I let go of Zari and take a couple of steps toward the street. Zari grabs my left arm and stumbles, still weak with grief. I grab her before she falls down. "Please," she whispers in my ear.

I turn around and look again at the two men on the other side of the street. Two women and three children have joined them and they're all walking away. I'm embarrassed and I can tell Ahmed is, too.

Faheemeh bursts into bitter tears, and her body trembles as she sits down on the sidewalk. Ahmed tries to calm her down, but she can't stop crying. Zari whispers to me to get Faheemeh some water. I help Zari settle on the ground next to Faheemeh and then hurry away. When I get back, Faheemeh points for me to sit next to her. She puts her arms around my shoulders as she continues to cry. "He'll listen to you. Please, tell him to take it easy when they get here, and promise me that you'll do the same. Promise me."

I promise, and walk up to Ahmed, who's smoking a cigarette a couple of steps away.

"Let's stay calm," I say.

Ahmed nods tensely.

A few minutes later a young boy walks up to me and hands me a piece of paper. He says a man asked him to give me the note. I look at the paper as Ahmed, Faheemeh, and Zari anxiously approach me. The note contains detailed directions to a grave. We start walking. We turn left on the second street, then right on the next road, and follow a roundabout that leads behind a building where they wash the bodies of the deceased. The closer we get to our destination, the harder and more wildly my heart pounds. Faheemeh and Zari are holding on to each other, and Ahmed is a couple of steps behind them. We reach an unmarked grave. It's the third from the building, the fourth from the curb, and a large round stone covers the bottom half of it, exactly as the note said.

I look at my friends and point to the grave. Zari's shoulders begin to shake violently. She is inconsolable in her grief. She sits down by the grave. Faheemeh sits next to her and utters incomprehensible prayers as tears stream from their eyes.

Zari leans over the grave and touches the wet mud with her hands. "He's just been put in there," she whispers as she turns around and looks at me. I sit down next to her and put my arms around her for just a split second. "They didn't just kill Doctor," Zari whispers to me. "They killed us all, didn't they?"

I look into her eyes. If I open my mouth I will cry, I know it.

"They destroyed our lives by killing him: his dad, his mom, and us," Zari says. "Nothing will ever be the same again, nothing will ever be the same." Then she slowly puts her arms around the grave as her face touches the sodden earth.

I stand up and take my place next to Ahmed. He and I look at each other. I can tell that both of us want to cry, but a promise must be kept, especially when it's made with your best friend. I failed to keep my promise to Doctor when he asked me to keep an eye on his girl; I'm not failing another friend.

I squint my eyes and hold my breath as my heart pounds. I look to our right and see a number of buildings. These are the private tombs of the rich, who can afford to build a structure around their final resting place. Great, tall columns, sandy stone steps, and large gates make these expensive crypts look imposing. I remember the words of the mullah by the gate. *In life there may be inequalities, but in death everyone is treated the same.*

What a joke. I look at Doctor's humble grave, and I can't believe that his body is buried only a few meters from the private tombs of the rich.

One of Doctor's favorite books was *Mother* by Maxim Gorky. He must be wondering why his mother has not come to see him. Does he know that his father is in the hospital? Does he wish I wasn't here?

I begin talking to him in my head. I tell him that I'm sorry for falling in love with his girl. It was my destiny. I know he doesn't believe in it, but I need to. I tell him that I will take care of Zari, and will love her for as long as I live. I tell him that I love him and that if this hadn't happened I would have quietly gone away, because I had no intention of stealing his girl. *Show me a sign,* I beg. *Let me know you understand, and that you forgive me.*

I feel someone standing behind me. I turn around and there is Iraj. He is pale, out of breath, and sweaty. He says he didn't have enough money to take a cab, so he took the bus and that's why he's late.

Ahmed and I are standing shoulder to shoulder. I take a step to my right, and Iraj steps between us. The three of us are now standing side by side. I look at Ahmed, no tears, just as he promised. I hear Faheemeh and Zari crying. Out of the corner of my eye I see a mullah approaching us. He asks if it would be okay for him to read a prayer out of the Koran. Ahmed reaches into his pocket for a few coins, and the mullah begins his sermon.

Ahmed, Iraj, and I sit down by the grave and say a final prayer for Doctor. It's October. A rush of cold wind coming from the north sends a shiver through me. The dark gray skies augment the heartrending emotions brought on by the worst day of our lives, so far.

I'm crying quietly in my room later that night when I hear a knock on my window. I look up and see Ahmed and Iraj standing outside on the terrace. I open the door and let them in. I can tell from their red eyes that I'm not the only one who's been crying. Ahmed lights up a couple of cigarettes and gives me one of them. Iraj says he wants one, too. Ahmed hesitates for a moment. I gesture for him to get on with it, and he does. Iraj smokes his cigarette like he's been a smoker all his life.

I tell them to wait there, then run downstairs and take my father's bottle of Smirnoff vodka out of the fridge. I also grab three shot glasses and a bottle of Coca-Cola. I'm glad my parents are out of town. They would have objected to everything we've done today. In my room, I open the bottle and tell Iraj and Ahmed that we need to replace it before my father comes back.

"Have you ever had this?" I ask.

"No." They shake their heads.

The first time I ever had vodka was with my dad, when I was sixteen. He poured me a shot and told me that he wanted me to have my first drink with him. He encouraged me not to ever hide anything from him. Perhaps it'd be better if I tell him what we did today instead of subtly replacing the bottle.

"One of my uncles says you can't call yourself a man until you've had your first shot of vodka," I say. "There are rituals you need to respect," I add, remembering my father talking about it. "The *saghi*, the one who pours the drinks, must be fair. He must serve everyone equally." I fill the shot glasses carefully, making sure that they all contain exactly the same amount of vodka. "You know how to drink this?" I ask them.

They shake their heads again.

"Pick up your shot glasses."

They do.

"You bang your glasses together, like this." The rim of my shot glass touches the middle of theirs. "You see, you're not supposed to let me do that. Banging glasses and making sure that your glass is not higher than your partner's at the moment of contact is a sign of respect."

Lecture dispensed, I chug my shot. Iraj and Ahmed drink theirs. I can tell that they feel as bad as I do as the vodka goes down, burning everything from our tongues all the way down to our belly buttons. We each take a sip out of the Coke bottle, and I fill our shot glasses again with the precision and accuracy of a longtime *saghi*.

"You have to have a couple in a row to make sure you get a good buzz," I say.

We drink our second and third shots, and I already feel the buzz. We sit there quietly for a while before Ahmed slurs, "Drinking today was the best idea you've ever had."

I acknowledge his praise with a nod.

"This is the best thing for killing pain." Then his eyes fill. "I know what you're thinking. But we're not in the cemetery anymore."

A lump grows larger and larger in my throat. "That was a courageous thing you did today," I say to Iraj, trying to hold back the tears.

Ahmed nods in agreement. I put my arm around Iraj's shoulders. "I really love you. I'm going to love you like my own little brother, okay? You'll be my little brother from now on."

Iraj, overwhelmed with emotions and inebriated with alcohol, begins to sob.

"Me, too," Ahmed cries out. "I will never give you a hard time again."

"You showing up today was a sure sign that despite what happens on a day-to-day basis, the human spirit is indestructible," I say. "No one can destroy it. Not the Shah, not the motherfucking SAVAK, not the CIA, nobody, I mean nobody can touch it." I burst into tears.

"I loved Doctor," Iraj slurs. "And I love you guys. I do, I do. I couldn't stand by and watch you put yourselves in harm's way. No way. And fuck those SAVAK bastards, and their Western masters, and the grand servant of the West. Fuck anyone who wants to put me in jail because I stood by my friends to mourn the death of a hero, screw them all. I don't care if I have to spend the rest of my life behind bars, I don't, I really don't. I learned today that friendship is worth making sacrifices for. Doctor proved that life is a small price to pay for your beliefs."

Iraj wipes the tears off his face with his shirtsleeves. He goes on. "I'm not sure what's going on in my heart right now, but I know that something big is happening in there, something that's trying to pull me inside; you know what I mean? Not sure what it is, but it's something. It's really something. That's how it happens, isn't it? I think so. Something happens inside you, and then that's it."

Ahmed and I watch him as he talks. "I love him like my little brother," I cry again like a little kid, completely drunk on vodka.

"Me, too," Ahmed whispers, and hugs Iraj sloppily.

A strange feeling is taking me over, one that's hard to describe. It must be what Iraj is calling "something."

15

The Rosebush

No one will ever know the price of the bullet that killed Doctor. His parents are forbidden to speak of it. The stone on his grave must be left blank except for his name. The family can visit the grave as often as they wish, but others should not be encouraged. Doctor will not be issued a death certificate, and all documents pertaining to his birth will be destroyed. As far as the world is concerned, Doctor never existed. His books and the rest of his belongings were taken away during his incarceration, and they will not be returned. I remember my grandma saying after the death of a distant family member that the earth grows cold. I guess what she meant is that burying a loved one prepares the family to move on to the next stage in the grieving process. This is why Islam encourages immediate burial of the deceased.

In Iran, it takes us a long time to move on. We mourn the death of a loved one for a whole year. We get together on the third, the seventh, and the fortieth day after someone has died. Tea, sherbet, and sweets are served. Friends, acquaintances, and family members show up with flowers to offer their condolences. The same type of gathering is repeated on the one-year anniversary of the death. Throughout the first year, the family members wear black and refrain from attending parties or celebrating the New Year or any other national holiday.

In the case of Doctor, Zari's family was told by the SAVAK that no one would be allowed to wear black and that there would be no gatherings permitted, especially on the fortieth day after his death, which happens to coincide with the birthday of the Shah.

I'm searching in my room for something when I accidentally find *The Gadfly*, the book Doctor gave me—the story of a young passionate revolutionary who is killed for his beliefs. I read it in less than two days. I'm gripped by its powerful nineteenth-century style of writing, and the passion and brilliance of its hero's struggle and sacrifice. I understand Doctor better as a result. I wish I had read this book when he was still alive! Did he know of the destiny that awaited him, and was that why he asked me to read it?

All of his books were destroyed except this one, this special gift that is in my possession now. I will never part with it. All the kids in the alley should hear the story of *The Gadfly*. They should all know Doctor the way I do. If I can do nothing else for him, I can tell everyone that Doctor was a revolutionary who was not afraid of losing his life. All who knew him should be proud of their association with him. They should feel special because it's not often that our paths cross with those of real heroes. I will tell everyone that the SAVAK has forbidden us to mourn him, out of fear that it may inspire us to live in a way that would make his death worthwhile.

The SAVAK arrests a few of Doctor's university pals, claiming that he identified them as participants in anti-regime activities. In spite of these fabricated accusations, stories of Doctor's bravery flood the neighborhood.

"He wouldn't let them blindfold him," one of the neighbors says.

"He kept yelling, 'Death to the Shah!' until they shot him," another boasts.

Everyone knows that the real cause of Doctor's arrest and execution will stay a mystery forever. The SAVAK will never release the real reason. In the absence of facts, speculation and rumors cover a range of explanations, from his involvement in a plot to overthrow the Shah to simply being a student activist. I tell Ahmed that I think his personal friendship with Golesorkhi—the Red Rose—must have played a role in his execution. "If asked about his friend," I say, "he would've been just as defiant: a red rose himself destroyed by the SAVAK." Then I tell Ahmed, for the first time, that Doctor was the person posting the posters of red roses all over the neighborhood the night of Golesorkhi's broadcast trial.

"Wow!" Ahmed shakes his head in amazement. "How come you never told me this before?" Before I have a chance to respond, he adds, "Never mind. I probably would've done the same thing."

I would love to do something special for Doctor, but can't think of a worthwhile way to commemorate his death without violating the SAVAK's instructions. As I'm thinking of the night I caught Doctor distributing the posters of the Red Rose, a thought flashes through my head, something that Ahmed would mastermind. I pace back and forth in my room all night until I finally make a decision and go out to the spot in the alley where Doctor was first struck, where his blood was first spilled.

The next morning I count the allowance money I have saved up and realize that I need to borrow money from Ahmed. He agrees to lend it to me without asking the reason for it. I go to a nursery and buy a rosebush and some fertilizer, bring them home in a taxi, and take everything to the basement without anyone seeing. In the basement I find an old rusted shovel and a pair of gardening gloves. I find the hose that my mom uses to water our plants, and connect it to a faucet close to the door. Late that night after I'm sure everyone is asleep, I go to the spot and dig a hole about thirty centimeters deep and forty centimeters wide. I make sure that the soil is dry and spread five centimeters of manure before setting the roots in the hole and covering it back up with the dirt. I water the plant well to make sure that the backfilled soil settles well around the roots, then I collect my tools and disappear into the house.

I sleep like a baby that night. The next morning I run downstairs and out into the alley. Everyone in the neighborhood has gathered around the plant, and they're all talking at the same time.

"Who planted this?"

"Why?"

"Yes, why a red rose?"

"Why here? It doesn't make any sense."

"Oh, a red rose! Remember the posters?"

"The posters? Oh, yes, the posters, I remember the posters."

"Red is the color of passion and the color of revolution."

"Red is also the color of love."

"And the color of blood."

Suddenly everyone quiets down as they remember that this is where Doctor's blood was spilled, and a reverent silence fills the air. Ahmed turns and looks at me. He doesn't say anything but his mute stare speaks volumes—after all, we Persians are masters of silent communication. I go inside the house and come back with a watering pot.

"We must take turns caring for this bush," someone says in the crowd, as I water the plant.

"Yes, we must," everyone agrees. "For Doctor."

16

The Width of the Alley

No one knows of Mr. Mehrbaan's status in prison. Mrs. Mehrbaan comes to our house every other day to spend time with my parents. She looks older than the first time I saw her, when the color of her dress, shoes, and purse matched, when her makeup was thoughtfully applied, and when her hair was clean and nicely groomed. Nowadays, she seems not to care very much about her appearance. She cries constantly, and speculates about her husband's physical and mental condition in prison. My mother does her best to provide comfort, and gives her a special herb tea designed to battle depression.

"It tastes bitter," Mrs. Mehrbaan complains politely.

"The more bitter the taste, the stronger its healing power," my mother explains, encouraging her friend to finish the drink.

Mrs. Mehrbaan says that being away from her husband is more difficult this time because she was getting used to having him around. They used to talk with regret about the lost years; little did they know that he was going to be gone again. How long will it be this time? He is not young anymore, and given his heart condition, God only knows if he can tolerate the mental and physical abuse that prisoners are subjected to on a daily basis.

What a waste this all is, Mrs. Mehrbaan continues. Everyone

knows that the Shah will never be overthrown. What the opposition
needs to do is find a way into the government and influence the decisions and the laws that impact those affected by the injustice. A revolution is out of the question, so why bother? She adds that Mr. Mehrbaan
used to express serious concerns about the new breed of prisoners in
the SAVAK's jails. He had told her that he was troubled by the strong
religious overtones in the thinking and philosophy of the younger
revolutionaries. He believed that the rise of religious fundamental-
ism would create insurmountable new barriers to attaining democracy in Iran. My dad nods and says that Mr. Mehrbaan was always
accurate in his analysis of political situations.

One evening, during the course of conversation, my mother inadvertently mentions Doctor's situation. I am sitting only a few meters
away from Mrs. Mehrbaan, and I see her face wash pale while ridges of
concern jump from her forehead, as if a sudden shock has been administered to her body. She hangs her head, takes a few short, abrupt
breaths, then falls over. I catch her right before her face hits the ground.
My father scolds my mother for mentioning Doctor as he rushes
toward us. "Good catch, son," he yells out. "Let's take her to the bedroom." Her body is limp and droopy, and her arms dangle in the air as
I carry her to the bedroom. She's heavy but I'm determined to carry her
without the help of my father, who's just a step behind us. My mother
runs to the kitchen to get one of her natural remedies. My heart is
pounding, and I'm sure that Mrs. Mehrbaan is dead from a heart attack.

The muscles in her face collapse, leaving her skin waxy and creased.
Her lips turn blue, as if she is not getting any oxygen. I lay her on the
bed and put my arm under her neck, trying to keep her head up. My
mother comes back with hot water and sugar, and uses a teaspoon to
feed the liquid to Mrs. Mehrbaan. My parents talk over each other,
issuing orders while fanning her with a newspaper, spraying cold
water in her face, and telling me to hold her head up.

Mrs. Mehrbaan regains consciousness within a few seconds, and begins to sob bitterly as she curses the Shah, his family, his SAVAK, the Americans and the British who support him and keep him in power.

When I go to bed, I struggle to fall asleep, worrying about Mr. Mehrbaan and his fate in the Shah's prison. Are they beating him up right now? Are they burning his skin again like they did the last time? Is he screaming? Crying for mercy? Or is he defiant and resolute in his hatred of the regime, like the Red Rose was, like Doctor probably was? I wish Ahmed would show up with his cigarettes.

When I finally fall asleep, I dream of the night they took Doctor away. I see the man with the radio. His eyes are staring, locked on me, his lips whispering into the radio, and his fist crashing into Doctor's cheek. I see his predatory eyes again, and again, and again. His eyebrows are thin. His forehead is wrinkled and his long hair is combed back neatly. I hate him. I want to run downstairs and stop him from kicking Doctor, but I can't move.

Then it's Doctor's eyes staring at me. He must be wondering where the getaway plane is, why I'm not sacrificing myself to save him and Zari, as Humphrey Bogart did in *Casablanca*. He must be wondering why I gave him away. The man with the radio blows me a kiss. I open my mouth, and my voice is ripped from its silence as I scream at the top of my lungs.

October is usually mild in Tehran, but this year it's been particularly cold. Although it's no longer possible to sleep on the roof, Ahmed and I still spend a lot of time up there. The colder the weather is, the quieter our alley, and the more peaceful our retreat into the depth of our souls to find answers to what seems utterly incomprehensible and unfair. I sense a change in Faheemeh, Ahmed, and myself. We've grown closer. Every day after Ahmed and I get out of our classes, we rush to Faheemeh's school to walk her home. We spend hours pacing the streets together, sometimes without speaking a single word, and yet at the end of the day we have a hard time saying good-bye. When we do talk, it's always about a future far, far away, a time when all of us are grown-ups, prosperous, educated, and traveling around the world. None of us wants to be present in the aftermath of Doctor's death.

When we talk, we discuss Doctor's parents, the SAVAK's ruthlessness, and the fact that it seems as if someone has sprinkled the dust of death over our neighborhood. We complain about the vulnerability of life, the absence of decency, and the seeming permanence of evil.

I never mention Zari, but Faheemeh senses what I'm not saying. She says that Zari spends most of her time at Doctor's house nursing his mother, who everyone says is "incurably insane."

"The poor woman doesn't eat anything, and doesn't talk," Faheemeh reports. "All day long she sits still and stares at the door, as if she's waiting for Doctor's arrival. She hugs one of Doctor's shirts, smells it, presses it against her cheeks, and quietly cries." Faheemeh adds that she is worried about the impact of all this on Zari's spirit. "I think she blames herself, as if she should have known about Doctor's activities and stopped him. She says she never paid attention to what he was doing. Anytime he tried to discuss it with her she dismissed it as political talk, which she hated."

"How can she blame herself?" I whisper, thinking that I should be blamed for everything.

"She can't believe how naïve she was about the Shah and the SAVAK," Faheemeh continues. "She used to argue with Doctor that the SAVAK organization probably didn't even exist, that it was, for the most part, the product of the university students' active imagination. That poor thing, she wishes she could take all that back."

One day, after we say good-bye to Faheemeh, Ahmed says that we should continue our walk because walking clears the mind and helps us see the big picture.

We walk for hours, and I feel that for the first time in my life I'm absorbing the universe around me: the narrow alleys; the earthen, unpaved roads; the ugly, lifeless television antennas on the roofs; and the mazelike way in which our alleys weave through each other. I notice the unusual loudness of life around us: children playing football, mothers calling them, cars with broken mufflers passing by, their horns honking. The craziness of it all reminds me of how our alley used to be before Doctor was taken away. Life, as I remember it, was like a colorful musical projected onto a movie screen. Now it's more like an old black-and-white photograph turned yellowish and creased.

On our way home, Ahmed stops at the corner of an alley and looks at the street sign on the wall.

"What is it?" I ask.

"Nothing," he says, and continues walking. At the next corner he stops again and looks at the sign for the next alley.

"What?" I ask again.

"Have you noticed how most of our streets and alleys are named after the Shah's family members?"

"Yes, I have."

"Most of these signs also tell you the size of each alley or street," he says, a perplexed look on his face.

"What do you mean?"

"Look—this street is called the Twenty Meters of Reza Pahlavi, meaning that this street is twenty meters wide. That street is the Twenty-one Meters of Farah." He looks at another sign, and starts to laugh. "This one is the Four Meters of Darabi. Darabi is not a member of the Shah's immediate family, so his metric allocation is smaller." He points to a large street several blocks away and says, "That one is the Sixty Meters of Shahpour. He's the oldest brother of the Shah, so he gets the big number."

I have no idea where Ahmed is going with this.

"Why do we need to know the size of each alley and street?" Ahmed asks.

I suggest that the size must be a factor in determining the value of the properties in each neighborhood. Ahmed's expression tells me that he knows I'm guessing.

"Are these measurements correct?" he asks. "Our alley is the Ten Meters of Shahnaz. Do you really think our alley is ten meters wide?"

"I don't know," I answer.

"I doubt it," he says, a worried look on his face. "What if it's not? We should measure the width of our alley."

"Why?"

"Well, what if our alley isn't ten meters wide?"

"Who cares?"

"I care," he says, his voice charged with emotion. "This could have a devastating effect on property values, you know?"

The way he tosses my bullshit back at me makes me laugh.

When we get back to our own alley, Ahmed goes inside his house and comes back out with a tape measure. He summons Iraj and another kid, and starts the process of measuring the width of the alley. He tells Iraj to hold one end of the tape, and asks the other kid to walk across the alley. A car comes through, and Ahmed waves at the driver to stop. He tells the driver that he's in the middle of something important, and that he appreciates the driver's patience. The driver says sure, and turns his engine off. Ahmed asks me if I think he should include the width of the sidewalks in his measurement. I say maybe he should measure it both ways.

Kids from all over the alley gather around Ahmed to find out what he's doing. A few more cars come through, and Ahmed stops them and notifies the drivers of his important mission, without being specific about the task or the reason for it. The drivers get out of their cars.

"It's twelve-point-two meters when you include the sidewalks," Ahmed yells to me. "Write it down."

I don't have paper or pencil, so I just shake my head.

"Okay, let's measure it excluding the sidewalks," he directs.

Iraj and the other kid start to move the tape. More cars have collected in the alley, and the commotion has attracted a lot of people. Ahmed's project has the alley blocked, and no one can get through.

"How wide is it?" Ahmed yells to Iraj.

"Nine and a half meters."

Ahmed turns to one of the adults and says, "I can't really trust that kid. Would you be kind enough to hold the end of the tape?" The adult walks over and takes the end of the tape away from Iraj, who runs to Ahmed to tell him he was doing it right. Ahmed smiles, points to me, and says, "Go stand by him." Iraj walks over. I can tell from his smile that he has suddenly realized what Ahmed is doing. Ahmed asks, "What is the measurement now?"

"Nine-point-six meters," says the adult.

Ahmed turns to Iraj and gives him a dirty look. Iraj smiles and shrugs his shoulders. Ahmed asks the second adult, "Are you at the edge of the sidewalk?"

"Yes," he answers.

Ahmed walks over and examines the placement of the tape. People randomly divide themselves into two groups and position themselves behind each of the tape holders. All eyes are on the tape and the position of the holders.

"This way, to the left," orders one guy, who has closed one eye trying to imagine a straight line between the two tape holders.

"No, no. Too far," another guy yells from the other side of the alley. The tape holder moves back a few centimeters. A number of people begin to argue that the line is now slightly slanted.

"Hard to tell," Ahmed says. "We're trying to figure out the straightness of an imaginary line. The Americans shot a man straight from the earth to the moon, and we can't draw a straight line." He then looks at Iraj and asks, "Do you know why the Americans were able to do that?"

Iraj nods vigorously and says, "Yes, sir, because Americans are the most disciplined nation in the world!"

One of the guys in the crowd says that he is a mason, and that he can do this with his eyes closed. He then takes one end of the tape in his hands and wiggles it around on the edge of the sidewalk a couple of times and says, "There, now you have a straight line." The line does look straight.

"What's the measurement?" Ahmed asks.

"Nine-point-four meters," responds the mason.

"And that's exactly my point! This alley is not ten meters wide," Ahmed crows in triumph.

I look around, and see at least fifty people gathered in the alley. Traffic has come to a complete halt but no one seems to care.

"Is that important?" asks one of the adults.

"Of course it's important!" Ahmed says with plenty of alarm in his voice. "This could have a devastating impact on property values. The prices of these homes are based on the width of the alley they were built in. The city could announce that everything in this alley is worth at least fifty thousand toomans less than what people are trying to sell them for."

"But the city doesn't get involved in such things," says one of the adults apprehensively.

"Are you sure?" another adult asks.

"Of course they do," somebody else yells.

"What should we do?"

"We should measure the width of every street that has a metric number in front of its name, and be prepared to present evidence that the homes in this city are all overpriced."

I want to laugh, but I control the urge. I see a spark in Ahmed's eyes, one that I know very well. One man says that he has no plan to sell his house, but should he decide to do so, the mayor himself couldn't get him to drop his price. A woman says that she and her husband just bought their house in this neighborhood, and if they knew the alley was narrower than advertised, they might have looked somewhere else. The mason tries to convince everyone that a few centimeters doesn't really matter, but no one listens to him. Ahmed has completely pulled himself out of the discussions. He looks at Iraj and me, and grins. We grin back.

17

Prove Your Innocence

The next morning I hear my mother whispering to my dad that she is scared to death that Ahmed and I are going to get ourselves in serious trouble. "I've heard them talk about killing the man with the radio," she reports, her voice tight with panic. "You need to talk to him, and to Ahmed, too. They're young and inexperienced, and very emotional right now. They can't go on like this." Then, as if she's afraid that someone might hear her, she whispers in a guarded tone, "Did you know that they went to Doctor's grave site?"

"No," Dad responds.

"What if the agents saw them? Oh, my God, I can't even imagine. Please, talk to them," she begs.

My father assures her that he will talk to us, but my mother continues. "There is a rumor in the alley that Pasha planted the rosebush outside the house. I know he's angry and depressed, and God knows what else he might be saying at school or to other kids in the alley!"

The next day, my father has a private conversation with Ahmed's father. A few minutes later we are summoned to Ahmed's living room, and my father tells us that he has to take care of some personal business up north, and he prefers not to go alone. He would appreciate it if Ahmed and I went along.

"One has to be careful all the time," Dad says as soon as we get on the road. "In this country being innocent doesn't protect you from suffering the fate of a criminal. That's because we have a lot of *nokars* in this country. Servitude and blind devotion is what a *nokar* subscribes to." Then he turns to me and asks, "Have I ever told you about Engineer Sadeghi?"

"No," I respond. "Who's he?"

"When you were about six years old, I was a Jungle Guard in Mazandaran," he begins.

I discreetly elbow Ahmed in the side. My dad always tells remarkable stories of his younger years. Ahmed nods a couple of times and winks without looking at me to let me know he's listening.

"The Shah had just nationalized the forests, and my job was to prevent the locals from cutting down the trees. One of the Shah's own brothers was breaking the law only a few kilometers from where I was stationed, but I didn't know anything about it. I was sitting in my office one day when a government inspector arrived from Tehran. His name was Engineer Sadeghi, a self-proclaimed man of high integrity and principles. He said that I had been accused of accepting a bribe to allow illegal forest shaving operations in the Kolahdasht area. If I were found guilty, which he was certain I would be, my punishment would be sixteen years in Evin Prison because disobeying the orders of the Shah was interpreted as treason by the high courts."

My father lights a cigarette and takes a huge puff. I can tell from the look on Ahmed's face that he wants a cigarette, too, but he is totally absorbed in my father's story.

"I told him that I had never taken a bribe in my life," my father continues. "He laughed and said that my denial was not out of character for a man of my corruptible standards. He asked me to surrender my badge and follow him to his jeep. He was taking me to Tehran to personally hear the sentencing I deserved. The accused has no rights in this country, so I did what I was told. I asked him if we could stop at my house to inform my wife of my predicament. He said no, and continued driving toward Tehran.

"He was a peculiar man, surprisingly loquacious and brutally honest. It didn't seem to matter to him that I was not interested in his long-winded stories about his ancestors who were as loyal as dogs to the family of the king. His father was a devoted servant to Reza Shah, as was his grandfather. He recalled Reza Shah telling his father that his family would be well provided for as long as the Pahlavis wore the crown. He claimed that the Sadeghis were a people of high integrity who wouldn't dream of accepting charity from anyone, including the king himself.

"He talked of his son and of his future daughter-in-law, whom he adored. They were to be married within a couple of months, and the prospect of having a grandchild, particularly a grandson, elated him.

"He said that men like me made him sick, that he never once in his life took a step down the wrong path, and he could not understand the cravings of men like me for money and power. He didn't understand the psychology of greed, and was in despair when he had to explain to his own son—the jewel of his life—why certain people would sink so low as to risk personal and family honor the way I had.

"I sat quietly and listened as he continued to tell me of his high regard for fairness and social equality, of decency and morality, and the inexplicable corruption of humanity. He told me of the bribes he had been offered as an inspector, and his refusal to accept a single rial throughout his long and unfaltering career. Once, he was offered a huge sum that would have financed his son's education at the finest university in the United States. He refused to accept the bribe, saying that he preferred an uneducated son to one whose quality of life was enhanced with money that came from illegal means. Another time, he turned down a new, fully furnished house in an affluent section of the capital city.

"He said he knew well that his enemies were lurking in the shadows, waiting for an opportune moment to strike, but his principles were unwavering, and he preferred death to a dishonorable life.

"I listened to him silently, thinking of the hardship that was to befall my wife and my dear child. What would my wife do? She hadn't worked a day in her life, and now she would be saddled with the burden of supporting the family. I had saved no money, and owned no property that could be sold. She was on her own. I could picture you getting slapped around by a master at a house or a shop, perhaps beaten for a small mistake you were bound to make as a child, or kicked just to be taught a lesson while I rotted in jail for a crime I did not commit. I was burning with pain while this imbecile, this self-appointed guardian of high principles and values, chattered away about his family's devotion to a tyrant. I looked at his face from the passenger side and saw a symbol of everything that had gone wrong in our country, and I knew what I must do.

"I could explode his skull with a single blow. My knuckles had cut down much bigger men in the ring, and now they were going to save my family from the greatest enemy we had ever faced. I clenched my fists and prepared myself.

"I knew that I needed a plan before discharging the fatal blow. I would hit him, then grab the steering wheel and move to his side to bring the car to a stop. I would throw his body on the backseat, get off the road, then bury his body in a ditch and burn his car before catching a ride back to my office. No one had seen us together, and he had an army of enemies. No one would ever suspect me, since I, too, had lived an honest life—a simple life that was about to be destroyed by this man without a single shred of evidence.

"He stopped the car right at the moment when I was ready to wipe his existence from the face of the earth. My silence had broken his rhythm. He told me that people in my predicament usually begged for forgiveness, or tried to make a deal or attempt to escape. He questioned, 'What is wrong with you, man? Have you no regard for your reputation? Feel no remorse? Have no shame? No fear? Feel no pain? Explain to me what it takes to stoop to your level.'

"I continued my silence as he got out of the car and shut the door behind him. He sat on the railing by the side of the road and lit a cigarette. I got out of the car and joined him without saying a word, still waiting for the best opportunity to discharge the fatal assault. He kept looking at the mountains and the little streams that ran through the valleys. He puffed on his cigarette. 'Are you innocent?' he asked.

"I looked at him for a while, then asked, 'Is that important to you? Isn't an accusation of wrongdoing as compelling as an admission of guilt to you? Aren't men like you responsible for the corruption of our value systems and for our national suspicion and reservation toward procedures of justice and fairness? Is it not true that men like you perpetuate the ugliness of our political and legal systems? No, I feel no remorse, no pain, no guilt, and no shame—for everything you mention is felt by one guilty of a crime.'

"'Let me be honest with you,' I continued. 'I was about to crush your skull before you stopped the car. And to be perfectly frank, I'm still thinking about it. Not for the unjustified pain you are about to cause me, but for the misery you are about to bestow on the lives of those most dear to me. I do not value your integrity or your unfaltering high standards because I resent your narrow-minded approach to an assumption of guilt. So I advise you to run, beg for mercy, or repent because your time on this earth is coming to an end.'

"He made no attempt to escape, despite seeing the anger and the anguish in my eyes. He put out his cigarette and lit another one. Suddenly, like a well-mannered man who had momentarily forgotten how to behave properly, he offered me a cigarette. I took one, and he respectfully lit it with his old lighter.

"'What do we do now?' he asked.

"I thought for a while, and said, 'Let's go back to the village and face my accusers.'

"He agreed, and walked to the driver's side of the car.

"'I drive,' I whispered. He turned around and looked at me, and I knew he had figured out what I was proposing.

"'Have they never met you?' he asked.

"'No,' I responded.

"We drove away without saying another word. I was surprised that he went along with my plan so readily. But I guess he had dealt with a lot of sinister characters in his life. And I guess, at least in his heart, I didn't fit the mold.

"I could tell that he was watching me as I drove through the gravel roads of the Alborz Mountains. We traversed narrow roadways made for horses and donkeys, through canyons and along rivers toward a little village known as Kolahdasht. I loved this area. There was peace in the meadows where the cows grazed. There was serenity in the rolling mountains, where you could see pristine streams running down the inclines, where every once in a while you could spot a deer climbing the slopes.

"The jeep was spotted from a couple of kilometers away. When we reached the outskirts of Kolahdasht, the *kad khoda*, the mayor, and half of the village were anxiously waiting to welcome us.

"I got out of the jeep and shook hands with the *kad khoda*, introducing myself as Engineer Sadeghi. The *kad khoda* was thrilled to meet a high-ranking official from the capital city. He invited me to follow him to his 'humble dwellings' for a cup of Lahijan tea. I looked at my passenger and barked at him to follow us. As Sadeghi was getting out of the car, I heard a man yell, 'How does it feel to get caught, you thief?'

"We entered the *kad khoda*'s house, followed by almost everyone who lived in the village. I was directed to a place in the room reserved for honorable guests, and Sadeghi was told to sit by the door. There were no chairs in the room. An old inexpensive Persian rug covered the floor. Cylindrical pillows were set on smelly sheepskins, which were laid on the carpet along walls that had been darkened by the smoke of Ghalyan and cigarettes.

"The *kad khoda* yelled at his daughter to bring his honorable guest a fresh cup of tea. 'Bring a cup for that man, too,' he directed, pointing to Engineer Sadeghi, who was playing the role of prisoner with the artistry of an accomplished actor.

"I know the people of this region well, and I know how important it is to them to come across as hospitable, so I was not surprised when the *kad khoda* pointed to Sadeghi and said, 'This man may be a thief, but he is my guest—and a guest will always be treated like a lover of God in my house.'

"A few of his helpers who were sitting in the room approved by nodding their heads. The *kad khoda*'s daughter brought us tea, sugar cubes, and sweets. He looked at me and said, 'Welcome to my humble dwellings, Mr. Engineer Sadeghi. It is seldom that I'm honored by the presence of a guest of your stature. I hope you will forgive my clumsy manners, and grant me the honor of hosting you tonight. As for him'— he gestured, pointing at Sadeghi—'rest assured that we have the proper facilities to keep him in check.'

"I thanked him for his invitation, and said that we must leave for Tehran immediately, that it was only in the spirit of fairness that I had brought him to this village to face his accusers before taking him to Tehran to suffer the consequences of his illegal acts.

"The *kad khoda* looked around the room and insisted that we stay the night. 'These are dangerous roads, especially at night. You will get lost, and it is cold. Besides, what would the people of this village say if I didn't show you the hospitality owed to a gentleman of your stature?' he said pleadingly.

"He looked around the room again, and everyone started nodding politely, insisting that we spend the night at the *kad khoda*'s house.

"I told him that we could discuss his proposal after we got the small business of this man's fate out of the way. I asked who was accusing him of taking a bribe, and whether or not he might be among us.

"One of the *kad khoda*'s helpers stood up and said that he was the accuser, and that he had seen the accused taking a bribe from his father-in-law.

"I asked if he had been present when the bribe was taken. He said that he had, and that he had seen the transaction with his own two eyes.

"I told him to look at the accused, Mr. Shahed, carefully, and then tell me with certainty that he saw him accepting the bribe from his father-in-law. The accuser walked over to Engineer Sadeghi and looked at him carefully. A couple of the people who were peering through the windows yelled, 'It's him, it's him! Tell the honorable Mr. Engineer that he was the man—tell him, tell him!' The man looked at Sadeghi for a few more seconds, then turned to me and said that he was sure the guilty party had been arrested. He and the accused had even smoked a cigarette together by the stream that runs through the village, and it was there that the accused told him he was going to use the money to buy a new car. The accuser then stuck his chest out and boasted that he would recognize this thief even with his eyes closed.

"'Why are you lying, man?' Sadeghi pleaded.

"'I'm not lying,' the accuser barked back. 'You are a liar, and a despicable one at that.'

"'Had you ever seen him before that day?' I asked.

"'No,' said the accuser.

"The *kad khoda* looked at me and said in a hushed tone that he had heard the accused had tried to implicate the family of his Imperial Majesty for shaving the forests. He said that the man had no shame, and should be locked up for the rest of his life.

"A couple of onlookers yelled, 'Lock him up, lock him up for the rest of his life!'

" 'Where's your father-in-law?' I asked the accuser.

" 'The gendarmes have him locked up. He denies having bribed anyone,' the accuser said.

" 'Is he wealthy?' I asked.

" 'He owns a house, and lives in it alone. I guess my wife and I have to move in now to protect the property until he pays his debt to society. He is old, your honor, and I doubt he will get out of prison alive. It's a shame, a shame.'

"I looked at Sadeghi, who seemed fascinated by the events unfolding. Another innocent man was in jail because of the greed of this detestable human being and the shameless cover-up efforts of the *kad khoda*. I asked if he had seen enough. He shook his head, completely appalled."

My father takes a deep breath, and stops talking. He reaches for another cigarette. I quickly pick up the lighter from the dashboard and light his cigarette. Dad recognizes my gesture of respect by tapping my hand a couple of times and shooting a smile my way. I can tell from the serious look on Ahmed's face that he has understood the wisdom in my father's story.

"This is an unfair world," my father whispers, "and unfortunately, in this country, being accused is as good as being guilty. I was lucky to end up with someone who, despite his *nokar*-like attitude toward the regime, was at least willing to listen. Not everyone is so lucky. Life is not fair all the time. You boys will remember that now, won't you?"

"What happened next, Dad?" I ask, wanting to reach over and hug him.

"I stood up and asked the accuser to come to me. When he did, I punched him as hard as I could."

Warm blood rushes through my veins as my eyes sparkle with pride and excitement. I laugh with satisfaction and joy. My dad is the wisest man I know. His indirect way of warning us of the potential dangers of a conflict with the government and its agents, without ever mentioning Doctor, was brilliant. That's the way of the Persians—we are masters in the art of implication, sometimes at the cost of the point getting lost on an unsophisticated listener. Facts seldom matter. The meaning and the message are always woven into the fabric of our discourse.

"Deep in each knot of a Persian rug is a statement of the hands that patiently drove the needle and the thread," I once heard my father say.

Winter of 1974
Roozbeh Psychiatric Hospital, Tehran

I wake up early in the morning, and the cocoon of comfort that the pill had woven around me is gone, replaced by anxiety and confusion.

"Apple Face, Apple Face!" I start to shout. A young nurse walks in. "Where is Apple Face?"

"She's at home, sleeping. Take it easy, will you? You're waking everyone up." She has a glass of water in one hand and a pill in the other. She tucks the pill in my mouth and brings the glass toward me. I spit the pill out and scream that I want Apple Face. The commotion brings two other nurses into the room. I am agitated, plagued by a pain that has no identifiable source. The nurses try to hold me down as a man in a white uniform enters the room. A few seconds later, I feel a pinch in my arm.

Apple Face is sitting next to me when I open my eyes.

"Did you miss me?" she asks.

"What's wrong with me?" I say.

"Nothing that can't be cured. It takes time, though."

"I'm hungry."

She hurries out of the room and comes back with a tray of food. I take a couple of bites, and then can't eat any more. She assists me into a wheelchair and takes me to a big room on the first floor. I realize for the first time that I am in a psychiatric ward. I see people walking aimlessly up and down the hallways. Some look at me, and others pass by as if they are floating in a different universe. Two male nurses try to help a young man into a wheelchair like mine. He shows me his teeth, and smiles. What am I doing in a mental institution? All my life I've been told to avoid crazy people, and now I am living among them. Apple Face rolls my wheelchair to a window, and sits next to me in a chair.

"Did you miss me last night?" she asks again.

"Where were you?"

"I was home. I have a small child, you know? She needs her mommy, too."

"How old is she?"

"Four and a half. She's really cute. Do you want to see a picture of her?"

I nod yes, and she shows me a picture of her daughter, Roshan, meaning "glowing" or "vibrant."

"She's pretty," I tell the proud mother.

"Thank you." She puts the picture back in her pocket and sits back in her chair.

"Why am I in a psychiatric ward?" I ask, hesitantly.

"You're here to be treated."

"For what?"

"You have some things to remember."

"Like what?"

"Be patient."

I look at my legs and at my wheelchair and wonder if I am paralyzed.

"Why am I in a wheelchair?" I ask.

Apple Face thinks for a few seconds. "You were weak, and you had tuned out. So it was easier and safer to put you in a wheelchair."

The old man on the other side of the room begins his chant again.

"What's wrong with him? Why's he here?" I ask, quietly.

"It's a sad story," she whispers.

"I want to know," I press.

"Maybe later."

"What does he mean by his chants?"

"I don't know."

I feel sorry for the old man, who is still looking at me.

"Will you get in trouble for spending so much time with me?" I ask Apple Face on the way back to my room.

"Doctors don't get in trouble for spending time with their favorite patients," she responds.

I assumed she was a nurse because she was a woman; I feel ashamed.

"I miss the old days, when doctors made house calls," she adds. "You got to know your patients, their family, their kids, where they lived and how. It's all about business now."

Back in my room, she helps me into bed and gives me a pill. She tells me that I can call her at home if I wake up in the middle of the night, and leaves her phone number by my bed. Feeling better knowing that a doctor is taking care of me, I fall promptly asleep.

I wake up in the middle of the night, and wish that Apple Face were with me. I think of her daughter, and suppress my need. The room is dark and I can't tell what time it is. I know that my parents were in the room while I was asleep because I see a new rose next to my bed. My mother brings me a single red rose every day. *There is something significant about the red rose, which I can't think of right now. My mind is so tired.* I close my eyes and try to think of why I am in the hospital. Suddenly, a sound from across the room startles me. I open my eyes and look toward the source of the sound. The silhouette of a man stands by the door. My heart beats fast, and I am gripped with such a strong fear that I can't utter a word to summon assistance. My body trembles.

"If I knew your pain, I would bear it." I recognize the old man's voice.

"Come here," I whisper. The old man slowly approaches my bed and sits in Apple Face's chair. His gaze is fixed on me.

"If I knew a way, I would find it."

"What does that mean?" I ask.

He sits there and stares at me with his sad black eyes that seem to be turning gray. His gaze is kind, and I am not afraid of him anymore.

"If I knew a song, I would sing it," he murmurs.

"Maybe someday you can tell me what that means, and why I'm here."

The old man says nothing.

"I can't figure it out," I whisper. "Is any of this real?"

I wait for a reaction from him, but he just stares at me.

"I don't feel connected to anything. It's like I just came into this world from another place, but I can't remember the place I came from, either. It seems as if I'm neither here nor there, not living but not dead. Is this what people mean when they say someone has lost his mind?"

The old man still doesn't say anything. I can't keep my eyes open, but I want to understand his cryptic chants. I want to know how he feels, what he thinks, why he is in my room, but I am too tired.

I can't tell how much later it is when I hear Apple Face talking to my parents in the hallway.

"What's going to happen when he remembers?" my father asks.

"It'll be devastating," Apple Face answers. My mother starts to cry, and I wonder about this thing I am supposed to remember that will be so devastating.

18

The Eyes of the Square

We continue our trip toward the province of Mazandaran, zigzagging up the dangerous roads of the Kandovan and down toward the north, where you can smell the heady salt of the Caspian Sea from miles away. Fifty kilometers per hour is the maximum speed you can travel through these mountains, even if you are the best driver in the world. My grandfather used to say that the Nazis built the winding Kandovan road to lacerate the much-detested "SS" shape into our psyche. The Russians tried to stop them, but they failed as they always do when faced with the brutality of the Western powers.

These roads are so treacherous that hundreds of people die every year trying to navigate them. According to one of my uncles, as a future engineer I'm destined to build the four-lane highway that will connect Tehran to Mazandaran, saving thousands of lives in the years to come. Throughout the journey, we see people stopped on the shoulders, cooling off their overheated radiators and snapping a picture or two of the breathtaking scenery—valleys and canyons that engrave the belly of Mother Nature.

We finally reach the village, our destination, but the gravel road makes it impossible to drive very fast. The people in the village look at us curiously, and some wave as we drive by. I'm reminded of Doctor,

who was intrigued by the lives of people in small villages, always talking about building roads, digging wells, and bringing electrical power
and other technologies to these remote areas.

The houses are built on the slopes of the mountains, and most of
them look small and worn down, thanks to their rusted tin roofs. The
whole village consists of a couple of small grocery stores, a coffeehouse,
a cheese-yogurt shop, a bakery, a butcher shop, a public bathhouse, and
a mosque—all conveniently built around an unusually large square. It
takes us less than three minutes to drive from one side of the village to
the other. The smell of burning wood and cow dung sears the inside of
my nose. There are horses and cows on the road, and we have to stop
frequently to let them cross. Ahmed has never been to this part of the
country, so he watches everything with quiet curiosity.

We stop outside a big house surrounded by tall walls, its main
entrance gated by gigantic metal doors. My father gets out with a smile
on his face. Soon, a man—Mr. Kasravi, an old friend of my father's—
comes out to greet us. "Don't let his easy demeanor fool you," my father whispers. "He is a very important man."

I remember Dad and Mr. Mehrbaan talking about him. He is the
richest man in the village, a landowner who also raises cattle and
sheep. He spends part of his time in Noshahr, a city by the Caspian
Sea, where he owns various stores and a large motel. His wife, Goli
Jaan, a simple-looking woman, rushes out to greet us. Soon, servants
and maids hurry toward us, dragging a sheep behind them. I know
what comes next. I try not to look when they slaughter the poor
creature under our feet. Out of the corner of my eye I see the animal
struggling and wonder if he knows we are responsible for his ill
fate.

Mr. Kasravi shakes my hand and embraces me as if he has known
me for years. He asks me if I remember him, and I politely say no. He
says that I used to call him "Uncle Kasravi" when I was very little. My
father smiles, and adds that I used to call Goli Jaan "Aunt Goli." Mr.

Kasravi shakes hands with Ahmed and welcomes him to his humble dwellings.

"You've grown so much," Goli Jaan says to me. "Look at you! You're a man now."

We are taken to a room designed for guests. Goli Jaan brings in a crystal bowl full of big red and green apples, oranges, and grapes. "Everything is from our own garden," she says proudly. "Please help yourselves. This is much better than the stuff you get in Tehran—fresh off the trees. I picked them myself just a few minutes ago. Go ahead, please eat."

Mr. Kasravi is tall, dark, and around fifty. He has an animated voice, and tends to repeat himself at the end of each sentence. It is almost impossible to listen to him with a straight face, especially with Ahmed around to pass amused looks to.

"So how are you, my friend? Really, how are you?" Mr. Kasravi asks my father. He and Goli Jaan have a son, Mustafa, who is around my age, as well as a four-year-old daughter named Shabnam. Both children are sitting on the floor on opposite sides of their father's chair. Goli Jaan finally sits down and asks about my mother: how she's doing, what she looks like now, if she still looks young for her age, why she didn't come along. Then she tells me how wonderful my mother is, and that she loves her and misses her a lot.

"Yes, she does," Mr. Kasravi confirms. "She always tells me that she misses your mom a lot."

Ahmed looks at me and covers his upper lip with his lower one to hide his smile. An elderly maid brings in tea. Goli Jaan insists that we drink our tea before it gets too cold. "This is Lahijan tea, the best in the world," she urges.

"What makes Lahijan tea the best in the world?" Ahmed asks in a whisper. "I always wondered about that."

"The taste, the aroma, and the Persian pride," I whisper back.

Ahmed smiles.

"I'm extremely excited to have you in my humble dwelling, and can't wait to show you around, really, I can't wait," Mr. Kasravi says. "Things have changed a lot around here," he tells my father. "Things aren't like they used to be, not at all like they used to be." Then he turns to Ahmed and me. "Do you know how to ride a horse?"

We both shake our heads no.

"Mustafa will be happy to teach you, very happy to teach you," he says as he looks at his son. Mustafa smiles and nods to let us know that he agrees.

"They're great athletes," my father says. "They will learn in no time."

Predictably, the adults begin to talk about the past. Mr. Kasravi turns to me and says, "Your father was a rebel, definitely a rebel. I always thought he would end up in prison and I would have to pull strings to get him out."

Dad shrugs his shoulders and mumbles, "Everything changes when you marry and have a child."

Then he talks about Mr. Mehrbaan. "He was our hotheaded radical," Mr. Kasravi remembers soberly. "We used to call him Karl because he reminded us of a young Karl Marx. It's tragic that he has spent most of his life behind bars. . . . Very tragic." Then Mr. Kasravi looks at Ahmed and me. "I also heard about your friend Doctor. I'm so sorry. I really am very sorry."

After tea we go to Mr. Kasravi's stable, where he has already picked a horse for each of us. Mustafa helps Ahmed and me get on our horses. I thank Mustafa, but he doesn't respond. He just smiles and walks to his own horse.

Riding a live animal, controlling it with the reins and seeing the world from that high up, feels weird to me. I glance at Ahmed. He's holding the reins tightly, his body seems tense, and his face looks anxious. "Don't they have bikes?" he whispers.

We ride our horses through the village square. The path we travel is
uneven, obviously beaten out by hooves and the wheels of *droshkies*—
horse-drawn carriages, cars, trucks, and tractors traveling in and out
of the village through the rainy season. Here and there we hear a
rooster crowing, a dog barking, or a cow mooing.

We ride out of the village and head toward the hills. Mustafa rides
ahead of everyone else. Every once in a while, he stops, turns around,
then looks at us and moves his right hand to indicate a march forward.

"What do you think he's doing?" I ask Ahmed in a whisper.

"He's scouting for Indians," Ahmed responds with a smirk. "I hear
Cochise got tired of getting killed by John Wayne in those damn
Zionist movies, so he finally said fuck it, and moved to this region."

I try not to laugh out loud.

Ahmed and I have a hard time keeping ourselves balanced on our
horses as they climb the slopes. I hear Ahmed mumbling profanities
under his breath, a grin on his face. Mr. Kasravi and my father ride a
few steps ahead of us, but far behind Mustafa.

"Get to know your horses and let them get to know you," Mr. Kasravi advises us over his shoulder.

Ahmed bends over and whispers in his horse's ears, "Hi, I'm
Ahmed. What's your name?" I tell him to stop fooling around.

When we get to the top of the hill, Mr. Kasravi points to the village and says, "That's the oldest square in our region. It was built about
three hundred years ago. There is something special about that square,
don't you think?"

I look back at the square, trying to figure out what's special
about it.

"You do know why they used to build squares in the centers of
most Iranian towns and villages, don't you?" he continues.

"Yes," I respond.

Ahmed shoots me a surprised look.

"In the old days, everything happened in the squares, happy occa-
sions as well as dreadful events," I say. "It was a gathering place."

My father shakes his head in confirmation. I think I notice a flash
of pride in his eyes. Mr. Kasravi smiles, encouraging me to continue.

"The square was also where they punished the criminals so people
could watch and learn: entertainment and education. Education because torture was used to deter potential criminals, and entertainment because people came from all over to watch these events."

Mr. Kasravi seems utterly impressed with my knowledge. He shakes
his head and says that I'm right. Then he speaks of the cruel punish-
ments administered to thousands of people during the Qajar regime.
"This was the most disgraceful period in our beloved country's history.
It was the Qajars and their backward policies that kept Iran from developing into a modern country. We could have been a superpower in
the world, yes, sir, a superpower." He takes a big puff on his cigarette.

Ahmed leans over and whispers to me, "Where the fuck did you
learn all this shit?"

"Books!" I whisper back. He immediately turns his head toward
the square. He knows I'm scolding him again for not reading.

"So what do you know about the Qajars?" Mr. Kasravi asks.

"There were seven kings in the dynasty, starting with Agha Mohammed Khan of Qajar and ending with Ahmed Shah, who was overthrown by the father of our current king in the 1920s," I say. Then in
a confident tone that surprises even me, I add, "I agree with you, Mr.
Kasravi. The Qajars' incompetence ruined Iran during their two-
hundred-year rule."

Mr. Kasravi looks at my father and nods. I throw a sideways look
at Ahmed, who shakes his head and whispers, "Son of a bitch."

"My father knew neighbors, relatives, and friends of the family who
were beaten, flogged, and hanged in that square," Mr. Kasravi says,
genuinely upset. "I wonder why no one has burned the place down,

why no one has driven a bulldozer over it. Maybe I should do that, yes, maybe I should."

The pensive look on his face makes me wonder if he's truly contemplating driving a bulldozer through the square.

"People forget how bad it used to be in this country. Did you know we had no prisons until the Shah's father overthrew the Qajar dynasty? Did you know that?"

I shake my head no.

"You dumb-ass son of a bitch!" Ahmed murmurs, as if feeling deep disappointment.

"No prisons, no prisons at all. Imprisonment was a totally foreign concept in our culture, a totally foreign concept. They'd cut people's hands off, amputate their legs, cut off their ears, and then kill them or release them. That's how criminals were punished."

"Wow," Ahmed whispers.

"Over six thousand prisons have been built in Iran since the Shah's father took over fifty years ago. People think that's bad, but I think it's better than having a few million people punished and humiliated in public. Penal torture and the public humiliation of criminals had to stop, it just had to stop. Even criminals have a right to dignity! I would've died if I saw Mehrbaan tortured and beaten in public," Mr. Kasravi says.

I suddenly realize the purpose of our trip. My father had no business to conduct here. Mr. Kasravi is giving us a history lesson, justifying what is happening in our political jails by comparing it to the abhorrent atrocities committed under the Qajars.

It's not proper to get mad at your father, but I feel a burning sensation in the pit of my stomach. I slow my horse to separate myself from the pack while thinking: Is abandoning public torture in favor of torture behind prison walls a great leap toward modernization and democracy? Did Mr. Mehrbaan feel less pain when the SAVAK agents were putting out their cigarettes on his chest, arms, and buttocks? I increase the distance between us even more by pulling back on the horse's reins.

The sun is out, but I can smell the scent of coming rain as clouds roll in off the sea. We soon reach a pristine mountain stream, where we water our horses and rest for a little while before heading back to Mr. Kasravi's house.

Night falls fast. Before dinner, Ahmed and I are sitting on the porch and my father and Mr. Kasravi are in the living room playing backgammon. We can hear them teasing each other and laughing.

Ahmed asks, "You know why your dad brought us on this trip, don't you?"

"Yes, I do."

"Are you angry?"

"He's my dad," I say. "I'm angry at our host."

"Take it easy, he meant well."

"I know."

Mrs. Kasravi has prepared a dinner fit to serve "a thousand kings," as my grandma used to say. Basmati rice, broiled chicken, lamb cooked in an underground oven, three different kinds of *khoreshts*, vegetables of all kinds, including radishes, mint, parsley, three different kinds of *naan*, along with goat cheese and yogurts mixed with dried mint and cucumbers, and four different kinds of *torshi*, including dilled garlic—which everyone says doesn't make your breath stink on account of the humidity up north.

Ahmed looks at the dinner and says to me, "I wouldn't mind getting adopted by this family, really, I wouldn't mind at all." I elbow him in the side. My father and Mr. Kasravi are drinking vodka with their dinner. Ahmed, Mustafa, and I are sitting next to one another, and we eat our food with the appetites of a pack of ravenous wolves. Ahmed and I try to start a conversation with Mustafa a couple of times during dinner, but he just looks at us and smiles.

"Do you think he can speak?" I ask Ahmed in a concerned whisper.

"Maybe his dad repeats everything because he speaks for both of them."

I bite my upper lip to hide my smile.

My father raises his glass and drinks to the hosts. Then he looks at Ahmed and me and raises his second glass to us, sending us a wink. Then, as if he's reading my mind, he leans close and says in a low voice, "Sorry for this afternoon. It didn't turn out the way I had planned."

I love my dad. I want to put my arms around his neck and kiss him on the cheeks, like I used to do when I was four or five years old.

The doorbell rings, and Mr. Kasravi goes to answer it. A few minutes later he comes back followed by a tall man of around fifty. He introduces the man as Mr. Mohtasham. We all stand up and shake hands with him.

"What a wonderful night for you to have come to my home, a wonderful night indeed," Mr. Kasravi says, pouring vodka for his new guest. "It is fabulous to have you here at the same time as my guests from Tehran."

I notice that Mr. Mohtasham does not speak.

Goli Jaan, who is also excited by the arrival of this unannounced visitor, brings in plates and silverware and insists that he start eating right away. Mr. Mohtasham keeps bobbing his head to express his gratitude. Mr. Kasravi turns to my father and says, "Mr. Mohtasham has taken the vow of silence. His Holiness is well known for his clairvoyance. He sees the future as you and I remember the past, that clearly, really—I'm not kidding you. All of his predictions have come true over the years, all of them." My father politely expresses his gratitude to God for granting him the honor of spending an evening in the presence of Mr. Mohtasham, while I wonder why one would vow not to speak if God has blessed him with such a magnificent power.

Pointing to me, Mr. Kasravi tells Mr. Mohtasham that I am a very special person, definitely very special, and that at the age of seventeen I have the maturity and the wisdom of an educated thirty-year-old man. Mr. Mohtasham stares at me as he chews his food. He reaches into his pocket and takes out a small notebook, writing, "He has *That*."

My heart sinks as memories of Doctor cloak my mind. Ahmed nudges me gently and discreetly with his elbow. "Trust it, you do," he says under his breath.

"What can you tell us about the future, Your Holiness?" asks Mr. Kasravi, as he drinks a shot of vodka to his guest's health.

Mr. Mohtasham looks around the room and focuses on Mustafa for a few seconds. The room is hushed with a tranquil excitement. I have a hard time believing that the holiest man in Iran, who by now must be giddy with vodka, is about to make predictions about the people in the room. Mr. Mohtasham writes on a piece of paper that Mustafa will follow in the footsteps of his father and will become a successful businessman.

Goli Jaan is overcome with joy. "*Enshallah*, God willing!" she whispers.

Ahmed looks at Mustafa and says, "Congratulations." Mustafa smiles back, but still doesn't say anything. Ahmed turns to me and whispers, "We'll take turns sleeping tonight. I don't trust this kid." I put my hand over my mouth to cover my grin.

Mr. Mohtasham looks at me. He writes that I will go to the United States to study. My father asks, "What will he study?" Mr. Mohtasham holds his hands in the shape of cylinders and looks through them. My heart jumps. He's saying that I will study something related to cameras! I'll become a filmmaker after all.

"You Zionist," I hear Ahmed whisper under his breath.

Before I am overtaken by too much joy, I remind myself that this is perhaps nothing more than a hoax. Drinking vodka isn't exactly known for enhancing clarity and insight. Mr. Mohtasham drinks another shot and then looks at Ahmed. He writes that Ahmed will get married at a very young age, and will have three beautiful daughters.

Ahmed says, "No sons? Then I'm not getting married." Everyone laughs.

Mr. Mohtasham tells Goli Jaan that she will live to be a hundred years old, and will enjoy a happy life with her children and husband. "God willing!" she whispers reverently. We are told that my father will live out his old age while searching for the true meaning of life and unity with God almighty. He will someday be regarded as one of the greatest poets in modern Iranian history. I wonder how he knows that my father writes poetry.

Mr. Kasravi will retire in a faraway place, with his family members around him.

"The future is bright as far as this group is concerned, very bright, thank God," says Mr. Kasravi. At that moment, Shabnam, Mr. and Mrs. Kasravi's four-year-old daughter, walks into the room. She runs to her mother to complain that she can't sleep. Mr. Mohtasham looks at Shabnam keenly for a long time.

"What is it, Your Holiness?" Mr. Kasravi pleads, picking up on the intensity of Mr. Mohtasham's gaze. "What do you see? What do you see? Please, tell us. Is my daughter in danger? Please, tell us, is she in danger?"

Mr. Mohtasham shakes his head no.

"Thank God. Then what is it? You must tell us. I insist."

Mr. Mohtasham looks at me as he drinks another shot of vodka. I begin to feel paranoid.

"What is it? What? Please, tell us, I beg you," pleads Goli Jaan.

Mr. Mohtasham starts to write, pointing at me. "He is not going to like this now because she is too young, but he will like it twenty years from now when he returns to Iran from the U.S."

"What? What is it that he is going to like, Your Holiness? Tell us, please, tell us!" begs Mr. Kasravi. Now everyone, including me, is curious to find out what I'm going to do to this poor four-year-old child twenty years from now.

"This young man will marry your daughter, and they will live many happy years together abroad," he writes in his notebook.

Everyone in the room applauds and cheers, and Ahmed and even Mustafa whistle. My father and Mr. Kasravi begin to laugh and drink more vodka to toast the occasion.

This is ludicrous, I think. *What nonsense! She is only four years old, and I'm seventeen. What a sick old man.* Goli Jaan hugs me and tells me that I'm a dream of a son-in-law. She runs to the kitchen and comes back with *espand*, a seed Persians burn to ward off evil, and she waves the seed around my head and then Shabnam's head, and pours the rest on the charcoal inside a grill that the elderly maid brings in behind her. Soon smoke fills the room, and the pleasant scent of *espand* fills my nostrils.

Mr. Kasravi pats me on the back and says that he will invite the whole village to the house the next night to celebrate my engagement to his daughter, the whole village. I feel I've gone pale. Mr. Kasravi starts laughing and tells me that he was only joking, really, only joking. Everyone laughs except my future wife, who keeps complaining to her mother that she is tired, but can't sleep.

19

Doctor's Candle

More than four weeks have passed since Doctor's execution, although it feels a lot longer than that. The trees have shed their leaves, the rosebush that I planted outside our house is bare, the days have become shorter, and the nights seem to fall into a deeper silence.

I haven't seen Zari since the day we came back from the cemetery, and I still can't think of Doctor without spiraling into an anxiety attack. I keep telling myself that one of these days, I'll go to his grave alone and spend the whole day talking to him about what happened that night. I'll tell him that I wish I'd ducked before the man with the radio saw me, that I would do anything to go back in time and correct my mistake. I'll say I'm sorry for falling in love with Zari, for spending most of my summer days at her house while he was away, and for betraying his trust in me. I'll apologize for dreaming about her now, for not being able to go through one minute of the day without thinking about her, for being mesmerized and spellbound by her.

I'm sitting against the wall that edges the roof and watching the sky. It's cool outside but I don't mind it at all. I've read about our solar system in science class, but the only way I can recognize any of the stars is through the names Ahmed and I have assigned to them, the names of the people who have *That. When I'm in the U.S., I'll communicate with my friends by talking to their stars every night.* The fact that I'll be seeing their stars even on the other side of the world somewhat lessens my anxiety of being away from them.

I've been reading Dostoyevsky's *Crime and Punishment* instead of doing my geometry homework. I still hate my major, and I still hate my teachers, but I don't hate Iraj anymore, even though he still looks at Ahmed's sister. Our new composition teacher, Mr. Rostami, has asked us to write a five-page paper on a subject of our choice. Ahmed suggests that I turn in his masterpiece on "Technology as the Mother of all Sciences." I politely decline. Instead, I write a paper about crime and punishment in Iran. I write that crime is an unlawful act of violence that can be committed by anyone, and that punishment is the consequence designed for criminals who don't have the economic means to cover it up. Throughout history, men of wealth and power have been exempt from facing the consequences of their evil deeds. Crime, therefore, can be defined as an offense committed by an individual of inferior status in society. Punishment is a consequence forced on the perpetrator of the crime only if he occupies one of the lower steps of the social ladder.

Mr. Rostami is standing in the back of the class watching me quietly over the frames of the large square glasses resting on the tip of his nose. His hands are clasped behind his back. "Who wrote this nonsense for you?" he demands.

"I wrote it myself," I say, looking angrily at him.

He starts walking toward me. "And you're proud of it?"

"Yes, I am," I say, keeping my gaze fixed on him.

A nervous buzz fills the room.

"Shut up," Mr. Rostami screams. Right at that moment the recess alarm sounds, but everyone remains seated, anxious to see what will happen next. Mr. Rostami orders everyone to leave the room. The class reluctantly complies. Ahmed and Iraj are sitting next to each other.

Iraj starts to get up, but Ahmed grabs the sleeve of his coat and pulls him down. "Get out," Mr. Rostami orders.

"We put the idea in his head," Ahmed says, ever my defender.

"Get the fuck out, you clown, or he'll be punished worse than you can imagine."

I motion for Ahmed and Iraj to leave the room. When a teacher uses a word like "fuck," you know he means business. Ahmed and Iraj leave, their eyes filled with concern.

After they are gone, Mr. Rostami walks up to me, his hands still clasped behind his back. I'm expecting him to slap me in the face. I'm ready to knock his arm off with a vicious block if he takes a shot at me, but instead he circles me a couple of times with a contemplative look on his face. "Don't you know you're not supposed to write shit like that?" he asks. His calm demeanor surprises me. "I have no choice but to report this. Do you understand?" he says in an agonized tone. His left eye begins to twitch.

"Why can't I write the truth?" I ask, gently.

Mr. Rostami shakes his head. "You can write what you want, but I have to feed my kids. Do you know what they would do to me if I didn't report this?"

"Who are they?" I ask.

"The system, the other teachers, the administration, the goddamn SAVAK; who the hell do you think?"

"It's unfair for you to get in trouble for what I wrote," I say, but I know full well that I'm acting naïve. Teachers are ordered by the administration not to tolerate dissent among students.

"You don't look like a stupid kid to me. You know you can't write stuff with political connotations, don't you?" He sighs in frustration.

I remain silent.

"I have no choice," he mumbles. "You understand? I have four kids. I have a hard time supporting them even now. Imagine what would happen to my family if I lost my job. I have to report this to Mr. Yazdi. Goddamn it, do you fucking understand?"

There's pain in his voice, and I can tell that he doesn't want to report me but he has no choice. "I understand," I say quietly. "Do what you need to do."

"Oh, you understand?" he asks angrily. "And you understand that I will stay up all night thinking about how I didn't have the courage to do the right thing? You understand that if they do something to you, I will have to live with it for the rest of my life?"

I think of how I inadvertently gave Doctor away. I nod my head.

"Give me your goddamn paper," he shouts.

I hand him my paper. He takes a lighter out of his pocket, sets it on fire and throws the ashes out the window. "Too bad I have to recall from memory what you wrote. Stay in the room. I have to go see the principal and the discipline teacher before the next session starts."

Then Mr. Rostami walks slowly out of the room. Ahmed and Iraj rush in. "Are you okay?" Ahmed asks.

I remain unspeaking for a while, thinking of Mr. Rostami's four children. The expression on his face and the measured pace with which he left the room were like that of a man walking toward the gallows.

"He has *That*," I whisper.

"What?" Iraj asks, bewildered. "Who has what?"

The next day, Mr. Yazdi asks my father to go to school to discuss the disturbing concepts presented in my paper. According to Mr. Rostami, my paper was not politically critical at all. However, its socially unacceptable position necessitated a discussion with my father. Mr. Rostami had confiscated my paper, but unfortunately lost it on the way to the principal's office. He was concerned that in my paper I had advocated tolerance for criminal activities, if the motives were justified. Mr. Rostami simply wanted my father to convince me of the inappropriateness of criminal behavior regardless of the motive.

When my father comes home in the evening, I expect him to talk to me about his encounter with Mr. Yazdi, but he remains surprisingly silent throughout the evening, and even during dinner, when he usually tells us about his day.

Thinking that I have gotten off easy, I go up on the roof immediately after dinner. I'm sitting beneath the short wall that separates my house from Zari's when my father walks up. He asks if I'm busy, and I say no. He sits down next to me and is silent for a long time.

Finally he says, "The events of Doctor's night are still bothering you, aren't they?" His eyes are sad, his voice dispirited. "Doctor was a good man. We all miss him. I know you were particularly close to him. Closer to him than everyone else in the alley."

I'm waiting for a big lecture, but he doesn't say anything else. I realize he's waiting for my response.

"What they did to Doctor wasn't fair," I say bitterly. "He wasn't a terrorist. He hadn't hurt anyone. Why do they kill young men like Doctor? Why do they take someone like Mr. Mehrbaan away for eighteen years?"

Dad pats me on the back. I know I'm lecturing the wrong guy, but I need to say what's in my heart.

"I hate the CIA. They're responsible for Doctor's death, and the deaths of all the other young people executed by the Shah. You know why, Dad? If you teach me how to kill, and I kill someone, you are as responsible as I am for my crime."

I know that I'm ranting, but I can't stop.

"Why doesn't God do something about this? Why do we have to wait so long for justice? That's not fair, Dad, is it? Do you know why God doesn't do anything about atrocities committed against innocent people like the Jews in Germany, or the followers of the prophet Mazdak, or the slaves of the Romans? Do you know why he doesn't do anything about the children who're dying every day in Palestine? Because God doesn't care, Dad."

I close my eyes, lower my head, and let the pain pour out from my chest and throat. It feels good to cry. My father puts his arms around me and I sink my head onto his chest like I used to do when I was a kid. Dad doesn't say a word. He understands that even his wisdom is no salve for my grief.

The next night I'm sitting beneath the short wall, reading the poetry of Hafiz, when I hear Zari's voice call to me from the other side of the wall.

"I heard what you said to your dad last night."

I want to jump up and look over the wall to see her, but I sense that she doesn't want to be seen.

"Were you on the roof?" I ask.

"I've been on the roof every night this week," she admits.

"Why didn't you say something?"

"I didn't want to interrupt your reading."

"What were you doing, sitting in the dark alone?"

"I wasn't alone. You were up here, too."

Knowing she's been nearby sends a rush of warmth through me. "How're you feeling?"

"I'm okay. What're you reading?"

"Hafiz."

"You promised to bring your book to my house and take a *fahll* for me, but you never did, remember?"

"I do," I say.

After a long pause she says, "Would you read something to me now?"

"Have you made a wish?"

She pauses for a few seconds, then says, "Done."

I open the book to a random page and begin to read.

Separation days and seclusion nights will end
I studied the secrets of the universe; your sadness shall rescind

A light night breeze floats over us, rustling the pages of the book and eliciting a soft sigh from Zari.

The arrogance and self-conceit displayed by fall
Oh the approach of spring, will end all
Glimmers of hope are seen from beyond the curtains
Dark nights are over and victory is certain

I stop reading, and my ears prick, scanning the silence for a hint of her response, but she remains silent.

"Did you like it?" I ask. She makes a soft humming noise to herself. Then she says, "Thank you for planting that rosebush out there."

I'm glad she knows. I don't care if everyone finds out, and I certainly don't care if the SAVAK shows up at my door tonight. I just hope they send the man with the radio so that I can make the members of the boxing fraternity proud. "The red rose will be our symbol of defiance from now on," I say, looking toward the alley where Doctor's blood was spilled.

"Okay," she whispers. "Would you read for me at night?"

"Yes," I whisper.

"Every night?"

"Every night."

And so every night, Zari and I get together on the roof. I never see her. She sits on her side of the wall, and I on mine. Ten centimeters of brick separate us, but I can almost feel her warmth. I press my palms against the wall and imagine I'm touching the curves of her face. I hear her breathe and occasionally move. Ahmed knows what is going on, and stays away. We're done with Hafiz, and she's asked me to read *The Rubaiyat of Omar Khayyam* to her.

After I finish reading a short Rubai, she asks, "Do you believe in God?"

"I don't know," I reply.

"It doesn't seem as if Khayyam believed in God."

"I don't think he did."

"Do you believe in destiny?" she asks.

"I do."

"Then you believe in God. You're just angry at him right now."

Her perception stings. "Why would I be angry at God?"

"Because of Doctor. I know you loved him a lot, despite . . ." She stops.

"Despite what?" I ask, my heart spinning as I bite my lower lip.

A long silence follows the awkward moment. Finally she says, "He used to tell me that I was the candle that lit up his nights."

I don't respond. "Doctor's Candle," I write on the first page of Khayyam's book over and over.

"They told us we couldn't wear black," she whispers, her voice wavering.

"I know," I say. "But we don't have to wear black to mourn him. That rosebush will be the symbol of our grief."

The night sky is drunk with stars, thick with the souls of loved ones, and I'm sure that she feels the magnetism of the inky heavens, that we are both staring into the riot of planets. My chest is tight with longing, as if I can breathe in but will never be allowed to breathe out.

"If you could go anywhere, where would you like to be?" she asks abruptly.

"I don't know," I say, but I think she knows I'm lying. I want to be on the other side of the wall. Ten centimeters east of my current location, that's all.

The next night she doesn't come to the roof. I stay up all night worrying. Is she okay? Have they arrested her, too? Will I ever see her again?

I'm tired and sleepy the following day in class. I haven't been doing my homework ever since Zari and I began getting together on the roof. This is a complete anomaly for me. My calculus teacher, Mr. Kermani, asks me to go to the board and gives me a problem that I have no clue how to solve. He tells me to hold my hands out. Reluctantly, I do, and he hits me over and over with his ruler. My fingers burn, my hands feel heavy, and I think I will die if he hits me one more time, but I won't give him the satisfaction of pulling my hands away. I fix my watery eyes on him because he personifies everything I hate. I wonder if my father would still insist that I major in mathematics if he knew what was happening to his only son. What would Mr. Kasravi say about all this if he saw what my teacher was doing to me in front of all the other students?

As my teacher hits me, I remember the eyes of the man with the radio—wide open, enraged, and evil. I see the same wicked look in Mr. Kermani's eyes. I remember the courage with which Doctor took punches and kicks from the son of a bitch with the radio, and I can feel my blood boiling.

For a second I consider punching Mr. Kermani in the face, but he's an old man, so I let him hit me until he's tired. When he stops to catch his breath, he screams at me, "Lower your shameless eyes, or I will pluck them out and send them to your stupid parents." Calling my parents stupid enrages me to the point of madness. "I know you're one of those kids who enjoys sitting by the fire and reading philosophical bullshit instead of learning proven formulas that might save this nation from the grip of backwardness." He spits out the words like he is shooting bullets at me. "During my honorable years of teaching, I have seen herds of pretenders like you who deem their burp to be a revolutionary manifesto. Every single one of you will end up in front of the firing squad, and that's why this country needs engineers and doctors instead of pseudo-intellectuals like you. And after they bury your bullet-infested, worthless body, I will show up in the cemetery and shit all over your grave, like I did with the moron you all called Doctor."

I hear a roaring of blood in my ears. I attack him with a snarl, my hands around his thin, ugly neck, and push him back until he's against the wall. I bring my right fist back, preparing to drive it into his face. I want to punch him once, just once. Fuck the sacred brotherhood of the boxing fraternity. I will put all my might into that single punch to make up for all the beatings I took on my hands, for the blows and kicks that Doctor took in the face, sides, and stomach. This single punch will be strong enough to make up for all the unjustified beatings that thousands of people endure in this godforsaken country every year.

I want to hit him, but he's old and weak. I remember my promise to Dad and force myself to drop my fist. I spit in his face instead, and walk out of the classroom.

I'm halfway down the hallway when I hear Mr. Yazdi calling my name. I turn around and see him right behind me. His arm is up, and he's about to serve me a vicious blow.

"I've had enough. Hit me, and I'll make this the last day of your fucking miserable life," I say.

Mr. Yazdi takes a step back. I detect fear in his eyes. He's a smart man. He wouldn't dream of taking me on—not now, not in front of all these kids watching us in the hallway. He orders me to go to his office. I see Ahmed running toward us. Mr. Yazdi barks at him to stay away. Ahmed ignores him and walks alongside me.

Mr. Moradi is attending to my calculus teacher, who is badly shaken, when we walk in. I'm expecting Mr. Moradi to take out his ruler, but instead he walks up to me and whispers sympathetically that I shouldn't have done what I did. Then he looks at Ahmed and says, "Why didn't you stop him?"

"It all happened too quickly," Ahmed responds.

Mr. Yazdi walks up to me. "Assaulting a teacher is the worst thing a student can do, do you understand?" he yells angrily. "I have no choice but to expel you. With this crime on your record, no school will ever accept you. Congratulations! You just destroyed your life."

"I don't give a damn," I yell back.

Mr. Yazdi takes a step toward me but then thinks better of it. Ahmed grabs his arm and tells him that he wants to talk to him and Mr. Kermani alone.

They walk to the opposite corner of the room, and I see Mr. Yazdi growing more and more agitated. Ahmed turns around and winks at me. Then Mr. Yazdi and my calculus teacher walk to another corner of the room and discuss the situation in low murmurs. Finally, Mr. Yazdi turns to us and yells, "Get the hell out of here." As we start walking toward the door he calls me and tells me, "Don't come to school for three days. And tell your father that I want to see him tomorrow."

"Tell him yourself," I say, and walk out.

Lots of students are in the hallway, and when we emerge, everyone cheers. I want to acknowledge them for their support but Ahmed grabs my hand and pulls me away. "What were you guys discussing in the corner?" I ask.

He gives me a dirty look and keeps on walking. When we're far away from the office, he stops and yells, "What the hell is wrong with you? You're determined to completely wreck your future, aren't you? I have a patent on the kind of shit you're pulling these days."

"You don't," I say. "I hate them. I hate them all. They killed Doctor. It wasn't the SAVAK. It was this screwed-up system, this goddamn country and its fucking people who can't get their act together to overthrow a tyrant. We're all a bunch of cowards or we would've rushed into the streets protesting his arrest the night I gave him away. Then maybe he'd still be alive."

Ahmed tries to put his hand on my shoulder to calm me down, but I knock his arm away and stalk out of the school.

20

A Kiss

My mother is crying when I get home. My dad is sitting in the yard by the *hose* smoking a cigarette. It's unusually cold for this time of year, late October, and I can see Mom's breath as she sobs. Dad looks angry, so I surmise that Mr. Yazdi must have phoned him. He stands up as soon as I walk into the yard.

"Before you say anything," I say, pointing a finger at him, "I didn't hit him. You told me it wasn't right to hit someone weaker. So I spat in his face instead because he called you and Mom stupid and he said that he couldn't wait to shit on my grave, as he did on Doctor's. I did what you would've done, fight. Like you did at the barracks and with Engineer Sadeghi. If that's wrong, then punish me."

Dad sits back down at the edge of the *hose*. He puffs on his cigarette and looks down at his feet. I watch him for a while, and when I'm sure he doesn't have anything to say, I walk toward the house. Mom is standing by the steps. I put my arms around her and hug her hard and kiss her on the cheeks and wipe the tears off her face. "Don't worry, Mom. I'm all grown up now and I know what I'm doing," I say.

She hides her face in my chest.

"I think you need to take me off the engine oil," I whisper in her ear, trying to cheer her up.

She pulls back and laughs nervously with teary eyes. Then she pounds lightly on my chest a couple of times and whispers something under her breath. I hug her again before walking up the steps to my room on the third floor.

I feel like an adult all of a sudden. I'm a man in control of my life, strong-willed, determined, and capable of choosing a path, just like my dad. I'll be in command of the life around me, making sure that I'm never treated like a child again by my parents or at school. I must figure out a way to take Zari with me to the United States. When we get there, I will work hard to support her. God, there is so much to be done, and I like the feeling of being responsible for it all.

I'm settling down at my usual spot on the roof when I hear Zari from the other side of the wall.

"Hello," she says.

"I've been worried about you," I chide. "I didn't know where you were, or what had happened to you."

"I'm okay. We went to the hospital to see Doctor's dad, and didn't get home till very late."

"How's he doing?"

"Not good."

"How're you doing?"

"Not good."

"I'm sorry."

I hear her sobs from the other side of the wall. "My parents send their regards. They think you're the only bright spot in my life right now."

"They do?"

"I do, too."

If this was last month, I would've thrown myself off the roof with

joy, but I'm a man now, so I contain myself. "I haven't done anything,"
I say, still wound up inside.

"No? Do you see anyone lined up out there to spend their every
evening with a depressed, miserable girl like me?"

I realize it's easier to take compliments when they're not given to
you face-to-face.

Zari is quiet for a while. Then she says, "Thank your girlfriend for
letting you spend so much time with me."

"Okay," I mumble.

"I can't wait to find out who she is."

"You will soon."

She doesn't respond to that.

After a long pause she says, "I'm going shopping tomorrow. Would
you like to go along? After school, of course."

"I can't think of anything else I'd rather do," I say. I don't say anything about my expulsion; I'm sure the subject will come up eventually.

The next day, I wait for her a couple of alleys down from ours. It's not
sensible for us to be seen together in our own alley, especially so soon
after Doctor's death.

"If we lived in the U.S. or Europe, we wouldn't worry about such
things, now would we?" I hear Ahmed's voice in the back of my head.
I should call him and apologize for being a jerk to him at school.

My heart is beating fast in anticipation of seeing Zari; my thoughts
are so scattered I can hardly think. When she shows up, we say hello
and start walking toward the bus stop. We're walking side by side. I
look at her and realize for the first time that she's a couple of centimeters shorter than I am.

Her face is drawn and tired, but she still looks like a doll. Her fair
complexion, her small pointed nose, her hair hanging like silk curtains on either side of her face, her long, blinking eyelashes, her large

blue eyes—everything is still there, except her crooked smile. This is the face I fell in love with. She turns and looks at me. I'm so excited by her presence that I want to tell her how much I love her, and that I want to spend the rest of my life walking next to her.

We don't say much on the bus. We sit next to each other, and our shoulders touch every time we pass over a bump. I look at her hands. She has thin, long fingers. I love her hands.

"Do you know what next week is?" she asks.

I know she is talking about the fortieth day of Doctor's death, the day we should have been allowed to get together to talk about him, to cry, to tell one another how much we miss him. The day we're forbidden to do all that. I look at Zari desperately, silently.

"It's the birthday of the Shah," she says, a sad smile on her face. "He'll be going from his palace to Amjadieh Stadium in an open motorcade. They expect five hundred thousand people in the streets. I want to see him."

"Why do you want to do that, especially on that day?"

"I've never seen him in person."

"He's like any other dictator," I scoff. "An arrogant, narcissistic, ruthless man whose cold gaze sends a chill down your spine. I hate him. You'll gain no insight into what has happened to Doctor from watching him drive by in a motorcade."

She is quiet for a while, perhaps a bit surprised by my blunt statement. "I still want to see him," she says.

"Okay, then I'll go with you."

"You've got a lot going on with school. You don't need this right now. I'd rather go alone."

"I'm going with you," I repeat, gently.

"Why?" she asks. "Why do you want to go along when you hate him so much?"

"Because I'd rather be with you in hell than without you in heaven." I look down at my own knees.

I can tell that she is staring at me. Then she reaches over and grabs my hand. "Pasha, I like being with you, too. You're a very special person. You truly have *That*, just like Ahmed said."

I squeeze her hand gently, and feel her squeeze mine back. I look into her eyes, and she returns my gaze.

"Your hands are warm," she whispers.

We get off the bus at Laleh Zar, the area in Tehran where there are thousands of shops, many theaters, nightclubs, and restaurants. The narrow streets and alleys are filled with people of all ages. The air is rich with the scent of cutlets, hamburgers, and liver being grilled on hot red charcoal.

Some vendors announce their specials:

"The best kebob in town, hurry up before it gets cold."

"Real British fabric for just ten toomans a meter; come and get it before it's all gone."

"Tickets, tickets to the greatest show in the universe with Jebelly, the greatest singer of our time."

"I like this area," Zari says. "It's so full of life."

In one of the stores she puts on a chador and asks me how she looks. I tell her that she looks like an angel. She laughs and buys it.

We go to an ice cream place and order two *paloodehs* with Akbar Mashdi ice cream, which is made with a special recipe that includes saffron, nonroasted salted pistachios, and rosewater.

"Did you know Faheemeh would've killed herself if they'd forced her to marry her neighbor?" she asks as we begin eating.

The thought of Faheemeh committing suicide makes me lose my appetite. "Suicide never solves anything," I say. "It certainly worsens things for those left behind. I can't imagine what that would've done to Ahmed!"

"I read a book about Socrates last year," Zari says softly, as she stares at her ice cream. "I was really intrigued by how he chose to stay in prison and die even when he had the chance to escape. Was he wrong to do that?"

I know where she's going with the argument; I don't respond.

"What about Golesorkhi?" she asks, now looking directly in my eyes. "In my opinion, both Golesorkhi and Socrates committed suicide, don't you agree?"

I remain quiet.

"Do you think Doctor . . ." She doesn't finish her sentence.

I shake my head in frustration. "I believe life's too precious to waste, especially when one has something worthwhile to fight for."

Zari watches me for a few seconds. "Am I making you angry?" she asks warily.

I shake my head no. She uses her spoon to mash her ice cream.

"Let's change the topic to something more pleasant," I suggest.

"Okay, let's," she says. "Are you still planning to go to America?"

"I said something more pleasant," I tease.

She starts to laugh. "I want you to go. I hope you become a famous filmmaker. Write a script and tell everyone the story of our alley. But promise to get someone famous to play me. Who's your favorite actress? Ingrid Bergman, right?"

"Yes, but she's too old to play you now. I have to get someone younger. The prettiest actress alive."

She turns red. Her eyes scan mine as if she is figuring out how the pieces of a puzzle fit together. Then she takes a bite of her ice cream.

"So what happened at school?" she asks.

"How did you find out?"

"Through Faheemeh."

"She has a big mouth," I say, and we both laugh. "Did it upset you?" I ask.

"Well, you picture a different kind of person when you hear about incidents like that. I wish you'd never do that again."

It feels good that she's worried about me. "He was asking for it," I say to prolong the moment.

"Promise me that you will never do anything like that again," she says, her eyes threatening.

I laugh and raise my right hand and put my left hand on my heart.

"Good boy," Zari says. Then she adds, "You know, I feel responsible for your lack of focus on school."

"You're the best thing I could be focusing on right now."

Zari blushes again.

Before we say good-bye she makes me promise to study harder. She wants to check my homework every night, when we get together on the roof. As she walks away, I curse the fact that the day has gone by so quickly.

That same evening, I'm sitting on the roof when Ahmed comes up. He sits next to me.

"Have you taken your rabies shot this year?" he asks.

We look at each other for a few seconds and then we both begin to laugh. I put my arms around him and hug him. "I'm really sorry," I say. "I will never yell at you again." He waves his arm to indicate that I shouldn't worry about it. Then I tell him every detail of my day with Zari. He's happy that I finally got a chance to spend time with her. He adds that he and Faheemeh will go to see the Shah's motorcade with us.

"I'm doing it to be with Zari," I say. "Otherwise, I'd rather fall off the roof and break my neck than lay eyes on the man responsible for Doctor's death."

"I feel exactly the same way."

We have a calculus exam two days after my expulsion ends. I study as hard as I can. It's important to me to deliver on the promise I made to Zari. When I go back to school, the students, and even our custodian, welcome me with open arms. "You showed that old hyena he can't treat smart kids that way," our custodian says. "I've seen him abuse so many good kids over the years. You're the only one who's ever stood up to him; good for you, really, good for you."

Ahmed says that kids at school have taken a creative license in retelling the story of my altercation with Mr. Kermani. He heard one kid tell another that I lifted Mr. Kermani with the intention of throwing him out the window before Mr. Yazdi stopped me. Some versions have Mr. Yazdi trying to slap me, but I used one of Dad's boxing techniques to fend him off. Then I threw him on the ground and almost choked him to death, before Mr. Moradi pulled me away from him.

"Why do they make up these stories?" I ask.

"Because they need a hero," Ahmed says without losing a beat. "And you, my friend, fit the bill."

Zari and I meet on the roof, finally on the same side of the short wall that separated us all those other nights. She asks me whether I've completed my homework. I show her my notebook, and she checks every page carefully. I watch those long, thin fingers turn the pages and swear I feel the heat radiating from her body. A strong bond has been established between us, and I feel so lucky that her parents don't mind me seeing her up on the roof.

She's trembling as she thumbs through my homework. I muster up enough courage to put my arms around her. She turns and looks at me, perhaps unsure of how she should react. Then she wiggles her body to make herself more comfortable in my embrace. She says, "This is how prehistoric people kept warm in the caves."

I remember Darwin's writings on prehistoric man. "Do you think our enjoyment of cuddling up is derived from that era?" I ask, and immediately wonder why I always ask stupid questions.

She laughs, "That, and probably other things."

I decide not to respond and I'm glad Ahmed wasn't around to hear my question. We sit in each other's arms for hours. Zari falls asleep with her head on my shoulder. I can't see her face, but she glows with a warmth that makes me feel wonderful inside. My father comes up to my room, sees us through the window, and leaves without saying a word. A few minutes later, Zari's mother comes up. My breath gets trapped in my chest. I'm expecting her to curse me and pull Zari away, but instead she smiles.

"She was tired, very tired," I whisper.

Mrs. Naderi slips back into the house. I am so relieved. I don't care if the whole world sees us now. I'm not hiding anything from anyone anymore. *Yes, we will get married and no one will object. This will be a relationship based on love and not outdated traditions.* I am jubilant.

Zari wakes up around eleven o'clock. She looks at me, and smiles.

"Have I been asleep long?"

"Not long enough."

"I haven't slept like this since . . ."

She doesn't finish her sentence, but caresses my shoulder and arm lovingly.

"Your arms must be hurting from supporting my heavy head. I'm sorry. You should have woken me up."

"I didn't mind. You sleep like an angel."

"You're so sweet."

"Your mother came up."

"What did she say?" she asks, somewhat alarmed.

"Nothing. She smiled and went back inside."

"She always lectured me about not having any physical contact with Doctor before we were married." She shakes her head. "This thing has changed everyone. I better go talk to her."

She stands up and hops over the short wall, disappearing into her house. I sit on the wall and think about how beautiful life can be. *God, I love her. Please don't ever take her away from me.* I realize that

I'm praying to the God I was cursing a few nights earlier, and beg His forgiveness.

I feel someone standing behind me. I turn and see Zari. She has the most radiant look on her face. Her head is slightly tilted to one side. In her gaze I discern a softening and serenity I've never seen before. She kisses my cheek and says, "Thank you," and walks slowly back to her house.

I ace my first calculus exam. The boy who is sitting next to me keeps looking at my test and copying my answers. Cheating on tests is customary at school. Almost everyone in my calculus class cheats, even the smart students. They hold their paper up, or sit crooked so that the person behind them can copy their answers. I wonder how we can explain this national impulse to cheat. Maybe it's more a matter of sharing than cheating. I've heard that people in the West compete at everything, and that you're either a loser or a winner. In my country, we don't have the same competitive spirit. Centuries of misery under the dominance of the Moguls, Arabs, and internal despotic rulers have conditioned us to stick together and help each other through unpleasant situations.

I let the boy next to me copy my answers.

Mr. Kermani doesn't look me in the eye when he's handing my exam back to me, after it's been graded a couple of days later. I don't think he looks in my direction even once during the entire day.

I'm already on the roof when Zari comes up and asks about my exam. I tell her that I got the highest grade in the class, and she laughs and looks toward the sky, as if she is thanking God.

"Why're you thanking God?" I tease. "I did all the hard work."

"You sure did. Good boy," she says as we sit next to each other with our backs to the wall. It's a cold night, and I put my arm around her without the slightest hesitation. She makes herself comfortable, fitting herself better into my embrace. "I'm so happy about your grade," she says.

"I feel like I could do anything if you demanded it," I tell her, and for once my words are confident.

She smiles.

We sit there for a long time without saying anything else. She falls asleep in my arms again. Her head is on my shoulder and her left hand on my chest, right on my heart; I hope my heartbeat doesn't keep her awake. Both my arms are around her. It's quiet and peaceful in the alley. A fall chill is in the air, making our cuddling that much more pleasant. I'm the happiest man in the universe.

I kiss her on the cheek. Her face is flushed, and I feel her breath on my neck. She opens her eyes. Our faces are a few centimeters away. Her eyes don't seem heavy and sagging. They must just have been closed, like she was relaxing in my arms, not sleeping. I can't stop myself. I kiss her on the lips, and she kisses me back. I feel her fingers caress my face, neck, and hair. Her lips are soft, warm, and full of love, a perfect match for mine. Her body moves against mine as she breathes and as our fingers lock. Could time freeze in this moment forever?

Then she suddenly stops, pushes me back, and runs to her house, crying, "It's not right, this is not right."

She doesn't come to the roof the next night. I stay up all night, pacing the roof. I look inside her yard but there is no sign of her. I climb onto her balcony and look inside her dark room.

It is cold out but I don't care. I will wait until she comes out. And when she does I'll tell her I'm sorry for that damn kiss, even though nothing has ever felt as good to me. I'll promise her that I will never take advantage of her friendship, unless she asks me to do it. I'll apologize and swear that I'll never kiss her again, not even after we get married. I'll tell her that I was out of line to move so fast so soon after Doctor's death.

Ahmed comes up on the roof and I tell him the story. For some reason seeing him makes me more frantic than when I was alone.

"I hope I'm not forever doomed to be without her," I say.

Ahmed laughs and shakes his head.

"Why are you laughing at me when I'm upset? You call yourself my friend?"

"Your best friend, asshole," he corrects me.

"Fuck you," I sulk.

"Listen," Ahmed says, still laughing, "you know what Faheemeh told me today?"

I don't answer.

"She said she's sure now that Zari is in love with you."

"What?" I shout. "What do you mean? Did Zari say that, or is Faheemeh speculating?"

"Faheemeh is a woman. Women don't speculate, they know."

"How?"

"Don't ask me. There're many things we know about women but can't explain, and this happens to be one of them."

I feel calmer. "But why doesn't she come to the roof?"

"Something's on her mind. Maybe Doctor, or she feels it's too soon, or that she's too old for you. Or maybe she doesn't know what to do with your cute ass."

"Shut up," I say, beginning to laugh. "Do you really think she's fallen in love with me?"

"Why not? You have *That*. Remember, lover boy?"

I throw my arms around Ahmed and hug him harder that I ever have before.

The next night I find an envelope on the roof in the spot where we used to sit. It's from Zari. The note inside reads, "My Dearest and Nearest: I adore you, but you should not be emotionally invested in me. I don't want you to get hurt. With all my love, Zari."

I suddenly feel as if I have been hit by a heavy fist, a blow infinitely more powerful than that of Mr. Kermani's ruler. A bottomless abyss has opened up in my heart, making the world feel like a very lonely place. I want to cry, but fight back the tears with all my determination, just as I did years ago, holding on to my broken shin. Except this time I am holding on to my heart. I look toward the door to the roof of her house. I know she's behind the glass window, sitting in the dark. I know she's watching me, just as Ahmed knew Faheemeh was behind the wall on the night they were auctioning her off.

The temperature has dropped quickly, mirroring the way my life feels to me. A cold wind howls through the alley as if to warn of more freezing days ahead, more miserable days to come. The skin on my face feels tight and my fingers are almost numb, even though I've been keeping them clenched in my pants pockets. I jump onto Zari's roof and walk to the large glass door that leads to her house. The windows are frost-covered, and I can't see in, but still I know she's on the other side. I use my fingers to scratch the frost off the glass. Backward, so she can read it on her side, my inscription reads, "I love you." I see her face through the letters. She's crying. She touches the glass with her hand and I press my palm to mirror hers, then she disappears from my sight.

I go back to the wall that separates our houses. I know she's watching me, and I'm determined to freeze to death if I have to, but I will not leave until she comes out. Ahmed joins me on the roof and wraps a blanket around me.

"It's cold. Why don't you go in for a few minutes? I'll sit here until she comes out," he says.

"No."

"Okay. Have it your way." He sits next to me.

"Go inside. You'll catch a cold," I tell him.

"You want a cigarette?" he asks, ignoring me.

"No," I snarl back.

"Remember the night I thought I had lost Faheemeh?" he asks.

I nod my head.

"I thought my life was over because I was losing her forever. You have the same look in your eyes, and I don't understand it. You guys have the rest of your lives together. All you need to do is be patient. Zari knows you love her, and I know she loves you, but you need to give her time. She'll do the right thing. Women always do."

"I don't want to wait," I say like a stubborn, spoiled kid. So much for being a man!

"Look, right now she needs to stay away from you. It's hard for her to accept that she's in love with you. She won't jump in your arms and pretend Doctor never existed less than forty days after his execution. So just tighten your belt, straighten your hat, and let's go about this the right way. Time, that's what she needs right now."

"Tomorrow is Doctor's fortieth day," I say in tears. "We were supposed to be together. I hate to see the Shah, but I don't want her to go alone."

Ahmed acts like he hasn't heard what I just said. "Be patient," he scolds. "Please, be patient."

"Don't yell at me," I say bitterly.

"Why not?" he yells, pointing his finger at me. "You, my dear friend, are supposed to have *That*. I ask you, is this the way a man with *That* behaves? You're not being a good role model for the rest of us."

"To hell with *That*," I say. "I'm tired of being told that I have *That*." To my annoyance, my eyes fill again. "I'm tired of it. Tired of pretending." I know that if I don't stop myself I'll go on a rant, as I always do when I'm emotional.

Ahmed lights another cigarette, lets out a stream of smoke and says, "Well, let's catch a cold together then. If you want to sit here all night long, I'll sit with you."

"Go inside," I say, wiping my eyes.

"No." He shakes his head.

A long time goes by and neither of us says anything. The night is cold and quiet, the skies are clear. I haven't slept for more than thirty-six hours. I am tired and my eyelids are heavy, my mind is numb. I think I fall asleep for just a few moments because images of the man with the radio clutter my mind. Again I see his eyes. I see his hair pulled back tight. At one point, I'm standing next to him. I'm trying to punch him but my arms feel heavy, too heavy to be raised. I wake up with a racing heart.

Zari is standing in front of me, and Ahmed is sitting next to me.

"Go inside," Zari pleads with me. "Please, go inside."

"No," I croak.

Ahmed stands up.

"Ahmed, please, take him inside."

"He's your problem now," Ahmed says, and heads toward his room.

"Why are you out here? You'll freeze to death," Zari scolds.

I have a lump in my throat, and I'm worried that I might burst into tears if I open my mouth. But it's time to say something. "I can't freeze to death because I've been living in hell since you decided not to speak to me." Then my voice chokes up. "I'm really sorry for that damn kiss."

She shakes her head as if she can't believe I'm apologizing.

"I will never kiss you again," I say. "Not even after we get married and have children."

She smiles and her eyes shine with tears.

"I want to be your friend, your comrade. I will mourn the death of Doctor with you for as long as you want me to."

She reaches over and touches my face lovingly.

"If there's a life after death, I'm living it. If there is a hell, I'm burning in it. I love you, and I always have, even before Doctor left on his trip. I've been living with love and guilt for a long time now. I don't want it to be like that anymore."

Zari touches my face again with her beautiful long fingers and wipes the tears off my cheeks. She puts her arms around me and holds me tight, and I swear I can feel her heart beat.

"This hurts a thousand times worse than breaking my shin," I whisper.

"Come with me."

I follow her to her room, where there is a bed, a small desk, a metal chair, and a whole bunch of books. A picture of her parents is framed on one wall, and the picture that Ahmed, Faheemeh, Zari, and I took by the *hose* is next to it.

"It seems like that picture was taken a thousand years ago," I whisper.

"It was," she says.

I sit on the chair with Ahmed's blanket wrapped around me. She slowly moves the blanket, sits on my lap, and wraps it back around us. I tell her that I love her, I can't live without her, and I will do anything to make sure that she's happy. She kisses my face, my eyes, and my lips. I taste the salty tears that roll down both our faces.

We spend the whole night in each other's arms. I say that some-day I want us to be married and have our own home and our own kids. She smiles, but doesn't say anything. Her eyes look lost every time I talk about the future. Ahmed is right. She needs time. And I will give her time until this lost look disappears from her eyes for-ever. I say that sometime down the road, way, way down the road, when we have kids, I hope that they have blue eyes just like their mother's because blue is the color of vastness, purity, and depth. She tightens her hold around my neck, and whispers that I'm sweet to remember that.

"I remember every word you've ever said," I whisper back.

We talk all night. Actually, I do most of the talking. I tell her that Faheemeh has been praying for us to become a couple, so that we could all be friends for the rest of our lives. She nods. Her silence makes me want to talk more. I tell her that I was up on the roof the night she and the Masked Angel were talking about me.

"How do you know we were talking about you?" she asks.

"Weren't you?"

"We were."

"I thought so." I smile.

"I miss her so much," she says. "You know, I haven't seen or talked to her since that night."

"How come?"

"Her parents are ill, and she has been consumed with nursing them."

"I think she would like to hear about you and me."

Zari doesn't say anything. The lost look in her eyes returns.

"After you and the Masked Angel went back inside the house, I sat on the roof and stared at the stars all night long," I say hurriedly, hoping to banish the look on her face, even if for just a few seconds. "It was a dark night, but your star was clearly visible."

"Where was yours in relation to mine?" she asks.

"I didn't find mine," I say. "I never do."

"You should've been able to find yourself because you have the biggest star up there. I call it Pasha's star. It's the biggest and the brightest, and the rest of us orbit around it."

I want to land a little kiss on her cheek but I'm afraid. She rests her head on my shoulder and I feel her lips touch my neck. I hold her tighter and my hands caress her back and her neck.

A few minutes pass. "When are you leaving for America?" she finally asks.

"I'm not going unless I can take you along."

"You can't plan your life around me. You have to go. I want you to. I want you away from this hellhole. You should stay in America forever. Make movies. Tell everyone our story, Doctor's story. People should know what happened."

I start to respond, but she puts her finger on my lips. "I want you to swear that you'll go to the States no matter what happens."

"No matter what happens? What do you mean? We've already had enough happen to us to last a lifetime. You and I will go to America together. Everything in my life will be planned with you in mind from now on."

"Don't say that," she pleads, the lost look back in her eyes.

"I will take you with me, and that's that. And you shouldn't worry about money because I'll work to support you. You were a great high school student, so I think you'll do very well in college. I personally think you'd make a great psychiatrist, or an anthropologist. Although I'd prefer that you be a heart surgeon so you can cure mine."

She looks at me, her pretty face frozen in concern. "What's wrong with your heart?" she asks.

I smile. "You've broken it." She smiles back and the lost look on her face finally fades, at least for now.

21

Lighting a Candle for Doctor

It's the day of the Shah's birthday, Doctor's fortieth day. Faheemeh, Zari, Ahmed, and I meet a couple of alleys down from ours and together we walk to the bus stop. Zari is wearing the chador we bought when we shopped at Laleh Zar. I tell her I hope she is wearing something warm under the chador because the weather is unusually cold for this time of year. She says she is.

We sit together on the bus, and Ahmed and Faheemeh sit a couple of rows behind us.

"Why are you wearing a chador?" I ask.

She doesn't answer for a few seconds before she looks at me, smiles, and says, "Because I want to look like an angel."

"You always do, with or without the chador," I shoot back without missing a beat. Then, I reach over and take her hand in mine.

The streets are not as crowded as I thought they might be. The bus skips some of the stops, no passengers to pick up and no one getting off. As we come closer to Amjadieh Stadium, traffic becomes more congested. There are more police cars and army jeeps, more traffic cops, and even more people.

We get off the bus on a street beyond which the buses are not allowed to go today. A dark cloud hangs over the mountain up north, which is visible from where we start our walk. A chilly wind threatens an imminent storm, as if nature, too, is mourning the fortieth day of Doctor's death and the birthday of the Shah.

The streets are filled with people waiting quietly, patiently, for their leader to drive by. Most of these people are government officials, students, and reluctant shop owners who have been ordered out onto the streets. The news agencies had reported that over five hundred thousand people were expected. This was obviously a lie, a total fabrication; perhaps wishful thinking on their part. I'm sure that the media will report an enthusiastic crowd, impatient and restless for the arrival of their king. I look around and what I see is people who want to go home, people who don't seem all that enthused about being out on the streets. Around certain corners, kids of different ages wave small flags, as their teachers instruct them to do. Every once in a while they are ordered to shout and to make happy noises as television cameras and photographers focus on them. Cops and soldiers can be seen everywhere.

There is a hum in the crowd, but it's certainly not one of excitement and jubilance. The shops are closed but their owners have been ordered, as they are every year, to decorate their doorways and their windows with blinking, colorful lights. Massive arches are built out of flowers on every block. Signs have been placed every few steps congratulating the Shah on his birthday and wishing him eternal life. On one section of the street a large group of men and women stand very close together. It's clear that they are government officials from the same administration, ordered to stay in a pack. Every few minutes the group chants in unison: "Long live the king, long live the king." Their chant sounds hollow and some of the people in the crowd giggle as if they're embarrassed.

We jostle through the crowd to a spot around a turn where we will have a great view of the motorcade when it appears. Zari looks a little pale. I ask her if she's okay, and she says there's nothing wrong.

I'm a Persian; we never believe anyone who says nothing is wrong. We're the people of intuition. We feel, smell, and taste trouble from a hundred kilometers away. We've been conditioned to worry because our history is full of atrocities committed against us by ruthless rulers. I reason that the anticipation of seeing the Shah, the man responsible for the death of her fiancé, is causing Zari's agitation.

We wait, and wait, and wait. It's cold outside, and I have a hard time standing still in the same spot.

I hear a man complaining in a low voice to his wife, "When is the son of a bitch coming, so we can go back to our warm homes?"

I look at Zari, and realize she's carrying something under her chador.

"What's that?" I ask, pointing.

"My purse," she says.

Ahmed looks at me. "Is anything wrong?"

"No."

He gives me the same distrustful look I gave Zari.

"What's wrong?" Faheemeh asks.

Ahmed shakes his head.

"Why are we here?" I ask Ahmed.

"To be with our angels," he says, laughing.

"We could have been with them someplace else." He agrees, but it's too late now. We wait to see how the Shah waves at people.

A loud cheer ripples down from farther up the street. A group of motorcyclists in uniform can be seen a few hundred meters away. "They're coming," I tell Zari. She looks pale, very pale.

"What's the matter?" I ask again.

"Nothing, honey. Nothing's wrong." She called me honey! I can't take my eyes off her white, tired face.

The motorcade gets closer and closer. Zari grabs my hand. "I love you," she shouts over the din. I think her words are meant to calm me down, but I know something is wrong. My heart races. I look around and can't see anything out of the ordinary. The motorcade is only a few meters away.

That's when I smell the gasoline. I look at Zari. Her chador has fallen off, and in her hands I see a small container of gasoline, which she is pouring onto her clothes.

I shout, "What're you doing?"

"I'm lighting a candle for Doctor. Today is the fortieth day of his death," she cries. "I love you."

Suddenly, time thickens, and we are all trapped in the horror of the moment. Zari runs out into the street, lights a match, and sets herself on fire. I run after her. "No, no, no!" I scream. The motorcade stops. The security guards take their guns out. Zari is running straight toward the Shah's car. The motorcycle officers quickly circle Zari's flaming form. She stops.

"Zari, Zari!" I scream. "Why? Why?"

Men in the crowd shout, and women beat themselves and cry, *"Ya Ali! Ya Ali! Ya Ali,"* a chant used when something devastating happens. I hear Faheemeh's frantic cries. I try to break through the cyclists to reach Zari, who is screaming and staggering in small, broken circles.

I hear Ahmed yelling, *"Ya Ali, Ya Ali!"* Zari turns toward the car carrying the Shah, and a security agent kicks her hard in the stomach, dropping her to the asphalt. She attempts to get up, but the pain keeps her down. She reaches inside one of her pockets and takes out a red rose and throws it toward the Shah's car. The sight of the flames drives me to the brink of insanity. I throw myself over her. I try to put the fire out with my arms and with my hands, realizing bitterly that the burning sensation I feel is no match for the one in my heart. Zari rocks from side to side, screaming and moaning.

I yell her name. "Zari, I love you. What have you done? Why? Why?"

Ahmed takes off his coat and throws it over her body, too. A man runs to us from the sidewalk and lays his jacket on her face. One of the soldiers comes at me with his rifle. Ahmed steps between us, and he hits Ahmed in the head with the butt of his rifle. Ahmed crumples. The motorcade drives past us. I hear the siren of an ambulance.

"I love you," Zari whispers, before passing out.

I'm beside myself. "Goddamn, son of a bitch!" I scream, and jump up and hit the soldier who hit Ahmed. He goes down like a crumbling brick wall. Another soldier attacks me. I punch him, too, and he drops to his knees. I'm screaming my shock and despair when I feel a sharp blow to the back of my head, and that's the last thing I remember.

22

Winter of 1974
Roozbeh Psychiatric Hospital, Tehran

Bridging the Gaps

Nights fall with a heaviness that deepens the hole in my heart, and I feel a million years old. There is a large tree outside my room whose barren branches tap against the windowpane like the knuckles of a ghost. I know who I am, and that I've been damaged, but it seems I can't move beyond these facts. I check my body for signs. The skin on my hands and elbows feels raw, but my ribs are no longer sore. My chest and arms feel small, so I know I've lost weight, and there's a deep bruise on the back of my head.

Everything about this place exudes a sense of sorrow, except for Apple Face, who is happy and jolly—although not when she is talking to my parents about me. I'm restless and in need of company, but I know that if I call the nurse, she will just give me another injection. It will make me feel warm for a few minutes, and then send me into a deep sleep, but I will awaken later consumed by fear and distress.

I hear a loud bang, and the power goes out. A moment of unnatural quiet is followed by a hushed chaos as the nurses scramble to put things right outside my room. I can't help but feel nocturnal, now that the world is as pitch black as the inside of my mind. I hear footsteps approach my door, then move away. I can't make out what the nurses are telling one another in the hallway, but the commotion intensifies as the seconds pass. The footsteps return, and the fear of the unknown coils around me like a snake as I sit up in bed. The door to my room opens with a soft squeak, and the old man walks in with a candle in his hand.

The flame jumps, licking up the oxygen in the room, and I see her, my little Zari, her face erupting in scarlet blisters as she gasps for air. The world inside me collapses, and my soul is ripped out at the roots.

I begin to scream, and it feels as if I will never be able to stop. I can't avoid the cascade of horrific memories that parade behind my closed eyes. Despite the pain that must have consumed her, Zari still struggled to reach the motorcade. Then the soldier kicked her, and the rifle butt crashed down on Ahmed's back, and she used her last breath to tell me she loved me. Apple Face has arrived by my bedside by the time this last realization strikes.

"Is she dead?" I ask, and Apple Face closes her eyes. I scream as loud as I can, trying to force the life out of my body. Apple Face tries to hug me, but I feel as if my skin has turned inside out and is now covered with sharp little needles. The nurses rush forward to hold me down, but Apple Face waves them back. I cry in her arms. I feel the warmth of my tears, and the ache in my chin and jaw from sobbing.

"How? How?" I scream.

"I don't know," Apple Face whispers.

"Damn you, God," I scream over and over, as I pull at my hospital gown. "Why?" I cry out. "Why? I want to know why."

Apple Face wipes her face with a handkerchief.

I yell, I bawl, I weep, but nothing lessens my pain. It hurts all over. I get out of bed and walk around aimlessly, trying to catch my breath. My skin feels too tight. There doesn't seem to be enough air in the room. Apple Face opens the window and fresh air rushes in. Then I sit down on the floor and weep, holding my head in my hands, rocking back and forth. Suddenly blood begins dripping from my lip onto the front of my gown. Apple Face sits down beside me. "You bit your lip, sweetheart," she whispers. "Please, be careful, please." She holds me in her arms, and asks a nurse for a tissue.

"Where is Ahmed?" I ask, as I cry on her shoulder.

"In jail," Apple Face whispers back, and I breathe a momentary sigh of relief before plummeting back into despair.

Hours later I still can't control my emotions. My parents come, and Apple Face tells them to step back into the hallway.

Then I slip into a haze, staring straight ahead for long periods of time. I can't cry anymore, there are no more tears, and I feel worn down inside. I think of the Shah's family and wonder if they talked about Zari at dinner that night. Did his son ask him who that woman was and why she set herself on fire and ran toward their car? I wonder if, two thousand years from now, a couple like Zari and me will sit in an ice cream parlor and talk about Zari's choice. Will they see me as a coward who should have embraced his lover as she caught on fire, and burned with her? I can't stop my mind as it races from thought to thought, from face to suffering face.

At some point Apple Face gives me an injection and I fall asleep.

When I wake, my parents are in the room having a quiet conversation with Apple Face. I remember Zari, and the world collapses anew on top of me. Tears rush to my eyes and something inside me twists, then snaps, discoloring the world so that it is an ugly place. I wonder how I'm going to get through the day, through the next five minutes. My mother must know what's going on in my head because as soon as I open my eyes, she begins to cry.

I think I reach for my sleeve, this time with my teeth. I don't feel the pain in my arm but recognize the blood that reddens my sheet. Apple Face rushes toward me. Then I see nurses, and the weeping faces of my parents, but I don't hear anything except a continuous hum.

I dream that Zari and I are sitting on either side of a tumbling brook. She's telling me that she loves me, and that I shouldn't mourn her death because death is not that much different from life. She says Doctor is not angry with me for falling in love with his girl, and begs me not to be angry at God, assuring me that God is kind, fair, and generous. She reminds me that there must be death so that there can be life, that there must be lies so that there can be truth, that there must be darkness so that there can be light. She wants me to know that she will always be beside me—but that I should forget her and try to live a long and prosperous life. I get up and try to cross the brook, but my steps take me nowhere.

I feel as if I'm dying when I wake up. Dr. Sana—my Apple Face—tries to calm me down. I hear every word she says, but don't understand. Apple Face doesn't go home that night. Her husband calls and Apple Face puts him on the speaker. He says hello to me. He has a deep but friendly voice. He says he's sorry, and that he is going to come and see me soon. I should hang in there and take heart, for all will be fine. His wife is a great doctor and she will make sure that I have the best care in the world. I don't say anything. After a while he says good-bye and hangs up, and I dissolve again. My life will not go on without Zari.

I like the tranquil feeling that has engulfed me when I open my eyes. My eyelids are so heavy I can hardly blink. My father says something about going to the northern part of Iran, where we have a villa on the foothills of the Alborz Mountains, with a view of the green waters of the Caspian Sea. Most of my parents' family members live in the northern states. Apple Face says that she will miss me when I leave. I hear their words but my mind is slow to process them.

They talk about when I get better, and I wonder how someone like me gets better.

"Time is the cure for all things," my father says to Apple Face, as he looks in my worn-out eyes. Time is the most precious commodity humans possess, and it no longer has any value for me. Suddenly, I succumb to a wave of anxiety. I am not aware I have moved until Apple Face runs toward me and holds my shoulders, and I feel yet another pinch in my arm.

Apple Face's husband comes to the hospital to see me. He's a young handsome man, tall and athletic with large black eyes, thick black eyebrows, and a mustache that makes him look like a young Mark Twain. Dr. Sana introduces him as Yahya, and he shakes my hand and sits in a chair by my bed. He has a pleasant disposition, and he tells me that he's been hearing a lot about me, and wanted to meet me in person. I'm not sure what to say in return. He says that he, Azar, and their child are planning to take a vacation in a couple of months, and that I should go with them. I gently shake my head no, realizing that Azar is Dr. Sana's first name.

I fall asleep while everyone is still in the room, and when I wake up the next morning I'm crushed that Zari didn't come to my dreams for another visit. She promised she'd always be beside me. Is she in the room now?

"I miss you," I say out loud, my voice thick, my words slurred and slow with tears. "How could you leave me in this miserable life without you? Why didn't you tell me? I broke my shin in three places when I was four and didn't cry; now I cry until I run out of tears."

I mumble that she owes me an explanation because when two people love each other they don't do stupid things like that. How would she have liked it if the situation were reversed? I'm sure she wouldn't have liked it because she begged me in my dream to live a long and happy life, and how can I do that when the sole source of my happiness has flown?

I sob loudly, and I don't care if the whole world hears me. I hope she can see me, and I hope she's sorry for what she did.

I cry myself to sleep. When I wake, the old man is sitting in a chair next to my bed. We stare into each other's eyes as he rocks back and forth.

"What has brought you here, my friend?" I whisper. "Have you lost someone, too?" The old man rocks forward and back, and the creak of the chair is almost soothing. "I cursed God last night," I tell him, "and he didn't bring the roof down on my head. I'm going to curse him again tonight, and the next night, and the night after that until he gets tired of hearing my insults. He's never going to bring her back to me, so I'm going to make him take me to her." I reach inside myself, looking for something to hang on to, but I feel myself drifting away.

23

Ahmed's Star

I spend a total of three months in the hospital. During this time, I learn to accept my fate, but lose my faith. I'm now an atheist, just like Doctor. I no longer blame God for anything—after all, how can you blame a being that doesn't exist?

Some afternoons I walk in the hallways or in the yard. Seeing the condition of some of the other patients and the degree of their suffering only intensifies my discontent.

I learn during this time that I was taken directly to a hospital from the scene of Zari's suicide. It took less than a week for the experts to decide that the blow to my head had not caused serious damage and the mild burns on my hands and arms did not require drastic intervention. The doctor who treated me believed that my silence and occasional outbursts were psychological and I was placed under Dr. Sana's care.

Apple Face believed that I had unconsciously wiped certain events from my memory, censoring anything that took place after I told Ahmed that I loved Zari. The world before that moment was less complex, so that's where time had stopped.

The SAVAK, which had thoroughly investigated Doctor's activities, knew that none of us was connected to his political group. Their interrogations of Ahmed confirmed their beliefs. The way Ahmed and I responded to Zari's situation at the scene further convinced the SAVAK that Zari committed the act without consulting any of us.

During my time at the institution, I also learn that Dr. Sana and her family are of the Baha'i faith. In the past four years, Islamic extremists burned down her home, and her husband was attacked and beaten up several times by strangers late at night. Yahya has bought two Dobermans to guard their home, but the fear remains. Dr. Sana says they will leave for Australia as soon as their immigration papers are in order. She can't handle the pain and suffering anymore, and she doesn't want her child to be raised in an atmosphere of constant fear and consternation. Her parents have already left the country, and it won't be long before her brothers and sisters leave, too.

During my stay at the hospital, I also learn the old man's story. He was an affluent, reputable merchant in Bazaar. His first wife died about fifteen years ago and left him with three sons, who lived with their brides in his huge house. The old man's sons were responsible for managing his business, and he spent most of his time alone and in dire need of a companion. Eventually he married a woman considerably younger than himself. She took care of him, and some even say she loved him very much. He adored her, and gave her anything she wanted. The young wife fit right in with the daughters-in-law, who were about the same age, give or take a couple of years. Then, a year ago, the old man was diagnosed with cancer. It was a devastating blow to the whole family.

The old man wanted to make sure that his loved ones were well taken care of after his death, so he rewrote his will and divided his property equally among his children and his young bride. This infuriated his oldest son.

One day, when the old man was out of the house, the oldest son went to the young bride's room and accused her of being a gold digger and a scoundrel. A thunderous fight broke out between the two, and attracted the other two sons into the room. The oldest son attacked her and beat her savagely. His brothers and their wives tried to intervene, but it was too late. She was dead by the time the police and the paramedics arrived. The oldest son is in jail for life, and the old man lost his mind the minute he learned of his wife's death. He's been here ever since. His condition is deteriorating fast.

"He doesn't have much time left," Apple Face says sadly.

While in the hospital, I learn that Ahmed has been released from prison. My father says the SAVAK has cleared all of us.

"Why didn't they go after me?" I ask.

"Well, first because of your condition. And second, they knew you had nothing to do with Doctor's activities."

"Then why did they keep Ahmed?"

"Only to make sure, and confirm what they already knew. It's not unusual for the SAVAK to do that."

The news of Ahmed's release fills me with an indescribable joy. This must be the first time I have smiled since hearing about Zari's death.

"Where is Zari buried?" I ask Dad, when I finally have the courage to do so.

"The family hasn't been notified yet," Dad says with a pained look in his eyes.

I don't sleep well that night. It's raining outside, and for the first time I think about Zari in a grave, out there in the rain. Shivers run down my spine. I remember her telling me that she will always be beside me, and I try to keep my mind busy with the thought of her nestled warm in my arms.

I suddenly remember my dream of Doctor walking into the trees with Ahmed and Zari. "He took Zari. He took Ahmed," I keep repeating to myself. A massive anxiety attack throws me into a state of delirium. I begin to sweat, and my body starts to shiver. Could they be lying to me, my parents and Apple Face? We Persians like to protect each other from bad news for as long as possible. A couple of years ago, a seventy-year-old man died in our alley. His daughter was a student at a London university at the time. Her family kept the death of her father from her for a year. Every time she called she was told that her father was out of town, on a business trip, out shopping, or at a relative's house. "Why does she need to know now?" they reasoned. "He's gone, and her grief will not bring him back. She is in the middle of her semester and doesn't need the distraction."

They must be lying to me about Ahmed. I think of the dream again. I was in a pasture with Zari, Faheemeh, and Ahmed. Doctor walked out of the woods nearby, reading the poetry of Rumi. He kept his distance from us. Zari leaned in and kissed me and then she and Ahmed followed Doctor into the woods. It all makes sense now. Ahmed is dead, too! I burst into tears and begin to scream and demand to see my father.

When my father comes to the hospital, I tell him that I want to see Ahmed's mother because if Ahmed is dead, she won't be able to hide it from me. My skin is too tight for my pain and I want to scream as loud as I can to free myself from the prison of my body. My father swears on my life that Ahmed is not dead. Ordinarily, my father would never swear on my life or tell a lie, but something tells me that he may under these circumstances. This is the kind of obligatory lie God forgives, according to my grandmother.

"Why hasn't he come to see me if he's alive?" I ask.

"Because it may not be safe," my father responds.

"I thought you said we're clear."

"You are."

"Then why is it dangerous for him to see me?"

My father seems flustered, struggling for an answer. I demand to see Ahmed's mother. Dad and Dr. Sana look at each other. Then they leave the room to talk.

Later that night I'm in my bed, tossing and turning. I hear Ahmed imitating Grandma: "If my husband were here, he would kick your ass!" I jump out of the bed and run toward him. He's standing by the door. We hold each other tightly for a while, just like my father and Mr. Mehrbaan did the first time they met after eighteen years. My father and Dr. Sana watch with moist eyes, and then they leave the room. Ahmed looks skinny and weak, as if he has not been fed for a long time.

"You've lost weight," I say.

"I've been exercising a lot lately," he says, a warm smile on his face.

"Exercising?"

"Yeah, you know." He looks uncomfortable with the topic, so I let it go.

"They told you not to see me, right?" I ask. "Otherwise, you would have come earlier."

"They never said it, but everyone, especially your dad, thought it'd be safer this way."

"We're not totally clear, are we?" I ask, referring to the SAVAK.

"We are. But with the SAVAK you never know."

"Why hasn't anyone from the SAVAK come to talk to me?"

"They know that we were just friends of Doctor's. They won't bother us anymore."

I shake my head and we're quiet for a while. Once we promised each other not to cry at Doctor's grave. Both of us are working hard to hold back our tears now. I ask Ahmed if Faheemeh is okay and he says that she is. He kisses my cheek and says it is from her. He and Faheemeh and everyone else in the alley have been taking great care of the rosebush I planted in Doctor's honor. People from all over come to the alley to see it. "They treat that plant like a consecrated memorial," he says.

"We have great people in our neighborhood."

After a few minutes, I ask Ahmed if they hurt him in jail, and he says that no one even touched him. I think he's lying but I don't pursue the subject. He says that he and Faheemeh can't wait for me to get out of here. Then we stare at each other, both of us knowing that we want to talk about Zari. I almost burst into tears. Ahmed puts his arms around me without saying anything.

"I'm okay, I'm okay," I respond. "How are her parents?"

"The Masked Angel is taking care of them."

I tell him about my dream, and about Zari telling me that Doctor has forgiven me for falling in love with his girl. I share how Zari said she would always be with me, and how I feel her presence all the time. I'm sure she's in the room with us right now, happy that we are together. And with that I break into bitter sobs.

Ahmed tells me to take heart and be strong. He says he doesn't know what the future holds for any of us, but that God always makes things right. I tell him that I don't believe in God and that if there is a God, he's got a lot of explaining to do when I get my hands on him. He shakes his head and smiles. I think he wants to bite the skin between his thumb and index finger, but he doesn't.

My father and Dr. Sana walk in. It's time for Ahmed to go.

"But it's only been a few minutes," I protest.

"We'll be spending lots of time together soon," Ahmed says. "Just like the old days, okay? Just like the old days."

We hug each other good-bye with moist eyes.

After they leave, I sit by the window and look at the sky. A brilliant, luminous star blinks at me from millions of miles away.

That must be Ahmed. He'll go on to live the life of a king, I just know it.

The memory of Zari pointing to the biggest star and claiming that it was me, the night before Doctor's fortieth day, chokes me up.

A week later, Dr. Sana tells me that her immigration application to Australia has finally been approved, and that she and her family will be flying out of the country as soon as their house is sold. I'll be released from the hospital in a few days. She's going to write me as soon as she settles in Sydney, and will even send me a ticket to visit them in their safe, new home.

24

The Color of Age

On the day of my release, I become more anxious as we drive closer
to our alley. I can't imagine what it will be like to be home again. Is
our house under surveillance? Have people been told not to interact
with me, and did my father choose a late hour for our arrival to avoid
the neighbors? As the car turns into the Ten Meters of Shahnaz, I remember the day Ahmed brought the neighborhood together to measure the width of the alley. I smile, and Dad notices.

"What're you smiling about?" he asks.

"Nothing," I respond, and ask him to slow down so that I can take
a good look at the neighborhood. Nostalgia envelops me as I think of
the past, when innocence ruled and wickedness existed only in the
minds of imaginative storytellers. Times when Iraj seemed evil because he looked at Ahmed's sister, and death was an alien state of
"not being" associated with the old.

Our neighborhood looks different, as if the brush of time has
painted everything the color of age. The alley seems darker and narrower than I remember it. The trees are bare and lifeless. February is
a cold month in Tehran. The wintry wind from the north blows and
traps the snow against the tall walls of the houses. The windows on
the homes with northern exposure seem frozen. I remember Mom

saying that those homes are a breeding ground for germs because they never get any sun. A smile creeps up on my face again, but then I see Zari's house from a distance. It too is dark and lifeless. An excruciating pain shatters my soul. It's unbearable to imagine the alley without her in it. Now I see the rosebush. It's standing tall but bare, like it's supposed to at this time of year.

We arrive at our house, and when my father stops the car, the brakes make a loud squeaking sound. My mother runs into the alley and, as I open the door, she scoops me into her arms. She hugs me, kisses me, and cries that she doesn't ever want to let go. I want to cry, but I don't. Before we enter the house, I look toward the roof.

"Where's Ahmed?" I ask.

My parents exchange a glance but don't say anything. My heart sinks and I involuntarily reach for my sleeves. Now what? What have they done to him? He wouldn't miss my arrival!

As we walk into the yard, I'm attacked by flying snowballs aimed at my chest, my head, and the rest of my body. "Get him, get him!" I hear two guys yelling. My mother turns the lights on in the yard, and Ahmed and Iraj come running toward me. They tackle me and throw me on the ground.

My mother laughs and warns, "Be careful, please, be careful. He's weak and his bones are fragile."

"Oh, leave them alone," my father says. "Let them have some fun."

Of course Ahmed and Iraj pay no attention to anyone. They turn me around, playfully punching me in the stomach and on the sides, piling snow over my face and body. I'm overwhelmed with joy. I kiss and hug them, too, but don't punch them back.

The lights in the neighbors' homes come on. Suddenly it feels as if the whole alley has come alive. "Welcome home," Ahmed's dad yells from the other side of the wall, as his mother prays.

Another man from a couple of houses down yells out, "We missed you."

I look around and see the neighbors at their windows, on their roofs and on the balconies of their homes. They wave, smile, and wish me well.

"Sleep well tonight," one neighbor says.

"Thank God he's home safe."

"We're playing soccer in the alley at nine a.m. sharp, okay?" I hear a kid yelling out. I nod, and wave back as we walk into the house. Ahmed and Iraj look so happy I want to hug them again. My father sits down with us as my mother goes to the kitchen to get tea and sweets. I look around and I can't believe I'm back in my own home. Our black-and-white television is right across from the door. The three ancient blue chairs are positioned around the little old sofa as if they're guarding it, and an old Kirman rug covers the floor. I notice that the bright blue wallpaper that my uncles helped put up five years ago is getting too old for this room and should be replaced. I try not to remember that blue was Zari's favorite color. The big grandfather clock, which never worked, is placed diagonally in the corner next to the huge brown oil heater. A large terrace lies between the living room and the yard. The lights in the yard are still on, and from where I'm sitting I have an unobstructed view of the *hose* and the olive tree that my father planted the day we moved in.

My mother brings us tea and tells us to drink it while it's still hot—but not too hot because drinking hot tea can cause liver cancer. Ahmed discreetly sniffs the tea for traces of powdered sorb. I chuckle.

Iraj informs me that Mr. Yazdi has retired and that Mr. Gorji, our religion teacher, has taken his place as principal. Things are very different at school now because Mr. Gorji is a strict disciplinarian, something no one knew about him when he was only a powerless religion teacher.

Every morning he makes the students line up and stand at attention while he lectures everyone via a bullhorn at full volume. In my mind, I can hear his pompous crowing. They also talk about a new algebra teacher named Mr. Sheidaee. He's a fourth-year physics student at the University of Tehran who believes that everything in the world can be explained by mathematical formulas, and that the governing laws of the universe are coded in the architecture of the pyramids of Egypt. It seems that Mr. Gorji hates Mr. Sheidaee's blasphemous theories.

"Everyone knows that Sheidaee's days as a schoolteacher are numbered," Ahmed says, "but he's putting up a good fight so far."

"To settle their differences, a few weeks ago they went out and drank vodka together," Iraj says.

Mr. Gorji used to lecture us that drinking alcohol was a sin and that drinkers were infidels who would burn in hell on the day of reckoning.

"How did you find out?" I ask, laughing at the ubiquitous hypocrisy of Mr. Gorji.

"Mr. Sheidaee told Ahmed!" Iraj says, laughing. "The next day, Ahmed praised Mr. Gorji in front of a whole bunch of students for setting aside his differences with Mr. Sheidaee and chugging a few drinks." I immediately begin to laugh as Iraj continues, "Ahmed said that all of us had learned a valuable lesson from them: that any quarrel can be peacefully resolved over a couple shots of vodka."

"Mr. Gorji left the room like a bullet from a six-shooter." Ahmed grins.

Iraj interrupts Ahmed. "The next thing we heard was Mr. Gorji calling Mr. Sheidaee an idiot and a blabbermouth, and Mr. Sheidaee calling Mr. Gorji a hypocrite and a charlatan."

I laugh as I picture Ahmed causing yet another major disturbance at school. It's the first time I've laughed so cheerfully in more than three months. My mother brings us more sweets and another round of tea.

"I don't miss being at school, especially if Mr. Gorji is the principal," I say quietly.

"Are you planning to come back?" Iraj asks.

"He can't," my father says. "He's already missed over three months. They won't let him in until next year."

Suddenly, I realize that I won't be graduating with Ahmed and Iraj. The thought of being in high school next year without my friends fills me with sadness.

Ahmed points to Iraj and asks, "Can you believe this guy is still growing? Look at how tall he is!" Sure enough, he's grown at least five centimeters. His upper lip is covered by thick, fuzzy hair that badly needs shaving.

"Why don't you shave your mustache?" I ask.

"My father thinks I'm too young to shave," he says, a bit embarrassed. "It'll ruin my skin, you know?"

Ahmed jokes, "Of course, the medical journals are full of stories of adults with bad skin, all because they started to shave too early." We all laugh, even Iraj.

My mother updates me on what's been happening in the alley while I've been gone. There have been far too many weddings, and pretty soon this neighborhood will be crawling with babies. Not that there's anything wrong with that, but she was just getting used to everything being quiet.

The neighbors ask about me all the time, and everyone wishes me the best. My father says that my uncles and aunts will be in town to see me within the next couple of weeks. He also mentions Mr. and Mrs. Kasravi, but doesn't say anything about the Mehrbaans. Is Mr. Mehrbaan still in jail? A more frightful thought goes through my head. *If something has happened to him, I don't want to know yet.* I take another sip of tea.

We stay up until three in the morning talking about everything except Zari and Doctor. Sometimes as others talk, my mind drifts away in the middle of the stories. Nothing feels right to me. The brush of age seems to have passed over my soul, and I feel as if there is nothing more for me to learn, and nothing else for me to look forward to. What can life teach me that I haven't already experienced?

It's finally time for bed. Iraj says good-bye and goes home, and Ahmed and I head up to my room on the third floor. We are finally alone. I look toward the roof, and let the tears fall down my face. Ahmed lowers his gaze.

"How is Faheemeh?" I ask.

"She misses you. We're going to see her tomorrow."

"I can't wait. Thank God you two are okay."

As soon as I say that, I remember that I don't believe in God anymore.

We stare at each other. We both know that sooner or later our conversation will turn to Zari. Finally he says, "Do you want to talk about it?"

I pause, then nod.

"We don't see her family very much anymore," he starts. "Her father leaves early in the morning and never speaks to anyone about her. Her mother never leaves the house, and they say she is sick all the time now. She spent a good deal of time in the hospital after . . ."

He pauses three heartbeats, then continues.

"I haven't seen her mother for a while, but everyone says it looks as if she has been hit by lightning. They say she hasn't been the same since that day. Her hair is gray, her face is wrinkled, and her hands shake uncontrollably, poor lady. You remember how lovely and vibrant she always was, right?"

I nod my head yes. Ahmed takes a deep breath and lights a cigarette. I light one, too. I think of my dad's dirty look, the one that hurts more than a thousand slaps in the face, but I no longer fear that look.

Ahmed continues. "They aren't allowed to wear black. Well, they don't need to; it looks so dark in that house. I wonder what Keivan will be like when he grows up. I walked to school with him once and tried to find out how he and his parents were doing, but he wouldn't say a word. He said he was told not to talk to anyone about Zari and what goes on in their house."

I remember the day we helped Keivan build a doghouse. I remember my clumsiness with the tools, pouring the drink all over my chest, Ahmed's insistence that I should talk to Zari, and the fiasco over *Su-vashun*. My heart wants to burst out of my chest. Those days feel like a century ago.

"The Masked Angel quit school and moved up here to take care of Zari's family," Ahmed says. "Everyone in the neighborhood says she's brought tranquility and sanity back into their lives."

"Do Faheemeh and she ever get together?" I ask.

"No." He shakes his head. "It's too hard for Faheemeh to be in that house anymore, you know what I mean?"

I think of the cherry tree, the red blanket, the little *hose* in their yard, and a teardrop rolls down my cheek. Ahmed puts his hand on my shoulder. "Are you okay?" he asks.

"Yes."

"Do you want to talk about this some other time?"

"No. I want you to continue."

"You sure?"

"Yeah."

"Okay, then." Ahmed takes a deep breath. "The Masked Angel doesn't associate with anyone. The rumor is that she takes care of the family until they go to bed, and then she goes into Zari's room and reads poetry all night. Can you imagine what it must be like for her to live in Zari's room?"

I remember that last night in her room, the picture of the four of us on the wall, the chair we sat on, the feel of Zari's body in my arms, the intoxicating scent of her hair. I wipe my tears away.

"Why don't they tell us where she's buried?"

"Because they're a bunch of bastards," he spits.

"The family never got her . . . the body?"

"No, never. As far as the world is concerned, it never happened. She didn't exist. It makes you want to scream, doesn't it? Fucking bastards! They do whatever they please, and there's nothing anyone can do."

"Did she make it to the hospital?" I ask, my voice a whisper.

Ahmed shakes his head. "I'm not sure anymore."

"Have her parents had any contact with the SAVAK?"

"I don't think so—not any that they've shared with the rest of the alley. As I said, they hardly ever talk to anyone. They don't accept company, and they rarely leave the house. Every time her name is mentioned, her father just cries. It breaks your heart. The man was an Olympic champion, for God's sake. Can anything be worse than losing your child?" Ahmed looks at me and stops himself.

"I'm sorry, I didn't mean it that way," he apologizes.

I shake my head to let him know he shouldn't worry. "Were her parents given any information about her at all?"

"Nothing that I know of. When I was in prison, I did hear that she was alive for a while—but you can't trust the information you receive in prison."

I wipe more tears from my face and wish that someone would either take the dagger out of my heart or push it in deeper to put an end to my miserable life.

"How long were you in jail?" I ask.

"Not long," he says, as if it wasn't a big deal.

"What did they do to you?"

"The regular stuff," he says with a flat, hollow laugh.

I can tell from his squinted eyes that he's not telling the truth. I watch him silently and persistently, to let him know he's not off the hook.

"They take you in because they want information," he finally explains, throwing his shoulders up as he talks—a tight, awkward gesture I've never seen him make before. "It wasn't anything out of the ordinary, I swear," he continues. "They kick you, punch you, and curse you out. You know, the regular stuff you hear people talk about."

I keep looking at him. I think he realizes that I'm still not satisfied with his answer, because finally he starts to elaborate without the shifty eye movements. He says his first days in jail were the hardest because he didn't know what had happened to me or to Zari, or if Faheemeh had also been arrested. The SAVAK investigators were nice to him in the beginning because they wanted to win him over and entice him into telling them about Zari. After all, he was just a confused kid to them. As he denied any association with the Communists, the banned political party known as the Toodeh, or any other political groups, they threatened to beat, torture, and even kill him.

One night, late, they woke him up in his cell and took him to a dark room, where they tied his hands behind his back, blindfolded him, and left him in an comfortable chair for two or three hours. Occasionally he would hear a couple of guards whispering, and then nothing. He was becoming more and more agitated as time went on, expecting the worst during the long periods of silence. Without warning, someone grabbed his knees and pulled them apart, and he felt a crushing blow to his groin. The pain was so devastating he instantly began to vomit. Minutes passed, and nothing else happened. Just when he was beginning to feel okay again, someone began to beat him with a long, thick cable. He didn't know what to do except scream and cry, but they wouldn't stop. The harder he screamed, the harder they hit him. He could feel welts rising on his back, shoulders, face, and head. He must have passed out as they were still beating him up.

Back in his cell he found a new prisoner who had also been savagely beaten a week or two earlier. His new friend's name was Javad. He was a young man of about twenty-three or twenty-four, tall, strong, and quite handsome. Javad told Ahmed everything about himself. He was a member of the Communist party and a student in the College of Law at Tehran University. A friend who had lost his life under torture had exposed him. He and his group were planning to rob a bank to finance their anti-regime activities. He had not been allowed to see his relatives, and wasn't sure they even knew he was still alive.

He showed Ahmed his maimed left hand and described in excruciating detail how they cut off two of his fingers in one night. Another night, he said, they stuck long, thick objects inside him and the pain was so overwhelming that he passed out. Javad was so bitter about what the SAVAK had done to him that he never stopped talking long enough to hear Ahmed's story. "These motherfuckers are servants of the West," he would say. "Don't you ever trust them, and don't you ever let them think that they have the upper hand."

Ahmed was beaten up every other night, each time more savagely than before. "They're not interested in investigating your crimes," Ahmed tells me now, puffing on his cigarette. "They want a confession, and they will do anything to get it. They told me they were going to cut off my fingers and my toes one at a time. They said to ask Javad how much it hurts, and I did. Javad didn't say anything. He just turned away and began to cry."

After each beating, Javad would tend to Ahmed's wounds while telling him about his vision of the future, which always included an armed rebellion against the Shah's regime. One night, he suggested to Ahmed that they should introduce their groups to each other. "It is only through the union of forces that a revolution can be successfully carried out in this country," Javad explained. "The government has created such an environment of suspicion and mistrust that revolutionary forces can only operate in isolated cells. That's because it's much easier to control and rule a small cell than a large one. Although there is always the risk of unwanted elements infiltrating larger groups, it is clear to me that you come from a well-organized, superbly trained group because you never talk about your comrades."

Ahmed shook his head and laughed. Javad wanted to know who Ahmed was, whom he was associated with, and if these "motherfucking servants of the West" had arrested anyone else from his group. Ahmed told him about Doctor, Zari, and me. He told him about our days under the cherry tree, Keivan's birthday party, and our nights on the roof. He told him that he loved Faheemeh, that I was his best friend, and that Zari was my first and only love. Zari's story touched Javad and made him cry while cursing the Shah and his "hell-bound" family.

Ahmed worried that Faheemeh's parents would force her to marry her neighbor while he was in prison. After all, they didn't know he was still alive. He told Javad that his heart broke every time he remembered me running after Zari with that look of total disbelief and horror on my face.

"That's the kind of stuff that crushes your spirit, breaks your heart, and weakens your soul," Javad cried. "It isn't fair for a young man to see what he saw on that ominous day." Ahmed said he wanted to smash his own skull in every time he thought of us under the cherry tree. Life was so good, and it had all come to a screeching halt when they took Doctor away.

During the days and nights Javad and Ahmed conversed, no one came to torture him. They would occasionally take Javad away, but he would come back promptly and without any visible signs of physical abuse on his face or body. Late one night, the agents took Javad away permanently. Ahmed never saw him again, and worried that they had executed his only friend and sympathizer in that hellhole. It wasn't until a couple of days before Ahmed was released that he learned that Javad was a SAVAK agent assigned to win his trust and expose his associations.

"They do that a lot, especially to the first-timers," he explained. "How are you supposed to know? He looked so genuine."

Ahmed says it wasn't being in prison that almost shattered his spirit, but the conflicting stories he heard about Zari, Faheemeh, and me. They told him all along that I had been executed, and that Zari was dead. Then they told him that she'd survived the fire, had confessed to being a *kharab-kar* during an interrogation, and died under torture. They had him believing that Faheemeh was arrested and was being gang-raped in the room next door at that very moment. They claimed that she would be raped repeatedly until Ahmed confessed to his crimes.

"I wished I could kill myself," he murmurs. "And I would've if I could've found a way."

It's getting light out as we walk out onto the roof. There is a thin sheet of ice covering it. We walk carefully, remembering Mom's mantra that hundreds of people fall off roofs every year. Looking toward Zari's room, I feel the weight of a mountain on my chest. The curtains are closed, but the light inside the room is on. My heart skips at the sign of life in that room. "Zari," I whisper.

Ahmed puts his hand on my shoulder. "I'm sorry," he says. "The Masked Angel must be doing her morning prayers."

The dawn chill makes me wish I was wearing something warmer. It's quiet outside, but here and there a light flickers, an infant cries for a brief moment, a door squeaks as the neighborhood gradually wakes up.

"I never used to notice these sounds," I say to Ahmed.

"Neither did I."

"How's your spirit now?"

"As strong as ever, now that I have you and Faheemeh back in my life. Those motherfuckers can kiss my ass if they think they can break me with a few bruises!"

"You still think about the stars?" I ask, looking toward the skies.

"Of course."

"You still have the biggest star up there. You'll go on to live the life of a king, with Faheemeh as your pretty queen in a big palace." I stop and take a deep breath. Ahmed lowers his head and stares at his toes. "The strength of our friendship is the only thing that has kept me sane. You're my brother, my comrade, and my friend for life."

Ahmed claps me on the back and smiles without saying anything, but I can tell from the soft expression on his face that he's deeply touched.

Out of the corner of my eye I see the Masked Angel walking out into Zari's yard. She's heading toward the bakery to buy hot fresh *lavash*, just like Zari used to. Her stride strikes me as unusually fast. I had heard from Zari that the Masked Angel was the calmest, most centered person in the world. I wonder why she's rushing, as if someone's chasing her. As I watch her, tears fill my eyes again. Ahmed asks if I want to go back inside, and I say no. He rubs the back of his neck with the palm of his right hand.

"I'm sorry," he says. "Life's not supposed to be like this at our age."

"I know."

"Promise me that you'll do your best to leave the past behind." As I nod, he extends his right hand. "Let's shake on it," he says, looking directly into my eyes. As we do, I remember the night before Doctor's funeral, when we vowed not to cry at the cemetery. I don't think I can keep my promise this time.

I look to the eastern end of the alley and see the Masked Angel returning. As I look at her burqa floating around her, I remember our religion teacher, Mr. Gorji, and his theories about unveiled women making themselves objects of sexual desire for men. I also remember thinking that Iraj was in love with Soraya, even though he had never seen her face.

"Is Iraj still . . . ?" I ask.

"Iraj is mesmerized by her," Ahmed says, smiling. I can't help but smile back.

The Masked Angel walks into the yard and shuts the door behind her. At that moment she looks up and sees Ahmed and me on the roof. She stops abruptly, as if she has run into an invisible brick wall, then rushes into the house.

"She must be shocked to see you," Ahmed says. "They've been worried about you, you should know that."

"We'll go to see them soon."

25

Caged Souls

It's been more than twenty-four hours since I've slept. Ahmed and I go downstairs and eat breakfast with my family. My mother keeps pushing food onto our plates because guys our age need to eat well or we won't grow strong. Ahmed says we better listen to her before she brings out the engine oil and the horse urine. I smile. My father has to go to work, but promises to come home early and take us out to dinner. We'll have chelo kebob—a skewer of ground beef mixed with onions and domestic Persian herbs, and a skewer of filet, served over basmati rice that has been prepared with butter, the savory Persian herb *somagh*, and baked tomatoes.

"I really don't want to go out, Dad," I tell him.

He nods. He says he understands, but I think he is surprised by my candor.

After breakfast, Ahmed and I step into the alley. Neighbors come over to say hello. I thank them for waiting up for me the night before to welcome me home. The men hug me and shake my hand. "You look great, you look great," one neighbor says.

"He looks fantastic," another interjects. "A little thin, but that's expected."

"Oh, yes, he looks thin, but his mother will nurse him into fine form in no time," Ahmed's mother says as she hugs and kisses me. "I missed you so much," she says, tears in her eyes. "I prayed for your safe return every day. Oh, if you only knew what your poor, helpless mother went through. She was like a lost soul the entire time you were away. A mother without her child is like a vein without blood." Then she whispers in my ear, "You should see Zari's mother. She looks like a ghost. Poor, poor woman."

Ahmed's grandmother is standing a couple of meters away. It seems she's aged twenty years in a matter of months. Ahmed whispers that Grandma's mental and physical state is deteriorating fast.

"My husband went away once," Grandma says. "For thirty years, or was it forty years? I never thought I'd see him again, but he came back." Then she turns to Ahmed and asks, "He did come back, didn't he?"

"Yeah, Grandma, he came back." Ahmed smiles gently as he puts his arm around her. "How could he stay away from a good-looking chick like you?"

Grandma looks at me and asks, "Where's your wife? Does she know you're back yet? I didn't know my husband was back for quite some time." Then she turns to Ahmed. "It was quite some time before I found out, wasn't it?"

Ahmed nods his head yes.

"It was quite some time before I found out, quite some time," she rambles. "Why didn't he let me know right away?"

"He wanted to surprise you, and show up when you least expected it," Ahmed reminds her. "What would be the point of going away if you couldn't surprise your own wife when you came back?"

"Oh, yeah!" Grandma says. "What would be the point?" She pauses, and then asks, "I was surprised, wasn't I?"

Ahmed turns to me. "You remember, don't you? Wasn't she surprised?"

Grandma is standing right next to me. I put my arm around her shoulders and say in her ear, "Grandma, you were very surprised. I'll never forget the way you smiled when you saw him."

Grandma's face lights up. "You should surprise your wife, too. She'd like that, just like I did." Then she slowly walks back toward Ahmed's house. "Yes, I remember being very surprised."

Ahmed winks at me and I wink back.

The kids in the alley are excited to see me. A couple of the younger ones keep their distance. After all, I've just been released from a mental hospital. Most of the kids, however, shake my hand and want to know if I still play soccer, and if I would like to play later on in the day. I thank them and tell them that I'm too tired, that it has been a long time since I've slept.

Ahmed and I go to his house. His mother brings us tea and sweets, and tells us that she's been dreaming of this day when we would be together again. She's a small woman with a thin face, skinny body, and pale complexion. She has the voice of a storyteller, kind, warm, and trusting. There is always a point—a lesson or a moral—to her stories. She talks of Ahmed's prison days as the worst of her life. "Life isn't the same when a piece of your heart is ripped away from you," she says. "It's a blessing and a curse to be a mother, that's for sure!"

Ahmed ducks his head. I guess he's embarrassed.

Ahmed's mother advises me to visit Zari's parents. "They've suffered a great deal. First Doctor, and then that rose of a girl. So young, so vibrant. It is unbelievable what has happened to that family. If there is a God, then there is a Day of Judgment, too, and her poor mother will see justice." She wipes the tears from her eyes. "Oh, yes, you should pay your respects soon," she continues. "I saw the Masked Angel watching you from the terrace on the third floor when everyone was gathered around you in the alley. I'm sure she has told the family that you are back. They probably expect you to pay them a visit today."

Ahmed says, "Yeah, we should do that." Then he turns to his

mother. "She saw him on her way back from the bakery today. We could tell she was surprised."

"The Masked Angel has been a godsend to that family," Ahmed's mother says. "They were devastated until she showed up and brought some peace back into their lives. She must be a true angel. God's ways are amazing, aren't they?"

I nod yes, thinking that if there is a God, he sure has an amazing way of showing his love for Doctor and Zari.

"Of course she will never fill the void that Zari has left in their lives," Ahmed's mother says. "That would be impossible because no one—and I mean no one—can replace your child. At least the Masked Angel is there to nurse them, and be a sister to Keivan. That poor boy! How they ever explained his sister's tragic loss to him, I'll never know. What a storm must be brewing inside him! God help him, I just hope he doesn't try to get revenge when he grows up. Thank God for the Masked Angel. I hear she spends most if not all of her time caring for him. She has devoted her life to that family. She never goes anywhere, never socializes with anyone. She is entirely focused on helping that family cope with the pain of losing their dear child. God bless her."

We hear Grandma walking toward us. Ahmed's mother shakes her head. "She's getting worse every day. Just a few days ago she fell down the basement stairs because she thought her husband, God bless his soul, was waiting for her at the bottom of the steps. It's a miracle she didn't break her neck. She sees him everywhere now.

"Life's short, way too short. Enjoy every breath you take because no one knows what comes next. Through the eyes of creation, the time each of us spends on this planet is no longer than a blink! We have to live our lives trusting in God's judgment. There's a reason for everything. My poor mother, bless her soul, used to say don't waste your time asking God why because God doesn't talk back. Somewhere down the road, though, he shows you signs that help you understand why things are the way they are."

I know what Ahmed's mother is doing, and I wish she would stop. I want to tell her that I don't believe in her arrogant God who's too good to talk to us, but that would be considered extremely rude. No matter how upset you are, you must never contradict your host. Even more important, you should never say anything religiously offensive.

Grandma walks in the room. She looks at me for a few seconds, and asks again if my wife knows I'm back yet.

Ahmed smiles and says, "He has no wife, Grandma."

"Oh!" says Grandma, her eyes hazy and befuddled. "I thought he was married to the girl next door," she says, "the one Grandpa used to give chocolate to."

"No, Grandma—" Ahmed tries to interject, but Grandma cuts him off.

"She is a nice girl. I like her a lot."

"I'm sorry," he whispers to me. "She doesn't know what's happened."

"That's okay, she's probably confusing me with Doctor."

"You should let your wife know you're back," Grandma says to me. "She has been waiting for you for quite some time. Just like I waited for Grandpa."

"Yes, Grandma. He will let her know," Ahmed soothes.

"She cries for him every night," Grandma says. "Poor girl, she cries every night. She is so sad."

"Okay, Grandma. We'll take care of it. We'll let her know," Ahmed says patiently.

"Yes, best to let her know," Grandma says, shuffling out of the room. "The poor girl should know. It breaks your heart to hear her cry like that."

The doorbell rings. When Ahmed answers it, Faheemeh pushes him aside and runs toward me. She jumps into my arms and kisses my face, over and over, as tears roll down her cheeks. I can feel her body shaking in my arms. She has cut her long black hair short, and it makes her look more grown up than she really is.

"What happened to your hair?" I say, laughing while trying to hold back my own tears.

"Needed a change, that's all," she whimpers, as she studies me through moist eyes. "You look like you've lost a lot of weight."

"I needed a change, too," I say.

She laughs, and hugs me hard.

"Thank God you're back, thank God for that," she says.

Ahmed's mother exchanges greetings with Faheemeh and asks if her parents are well. Soon she goes to the kitchen to start lunch.

Faheemeh puts her arm around my shoulders. She bites her lower lip as she quietly sheds tears and wipes her face with a white handkerchief. "Ahmed and I talked about you every day you were away," she says. "We missed you dearly, and couldn't wait for you to come home. Everyone in the neighborhood knew what happened to us, including my parents and brothers. My mother and father were genuinely worried for you, and prayed for your health and your safe return." She asks me how I feel, and before I have a chance to answer, she hugs me again and breaks into bitter sobs.

"We'll make it through this together," she says. "I don't know how, but we'll make it. I promise. Our recovery may be slow, but it will happen, I'm sure of it."

It feels wonderful to be with Ahmed and Faheemeh again. They look more mature than I remember. They appear to be totally aware of each other in the way that only married couples are. Gone are Ahmed's boyish antics and youthful mannerisms. Sitting next to her, he's like a man, confident, determined, with an air about him that makes it obvious that Faheemeh is his woman. The girlish disposition that made Faheemeh look like a teenager fallen in love for the first time is gone, too. She is a woman now, mature, serene, and aware that she is the subject of someone's unconditional affection and devotion. I wonder if Zari and I ever would have gotten to this point if she were still with us.

Faheemeh starts to talk about that day. She remembers fainting on the sidewalk after the soldiers attacked Ahmed and me, but she doesn't remember anything after that. A couple of the families who were standing close to us, and witnessed everything, shielded her from the agents who were roaming the crowds to learn about "the three crazy kids responsible for this nonsense." The people who took her home told her parents everything. Her older brother yelled and cursed when he learned that she was with Zari, Ahmed, and me. But when he heard about what had happened to the three of us, he hugged her, showered her with kisses, and thanked God that she was safe.

Faheemeh was sick for a long time. She couldn't eat or sleep. The images of that day still haunt her, and she often finds herself crying without a cause. Her parents tried to send her to England to stay with a distant cousin for a while, but she refused to go.

"You know what kills you?" she asks. "Not knowing, that's what kills you. I went to Evin Prison every day. I was sure I would have to come up with the cost of the bullets before I could get your bodies back." She bites the skin between her thumb and her index finger. She says she couldn't start mourning for Zari because of her uncertainty about our situations. "I couldn't go on until I had a sense of the total loss in my life," she says, as she breaks down into another bitter fit of weeping. "I miss her so much! I just wish I knew why she did it. She seemed so in love with you. I wouldn't have guessed it in a million years."

I tell them that I should have known and that a few days before it all happened, Zari and I talked about Socrates and Golesorkhi. I tell them how she talked about death and suicide when we were out having an ice cream, and how I changed the topic because I thought it was depressing.

"Perhaps if I had listened, I would've suspected something," I say, nervously reaching for my sleeves. Ahmed grabs my hand.

"Don't do that," he whispers.

"Don't blame yourself," Faheemeh begs. "No one could've guessed what she was up to from a conversation like that."

"I wouldn't have interpreted anything Zari said as a sign of what she was about to do," Ahmed says. "This came out of nowhere. You can't, you can't, you can't blame yourself," he warns emphatically.

"Why did she do it?" I ask. "She said she loved me. How can you do this to someone you love? I don't understand."

I say I don't understand, but I do. As inconceivable as her action was, it must have seemed the only way for her to shout her defiance of the Shah, making the ultimate sacrifice for a greater good, a red rose action, a Socrates decision, a heroic gesture, signifying the triviality of life without freedom.

After lunch I ask how Ahmed and Faheemeh met after Ahmed was released. He shakes his head and starts to laugh. Faheemeh follows suit.

"He came to our house," she starts. "My brother opened the door." She stops and looks at Ahmed to continue.

Ahmed shrugs his shoulders. "I'm so glad I didn't have to violate our pledge to the sacred brotherhood of the boxing fraternity."

Faheemeh smiles and hits Ahmed in the shoulder with the back of her hand. "My dear brother," she says. "You weren't going to man-handle the poor kid, were you?"

"He wasn't a kid when he was beating me up a few months earlier," Ahmed says sarcastically.

"He's just a kid," Faheemeh laughingly protests.

"Anyway," Ahmed says, "lucky for the 'kid,' he got out of my way. By then she was already halfway to the door, screaming and yelling my name. Boy, you should've been there! She made quite a scene. Everyone came out of their homes to see what was going on."

"A couple of days later our parents got together and announced to the neighbors that we were engaged," Faheemeh says as she jubilantly shows me her engagement ring.

"I can't believe I didn't notice that before," I say, putting my arms around her and Ahmed at the same time.

"We didn't want to have an engagement party without you," Ahmed says. "Besides, we want to wait until Zari's one-year anniversary."

I'm extremely happy for them. Theirs is the first good news I've heard in many months.

On the way to Zari's house, we stop at the spot where I planted Doctor's rosebush. "Everyone took care of it," Ahmed whispers. "For Doctor, for Zari, and for you."

I shake my head in appreciation. "We'll never let this bush die," I say.

"We won't," Ahmed confirms.

We arrive at Zari's house. A series of images flashes in my head, including the first day Faheemeh rang the bell to begin our remarkable summer together. I'll never forget the joyful smile on Zari's face when she first opened the door. She and Faheemeh hugged. Then she looked toward us and winked before walking back into the house and closing the door behind her. It's so heart-wrenching to know that Zari will never be answering a doorbell in that house again.

I ring the bell with shaking hands, and Zari's father opens the door. He stands in the doorway and stares at me with sad eyes. I say a tentative hello. He takes a step toward me and hugs me so tightly that I fear he may crush my ribs. He holds me for a long time, and I can feel his body shaking. When he lets go of me, I see tears in his eyes. He steps aside and we walk into the yard.

As Mr. Naderi shuts the door, I see Zari's mother walking gingerly toward us. The brush of age has touched her, too, creasing her face and turning her hair gray, just as Ahmed had warned. She looks like an unhealthy old woman nursing not just a fatigued, exhausted body but also a haunted spirit and a tormented soul. I go to her, and she hugs me, and we begin to cry in each other's arms.

There is no pain like the pain of losing your child, my mother's voice echoes in my head.

After a few seconds, Zari's mother grabs my shoulders and gently pushes me away from her to gaze into my teary eyes. I recognize traces of Zari's features in her kind, sorrow-worn face. Underneath the veil of grief I can see the blue eyes, the well-shaped chin, the lovely cheekbones.

Zari's mother wipes the tears from my face with her fingers and tells me to be courageous. "You're too young to harbor a pain like this in your heart for too long," she says. "My dear, dear boy, I wish you knew how I feel about you and about what you were doing for my dear Zari." I nod while remembering the night she saw her daughter in my arms up on the roof.

"You need to let go of the past, and focus on the future," Mrs. Naderi says. She hugs me again, and whispers, "I know you're strong enough to move on. Leave this country as you promised Zari you would. You need to go to the States and get a college education, because only educated people can save this country. While there, tell every American what their government's senseless support of a dictator has done to the Iranian mothers. Tell them that there will be no end to these atrocities until they stop paying for our oil with the blood of our children. Promise me that you will do your part toward emancipating our people, because you owe it to Doctor and Zari."

I nod yes, but I'm not sure in my heart that I can ever leave this alley. After Zari, what does it matter if I have an education? How can I go to the United States, the country that has supported the man responsible for the death of my angel?

We walk past the cherry tree and enter the house. On the way to the living room I notice that there are a number of boxes in the hallway. "Are you moving?" I ask Mrs. Naderi.

"Not for a while, but not a day too soon," she says. "You can imagine how difficult it's been for us to continue living in this house."

The thought of another family occupying the house in which my Zari lived fills me with pain.

The living room is exactly the way I remember it from the night of Keivan's party. The picture of Zari and Doctor is still on the shelf. We almost kissed looking at that picture. I try to peel my eyes away from the shelf before I burst into tears.

The floor is covered with an inexpensive Kashan rug. There are large cylindrical pillows around the room on small Turkmen sitting mats. A steaming samovar is in one corner of the room, a teakettle on top of it. Six small old Persian teacups with worn-out gold rings around their bases are set on a brass tray next to a neat pile of matching saucers. The smell of the freshly brewed tea makes the room feel cozy and warm.

Zari's mother pours us tea from the samovar as Mr. Naderi smokes his cigarette quietly. Out of the corner of my eye, I see the Masked Angel in the hallway whispering something in Keivan's ear. Zari's mother waves at Keivan and says, "Come here, honey. Come say hello to our guests."

Keivan walks up to me. Zari's mother prompts, "Say hello, dear."

Keivan says hello and hugs me, clasping his little arms firmly around my neck. I hug him back and whisper in his ear that I missed him. He says he missed me, too, and then he turns around and looks at the Masked Angel in the hallway, who's preparing a tray of sweets. Keivan sits next to me and places his elbow on his thigh and his hand under his chin. I put my arm around him and squeeze his shoulders a couple of times. Zari's mother smiles and says that Keivan has been a great help to Cousin Soraya while his poor, heartbroken mother was dealing with pain no mother should ever have to deal with. Keivan shrugs his shoulders and smiles, understanding that his mother is paying him a compliment.

"Children are the most precious things in the world, if you ask me," Zari's mother says. Then she turns her head toward the ceiling and begs God not to ever deprive any parent of the joy of raising their kids.

I want to ask why she's praying to a God who robbed her of her child, why she hasn't boycotted him, written him off. I remember the night on the roof when I told my father that God wasn't fair because he never reacted to those who committed atrocities against humanity, especially the young. That night Zari was sitting beneath the short wall, listening to us. I look at her picture on the shelf and feel the muscles around my heart tighten up. I want to scream and pull on my skin to free up some room for the pain that is bloating me.

Mrs. Naderi starts to talk about Doctor's family. "His mother is now in an institution with no prospect of recovering from her mental illness," she says. "His father died a couple of months ago; God bless his soul. He was the lucky one, if you ask me. It's not a good thing to outlive your own child. Nothing is more painful, nothing. The last few months he wasn't really living, he was just breathing. Death is a blessing at a time like that." Mrs. Naderi shakes her head and wipes the tears from her face.

The Masked Angel enters the room carrying a tray full of sweets. She whispers hello, and Ahmed, Faheemeh, and I get up to greet her. She points to us, and with a gesture of her hand pleads with us to sit down as she and Faheemeh hug and exchange pleasantries. She whispers so quietly that I have a hard time hearing her.

Mr. Naderi smiles as the Masked Angel sits down on a pillow only a few centimeters away from him. He whispers something to her, and she shakes her head no. Then he looks at me. I wish I knew what just passed between them.

Mr. Naderi's silence is certainly odd, and uncharacteristic of the talkative, somewhat philosophical man I once knew. He has always been a kind man, gifted with a gentle soul and cursed with a rugged face that looks anything but friendly. The hardship he has endured has not marred his Olympian body, and he still looks like a formidable wrestling champion, with broken ears and a face that has been rubbed into the mat a few too many times. He and my father used to talk about their matches and opponents in great detail. I always enjoyed Mr. Naderi's exciting stories told in his deep, scratchy voice. What a stark contrast his present demeanor is to the happy-go-lucky ex-champion of a few months ago!

Zari's mother says that the Masked Angel has been struggling with a bad cold that won't go away. "The poor thing has lost her voice, and coughs all night long. She has to see a doctor," she says. "But the young are too stubborn, and think they can overcome everything. God bless her, there isn't a day that I don't burn *espand* for her to keep the evil spirits away! I don't know what we would have done without her."

I can tell from the movement of the Masked Angel's eyes behind the little holes in her burqa that she is looking at me. This is the first time she has seen me up close. She must be curious about the boy her best friend and cousin fell in love with. I sense a distinct nervousness in her demeanor. I would almost swear that she is shaking under her veil. Mr. Naderi whispers something to her again, and she whispers back.

They must be very close. She must be filling the void that Zari's death has left in his life. The poor man adored his daughter, always referring to her as his reason for living. She was the center of his universe, the sun that brightened his days and the moon that lit his dark nights. In the evenings, when he came home from work, Zari ran up to the door and clasped her arms around his muscular neck to embrace him, and that was enough to make him feel rested and at peace. And on Friday afternoons, Zari brought him tea in the yard as he sat by the *hose* in the shadow of the cherry tree and read the newspaper. He always talked about his dreams of having grandchildren. "Two grandsons," he would say. "I'll teach them how to wrestle and carry on the family tradition. Wrestling is the best sport in the world!"

And now the two people who could have fulfilled his dreams are gone. Maybe the Masked Angel can someday give him an experience close to what he would have had with Zari.

Mrs. Naderi repeats that Soraya has been the pillar that has kept the family from collapsing. "Dear God, never deprive anyone of the joy of raising their child," she prays again, "and damn the Devil of the Middle East, the servant of the West, and the destroyer of young lives."

We all hang our heads in silence. Then Mr. Naderi sighs and lights up another cigarette. Brokenhearted over the outlook of someone else occupying their house, I ask, "May I ask where you're moving to?"

"To Bandar Abbas."

My heart sinks. The government exiles its unruly employees to Bandar Abbas, a town on the Persian Gulf famous for its intolerable heat and humidity.

"Why Bandar Abbas?" Ahmed asks.

Mrs. Naderi looks at her husband, but doesn't say anything.

"Who would ever forget Zari if her family continued to live in this alley?" I answer gently, although I'm furious at the thought of them in exile.

Ahmed suddenly gets it. He seems embarrassed by his question.

"But the SAVAK is wrong," I say. "No one will ever forget her anyway. Not her and not Doctor. People in this country don't forget and never forgive."

Mr. Naderi's eyes fill. His pain-worn eyes are frozen on me as he puts out his cigarette and lights another.

I wish I had the courage to tell them about myself and Zari, but love is a private matter, and the vault of the heart is not to be opened lightly, nor the treasure of love exposed. I always wondered why, despite our passionate spirit as a nation whose poetry is filled with declarations of love, our reality is one of guarded emotions when it comes to members of the opposite sex. Although Mrs. Naderi saw Zari and me in each other's arms, she will never talk about it, and neither will I. It doesn't matter that their daughter was the center of my universe, or that I have grieved her loss every waking moment of the last few months. Some things must remain sealed in the cage of the soul.

I look toward the Masked Angel, and realize that she is still looking at me. Her eyes blink fast behind the dark lace panel in the front of her burqa—eyes that remind me of the eyes of my own angel, except that they don't smile like hers.

We sit in that room for hours without saying much, taking refuge and comfort in the fact that we share a common pain. And for the first time since Doctor's death, we are able to mourn together.

26

The Eyes of an Angel

The weather is unusually warm and springlike for this time of year, the middle of *Esphand*, the end of February, but my mother insists that I wear warm winter clothes when I go out. "This weather can turn on you without notice," she says. "It's warm one minute and then suddenly it starts to snow." She brings out a bottle of herbal juice from her medicine cabinet and insists that I swallow two full teaspoons of it. "This will boost your immune system, which has been weakened in the last few months."

It's good to know some things never change.

The whole world has heard that I'm out of the hospital, and they all want to see me. Everyone has decided to come for a visit at the end of this week. My mother is busy preparing the house. She dusts, sweeps, washes the sheets, and tries to figure out where everyone will sleep and what she will serve for every meal. She names the guests without counting them: "Mr. and Mrs. Kasravi, your two aunts and two uncles, Mrs. Mehrbaan, and your grandparents from your father's side— however many that is."

"That's nine," my father says.

"Don't count! Don't you know it's inauspicious to count people?" she scolds, a concerned look on her face.

"Why?" my father asks, shaking his head in exasperation.

"I don't know. It just is." Then she turns to me and says, "They're all coming to see you, aren't you excited?"

"I am," I say. But I wish I knew why people feel they need to visit someone who's sick. When I'm not feeling well, the last thing I need is people telling me that I look good, and that all will be okay. The forced smiles and laughter will drive me insane.

My father seems unusually agitated and restless. He follows my mother around without helping her, and I can tell he's getting on her nerves.

"Do we have enough vodka?" he asks at least three times. "There'll be a lot of drinking and celebrating tonight. We'll all be drinking, including Pasha."

I remember the last time I drank vodka—the night of Doctor's funeral—and the idea doesn't strike me as celebratory.

Mother says, "Yes, there is plenty of vodka."

"Is Mrs. Mehrbaan coming?" he frets.

"Yes, I told you that already."

"Did you talk to her personally?"

She gives my father a dirty look.

"Did she say she is coming for sure, or that she would think about it?"

My mother turns around, looks at my father and starts to say something, but decides against it. Instead she throws her arms up in the air, mumbles something under her breath, and walks away. I wonder why my father is so concerned about Mrs. Mehrbaan.

"Okay then, I'm going to check to make sure we have enough vodka," my father says, as he walks toward the refrigerator.

My paternal aunts, uncles, and grandparents arrive a few minutes before noon. They hug me, kiss me, and tell me how glad they are that

I'm home again. They say I look great and that I will soon look even better, thanks to my mother's superb cooking.

All my aunts and uncles are in their thirties, but only my aunt Mateen is married. She is the largest woman in our family, and the kindest woman on the planet. Her first husband died tragically four years after they were married in a head-on accident on a pilgrimage to Imam Reza's mausoleum. Aunt Mateen was single for ten years, but eventually fell in love again and married Mr. Jamshidi, a middle-aged man who owns a dairy factory in the northeastern city of Mashhad. One year after their wedding, she found out that Mr. Jamshidi was already married. She cried day and night, threatened to kill him, asked him for a divorce, and even locked him out of the house for a few days. Eventually, however, she decided that being married to a bigamist was not so bad, as long as he loved her, respected her, and was faithful to her. So Aunt Mateen told Mr. Jamshidi that if she ever caught him with his first wife, she would circumcise him, little by little, until he was little more than a eunuch. Everyone in the family says that Mr. Jamshidi is the most faithful man on the planet, not because he doesn't like women, but because he knows my aunt is a serious lady with extremely sharp knives in her kitchen cabinet.

Aunt Maryam is a pretty woman, with a face that looks more European than Iranian. When my grandparents aren't around, her brothers tease her that she is an illegitimate child, perhaps conceived by the Russian soldiers who were occupying the north during World War II. Aunt Maryam always shakes her head and laughs. She has a great sense of humor, and I have always liked her a lot. Aunt Maryam is almost always argumentative and sometimes even contentious toward her brother, my uncle Mansoor. Sometimes they don't talk for months, and although they live in the same alley, they avoid each other at all costs.

It's fascinating to watch the two of them argue because neither of them ever gets a chance to finish a sentence. So now when they fight, instead of talking they write letters to each other, which they read to the entire family before mailing to the intended receiver. Their letters always start with an expression of love, but quickly disintegrate into bitter disclosures of the sacrifices one has made for the sake of the other.

"Dear Sister," Uncle Mansoor once wrote, "I've heard you told everyone that I don't love you. Bullshit! You know that I do. I've always loved you, but I never will again. In fact, no brother—and I mean no brother in the world—could love his sister as much as I have loved you! Remember when your tonsils were taken out, and you were in bed crying for ice cream? Who ran six kilometers in the rain to get it for you? Do you recall the time you twisted your ankle on the way home from school? Who carried you home on his back? Don't I always check up on you, and ask you if you need anything when I'm going to the market? Have you ever done anything for me, or for anybody else? You are so selfish. I will never love you again!"

Aunt Maryam responded with a letter of her own. "Dear Brother Mansoor," she wrote back. "You never loved anyone but yourself. You are the selfish one. I have sacrificed my life for you. I mended for you, cooked for you, cleaned for you, washed dishes for you. I can fill a book listing what I have done for you. Maybe two books! I will never do any of those things for you again because you are selfish and you don't understand the love of a sister. Too bad for you. Good-bye forever. No one will hear your name from my lips again, no one. I will forget that I ever had a brother named, well, whatever your name is! Good-bye."

Of course, someone always intervenes and the two kiss and make up, promising never to discuss the stupid conflict again.

"It's water under the bridge," Uncle Mansoor says.

"What's past is past," Aunt Maryam agrees.

"Only a fool reopens a wound that's already healed."

"Who hasn't had a fight with her brother? Fighting is the salt of life; a small amount makes life more delicious!"

They go on as if nothing ever happened until the next time they fight, and then all the old issues resurface.

My two uncles look like twins, even though they were born two years apart. They both have thick mustaches that mirror the darkness of their black hair. They are big and muscular, and often in trouble with the local police in Noshahr, the town they live in, because they fight strangers all the time. My father says my uncles are a picture of what my grandpa was like in his youth. Now, of course, he is a quiet, skinny man who walks with the aid of a cane and always wears a gray suit. He was a revolutionary activist during Mosaddegh's era, and hated the Shah and his "pseudo reform policies" that only strengthened his position as the sole authoritarian voice in Iran. Grandpa, like many in his generation, hates the British with a passion that makes his face red every time someone mentions Churchill's name.

"The goddamn colonialist, he regarded the Indians the same way Hitler viewed the Jews," he says of the British prime minister. "Given the chance, he would have incinerated the Indians just like Hitler did the Jews!"

As an atheist, Grandpa also hates organized religion. "Show me an honest clergyman, and I'll show you a skunk that doesn't stink," he says every time there's a discussion of religion.

My father always laughs at his remarks. "Thank God he hates everybody equally: the mullahs, the priests, the monks, the rabbis, and the politicians."

"There is no God," Grandpa whispers bitterly every time Grandma prays. "Haven't you learned that yet? Marx tried to tell everyone, but only a few of us listened." Every time Grandpa says something blasphemous, Grandma bites the skin between her thumb and index finger without looking in his direction. She's lived with him for too long to think that she could influence his beliefs.

Grandpa never watches television or listens to the news on the radio. My father says he has a collection of magazines and newspapers from Mosaddegh's era that he guards with his life. Every morning he takes one of the papers out of the box by his bed and reads it, cover to cover, as if it's fresh off the press. I wonder how many times he's read each article by now.

Grandpa kisses my closed eyes, then sits in a chair by the grandfather clock that hasn't worked for years and asks my grandma for a cup of tea. My mother tells Grandma to sit still and runs to the kitchen to bring tea, sweets, and fruits. Grandpa looks at the clock beside him, and I whisper that the time is wrong. He looks at me, and then looks at the clock again, but doesn't say anything. After a few seconds, I hear him whispering, "It's not wrong, it just shows a different time!"

"Thank God you're back; thank God you're okay," Grandma repeats, her hands shaking as she reaches over to touch my face.

Grandpa whispers something under his breath, as he does every time Grandma mentions God; my father and uncles chuckle. Grandpa then turns around and looks at the broken grandfather clock again.

All the attention is on me now, and I don't like it. I can tell from everyone's eyes that they are saddened by my frail appearance, but no one wants me to think so. Every time I catch someone looking at me, they smile and try to look happy—except Aunt Mateen, who just hides her face so that I can't see her tears.

Just as everyone begins to drink their tea, the doorbell rings and Mr. and Mrs. Kasravi walk into the yard. Mr. Kasravi is carrying Shabnam, my future wife, in his arms. Everyone runs to the door and creates a happy commotion by all talking at the same time.

"How was the trip?"

"It was fine."

"Oh, God, you guys must be tired!"

"That's a devil of a road. If someone just added a few lanes to that damn highway, the trip itself wouldn't be more than ninety minutes long."

"My nephew is destined to build a four-lane highway that will connect Tehran to Noshahr," Uncle Mansoor interjects.

"Mosaddegh wanted to do that, before the Americans and the British arranged a coup."

"Yeah, that's a tiring trip, really, really tiring."

"Come in, come in! The tea is ready."

Mr. Kasravi sets Shabnam down and hugs me. "So how are you, my boy? Really, how are you?" he asks. "I called every day to get an update on you. I'm so glad you're back, really glad!"

Goli Jaan looks at me and begins to cry. "You have lost so much weight!" she says. "You better come up to see us soon. The clean air of the mountains would do you lots of good."

My father leads the way to the living room, and everyone follows. As we are walking through the yard, I look up and see the Masked Angel on the balcony of the third floor. She steps back as soon as she realizes she's been spotted. In the living room, Aunt Mateen sits next to me, puts her arm around my shoulder, and whispers, "How do you feel, dear?"

"Oh, he's fine," Uncle Mansoor says boisterously. "Look at him, he's a strong kid."

"Yes, he is," says Mr. Kasravi. "My future son-in-law is most certainly very strong."

Aunt Mateen looks at my frail body and shakes her head as she tries to hold back her tears.

"Don't do that," Uncle Mansoor chides. "The kid is going to think there is something wrong with him."

"Yeah, he'll be boxing in no time," Uncle Majeed says.

Uncle Mansoor interrupts Uncle Majeed. He's so happy that I've learned the basics of boxing from my father. Now he intends to teach me the advanced stuff. Everyone, including Dad, laughs. Then Uncle Mansoor says while I'm studying civil engineering at the university in the U.S. and making plans to build the four-lane European-style high-way that will connect Tehran to Noshahr, I'll be beating the living day-lights out of my opponents in the ring. A large grin flashes on his face.

Aunt Maryam tells me that she loves me, and that she can't wait to host me in her home so that she can feed me kebob, rice, fresh veg-etables, homemade yogurt, and her special salad of cucumber, salt, pepper, and mint, followed by some nice Lahijan tea. Then I'll be ready to play tennis. Yes, tennis—because boxing is the sport of fools and I'm too smart to follow in the footsteps of her crazy brothers, who take pride in beating people up. She tells me to forget everything my father has taught me and prepare for my tennis lessons, which she will pay for out of her own pocket. My mom uses this opportunity to give my dad a dirty look, which he ignores completely. A heated argu-ment ensues with Aunt Maryam shaking both her head and her fin-ger vigorously.

Now everybody is talking at the same time and nobody seems to be listening to anybody else.

My father watches everyone without saying anything. I can tell from the anxious look on his face and the frequency with which he glances toward the door that he is impatiently awaiting Mrs. Mehrbaan's ar-rival. I still don't understand why he's so eager to see her.

"Look at your noses, both of you!" Aunt Maryam says to her two brothers. "Do you have any idea how our mother cried when she saw your broken noses?" Grandma looks at her two sons, shakes her head, and says a prayer. Grandpa shakes his head and whispers profanity under his breath, prompting Grandma to bite the skin between her thumb and index finger.

"It's not shameful for a man to have an ugly, broken nose," Uncle Mansoor argues. "A man's not supposed to be pretty."

"Oh, for God's sake!" cries out Aunt Maryam.

"Besides, nobody can even tell that my nose is broken! See, it's like I don't have a bone in there," Uncle Mansoor says, putting his finger on the tip of his nose and pushing down. His nostrils come together, making him look like an old man, and I begin to laugh. Everyone notices that I'm laughing, and they all join me with relieved expressions on their faces. My mother comes out of the kitchen with more tea.

The doorbell rings again, and Mrs. Mehrbaan walks in. Like Zari's mother, she looks much older than I remember her. The mood in the house becomes somber as soon as she enters. My father is excited to see her. He runs ahead of everyone to greet her. "I'm so glad you're here," he says. "I was so worried that you might have decided not to come."

She ignores my father completely and pushes through the crowd toward me. "I get to see Pasha first," she says. "I get to see him first. How're you, my dear?" She hugs me and whispers, "We missed you very much. I prayed for your safe return every day. I wish Mehrbaan were here to see you, too. I don't know if anyone has told him in jail. I would have told him myself, but they won't let me see him. They won't even tell me where he is. Oh, your poor dad has tried so hard to get some information, but they won't tell us anything."

"I hope they release Uncle Mehrbaan soon," I say.

Mrs. Mehrbaan hugs me again. "Oh, God, I hope so, my son, I really hope so," she whispers.

Right at that moment, Ahmed and Faheemeh arrive. "Look, our soon-to-be bride and groom just walked in!" my father says joyfully. Mr. Kasravi runs ahead of everyone to greet them. The chaotic din of everyone talking over one another is restored. Faheemeh is introduced to everyone, and they take turns hugging her and welcoming her to the house. Uncle Majeed thanks Faheemeh for having mercy on a guy like Ahmed, whose shortcomings he can count on the fingers of one hand. He counts one, two, three, four, five on one hand—and then six, seven, and on using the same hand. Everyone laughs, and Uncle Majeed puts his arms around Ahmed and says to Faheemeh that she has landed one of the best men in the world. Faheemeh smiles and thanks him. I hug Faheemeh, and as we start walking toward the living room, I look up toward the roof and see that the Masked Angel has returned to the balcony of the third floor.

Inside the house, Mrs. Mehrbaan tells Faheemeh that she is very happy that Ahmed has been released. "I know how difficult it is to be away from the person you love the most. God knows I have been through that. The first time they took him away, I was young and he was young. We were both full of idealistic plans and the future seemed like a road that had no end. But this time it's different. We're getting old, and desperately need each other's companionship." I'm surprised that Mrs. Mehrbaan delivers this long speech without shedding any tears. The passage of time has hardened her quite a bit.

My father brings out a bottle of vodka and says that it's time for a celebration. He pours drinks for all the men and raises his shot glass to say, "To my son's return," and then he turns to Ahmed and Faheemeh, "and to my other son's engagement." We all drink up. My mother looks anxiously at Ahmed and me. I know she thinks we're too young to drink, but she would never say anything to embarrass us. The bitter taste of the vodka makes me squirm, and again reminds me of the night of Doctor's funeral. Everyone laughs at the face I make. Dad immediately tops off the shot glasses again and says, "This one we drink to the return of Mehrbaan." We all chug our drinks.

The women join my mother in the kitchen to help her serve lunch. My father calls my mother into the hallway and asks nervously if it's not too soon to be serving lunch. My mother, who has never known my father to interfere in her affairs, gives him an exasperated look and walks away. My father checks his watch, only to realize that he's not wearing one. He then looks at the broken grandfather clock and whispers something under his breath.

I ask Dad if there is something wrong. He answers there isn't. And of course my suspicion is only heightened by his denial. But what can it be? His uncharacteristic behavior makes me wonder if he's on some kind of drug.

My father complains that it's too early to serve lunch, a domestic decision he would never get involved in under ordinary circumstances. The guests respond that they're hungry.

"It's almost two o'clock in the afternoon," Uncle Majeed objects.

"It is?" My father looks at his empty wrist again. Then he comes back into the room and fills everyone's glasses, raises his, and says, "Here's to friendship."

Everyone downs their drinks.

My father asks me what time it is. This time I look right into his eyes to see if I can detect an ailment. Is he fatigued? Losing his mind? Already drunk? I just hope he's not sick. As if in response, the doorbell rings. My father tells me to go to the yard to open the door, then runs to the kitchen to ask everyone to come out because we have a new guest.

As I'm walking toward the door, I turn around and look to see if the Masked Angel is still on the balcony of Zari's house. There's no one up there.

I open the door, and am shocked to see Mr. Mehrbaan in the alley. He jumps forward and hugs me, almost as hard as Zari's father did when we visited their house. Pandemonium breaks out inside the house. Everyone starts screaming with excitement and running toward the door.

Mrs. Mehrbaan is the first one to reach us. I get out of the way as husband and wife fall into each other's arms. Everyone is in the yard now and talking at the same time, except for my father, who quietly watches the scene from the terrace on the first floor. Obviously he knew that Mr. Mehrbaan was getting released today. The frantic look in his eyes has faded. I watch him for a long time. He doesn't know that I'm watching him; he also doesn't know that I hope someday I can be just like him.

As others try to hug Mr. Mehrbaan, Mrs. Mehrbaan sits down on the ground and weeps.

"Thank God, thank God!" she cries out, beating her chest. "I never thought I would see this day." My mother hugs her and tells her that she should be laughing because her man is safe and free. But Mrs. Mehrbaan is caught in a fit of emotion that won't soon subside. Mr. Kasravi hugs Mr. Mehrbaan and tells him he's happy to see his old friend safe and healthy. Grandma says we need to burn some *espand* to keep the devil away, and Grandpa shoots her a dirty look.

Finally, my father and Mr. Mehrbaan hug. They laugh and whisper things to each other. Mrs. Mehrbaan is still sitting on the floor, rocking gently and crying. Her hands shake, her eyebrows twitch, and she sputters wetly.

I look toward the roof and discover that the Masked Angel has returned to her post on the third-floor balcony. Does she know what is going on, and is she crying, too? As soon as she again realizes that I'm looking at her, she steps back into the shadows.

We all go to the living room. "This is the best day of my life," my father keeps saying. "My best friends are here, my family is here, and my two sons are here." He points at Ahmed and me.

My father pours still more vodka for everyone and we all drink to Mr. Mehrbaan. He throws back his drink, wipes his thick mustache on the sleeve of his coat, and looks at his wife, biting his lips to hold back the tears. All the women start to cry, too, as the men turn their heads away politely. I hear my grandpa whispering something to the effect that our predicament is the fault of the damn British.

Mrs. Mehrbaan doesn't take her eyes off her husband. She whispers prayers as she wipes her tears away. My father breaks the silence by asking Mr. Mehrbaan how he is doing. He shakes his head and whispers that he is okay, then breaks out into a bitter sob. I know that sob; I remember it from my hospital days. That sob speaks of a broken heart and a shattered spirit, of a pain too violent to be verbalized, except in the choked language of tears. I wish my father would pour us another drink! The bitter taste of vodka doesn't bother me anymore and I welcome its numbing effect on my nerves, just as it had on the night of Doctor's funeral.

Ahmed seems touched by all that has happened in our little house today. He is in awe of Mr. Mehrbaan. I'm glad that he finally got a chance to meet him. And I'm sure they have a lot to compare notes about as two men who had been wrongfully jailed.

"Why did they take you away?" Mrs. Mehrbaan asks as her voice chokes up.

"They never tell you why," he says.

My two aunts are sitting next to each other near Mrs. Mehrbaan. They're holding each other's hands as tears roll down their faces. My uncles smoke their cigarettes and are uncharacteristically quiet. My future wife is sitting on her mother's lap playing with a doll. Will she remember this day when she grows up? Mr. Kasravi is sitting on the floor by my father, and I have no doubt that he wants to say something about the Qajars and their backward policies, but knows better than to interrupt this moment that belongs to the Mehrbaans.

Lunch is followed by more drinking, which is followed by dinner and still more drinking. I'm totally drunk, and so is every other male in the house. Mrs. Mehrbaan sits next to her husband, and even though it's considered rude in our culture for couples to be affectionate in public, Mr. Mehrbaan puts his arm around her shoulders and holds her close.

I have no recollection of when Ahmed and Faheemeh left, or how I got to bed. When I open my eyes, I'm lying on a mattress in the living room remembering a very strange dream I just had. An orange grove lies at the foot of a mountain, with a river flowing through it from the south to the north. Dark clouds are rapidly approaching the mountain from the west, and far, far off a stroke of lightning illuminates the skies as drops of rain, one by one, dance their way to the ground. The slopes are covered with white, fragrant orange blossoms that blanket the ground like snow. A dazzling glare makes it difficult to see straight down the mountain. Suddenly, the outline of a figure appears on the incline. I squint to get a better glimpse of who might be approaching me, but the glare is too bright. I recognize the eyes of the Masked Angel behind the lace of a white burqa, blinking rhythmically to the beat of my heart. It all reminds me of the picture Zari drew of my mystery woman, in the setting I had so clumsily described to her in the kitchen the first time we were alone.

The white figure stops a couple of meters away from me. Her large blue eyes stare into mine.

The wind picks up, blowing blossoms into the air in a whirling blizzard of heady scent. The Masked Angel struggles to keep her balance. I reach to grab her hand under her burqa, but she floats away from me, propelled back by the wind. I try to hold on to her, but unmerciful Mother Nature circles her, blowing away the Masked Angel's burqa. I squint to catch a glimpse of her but the stormy riot of white blossoms makes it impossible to see.

What a strange dream.

Then I wonder why the SAVAK won't tell us where Zari is buried. What's the harm in that? A lump crawls into my throat. I look at the clock again. I wish I were smart enough to fix it.

27

Shade in Shadow

I'm sitting in the living room, staring out the window at our yard, and as usual am lost in my own thoughts. I hear Dad talking to Mom: "Time flies. He'll get over this before we know it, I'm sure of it."

Time flies? How absurd! So not only is time the most precious human commodity and the cure of all pains, it flies, too!

Ahmed, Iraj, and the rest of the kids in the alley spend all day in class. I don't miss school, but being alone bothers me a lot. I've told Dad that I won't go back to our school next year without Ahmed and Iraj. He understands and he's making arrangements for me to leave for the States in just a few short months. "It's not safe for you to remain in Iran," he says. "You never know when the SAVAK may decide to revisit this case because a new detainee says something that implicates Doctor."

The thought of leaving Iran and being alone in a country twelve thousand miles away doesn't appeal to me, either.

During the days, the majority of my time is spent on the third floor of our house, where I'm free to clutch the pillow I've come to depend on, regardless of whether I'm sitting, lying down, or pacing back and forth in my room. The tighter I hold it, the calmer I feel. It provides a much-needed buffer between my surroundings and me. Sometimes I find myself sitting in one spot for hours, staring at nothing, thinking of nothing, feeling nothing, and, most disturbingly, caring about nothing. A persistent silence has taken over my life. Life moves on, and I seem to be standing still, defying its demand for change. I live in my life without touching it, without feeling it, and certainly without appreciating it.

From time to time, I wish that I could go back to when every memory of the past looked like a chapter in a fairy tale. Sometimes, out of boredom, I pick up a book to read, only to realize that I'm just staring, eyes unfocused, at the pages. Not long ago I was celebrating taking control of my life, like a man. That all seems like a joke to me now.

A few days after my strange dream, I remember the night Zari drew the picture of me staring at the faceless girl floating toward the mountains. I remember pinning the drawing to the wall. I see the hole in the plaster where it used to hang. I look behind the books on the shelf, inside the briefcase that my father bought me in my first year of high school, but the drawing has vanished.

I ask my mother about the picture, and she says she doesn't know anything about it, while my father says he would never take anything out of my room without asking me first. I cover the hole in the wall, and wish someone could do the same with the one in my heart.

Some nights, after everyone has gone to bed, I look out the window of my room to where Zari and I used to sit. I remember holding her in my arms, her head on my shoulder and her eyes closed. My eyes fill quickly, and I feel short of breath, as if a heavy object has been placed on my chest. The feeling is so real that the only way for me to escape the illusion is to get up and walk. I usually end up on the terrace, where I try to keep my glance from falling on anything that might remind me of Zari, but my eyes eventually wander toward her room. Her lights are always on, and the curtains are always pulled shut. Sometimes I can see the Masked Angel's shadow behind the curtains. Her silhouette flows through the prayer movements: hands up by the ears, then body bending forward, and eventually sitting down with her head on the *mohr*. The weather is cold and I can see my breath, but I still would rather be outside than in my room, where the walls seem to close in on me at times.

One night, the window to Zari's room is open and I hear the Masked Angel reciting a poem. I remember Zari telling me that she had memorized Hafiz's entire *Divan*. I try to listen to her voice, but all I hear is a constricted whisper. I look around. The moon is fastened to the belly of the sky, and the night outside my window is drowned in moonlight. The buildings cast shadows that seem bolted to something that itself is bolted to everything else. It's in these shadows that I feel Zari is keeping her promise of being with me. I burn with a desire to penetrate the darkness and merge with the shadows. I search for her in the darkest areas, intently fixing my glance at one spot and then the next, hoping that she's watching me and that we might make brief eye contact. I feel her presence, and I want to leave the room, but I'm afraid of not finding her.

On another evening, I'm sitting in my room by the window and looking toward the terrace of Zari's house when suddenly someone moves in the shadows. My heart leaps. It looked as if someone glided from one spot to another: a shift in location, a quick displacement, and then a permanent pause. The moving person is now static, fixed in one spot. Is it my imagination, or is someone out there? I remember Apple Face talking about an illness that makes people hallucinate. Am I losing my mind?

I concentrate on dilating my eyes to better explore the shape that fades in and out of the darkness, but I'm not sure that the silhouette I'm staring at has a real outline. The more I look into the night, the less certain I am that the piece of darkness that has attracted my attention is anything more than night framed by itself. I get up and switch off the light in my room. I come back and sit in the same spot as before, searching for the outline. There is nothing out there. Even the silhouette is gone.

It's a mild but pitch-black night. I walk quietly out onto the terrace and look toward Zari's room. The lights are off. The window to her room is open, and as the wind blows through, the curtains move like a woman in the arms of an accomplished dance partner. I sit on the short wall that separates our homes. I remember how she and I used to sit together on her side of the wall and read poetry. I slide down on her terrace and sit at the same spot, pretending that she is sitting next to me. I'm suddenly catapulted into a sea of melancholy. I land smoothly and without much of a splash, just a sudden surge of pain and a flood of tears. I lean my head against the wall, close my eyes, and collapse inside myself.

Zari and I are walking up a hill that's engulfed in a hazy mist. Down below, the prairies are wrapped in withered green weeds. The wind blows in more than one direction and the grass bends and twists passively. The skies above are an inky blue and free of the charcoal darkness that normally accentuates the luster of the stars at night. There's a marvelous scent in the air, refreshing and clean, that leaves my nostrils craving more, my lungs longing for a finer share.

Is this really a dream?

Zari is wearing a white cotton dress and I'm in a dark suit. She turns and looks at me. I have my right arm around her waist. She rests her head on my shoulder, and her face touches mine. I kiss her face over and over and whisper that I love her, and that I don't ever want to be without her. If this is a dream, I don't want to wake up.

Zari tells me that this is not a dream.

Then we are on the terrace of her house. She's sitting behind me, holding my head to her chest with her arms wrapped around my neck. I can't see her face.

"It's cool out," she whispers. "And you're not wearing much. Don't you know that I don't want my sweetheart to catch a cold?"

I press myself against her and she tightens her grip on me. I keep my eyes closed. I don't want to test her existence by opening them. Her voice is all I need.

"I will keep you warm with the heat of my own body until the sun comes up, and then I must go," she says.

"I don't want you to leave," I cry.

She touches my face, kisses my cheeks, and assures me that she is never far away, never too far. In the merest whisper she says she loves me, but I'm not to mourn her loss; this is what was meant to be. She is glad I visited her parents, and was strong enough not to cry in their presence.

You are my angel, I tell her, but she replies that no one can see an angel. No one can hear or feel an angel.

So, I tell myself, if I hear Zari's sweet voice and if I feel her warm weight, I must be dreaming. I want to turn to embrace her, but a paralyzing heaviness engulfs my entire being.

When I open my eyes, I can't remember where I am. I look around and realize that I'm sitting under the wall on Zari's terrace. The sun is coming up in the east, and the air has a chill that makes me want to crawl under the covers. Then I notice that a blanket is wrapped around me. It's not one of our blankets, and I certainly don't remember coming out of my room with it. I look toward Zari's room, and see that her window is shut. *Did the Masked Angel wrap the blanket around me, or was it Ahmed?* Ahmed would have woken me up. The blanket has a sweet fragrance, a brand of women's perfume unknown to me. Is this Zari's blanket? Did she once wind it around her beautiful body to keep herself warm at night? Maybe it was she who wrapped it around me last night!

The location of the sun tells me it must be around six in the morning. I look toward the alley, and see the Masked Angel walking back toward the house from the bakery. She's carrying two large pieces of *Barbari* bread.

She walks fast. Much faster than Zari used to.

She enters the yard and shuts the door behind her. Once she disappears inside the house, I fold the blanket and leave it on the wall between our homes. I go to my room and crawl into my bed, consumed with my dream of Zari. The gloom of loneliness crushes my soul. I tell myself that I was sleeping in her arms last night, and realize that even this outrageous lie doesn't make me feel better.

The next evening finds me once more sitting in my room, hugging my pillow and looking out the window. It's a dark, cloudy night with no sign of the moon and the weight of eventual rain in the air. Although it's quiet, a persistent hum from an unidentifiable source soothes the ears and calms the soul. I look toward Zari's balcony, searching for the silhouette that had sculpted a piece of the night into a hopeful illusion the evening before. Maybe if I look hard enough, I can find it. Maybe if I dilate my eyes and watch more carefully, it will appear again.

There it is—a shade, a trace, liquid night outlined. I watch it intently, waiting for it to move like it did last night. Maybe if I could float through my window gently, it would not be scared away. Whatever it is, it's motionless, completely stagnant in time and space, and it's watching me back. Suddenly, the wind blows and the curtains at my window fly into my face. Outside, a piece of the darkness vibrates as the dark air flutters, and night itself trembles. The shadow solidifies and dances to the tune of the wind. I know whatever was out there moved, I'm sure of it. I am not hallucinating. The hair on the back of my neck stands up.

I run out onto the balcony, but it's empty. I stand for a long time, looking around. Finally, I cross over to Zari's side and sit in our spot. I look toward her room. The lights are on, but the window is shut and covered. After a few minutes rain starts to fall, and the temperature falls quickly. The lights in most of the alley are off. I look at my watch: eleven thirty.

Behind Zari's curtain, the Masked Angel moves from one side of the room to the other, and I glimpse her profile for a split second. She's not wearing her burqa, but she passes by the window too quickly for me to see her face. I'm dying to know what she looks like. She lives in the room where my Zari used to live, sleeping in her bed, sitting in the same chair I sat in while holding her in my arms. I walk up to Zari's window and peep through the opening in the curtain. My heart races and the blood rushes to my head. My hands are shaking, my knees weak from excitement, and the surface of my skin goes cold.

The Masked Angel is sitting in the middle of the room with her back to the window. Her head is lowered and she's reading a book: Hafiz's *Divan*, the one she has memorized.

Why is she reading the book if she has memorized it?

She's wearing a long dark dress that drapes her body from the neck to the ankles. A blue scarf covers her head and hides her hair. The black burqa is on a chair by the round table. The blanket that was wrapped around me the night before is by the bed. I look to the other side of the room and see the little notebook that contains Zari's drawings. Oh, what I would give to possess that notebook!

Suddenly, the Masked Angel lifts her head from the book and stares straight ahead, as if she knows someone is watching her through the window. I want to run back to my terrace, but my feet are glued to the ground. I can see her shoulders rise and fall as she breathes. She turns slightly to one side for a split second, and then lowers her head and continues to read.

Thanking God that she didn't turn around, I creep back to my room.

28

An Incurable Disease

It's been over a month since I was released from the hospital. The Persian New Year, celebrated on the first day of spring, has brought a tremendous energy to the neighborhood. The schools are closed for the first thirteen days of the year, when people travel, visit each other, exchange gifts, and forget and forgive old quarrels. The spirit of the New Year even moves the Shah, causing him to forgive a number of political prisoners and to pardon some common criminals. I wonder if he would've ever pardoned Doctor. Even my aunt and uncle make up and forget about their differences. I, however, am still trapped in the dark winter of my life, and I can't find a way out. Ahmed and Iraj stop over often. I enjoy their company, but sometimes as they're talking, I drift away and tune them out, just as everything outside of me gets blocked out.

Early one evening, I'm outside my room on the terrace when I hear Ahmed's grandma.

"He's coming to take me away," she declares from the balcony of Ahmed's house.

"Who's coming, Grandma?" I call.

Her wrinkled forehead tightens up as she says, "My husband. He's giving me a New Year's present by taking me away."

"Oh," I say, feeling sad for her, but wishing that Zari or Doctor would come to me with the same present.

I notice that she has a touch of makeup on her face. "You look nice, Grandma," I tell her.

"I wanted to look good for him," she says. "You know, we talk every night, but he doesn't let me see him."

"Do you see him, Grandma?" I ask, thinking about my own Zari, gliding in the night shadows.

"Oh, yes, I see him every night ever since he went away," she says, the trace of a sad smile on her face. "You see him, too, don't you?"

"Where do you look for him?"

Grandma squints at me, as if she doesn't understand my question.

"Does he hide in the dark?" I prompt. "Does he ever move, or does he stay still?"

"Still?" she asks, obviously not understanding what I'm talking about. She shuffles to the edge of the balcony, and again I hear my mother's voice in the back of my mind. *Hundreds of people fall off these damn roofs every year.* I quickly move closer to Grandma to make sure that I can catch her in case she loses her balance.

"He wants me to go away with him this time," she whispers, a serious look in her eyes.

"Has he ever talked to you?" I ask.

"Talked to me?"

"Yeah."

Grandma thinks for a while. "I don't know. I'm hard of hearing. If he does, I don't hear him."

"But you hear my wife crying, don't you?"

"Your wife? Why does she cry?"

I look at Grandma's confused face and wish I hadn't brought up the subject.

"You shouldn't let your wife cry," she says. "My husband never let me cry. He never did."

"Yes, Grandma."

"You know how he and I met?" she says, a crooked little smile dawning on her face.

"At the American embassy?"

"American embassy?" she murmurs blankly.

"No, Grandma," I correct myself, "I don't know. How did you meet?"

"Would you like me to tell you?" she says, animated now.

"Yes, please."

"When I was seventeen," she begins, "I was diagnosed with an incurable disease. An incurable disease, they called it. My poor mother prayed day and night, asking God to have mercy on me, as if God had nothing better to do!" Suddenly a bewildered expression creeps over Grandma's face. "Have you ever been seventeen years old?" she asks.

"Yes, Grandma."

"Oh," she mumbles. "Never had an incurable disease though, right?"

"No, Grandma. I never did."

She thinks for a while, as if she's lost track of where she is in the story. Finally she asks, "Do you think heaven and hell are connected?"

"What?" I ask.

"My mother used to say that God dug a huge hole in the ground and filled it with fire, then built heaven on top of it. But that doesn't make any sense, does it? That would make the floor of heaven too hot to pray on, don't you think?"

I want to laugh, but I hold it in.

"But then, if heaven and hell aren't connected," she continues, "what's in between them?" She turns around and looks at me inquisitively. I shrug my shoulders to indicate that I don't know the answer.

"My poor mother used to cry all night long because I had an

incurable disease, and I was going to die and go to heaven," she says, "wherever the hell heaven is. She fasted and gave money to the poor, she sacrificed a lamb a month and gave the most tender meat to the poor. She cooked a special soup called *aash* and fed it to the poor, and all along I'm thinking, 'I'm the one who's dying, why are the poor getting all the treats?'"

Grandma smiles, realizing she has made a clever joke, and I grin encouragingly at her.

"I had a horrible pain in my stomach all the time," she says. "On top of that, I couldn't keep food down and always threw up everything that touched my lips. Life couldn't be more miserable, and all of this when I was only seventeen years old." She shakes her head. "Seventeen's not a good age. That's when you realize that you have a heart. That's when feelings get in the way of thinking." She pauses for a while.

"Ahmed's grandpa lived a few doors down from us. He was a young, handsome man, a very handsome man. Every time I saw him, I cried and cried and cried." She pauses for a while again, staring into the night. Finally she says, "Did I tell you that he's coming back to take me away?"

"Yes, Grandma."

"He came back before, but I couldn't go. This time I'd like to go with him, I really would." Grandma is silent for a long time. She looks down into the yard and takes a deep breath. I inch closer to her, fearing that she may lose her balance and fall off the edge. The look on her face is so confused that I can't possibly guess where her mind is. Finally she says, "One day, I climbed a big hill behind my father's house, and threw myself off a cliff."

"You threw yourself off a cliff?" I ask, moving closer still.

"What good is life if you have to live without the person you love? I remember now. I didn't have an incurable disease—I was in love. But then, love is an incurable disease, don't you think?"

In a whisper I agree that it is.

"Yes, of course. That's why all famous lovers die at the end of their stories."

Suddenly, Grandma seems totally cognizant of everything around her. The dazed, fuzzy look that made her seem half-witted and lost is replaced by the alert expression of an individual in full control of her faculties. She is sitting so close to me that I can count the number of wrinkles on her face, a face I've seen many times but never really looked at. She runs her fingers through her amazingly long gray hair and murmurs something under her breath. She was once tall and thin, but has grown stooped with age. Her eyes are a pale brown that borders on gray, the same color as my grandpa's eyes. I can tell from the shape of her long chin and the way she swallows the saliva in her mouth that she's wearing dentures.

She seems more like a portrait than a person, and I've learned to love her dearly.

"My father's home was built near a cliff. Did I tell you that already?" she asks in a voice that is scratchy but kind, like my own grandmother's voice.

"Yes, you did, Grandma."

"I was in the air forever, thinking I was going to die for sure. Who can survive a fall like that? I lost consciousness in the air. When I opened my eyes, I found myself in his arms. He saw me jumping off the cliff, and he caught me."

"That's wonderful, Grandma. He must have been a very strong man."

"Oh, yes, the strongest man in the world," Grandma remembers with a faraway smile.

"That's right," I hear Ahmed's voice affirm from the darkness, "he caught my grandma in the air. He was the strongest man in the world."

"He's coming to take me away," Grandma tells Ahmed.

"Yes, Grandma. I told you he'll be back soon," Ahmed says, hugging her frail, bent frame.

"He wants to surprise me," she says, buried in Ahmed's embrace. "And someday we'll come back and surprise you two. That would be nice now, wouldn't it?"

"Very nice," Ahmed agrees, and I nod. She starts limping back toward the house.

"That would be very nice. Yes, very nice indeed," she mumbles as she disappears inside.

Ahmed shakes his head and smiles. "My grandma's stories are getting more creative and amusing. She is an amazing person. Did you know she was one of the first women in her town to do away with the chador?"

"No!" I reply, surprised.

"Most people don't know it, but she was. And in Ghamsar, of all places! Not the most progressive city in the world." A sad smile softens his face. "She was the first woman in her town to get a high school diploma. She was rebellious, tough-minded, and hard as a rock. Her parents married her off to my grandpa to get rid of her." Ahmed smirks. "Grandma didn't want him, hated him. In fifty years she never said an affectionate word to him, not that he expected it."

I shake my head. Grandma's endless dreams of Grandpa remind me a bit too much of my nightly search for Zari in the shadows. I wonder if someday I'll be wandering around the neighborhood making up stories about Zari being a college professor or saving cats from burning buildings.

"He was a good man, and put up with her patiently," Ahmed continues. "I think he was the only one who took her seriously. He never complained about her, either. Some of Grandpa's friends thought he was a weak man. Neighbors in Ghamsar would say that he wasn't a man at all, that he couldn't take her in bed and that's why she was as aggressive as she was. Grandpa didn't mind, didn't listen to any of it—but she did. So she had four kids in a row."

A sly expression creeps over Ahmed's face.

"I wonder if those were the only times she let him have her."

I smile.

"Did you know that she's an atheist?" Ahmed asks.

"No."

"A woman of her age, with her upbringing in Ghamsar, not believing in God? Can you imagine? She's lucky she wasn't stoned to death. My dad says she has never prayed for anything, but that all of her wishes have come true."

"How?"

"Grandpa," Ahmed says, lighting up a cigarette. "He was the God she never worshipped, and now she sees him everywhere."

29

An Angel Calling

My mother brings up hot tea, but I pretend to be asleep in my chair. She leaves the room without waking me up. I've told her that I fall asleep faster when I'm not in bed. Lying in bed seems to shift my brain into hyperactive chaos. I toss and turn and get frustrated, so I end up back in the chair with a book, dozing off after reading only a few pages.

I don't know what time I really fall asleep, but my much-needed rest is suddenly interrupted by a woman's cry. I'm not sure where the sound has come from, but I feel the hair on the back of my neck rise. It was undoubtedly the cry of a woman, and it definitely came from outside my window. I want to open my eyes and look outside, but I'm too tired. I listen carefully, only to hear the silence of an undisturbed night. I remember Ahmed's grandma saying that she heard the girl next door crying. *Your wife misses you. She cries for you every night, like I cry for Grandpa.* A shiver ripples down my spine.

I hear another soft cry, this one from directly outside my window. A chill sweeps through me, and I begin to shake uncontrollably. I open my eyes and look at my watch. It's four in the morning.

There is another cry. I throw my pillow on the ground and rush outside to the terrace. I'm afraid to look toward Zari's room, but that's where my attention is drawn. Her window is open, but the curtains are shut tight. Who's crying, and why? Is it the Masked Angel? Why would she cry? Does she miss Zari? Maybe she's homesick and misses her parents. Maybe she's in love with a man back home and misses him. No, that can't be; she doesn't strike me as that kind of woman.

I listen carefully and attentively, but hear nothing more. I sit on the short wall that separates my balcony from Zari's and wonder whether I should walk up to her window and look inside. A mild breeze moves her curtains; the light in her room is off. Should I cross over? What's the use? It's too dark, and I won't be able to see anything.

The pounding of my heart fills my ears and chest. Suddenly, something moves beneath the short wall on Zari's balcony. I look down—it's the Masked Angel. She's sitting motionless in the same spot where Zari and I used to sit, where I was sitting a few nights earlier dreaming of being with Zari. I want to say something, but my voice has died. I want to walk back to my room before she looks up, but I can't move, just like the night Doctor was taken away.

Gracefully and silently, she stands up, as if she knew all along that I was there, as if she expected me to be there. She turns toward me. The moonlight penetrates the black lace that makes up the front of her burqa, and beneath it two moist, turquoise eyes shine like stars in a velvet sea of darkness. She breathes gently, and I feel there's not enough oxygen in the universe to fill my lungs. The Masked Angel is about the same height, maybe even the same shape, although the veil makes it impossible to know for sure. It's amazing how long a moment of utter stillness can last!

Suddenly a mild wind blows from the south and shifts her black burqa, reminding me of the evening when a piece of night fluttered outside my window. Oh, my God, could that have been the Masked Angel, woven into the darkness of the night, seamlessly riding the shadows, watching me rock back and forth in my chair?

The Masked Angel turns and starts walking back toward Zari's room. The tail of her burqa drags behind her, collecting dust from the concrete. Her head is turned toward me as she walks away. I want to tell her to stop, but my voice is hiding. She enters the house and closes the glass door behind her. I sit for some time on the edge of the wall that separates our houses. Is the Masked Angel watching me at night? Why? What curiosity draws her to me? What did Zari tell her? Maybe she wants to see how badly I hurt.

Hours go by, but I'm sleepless.

30

Enshallah

Ahmed wasn't kidding when he said that no one could break his spirit by beating him up in a stinking jail. He's more defiant and rebellious than ever. He says what he wants, and does what pleases him. According to Iraj, he openly criticizes the school officials, especially Mr. Gorji, our onetime powerless religion teacher turned maniacal school principal.

"He's a fascist," Ahmed told everyone on the school grounds a week or so ago, when Mr. Gorji was standing only a few meters away.

"Who's a fascist, Ahmed?" Mr. Gorji asked.

"Mussolini, sir. Mussolini was a fascist; Idi Amin is a fascist. There are a lot of fascists in the world, sir. A whole lot of fascists!" Mr. Gorji looked at his rosary, said a prayer, and walked away. "And you're a fascist, sir," Ahmed whispers. Mr. Gorji turned around and looked at Ahmed, who smiled as if he was not afraid of Mr. Gorji's wrath at all.

"What's he going to do to me?" Ahmed asked Faheemeh, who was worried Ahmed was going too far.

"He'll make trouble for you, honey," Faheemeh said, while pleading with me to reason with him. "Don't you think? Please, tell him to stop this nonsense."

One day, Mr. Gorji told Ahmed that he needed to get a haircut.

"My barber has left on vacation, Mr. Gorji," Ahmed sniped.

"Really? Where to?"

"He's gone to Afghanistan. He's a drug smuggler, you know!"

Ahmed claims later he could tell Gorji wanted to slap him.

"The length of my hair is none of his business, don't you think? Who does the son of a bitch think he is? He's a control freak. Didn't you tell me once that fascists are control freaks?"

"No," I said, "you and I talked about anarchy, not fascism."

"All right, then. I must have read it somewhere. Fascists are control freaks. That should be the definition of fascism in the dictionary."

Faheemeh pleaded with him to stop. "You're not going to win a war with your principal, so why do this?"

"Because I hate the son of a bitch," Ahmed said.

Ahmed's hatred for Mr. Gorji costs him dearly. The next afternoon Ahmed comes home with his head shaved. Mr. Gorji brought a barber to school and forced Ahmed to get a number-two buzz cut while all the students and teachers watched in disbelief.

"He walked around in the yard, staring into the eyes of the kids who had gathered around us, telling them that he is the ultimate authority at school and that his decisions and commands should never be challenged," Ahmed recalls. The dejected look in Ahmed's eyes and the dispirited tone of his voice tell me that he is having a difficult time with the humiliating experience.

"Did you put up a fight?" I ask.

"No," he says. "I would have lost anyway. There's no sense fighting powerful people because you will lose. You wait for the right moment to strike back and get even."

"I'm sorry," I say.

A few minutes later Faheemeh comes over. She looks at Ahmed's head with a shocked look on her face.

"What did you do to yourself?" she asks, holding her fingers in front of her mouth.

"Gorji cut my hair," Ahmed says, forcing a grin.

"How?"

"With a pair of clippers!" Ahmed responds, exasperated. Faheemeh tries to hold back her laughter.

"You didn't hit him, did you?" she asks.

"No"—he scowls—"but I should have."

"Well, I'm glad you didn't," Faheemeh says. "Did you say anything?"

"Yeah, after he was done, I looked in a mirror and asked if he could bring the sideburns up a little bit."

Faheemeh puts her hand over her mouth and giggles. Ahmed looks at her with surprise.

"I'm sorry, but you look really funny!" she says, and finally laughs.

Ahmed widens his eyes at me. "She's laughing!"

I give an exaggerated shrug, hiding my grin.

"She is mocking me!" Ahmed says.

"No, no, no," Faheemeh soothes, then lets out a loud, boisterous laugh. "I just think you look really cute."

Ahmed looks at me.

"You do look cute," I say.

"I do?" he asks. "Really? How cute?"

"Really, really cute," Faheemeh says.

Ahmed turns back to me, and I nod my head in all seriousness to confirm.

"Yeah, you're right," he says, walking around proudly. "We'll call this the Ahmed Buzz and offer a free one to the kids in the alley. But only the kids in our own alley. Everybody else has to pay." He looks at me. "Hey, you, you're my first customer!" He runs inside the house and comes back with a pair of scissors in his hands and starts chasing me around the yard as Faheemeh laughs.

"Come here, you son of a bitch!" he yells. "I order you to get a haircut! Are you disobeying my supreme command? How dare you! You bastard son of a bitch!"

In the following days, Ahmed tries to avoid Mr. Gorji as much as possible. Knowing Ahmed, I'm sure he's formulating a plan of attack. Mr. Gorji, in turn, shows up in almost all of Ahmed's classes and sits in the back observing the teachers and the students.

"Yesterday, Gorji came to Mr. Bana's geometry class," Ahmed says. "From the second he walked in, I knew something was up. All the kids knew it, too. They all sat in their chairs with their backs straight, unsure where the ax was going to fall. But I knew. Gorji walked up to Mr. Bana and whispered something in his ear, then proceeded to the back of the room, where he had a good view of everyone. Mr. Bana didn't seem happy about what he was asked to do. He shifted his weight from one foot to the other a couple of times, nervously looked at Mr. Gorji, walked back and forth in front of his desk, then finally whispered my name and asked me to go to the board. Bana asked me to solve a theorem I'd never seen before." Ahmed looks down at his feet while touching his shaved head.

"What happened?" I ask.

"I couldn't solve it, of course. So he gave me a zero and Mr. Gorji walked out with a satisfied smile on his face."

"I'm sorry, honey," Faheemeh says.

Ahmed turns to me. "You remember how much we used to hate Mr. Bana? Now we all like him. Isn't that strange? Gorji makes everyone else look good. It's like having pain in multiple parts of your body. You only feel the one that hurts the most."

He then shakes his head, takes a deep breath, and says, "This zealot fraud is making the autocrats of yesterday look like angels of mercy. Isn't that bizarre?"

"What does Moradi think about all of this?" I ask, referring to our discipline teacher.

"Moradi is totally powerless. Gorji hates Moradi because he likes the Americans. According to Gorji, there's no nation in the world more deserving of hatred than the Americans, with the possible exception of the Israelis."

"I don't want to tell you what to do, but I think you need to find a way to make peace with him," Faheemeh says.

Ahmed ignores Faheemeh's comment. "Can you believe that bastard? He's going to show up in all of my classes and get me in trouble!"

"I'm so sorry, honey," Faheemeh says, beginning to cry.

"Oh, sweetheart," Ahmed soothes with a gentle smile on his face, "don't worry. Please, don't."

Faheemeh's tears have a strong impact on Ahmed because from that day on, he doesn't say much about his battles with Mr. Gorji. However, I notice that he reads the Koran all the time.

"Becoming religious?" I ask.

"Of course," he says with a smirk on his face.

I wonder what he's up to, but don't dare to ask. One night I hear him reciting verses out loud.

"You memorized all that?" I ask, impressed.

"Yep," he responds.

"How come?"

"Enshallah—God willing—you will find out soon." Then he smiles and walks away while reciting another verse.

I learn the reason for Ahmed's preoccupation with the Koran the following day, after school, when I hear the whole story. Mr. Gorji showed up at Mr. Bana's class, said hello to everyone, recited a prayer, then proceeded to the back of the classroom, where he signaled Mr. Bana to call on Ahmed. Mr. Bana, who didn't approve of Mr. Gorji's tactics and frequent visits to his class, looked understandably dejected. Ahmed immediately raised his hand and asked loudly if he could ask a question.

"Sure," said Mr. Bana.

"The question is for Mr. Gorji," Ahmed said.

"Yes," Mr. Gorji replied, "you may ask your question."

Ahmed recited a verse out of the Koran, and asked Mr. Gorji for a literal translation and commentary. Mr. Gorji, who doesn't speak Arabic, and only knows certain verses by memory, shook his head and coughed a couple of times to clear his throat, then said that Ahmed's accent made it difficult for him to understand which verse he was reciting. Ahmed took a small Koran out of his pocket, kissed it, pointed to a page, and said, "It's this one, sir. Here, would you like to read it?"

Mr. Gorji stood motionless, staring at Ahmed and knowing full well the fate that awaited him from now on if he ever stepped into another one of Ahmed's classes. Ahmed swore that he could see the sweat running down Gorji's face. After a long and agonizing moment, Mr. Gorji excused himself and left the room quickly. Laughter, applause, loud screams, and whistles followed his departure. Even Mr. Bana laughed and bowed to Ahmed!

"He won't be coming to my classes anymore," Ahmed says. "And I'm not done yet, I promise! Pretty soon I'll be following him in the yard, into his office, into the bathroom; I'll be wherever he is, reciting the Koran and asking him questions. I'll do whatever I can to embarrass him. I'll memorize every word of our holy book and expose the son of a bitch for the no-good pretender that he is. That's the way to deal with the Mr. Gorjis of the world, that powerless religious teacher turned emperor."

31

That Is All

I'm dozing off in the chair in my bedroom when a loud scream wakes me. This one is a far cry from the soft sobs of the Masked Angel. I recognize Ahmed's voice. I struggle against a fearful paralysis and haul myself to my feet. More noises begin to fill the alley: doors opening and closing, people running, women crying, and men huffing and puffing. I run out the door and onto the terrace.

"Oh, my God, oh, my God!" cries a woman, whose voice I recognize as Ahmed's mother's.

"Grandma, Grandma!" I hear Ahmed screaming.

I run to the edge of the terrace and see neighbors in the alley, rushing toward Ahmed's house. In Ahmed's yard, Grandma's body is lying on the ground, her entire family gathered around her. I cross over to Ahmed's terrace and head down the stairs, skipping two or three steps at a time.

Many of the neighbors are already in the yard when I finally reach the ground floor. Ahmed is leaning against a wall, his eyes bleary with tears. He slides slowly down and slumps on the ground. When he notices my presence, he shakes his head in disbelief and anguish, as Iraj sits down next to him and puts his arm around him. Iraj's mother and a number of other women attend to Ahmed's mother, who is crying next to Grandma's body. Ahmed's father whispers prayers as a number of men try to console him.

The yard seems dark, and there's an uncomfortable chill in the air that I recognize from my previous encounters with death. The light from the living room makes the single tree in Ahmed's yard cast a grotesque shadow, in which Grandma's twisted body rests.

Zari's parents enter the yard at the same moment that I look toward the roof and see the Masked Angel in her black burqa looking down at the commotion. She must notice me because as usual she immediately takes a step back and melts into the shadows.

Grandma's skull is crushed, her joints wrenched from the force of the impact. The neighbors walk around carefully to avoid stepping in the blood that peppers the yard. It's difficult for me to accept Grandma's death. Only a couple of nights ago she unleashed her imagination and told me improbable stories of her childhood and her late husband. A wave of grief and anxiety crashes over my heart, for Grandma's death is a painful reminder of the anguish I have bottled up inside me from the loss of Doctor and Zari. *Why is life so cruel?*

Ahmed's father cries, "I told her to stay away from that damn roof. She must have walked right off the edge."

Iraj shakes his head and bites the thick hair on his upper lip. Ahmed whispers, "Grandpa didn't catch her this time."

"What should we do?" one of the neighbors asks another.

"It's too late to call an ambulance."

"Oh, for sure, but we should call one anyway."

"Poor woman must have thought her husband was down in the yard."

In the next two days, people come from all over to offer their condolences to Ahmed's family. In times like these, men don't shave their beards out of respect for the dead, and women wear little or no makeup. Kids are kept away, and no one plays music. The faces are somber.

Faheemeh's parents come over to help receive the visitors. They seem sympathetic and kind. Ahmed's mother serves *aash*, with the help of my mother and some of the other female relatives and neighbors. Ahmed's father chain-smokes. Every once in a while he uses his white handkerchief to wipe the tears from his eyes as he receives friends and relatives.

The night before the funeral, Ahmed and I go onto the roof. The crescent-shaped moon, which hangs from the belly of the star-crowded sky, looks like a neon cradle designed to outshine everything around it. The neighborhood appears quiet and subdued, as if it has collapsed under the weight of all the grief it has experienced in the past few months. Somehow the dark shadows of the homes and the trees seem longer, and the twinkle of the city lights flicker frail and lifeless. It's as if someone has sprinkled the dust of death over the alley once again. Ahmed lights a cigarette and offers me one, too. I accept.

"She was a good woman," Ahmed says.

"Yes, she was."

"But everyone has to die sometime, right?"

"Right."

"Her time must have come," he says, taking a long draw off his cigarette.

"Yeah."

"But why did she have to go this way? Why couldn't she die peacefully in bed? Why is God so cruel?" He stops talking, an apologetic look on his face. "I shouldn't be saying things like this after what you've gone through. I'm sorry."

"It's okay," I say. "I've actually been feeling very close to Grandma lately. It was almost as if our lives were on a parallel course."

"God, don't say that," Ahmed says. "I don't want you to fall off the roof someday."

"No, no. I mean I could feel her anguish and the pain of permanent

separation, the loss. I had begun to feel as if maybe she wasn't so disconnected from reality."

"What do you mean?"

"All the talk about seeing Grandpa." I pause as the expression on
Ahmed's face grows worried. "I mean, people can't just die, right?"
Ahmed doesn't respond. "Grandma's insistence that Zari was waiting
for me . . . well, sometimes I think I see her in the shadows at night."

The look on Ahmed's face becomes even more alarmed. He's quiet
for a long time before he says, "I wonder what it's like to be dead?"

I think he's trying to avoid talking about my crazy thoughts. I
don't say anything, but remember Mr. Gorji talking about death
as the ultimate source of terror. "The afterlife is designed to punish
wrongdoers, who will be condemned to an eternally unimaginable
torture," he once said with fire in his eyes. I remember Grandma asking whether hell was built beneath heaven, and a smile flashes on my
face, but disappears just as quickly. Ahmed looks toward the spot
where Grandma presumably fell off the balcony. His face contorts as
he tries to hold back his tears.

"God bless her soul," he whispers as he looks toward the skies.
"Watch out, Grandpa!"

The next day, we all go to the cemetery. Ahmed, Iraj, and I sit in the
back of my father's Jeep, and my mother and Faheemeh sit in front.
Every once in a while, Faheemeh turns around and looks at Ahmed.
Then she reaches over to touch his hand or pat him on the knee.

I remember the day we went to the cemetery for Doctor. I remember Iraj's face as he was running behind the taxi. I feel good that this
time he's with us. The streets are full of cars, and the scent of exhaust
fumes sets my heart stuttering with the memory of Zari's last moments. The sky is gray and painted by dark clouds bloated with rain.
The sidewalks are crowded with pedestrians who seem to be rushing
to escape the inevitable downpour. We don't say much, except at one

point my father says that Grandma was a great lady and we all murmur our agreement.

All the neighbors are at the cemetery, including Zari's parents.
Everyone is dressed in black out of respect for Grandma's death. It's
great to be able to wear black for a change—we can finally grieve not
only Grandma, but also Zari and Doctor. Zari's parents extend their
apologies to Ahmed's mother for the Masked Angel's absence, explaining that she had to stay home to take care of Keivan. "It wasn't
appropriate to bring him to the cemetery," Zari's mother says. "He's
still too young."

Everyone is gathered around a hole that has been dug in the
ground. Most of the women are on one side of the grave, and the men
are standing on the other side. Ahmed's mother cries quietly and
whispers to my mother that she's worried about her husband. Grandma
was the only family he had left.

"She lived a good life," somebody tells Ahmed's mother.

"Yes, she did," another woman agrees.

"Look around you," the first woman says. "This place is full of
young people. God bless them all, and God bless Grandma's soul. She
lived her life as she pleased, and thank God it was long and fruitful."

I wonder how many of these neighbors know the story of Grandma
throwing herself off a cliff. I doubt that any of them do.

The cry of "There is no God but the almighty God!" is suddenly
heard from a distance, the signal that Grandma's body is being carried to her permanent resting place. Pandemonium breaks out at the
graveside. Everyone begins crying, including the women who were
consoling Ahmed's mother. Ahmed runs toward the group that is
carrying Grandma's coffin. Iraj and I run behind him, lending our
shoulders and arms to hold the coffin up in the air. The wood feels un-
naturally cold and rough on my neck. I think about Grandma's lifeless
body overhead, and a rush of blood makes me shake uncontrollably
as my face grows hot. At first, dizziness takes over, and then I feel the

energy and strength drain from my body like water through a sieve. I let go of the coffin and fall behind the procession, walking dazedly behind the crowd. Nobody notices my sudden weakness. The anxiety that overtakes me reminds me of my early days in the hospital. I wonder if Zari is buried in the same area, in a grave without a name.

Grandma's coffin is placed on the ground and everyone gathers around it, beating themselves, crying, and shaking their heads. Ahmed's father kneels down and fills his fists with the black dirt that's piled up next to the hole in the ground, pouring it over his head while sobbing inconsolably. Ahmed hugs his father from behind and cries along with him. A clergyman with a thick gray beard, wearing a black robe and a green turban, chants a few incomprehensible verses as he looks at my father, who is reaching inside his pocket to pay him. The clergyman's chants become more passionate when he realizes that he will be receiving a good sum for his services.

I'm not sure why I feel the way I do. The present seems disconnected from the past, as if there were a sudden disruption in the continuity of time. I see a group of strangers using old rusty shovels to pile dirt on Grandma's body, which is already in the ground. I look to my left and see the burial places of the rich. The columns and the steps of those structures revive a vivid memory of the day Zari, Faheemeh, Ahmed, and I came to this cemetery. I look to the right and see the little turnabout that we crossed to get to Doctor's grave. I don't know how long I gaze in that direction, because the next thing I know I'm staring at Doctor's name on his gravestone. His grave looks desolate and dismal compared to the ones around it, which are adorned with memorials, pictures, and sometimes even a poem dedicated to the deceased.

"I'm sorry I haven't come to visit," I whisper. "A lot has happened since . . . since you left."

His name is spelled "Ramin Sobhi," and the *R* in his first name is already worn out, indicating the inferior quality of the stone placed on his grave. A thick layer of dust covers the stone, making it obvious that no one has visited Doctor in a while. I take a handkerchief from my pocket and wipe the dust off, slowly and meticulously. "I'm so sorry that I haven't come to see you," I whisper. "You know, I planted a rosebush for you in honor of what you did for Golesorkhi, and you should see how everyone in the neighborhood takes care of it. That's great, isn't it? Nobody will ever forget you, Doctor."

A few meters away, water drips at a rapid rate from a faucet into a tin bucket. I lift the bucket and carry it to Doctor's grave, pouring the water on the stone. The soil around the grave absorbs the water quickly. Using my handkerchief again, I clean up the stone, then sit by the grave and remember when Doctor was alive.

I remember his bright smile, his round thick glasses, his passion for books, and his cheerful attitude toward Grandma. I wonder if he knows she's dead now, and buried only a few meters away. I want to say a few words to him about what happened between Zari and me, but quickly realize that by now he knows all there is to know, and has forgiven both of us: me for falling in love with her and she for letting me.

"She must have really loved you," I whisper, looking at Doctor's grave. "She gave her life to be with you. I'd give my life to be with her, but you two are together now, the way you should have been here in this world."

As I look at Doctor's grave, I remember the nights Zari came to the yard, occupying herself with chores that didn't need to be done while I watched from the roof. She looked up at me, but never said a word or even flashed a smile. What we had was a forbidden love— sweet, secretive, and intoxicating. I smile as tears roll down my face. I don't feel ashamed of loving Zari anymore because there's nothing wrong with loving someone who is worthy of being loved.

I touch a place on Doctor's stone where a little piece has chipped away. "When I get a job and have some money, I'll replace this stone for you," I whisper. "'Doctor'—that's what the inscription will read.

Pretty soon people will start to wonder why 'Doctor' and not a name. 'Who was he?' they'll ask. 'What happened to him? How old was he when they shot him? What did he look like? Was he tortured before he was killed? What happened to those who loved him?'

"And I'll tell your story to everyone I meet. Then pretty soon everyone will know that your father had a heart attack, and your mother lost her mind with grief. 'Poor woman,' people will say. They will talk about Zari and her courage, her defiance, and her self-sacrifice. 'That poor girl must have loved him very much! This is so unfair. How can we let things like this happen?' Then people will tell their children, their friends, and their neighbors. And the news will spread, and everyone will know the truth the SAVAK has been trying to hide by preventing us from grieving your loss, by destroying documents of your existence, by confiscating and probably burning your books."

I then look down at his grave and smile.

"Thank you for teaching me about *That*, Doctor," I whisper. "I think I know what it means now."

As I pause I can picture his smiling face, his nodding head.

"It's all about honor, friendship, love, giving it all you have, living an alert life and not pretending ignorance because it's an easier way out—all those things packaged together, isn't it? I feel fortunate to be surrounded by people who have *That*. You, Zari, Ahmed, Iraj, my parents, and Faheemeh; I've lived a wonderful life in that way."

I touch the chipped *R* of his name as I fight back tears.

"I take solace in knowing that you and Zari aren't dead. Because people with *That* never die, they don't cease to exist; they continue to live on in our hearts and minds, where existence matters."

The tears roll freely now and I know there is nothing I can do to stop them.

"Do you remember asking me what the most precious thing a human possessed was? I said, 'Life.' You smiled and said, 'Time.' Do you remember that, Doctor?"

A mild wind blows and a single leaf falls on Doctor's grave. I pick it up, look at it, and place it at the foot of his grave.

"I've been doing a lot of thinking about our discussion that day," I say. "And with all due respect, I think both of us were wrong. The most precious thing a human can possess is *That.*"

Just then, I feel someone behind me. I turn and see Ahmed, Faheemeh, and Iraj. They sit down next to me without saying a word. Faheemeh puts her arm around me. Seconds later, my parents come to the grave with red roses in their hands. My father winks at me as he sits down by the grave, places the roses on Doctor's clean stone, and says a final prayer. My mother does the same. One by one, our neighbors join us—a sea of people, everyone in the alley, and all with single red roses in their hands. I don't think anyone cares that the SAVAK might be watching. We should have been allowed to mourn Doctor's death a long time ago.

32

Another Dawn

The day after Grandma's funeral, I wake up to a beautiful April morning. Sunlight spills through the opening in the curtains and warms my face. I hear birds outside chirping and celebrating the glorious spring day. Last night, I slept like a baby for the first time in many, many nights.

I feel refreshed, rested, and full of energy, as if I'm ready to go out and run a few kilometers, something I haven't felt like doing in months.

I hear kids yelling and screaming in the alley. I walk out onto the terrace and breathe in the fresh air. I stretch my arms to the sides and make a loud noise as I exhale. A strange hope fills my heart. At the edge of the balcony, I look down into our yard. The tree my father planted the first day we moved here is beginning to sprout leaves.

I'm not the only one enjoying the day. The alley seems crowded with people of all ages, just as I remember it before Doctor's arrest. Iraj is sitting on the sidewalk playing a game of chess against himself. I promise myself I will challenge him later today; not that I can win, I just want to get back in the game. Occasionally he throws a nervous look toward Zari's house, perhaps anxious to see the Masked Angel. A group of kids is playing soccer. One kid pushes another down during a play, and a brief scuffle ensues, then a shouting match. The incident reminds me of Ahmed's ploy to get back in the goalie position last summer. That feels like a million years ago.

Groups of women have gathered in different parts of the alley: the east, west, and central gossip committees, as Ahmed used to call them. They all talk at the same time, and they all laugh and interact as if they understand one another despite the chaos.

Then I see a man walking to the rosebush with a bucket of water. Iraj quits his game and runs up to him, and together they water my plant. Tears roll down my cheeks—tears of joy.

I look down the alley and see Aboli and a couple of other kids ringing the bell of a house and running away. I start to laugh out loud, remembering the little trick he played on my poor Dad.

I close my eyes and take a deep breath. In that placid state a soothing thought slowly creeps into my mind: *I need to go away*. For weeks I have been fighting the idea, but the more I let go of myself, the more comfortable I am with the thought. I will go to the United States. There I can restart my life. I will live alone and go to school, busying myself with learning English and getting to know the Western culture. There is so much I need to understand. I hope Doctor and Zari don't feel betrayed. I hope not.

I go downstairs for breakfast. In the living room, a repairman is fixing the old grandfather clock. He's pulled the clock out into the middle of the room and is in the process of examining a number of its dismantled parts.

"What's going on?" I ask.

"We either need to fix this damn thing or throw it away," my father explains.

"It's too good to throw away, sir," the clock repairman says. "They don't make this brand anymore. This is an antique."

"What do you think?" my father asks me.

I approach the clock and touch its coarse and bumpy surface. "We should keep it. So what if it doesn't work? It's a nice piece. Besides, it was given to you and Mom as your wedding present."

Dad nods thoughtfully. "It was the only present we got. I used to wind it first thing every day as I had my morning tea." He smiles and then turns to the repairman. "We're keeping the clock no matter what the outcome of your efforts."

At breakfast, I tell my father that now I really do want to go to the United States.

"It would be best," he agrees. "I always wanted you to go there to become a civil engineer. Yes, a civil engineer, and then you can come back and build the European-style highway that connects Tehran to Noshahr!"

"I want to be a filmmaker, Dad," I say, looking directly in his eyes.

He stares at me for a little while. "Well, maybe you can double major in college," he says, still enthused about my agreement to go abroad.

My mother doesn't receive the news as well. Although she doesn't say anything to discourage me, she gets a thoughtful, mentally preoccupied look on her face. She walks around aimlessly, dusting the shelves, the picture frames, the TV screen, the grandfather clock, and everything else in the room. Then she begins again with the shelves.

"You just dusted those," my father points out.

She looks at him without speaking, and moves on to the picture frames.

The news of my departure travels through the neighborhood like water through a floodgate. By now almost everyone in the alley has learned that I'm preparing to leave for the United States. Grown-ups wish me good luck and express a wishful desire to go, too. Almost everyone has a friend or a relative who is either currently living there or did at one time.

"The U.S. is a great place," one of my neighbors comments. "My cousin just came back from Washington, where the government has installed hot water pipes under the streets to keep the roadways from freezing during harsh winters."

Another neighbor sighs with amazement. "How clever, how clever," he repeats with a dreamy look on his face.

Another neighbor confirms that technologically Americans are more advanced than we are, but not culturally. Children, he claims, are kicked out of the house when they turn eighteen. A few people gasp and shake their heads as the man continues by saying that the more compassionate parents ask their kids for rent money and charge them a fee for their food. "That's why the crime rate is so high in the States," he claims. "Being out on your own, without the supervision of your parents and away from the warmth and security of your own home, of course you're more inclined to gravitate toward crime!"

"Yeah, they call that independence," says another man. "They teach their kids from an early age to be independent."

"That's not independence, that's bullshit!"

Ahmed, who is standing next to me, turns to Iraj and says, "I wish my parents would kick me out soon." Both Iraj and I chuckle.

Days pass quickly. Ahmed's family learns to cope with the tragic loss of Grandma. They slowly find their way back into the groove of the alley's everyday life. Not much happens in Zari's house, except that her father goes to work every morning and returns at night to a wife who has chosen to spend the rest of her life at home. Keivan plays in the yard by himself, subjected to a lonely childhood apart from the other kids in our alley. Occasionally I hear him giggle when he is playing ball with the Masked Angel—just like he used to do with his sister.

My father meets regularly with Mr. Mehrbaan and Mr. Kasravi to arrange for my immigration to the United States. The contacts in the Passport Administration Office deliver as promised, and I now own a passport. The next step in the process is to obtain a valid student visa from the American embassy, which requires an I-20, a letter of acceptance from an accredited university or college in the U.S. This is where Mr. Mehrbaan plays a crucial role. Some of his exiled comrades in the Unites States will be obtaining an I-20 for me from a college in Los Angeles. Mr. Kasravi also knows people in the Education Department who can help with fabricating a high school diploma and a high score on the *Ezam* English-language test so that my request for a student visa will be granted.

Mr. Kasravi tries to calm me down when I express concern over getting a fake high school diploma. I worry that if the authorities found out, I could be banned from ever attending college.

"You see, you can move a mountain in this country if you know the right people, you really can," Mr. Kasravi says.

"And why not?" Mr. Mehrbaan adds. "When you're cheated out of life, you cheat back to get even. That's how things work in countries like ours. They stopped you from attending school, so we fake a diploma to make up for the lost time."

I don't feel comfortable with the ploy but go along anyway. I want to leave Iran more than ever. I can't go back to my school without Ahmed and Iraj, and I can't stay in this alley after Zari's parents move to Bandar Abbas.

Ahmed and Faheemeh are happy to see the renewed hope in me, but they're also sad to see me go. Although I can see it in their eyes, they never say anything to discourage me.

"You'll go away for a while, study at the finest university in the States, and come back as an educated man," Ahmed says, smiling.

"Yes, we'll pick up exactly where we left off," Faheemeh agrees enthusiastically. "It'll be like you never left, except that you'll probably be an uncle by then."

My mother is not excited about any of this. "He doesn't speak any

English," she frets. "How is he going to find his way around at the airport when his plane lands? How will he ask for food? How will he know what to eat or how to get around?"

"Oh, come now," my father says. "You underestimate him! Thousands of young people make this trip every year. He's probably more capable than all of them put together. He's the most resilient kid I know."

"Oh, yes," Mr. Kasravi confirms. "He's a very smart kid, really, the smartest kid I know."

I look at Mr. Kasravi and smile to let him know I appreciate his compliments. Mrs. Mehrbaan tries to console my mother by telling her that college will be over before she knows it, and I'll be back in no time with the prospect of a great future. "At least you know he is going to a good place. God forbid, what if he was going to jail?" All three ladies immediately bite the skin between their thumbs and index fingers.

"An educated guy like him? My God, can you imagine? Girls will throw themselves at his feet!" Mr. Mehrbaan says, shooting me a wink.

"No, no, no," Mrs. Kasravi interrupts. "He is destined to marry my Shabnam."

Everyone laughs, including my mother. I think of Zari and feel a lump in my throat.

Everything is settled. I'm supposed to leave in a month. My father shows me the ticket for my flight, his face beaming. "You'll land in Los Angeles and will be picked up by a few relatives of your uncle Mehrbaan," he says. "They will arrange for you to get an apartment, and sign you up at USC. Are you comfortable with all this?" he asks suddenly, as if he's not sure himself that I will be able to handle living alone in the U.S., despite what he told my mother.

"Yes," I say automatically. In truth, despite the many plans I've made, the future seems like a fogged-up mirror to me. I'm there, but not clearly visible or recognizable. When I think of the United States, all I envision are the streets in the movies and the television shows I've seen. I decide the best way for me to deal with the uncertainty is not to think about it, to suppress my guilt about seeking a better future in the country that has ruined my past.

My mother says I need to say good-bye to our friends and relatives in Tehran. She turns her head and blows her nose as she wipes the tears from her face. She'll invite everyone over for a farewell dinner.

"That would be much better, and a lot easier on you," she explains.

The day before my good-bye party and a week before my departure, I'm looking into Zari's yard from my vantage point on the roof when I decide that I need to tell Mr. and Mrs. Naderi about everything that happened between Zari and me. It would be good for them to know that my intentions were totally honorable, and that I loved Zari more than life itself.

Ahmed agrees with my plan. He thinks they'll be moving soon because he has been witnessing strange activities in their house. Strangers are coming and going at odd hours of the day and night— they must be the SAVAK agents. They plan these kinds of exiles carefully to ensure that they are carried out as inconspicuously as possible, since according to official claims the SAVAK hardly exists. For months now, there have been rumors in the alley that Mr. Naderi must move to a warmer region for his health.

I ring the bell to their house, and the Masked Angel opens the door. I say hello, and she whispers an inaudible hello in return. As always, she's wearing her burqa, and I can barely see her eyes behind the lace. Her downcast gaze and hunched shoulders tell me that she's uncomfortable in my presence. I quickly look away to ease her tension. "I'm here to see Mr. and Mrs. Naderi," I whisper. "I'm leaving in a few days, and I'd like to say good-bye to them."

The Masked Angel stands in the doorway without moving or saying anything.

"May I see them?" I ask.

She steps quickly out of the way and gestures for me to enter the house. I try not to look at the cherry tree as we walk through the yard. The Masked Angel leads the way toward the living room and whispers that her uncle and aunt are on the third floor, and that she will get them for me.

There are boxes everywhere, signaling their imminent departure. I stand in the middle of the room, unsure what to do, as she quickly disappears down the hallway. I'm reminded once again of Keivan's birthday party. The house was full of kids running around, playing, screaming, laughing, and bitterly complaining about one another. Zari snuck up close to me as Ahmed was keeping everyone busy with the Who Am I? game. *"I hope your girlfriend doesn't mind that you're helping me out tonight,"* Zari had said, leaning forward to see my eyes.

"My girlfriend?" I'd asked.

"Yeah, the one who's softer than . . ."

The lump is back in my throat.

There was so much activity and so much life in this house on that warm summer day. This empty room is such a stark contrast. A few meters away, on a small round table that is placed close to the samovar, I see Zari's notebook of drawings. I walk over to the table and pick up the book. Page by page, I look at each drawing and remember every word Zari uttered to describe them.

"This is a picture of you guys playing soccer in the alley. Can you guess which one is you?"

"Which one?"

"You weren't there that day!"

Toward the end of the book, I come across the picture she drew of my mystery woman and me. What is this picture doing here? I've been looking for it ever since I came back from the hospital. I know that I pinned it to the wall of my bedroom and stared at it every night, fantasizing a million ways to give it to her without saying a word—just as she had instructed me to do. I imagined her face as she was taking the picture from me: those smiling eyes looking directly at me, cheeks blushing with excitement, and her sigh of relief at knowing that she was the woman of my dreams.

Just then, Mr. and Mrs. Naderi walk into the room. I quickly place the drawing book back on the table. Zari's parents embrace me and tell me to sit down and make myself comfortable. Mrs. Naderi pours me a cup of tea, and tells me she's happy I'm going away. Life has been too hard for me in this country, and being away will do me a lot of good, especially if I focus my efforts on my studies, away from all that has happened here. Her family will miss me, but this is exactly what I should be doing.

Mr. Naderi nods in agreement as he lights a cigarette.

"Would you study medicine or engineering?" he asks, as if no other academic major is a viable option. Before I have a chance to respond he adds, "Study hard because education is the only cure for ignorance, and it's up to people like you to liberate this country from the disease of dictatorship and help construct a better future for kids like Keivan."

The Masked Angel enters the room with a plate of sweets, which she places in front of me and whispers, "Please, help yourself." She then proceeds to the other side of the room and sits down on the floor close to Mrs. Naderi, in front of the round table where Zari's drawing book lies. Mr. Naderi says that he and his family are very happy for me, and they hope that I won't forget them while I'm away. I shake my head no.

Mrs. Naderi wants to know where I'm going, how long I will be gone, and what I will study. Am I anxious about being in a foreign country, and how do my parents—especially my mother—feel about it? The Masked Angel's eyes are fixed on me as I answer Mrs. Naderi's questions. I can see them blinking fast behind the veil. But I look mostly at Mr. and Mrs. Naderi because the Masked Angel becomes visibly uncomfortable every time I glance in her direction. I tell them that I hope to get a degree in three years, that I will miss Iran, the alley, and all my friends, relatives, and neighbors. I express my wish that I were leaving under different circumstances. I pause, beginning to sweat at the thought of revealing the secret I never thought I'd share with anyone but my best friends. My hands start to shake, and my face feels hot.

"I would like permission to speak candidly about my relationship with Zari," I whisper.

No one says anything, and I begin to feel that maybe I should stop right there. My palms are sweaty, and I can feel the heat from my flushed face. I wonder why telling the truth is so hard. I understand now why my uncle and aunt write instead of talking when they have uncomfortable topics to discuss! But I have to go on. It's too late to stop now.

I drop my gaze to avoid eye contact with anyone in the room, and begin my story. I say that I always thought Zari was a special girl. As a boy, I was impressed with the way she handled herself. Of course, her engagement to Doctor, the greatest guy in our neighborhood, also elevated her status in my eyes. I say that I used to watch the two of them from the roof of our house, and although I couldn't hear what they were talking about, I knew they always discussed important topics because intelligent people wouldn't waste time on frivolous things.

I look up and notice a stoic expression on both Mr. and Mrs. Naderi's faces. Not daring to look at the Masked Angel, I hang my head and continue.

"I loved Doctor. He was an extraordinary man, a great man. He had *That*." Finally I look up at the Masked Angel. I can tell from the sounds that come from under her burqa that she's weeping.

"And of course Zari, being engaged to my friend and mentor, al-

ways had a special place in my heart. I mean, she was Doctor's fiancée, right?" I repeat as if I'm trying to drive that point home. "It was
impossible for me to think of her as anything but Doctor's future
wife." Then I pause for a long time because I don't know what else to
say.

The silence in the room weighs heavily on me. This is a lot harder
than what Ahmed did for Faheemeh. I would gladly take the beating
he took instead of this, as there's nothing more disgraceful than falling in love with your friend's fiancée and having to admit it.

Mr. Naderi lights a cigarette, clears his throat, and asks, "What
are you trying to say, my son?"

I shake my head, mute and ashamed.

"Damn those bastards that have destroyed the lives and hopes of
so many young people!" Mrs. Naderi cries out.

Out of the corner of my eye I see her wiping the tears from her
face with a white handkerchief.

"You don't need to say any more if it makes you uncomfortable,"
Mr. Naderi assures me in a soothing tone. "I'm pretty sure we know
everything already."

Mrs. Naderi nods her head in mute agreement as the Masked Angel touches her face under her burqa, wiping her own tears away.

"This tragedy has destroyed so many lives so unnecessarily, so
unfairly," Mrs. Naderi says. "No one—and I mean no one—should
feel ashamed of anything. We could only wish that the thoughts that
have made you feel shameful were the worst that had happened to us.
Damn the devil."

"I loved her very much," I finally blurt, as tears stream down my
face. "She was my life, she was my future."

Mr. Naderi blows the smoke out of his lungs, clears his throat, and
says, "Listen, my son. Life is like a boat without sails: there is no telling where this boat will take us or which shore we'll end up on. Sometimes it is wise not to fight the wind and accept things as they are, as

painful as they may be, trusting in the wisdom of God and believing in the certainty of fate. No one can justify the pain we have all endured, and nothing can ever take the pain away. God knows, I wish I could offer you an alternative."

He stops abruptly, draws deeply on his cigarette, glances at the Masked Angel, who is still quietly crying under her veil, and shakes his head. "I swear on your love for Zari—the light of my eyes and the breath in my lungs—that we all wish for an alternative. Maybe someday this will all make sense, but it doesn't right now." He hangs his head, brushes at his eyes, and continues to smoke his cigarette.

The Masked Angel walks up to Mr. Naderi, puts her arms around him, and whispers something in his ear that momentarily calms him down. Mr. Naderi's condition surprises me, but I don't know what to make of it.

"What he means to say," Mrs. Naderi adds, "is that you will always be welcome in our home. We know how you felt about Zari, and you needn't feel ashamed of it. We know that she loved you, too. That's all I am going to say." She rocks from side to side and slaps her side a couple of times in frustration. "It's hard for us to talk about this. I am sorry. What we are left with are lost hopes and destroyed dreams. It's really so hard for us to talk about."

Mr. Naderi breaks into a bitter sob, and the Masked Angel hugs him harder and whispers louder and louder, "Don't cry, don't cry. Please, don't cry. For my sake, don't cry. I beg you to stop." I see her eyes behind the lace of her burqa, those angelic, sad eyes that now look very familiar to me. I remember them from the picture in Zari's photo album. She turns her head the other way and walks toward the doorway. Mr. Naderi keeps saying that he's sorry while still crying.

"Thank God you have her," I say, pointing at the Masked Angel, who is about to exit the room. "She was like a sister to Zari."

Mr. Naderi shakes his head and whispers, "Yes, thank God we have her!"

Then Mr. and Mrs. Naderi both hug me as I get up to leave. "You won't be here when I get back," I cry out.

"No," Mr. Naderi confirms.

"How can I find you?" I ask, sobbing like a child who's being separated from his parents forever.

"We will find you," Mr. Naderi says. "I swear on Zari's love for you that we will find you."

Zari's love for me. The sentence tears at my heart. Something inside me is ripped in two. I can't possibly leave the country, and then I think of Mr. and Mrs. Naderi, Keivan, and the Masked Angel no longer living here, and I know that I must leave as soon as possible.

Moments later I'm back in my own house with a heavy heart.

33

One More, Please

That same day, my mother asks if I would like to go shopping with her. I say that I want to, but I'm tired and would like to stay home and enjoy my last days in the house. She hugs me and says, "I will miss you."

"I'll miss you, too, Mom."

"Oh, no, no, no. You, my dear, have no idea how a mother can miss her child. So don't give me that 'I'll miss you, too, Mom.'"

I nod.

"As hard as this is for me," she says, while trying to smile instead of cry, "I know that this is the best thing for you. So, I plan to visit you as often as I can, even if it means selling the house, the family car, and all of my jewelry—because we can't be torn away from our heart for four years now, can we?"

I hug her. "Four years is nothing. It'll go by in a wink. You should be happy that you're getting a break from me."

She smiles and utters something between a laugh and a cry. "You do have a point," she says.

After she leaves, I sit in a chair by the *hose* in our yard. As the spring sun lulls me into a state of semi-unconsciousness, I think of what happened in Zari's house. As painful as the experience was, I'm glad that I went over and talked with the Naderis. I feel right about my decision. It was the adult thing to do, and I'm glad I didn't take the letter-writing route after all.

Ahmed will soon come over, and as much as I enjoy his company, I want to delight in the quiet serenity of my surroundings. I close my eyes and let my thoughts wander. Even at rest, my mind is in a hyperactive state. I distinctly hear a car with a broken muffler pass through the alley. There's a long silence, and then the chirping of a few birds. A few minutes later a couple of cats hiss at each other, and then a throaty growling noise, then nothing. A roaring airplane passes by overhead, followed by another uninterrupted period of silence. Then, I hear a child's giggle and a woman's muffled voice asking him to be quiet. Then another giggle, and another, and finally a young woman's whisper from the other side of the wall in Zari's yard. The hair on the back of my neck stands up. A shiver slides down my spine, and suddenly I'm wide awake.

"One more story, please, just one more!" the child whispers.

"Hush!" is the response.

I open my eyes and listen. Nothing.

"Zari!" I say involuntarily. I turn and look at the wall behind me as I listen with every fiber of my being to the unusual silence that has filled the air. I walk up to the wall that separates Zari's house from mine. I put my ear against it and listen—nothing but absolute quiet. Was this a dream? It must have been, and I'm probably still dreaming, otherwise how could the whole world plunge into a state of total noiselessness? I look around and touch the brick wall with my hands to ensure that I'm functioning in a world made of solid materials. I'm not dreaming.

I wish I could see into Zari's yard. I run toward the steps that connect the yard to the terrace on the first floor, and then up the steps to the second and third floor, skipping two or three steps at a time. I open the door to the balcony and rush to the edge where I can see down into her yard.

No one is there.

I lean over the edge to see if I can see anyone on her first-floor ter-race. There's no one. I look toward Zari's room on the third floor. The curtains are pulled tight. I pace back and forth on the balcony as my whole body tingles.

"It was only a dream," I whisper to myself. "Besides, what if Keivan was just begging the Masked Angel for one more story, like he used to do when his sister was alive?"

I look into her yard again. I want to tell myself that my suspicion is absurd, preposterous, and downright stupid—but I don't. My tor-mented heart defies my logical mind.

She wouldn't do that to me, I keep thinking. She would never in-flict so much pain on me, no matter what the circumstances.

But what if the Masked Angel is my Zari, hiding her scorched face under a veil? Why would she do that? Does she not know how miser-able my life has been without her? Does she not know the pain that her absence has caused me? I hunch down and lean back against the short wall, biting my hands to hold back my whimpers.

"God, please, I want my Zari back!" I cry, belatedly remembering that I don't believe in God anymore.

I look into the empty yard again, and can't believe how everything seems to have come to a standstill, as if the world is holding its breath in anticipation of an answer to this mystery. I run to my room and look around, unsure of what I'm hoping to find. I run back onto the terrace and take a deep breath of the fresh air. I wish Ahmed and Faheemeh were here. I sit on the short wall and try to put the pieces of the puzzle together methodically, but I'm overwhelmed by a storm of emotions that blows me farther and farther from the shores of reason.

I try to focus on the moment I heard Keivan's whisper, *"One more story, please..."* Was that a dream? Did I really hear him? What did I hear before that? The car with the broken muffler! Does anyone own a car with a broken muffler in our neighborhood? If that sound was real, then Keivan's whisper was real, too. What else did I hear? The

cats fighting and hissing at each other. I look in the neighbors' yards
for the cats. The growling must have been real. Why would I dream of
two cats fighting? But none of our neighbors own cats; they must
have been strays.

I think of the shadow that watches me at night. I already know it's
the Masked Angel, but why would she watch me unless she were
actually my own Zari? It was her veil the other night that moved with
the force of the wind, I know that now, too. Everything is beginning
to make sense. "The Masked Angel never rushes anything," Faheemeh
once said. "She glides like the spring breeze—calm, gentle, and deliberate. There is nothing expeditious about her." Then why does she
walk so fast every time I see her coming back from the bakery in the
morning? The person under the veil is not the Masked Angel. It is
Zari, hiding from me, either because she was told by the SAVAK to do
so, or because she doesn't want me to see her charred face. Oh, my
poor, dear little Zari!

She told me once that she wanted to become an expert in inter-
preting the poetry of Hafiz. How could I not see it all these nights,
staring at her through the opening in the curtain? The Masked Angel
has all of Hafiz memorized. She wouldn't be reading his *Divan* because it's all in her head. It's Zari who reads the book, trying to fill the
lonely nights. And earlier today, I found the picture Zari had drawn
of me and my mystery woman in their house. Somehow Zari must
have taken it out of my room when I was in the hospital. And then the
outburst of Mr. Naderi—it's all making sense now. He said he wished
he could offer me an alternative, and that's when Zari walked up to
him, hugged him, and whispered something in his ear. The Masked
Angel would be too religious to embrace a man who is not a blood
relative!

I bend over and cry with joy and sorrow, exaltation, and misery. I
close my eyes and tip my head to the skies, realizing that, for the first
time since the day I gained consciousness in the hospital, a heavy

burden has been lifted from my chest. The air I inhale seems to go down easier, at least for now.

What should I do? I need a plan of attack. Where is Ahmed when I need him? Does he know? Maybe he and Faheemeh know what has been going on but haven't said anything to protect me and Zari from the SAVAK. Then it suddenly dawns on me that I'll be leaving for the United States in less than a week. That cannot happen, now that I have my Zari back! Given the circumstances, the trip must be called off. We must call all the guests and cancel the good-bye party. But how do I get to the Masked Angel and uncover the truth? This will be embarrassing for her family, and there may also be safety ramifications as far as the SAVAK is concerned. I need to approach her carefully. I don't want the SAVAK to take my angel away again.

I run downstairs and drink a couple shots of my father's vodka, which immediately warms me up and calms me down. "To you, my love," I whisper. "Resurrected, I hope and pray, from nothingness back into my life."

I climb over onto Zari's side of the wall and sit in the same spot where we used to sit. I remember the dream I had the last time I sat under this wall. I'm sure now that the experience was not a dream. She was sitting behind me, holding me in her arms. She said she wanted to keep her sweetheart warm. My poor little Zari. *Oh, God, I love you so much. I miss you so desperately.*

I was cold and delirious that night, and Zari saw me through the window and came out with a blanket. She wrapped it around me and hugged me all night long, keeping me warm and whispering in my ear that she was afraid that her sweetheart might catch a cold, and that she was going to make sure he didn't. That certainly was not a dream!

My mind races from one topic to another. I can't focus on one thought for long. The memories of the day she set herself on fire rush through my head. The days in the hospital and the suffocating depression that devoured me, the fear that Ahmed was lost, the old man, Apple Face . . . *Oh, my God, why is life so cruel?* If I had to live through all that again, I don't think I would make it.

Then my thoughts turn to Zari, alive next door, breathing the same oxygen as me, and perhaps thinking of me at this very moment. No wonder I've felt her presence so strongly. These were the conditions that drew me to her window every night. And why would I dream of being on top of a mountain with the Masked Angel if it wasn't for the fact that, deep down, Zari wants to unveil herself in my presence?

The vodka I drank gives me the courage to walk up to Zari's window. The curtain is half open, and I get a good look into the dark room. The Masked Angel's burqa is on Zari's bed, so I know she's in the room, or at least in the house. I return to my room.

The doorbell to our house rings. It's Iraj. I'm so excited about my new discovery and I want to tell him all about it, but as always he begins to talk before I have a chance to say anything. He's not the person I need to be talking to, anyway. We sit by the *hose* in my yard. He shows me a new book he's purchased, a biography of his hero, Thomas Edison. He is deeply disturbed by the author's account of Edison's life.

"According to this guy, Edison was a crook," Iraj says. "He used to hire hoodlums who forced young inventors to sell their inventions to him for pennies, or face a vicious beating!" Iraj is having a hard time believing these outrageous lies, but he swears that if these accusations are true, he will give up his dream of becoming an inventor in favor of being an honest politician.

According to his father and his uncle, the Shah's days are numbered because people are fed up with his dictatorial ways and the inhumane treatment of political dissidents. Even the leaders in the army feel that he has gone too far. Iraj's uncle, a general in the American-backed army of the Shah, was involved in negotiations to purchase a number of F-16s from the American government. These fighter jets would make Iran the superpower of the Middle East—exactly what the Americans always wanted. The Israelis would have been their first choice, of course, but it's better to have a Muslim state carry your stick than a Jewish one that's hated by millions of people in the region. Iraj says his father believes that the closer the Shah gets to the West, the less popular he becomes in the Middle East. The biggest threat to the Shah, however, is Israel. The Israelis must be getting nervous that a military powerhouse is developing in their backyard. Sooner or later, they will use the rich Jewish lobbyists to turn Washington against the Shah.

I want to tell Iraj that I'm not interested in hearing his father's political theories, but I don't. My God, why can't he leave me alone? Why did he have to show up now? Aren't there more important things in life than the political situation in Iran? I don't yell at Iraj only because I remember his sweaty face at the cemetery, tired from all the running to join us at Doctor's grave site, despite knowing that the SAVAK was watching.

To my surprise, Iraj switches gears and starts talking about the Masked Angel. He's been depressed lately because he finds it impossible to get her attention. To make matters worse, no one takes his love for her seriously. I don't tell him that the woman under the burqa is Zari and not the Masked Angel. I can't reveal that yet. What if they have an agreement with the SAVAK for Zari to remain incognito and I blow her cover?

Iraj says he's tired of people criticizing his love for the Masked Angel. Everyone wonders how he could love a woman he's never seen, but does that really matter?

"One's not supposed to fall in love with how a person looks," Iraj argues. "That's superficial love. True love is about accepting someone's inner goodness. People criticize me because I don't know her personally, but do I need to know her to believe in her goodness? Isn't it true that genuine love is about respect for one's character and disposition? Shouldn't people marry based on the compatibility of their temperaments? If so, then everything I know about the Masked Angel makes her a perfect bride for me."

The Masked Angel! Poor kid; if only he knew. Iraj continues to talk, but I tune him out. I occasionally nod in agreement as I drift further and further away.

He finally leaves and I run back up to the roof. The lights in Zari's house are off. I know the family doesn't go to bed this early, so they must be hiding from me. They can't reveal the Masked Angel's true identity. They must've made an agreement with the SAVAK. Yes, that's how they saved her from going to jail and that's why there is no grave. I look into Zari's room. The Masked Angel's burqa is still on the bed.

34

In the Silence of the Night

At dinner that night, I'm so preoccupied with thoughts of Zari that my father asks me if I'm okay. "Yes," I say, playing with my food.

My father puts his spoon back on his plate. "Are you getting nervous about your trip?"

I know I can't tell my parents about the events of the afternoon, so I nod yes.

"It's normal, you know?" Dad says. "This is a big step, and your apprehension is totally understandable. It isn't easy to pack up and move to the other side of the world, where you don't speak the language, don't know anyone, and don't know the culture. I'd be nervous, too!"

From the corner of my eye, I see my mother begin to cry. My father clears his throat and continues. "My father used to say that life is like a laboratory in which people's true characters are tested. He believed that the greater the person, the greater the tests they faced." He lights up a cigarette and takes a huge puff; I have to check myself from asking if I can have one.

"Nobody in our family has ever been tested as you have been. I'm so proud of you for the way you have handled things. You've experienced more in a couple of years than most people do in a lifetime.

Your mother and I are very proud of you, very proud. Tomorrow, this house will be full of people who love you. People who are happy to see you go, but will be even happier when you come back as an engineer. 'Mr. Engineer,' that's what everyone will call you for the rest of your life. You'll be an icon of success, a role model for many in this community. You're opening a door no one in our family has ever been through, but I assure you that you won't be the only one to pass through it! As you pave the way, others will follow in your footsteps. Your courage and determination will be an inspiration. Your success will make many lives better. You truly have *That*, my son."

I look at him with a blank look on my face. The U.S., the laboratory of life, the test of greatness; if he only knew what thoughts were brewing in my head now!

My father continues talking, but I'm not listening anymore even though it's impolite to be distracted when your father speaks. I hear words like U.S., airplane, civil engineering, four-lane highway, and Noshahr and Tehran, and I'm beginning to lose my patience with all the bullshit I've been hearing ever since I was four years old. I think, *Fuck the United States, the airplane ride, the goddamn civil engineering degree, and the fucking four-lane highway that connects one fucking dump of a town to another.*

Then I think about Zari, my beloved, who is embarrassed to show her charred face, or forced by the government to hide her true identity. My angel who has accepted a life of solitude and loneliness. These are not hypotheses anymore. These are facts—not my perceptions, but reality.

Ahmed's poor grandma knew what she was talking about. Why didn't anyone ever listen to her? She kept telling us that the girl next door cried every night, longing for her husband. The girl next door was Zari, and I was the husband. I can't believe that I thought my sweetheart was dead. I bite the space between my thumb and index finger. There is no doubt that everyone will think I'm crazy when I announce that Zari is alive and hiding beneath the Masked Angel's veil, but I don't care. I know what I know, and I know what I heard. It was Zari's voice that hushed Keivan when he begged for one more story. The Masked Angel is Zari—I have no doubt about it.

The thought of Zari alive fills me with such joy and excitement that I suddenly find myself leaning back with my arms stretched out wide to the sides, eyes closed and face pointed at the ceiling, as if welcoming the sun's embrace. I feel the warmth of her body against mine as I did on the nights she fell asleep in my arms. I feel her breath on my neck where her face rested. I hear her heart like the beating of wings. *Thank you, God, for bringing my Zari back to me! Forgive me for doubting your wisdom and magnanimity. Forgive me for living a godless life. Let me be your servant, and I promise to make up for my stupid ways.*

I open my eyes and notice that both my parents are watching me. I sit forward quickly and hang my head without saying anything. I expect my father to ask me what's wrong, but he doesn't. My mother whispers, "It's too much pressure for him. He's been acting strange since this morning." She reaches over and touches my forehead. "He's not hot," she mumbles. "He must be burning from the inside, my poor child."

"Stop it," my father snaps with more impatience.

He leaves the room as my mother touches my face gently with her fingertips and whispers worriedly, "What's wrong?"

"She's alive." I'm unable to contain myself.

"Who's alive, sweetheart?"

"My Masked Angel," I whisper.

"Of course she's alive," she says, thinking I mean Soraya.

"I'm not crazy," I murmur, looking to the hallway, where I can hear my father approaching.

"Oh, God," my mother soothes. "You were never crazy. You've just been through a lot, that's all." My father enters the room with a glass of water in his hands. He gives me a pill, and tells me to take it.

"What is it?" my mother asks.

"Valium," he says. "It will calm him down."

I've never taken Valium before, but it must be better than anything my mom would give me, so I swallow the pill without arguing.

It isn't long before a sense of numbness envelops me. I'm reminded of my hospital days, when a sensation of tranquility was followed by a painful awakening to a somber and austere reality. Before I lose consciousness, I want to make sure my mother is okay.

"Why're you crying, Mom?" I ask. "Please, stop. Zari is alive. I don't need to go to the States anymore. Isn't that grand? Doesn't that make you happy?"

Mom grabs my face in both hands and leans her forehead against mine as she weeps bitterly. "My sweetheart, my little child. What has happened to you?"

"If I ever go anywhere it'd be with Zari, Ahmed, and Faheemeh, and only for a short time. Just on vacation. Isn't that great? I'll be very happy from now on, just like I used to be, before this nightmare began. Isn't that great, Mom?"

She nods. "Yes, it is, my sweetheart."

"Living is like being lost in the desert where the stars are the only guide you can count on," I continue, my lips dry, but a river flowing from my eyes. "You and Dad, Zari, Faheemeh, and Ahmed are the stars that guide me. You all have *That*. And someday I'll write a book about everything that's happened."

Then I turn to my father and slur, "Do you believe in destiny, Dad?" My voice feels distorted to me. I don't remember hearing my father's answer.

I wake up on a mattress in the living room—sweaty, hot, drowsy, and aching. My parents are asleep on the floor a couple of meters away. The lights in the room are off, but the moonlight spilling through the curtains makes everything visible. I look toward the grandfather clock that my father had repaired a few days earlier, and the time reads three thirty, while my watch says it's ten thirty. I see the pendulum moving sluggishly from one side to the other, and wonder why my father and I bothered to try and fix this poor old clock that has long outlived its usefulness.

My mind spins itself dizzy with thoughts about time. To stop it, I get out of bed and head up the steps toward the terrace on the third floor. I will hide there in the dark and wait for Zari to come out, as she often does, to watch me. When she appears, I'll confront her and reveal that I know the truth.

When I get to the third floor I look out through the window to see if she is already on the terrace. God's round, glowing orb of light has lit the sky, and I have a great view of everything outside, but the terrace is barren. I cross over the short wall between our houses and move to the extreme south side of the terrace to sit down in the shadows. I look at my watch—still ten thirty.

It's a quiet night, so quiet you could hear the falling of a leaf, the squeak of a door, or the sound of the night itself breathing through the mild breeze that starts and stops. I sit patiently there in the dark, my chest expanding with a balloon of anticipation, anxiety, and hope. I look at my watch. It's still ten thirty. I wonder how long I'll have to wait.

As I'm sitting in the dark on the balcony of Zari's house, I hope that my parents don't wake up, because they will undoubtedly panic, rush upstairs, and potentially ruin my plans to expose Zari. A familiar anxiety, similar to the panic attacks I used to experience in the hospital, sweeps through me. Maybe I'm losing my mind. God, I hope not!

But I'm beginning to lose my patience. Maybe I should just storm into her house and demand to see her. I look at my watch, and it still says ten thirty. I shake my wrist and tap the watch. I hear the soft squeak of a door opening. My heartbeat throbs in my ears so fiercely that I fear the whole neighborhood will be woken up. I place my hands on my chest and push down hard to calm myself. I hear her muffled footsteps on the terrace, accompanied by the whispery rustle of her burqa dragging behind her on the cement. She's still out of my sight, but her long shadow stretches away from the door, rushing toward the edge of the terrace, then contracting suddenly as she crouches low. The weight of the moment turns me to stone, unable to speak or even breathe.

She has a good view of my room from where she sits, and I conclude that she's waiting for my light to come on. Maybe this wasn't the best place for me to hide. What is the benefit if I can't see what she's doing?

Suddenly, her shadow extends again and she comes into view, moving slowly from my right to my left, toward the spot where we used to sit together under the short wall. Her figure, enshrouded in the black burqa and illuminated by the full moon behind her, seems taller than I remember it. She looks over the wall toward my room, then she stands up on her tiptoes and stretches her neck to try and improve her view. She stands there for a while, then moves to the edge of the terrace and leans over to look into my yard. I'm certain now that she's spying on me, and that it was she who watched me every night from the safety of the shadows. She returns to our spot, casts one more look at my room, and sits down. I can feel my blood coursing through me, pulsing with an intensity that makes me as weak as water.

She starts fussing with the front of her burqa, as if she's removing the lace that lines the mask section of her veil. Her fingers work quickly, but it seems she is struggling to untie a hidden knot. Her hands are thin, pale, and slender, just like Zari's. My God, if she succeeds, I may be able to see her face! With a flick of her hand, she throws the lace back and begins to scratch the top of her head. I strain to see her face, but her arm shields my view.

After a few moments her arm slides down, but now the side of her veil blocks her face. All I can see is the velvet silhouette of her profile, motionless like a model posing for a painter. After a few seconds, she leans back against the wall. Although I can't see her face, I can tell that her eyes are closed and her lips are moving, perhaps reciting a poem from Hafiz or Khayyam—maybe even one of the ones I read to her. Her chest rises and falls, and I can almost see her breath as it comes and goes. Suddenly, she perks up, as if she's heard a sound. I can tell from the direction of her gaze that she thinks the sound came from my house. I hope my parents are not on their way up. I know she would run back to her house if she saw them.

I concentrate hard on seeing her face. Her head is tilted to the right, as if she's looking over her shoulder toward my room, anticipating my arrival. I can tell from the position of her body and the way she wiggles around that she's anxious and distracted by the sound she thought she heard. After a few uneventful seconds, she leans back against the wall again.

I wrestle with the idea of coming out of the dark and into the moonlight. We would look into each other's eyes, but wouldn't say anything. What could either of us possibly say? It would be too beautiful a moment to ruin with words. I would walk up to her, extend my hand, and help her up. We would embrace forever. But what if she tried to run away? I'd grab her and tell her that the nightmare is over, that I don't care what she looks like, and that she will be mine for the rest of our lives!

"Yes," I accidentally whisper.

Her head snaps up and fixes on where I'm sitting. Her eyes glow radiantly with borrowed moonlight—undoubtedly the same eyes that have watched me every night. Her gaze is fierce and penetrating, predatory and skittish, like a startled cat's. Instead of running away, she calmly reaches over her head and pulls the lace down in front of her face, transforming herself back into the Masked Angel. The steady finality of her movements reminds me of her characteristic confidence.

I stand up and step out into the moonlight. She sits motionless, and her pull on me is magnetic. I walk slowly up to her and, after a momentary pause, I fold my body neatly to sit next to her. Her blinking eyes stare at me from behind the lace of her burqa, and my heart adjusts its rhythm to match their cadence. My eyes fill.

"Don't cry," she whispers.

I search for a familiar ring in that whisper.

"Please, don't cry," she repeats.

"Is it you?" I ask.

She turns her head, hiding her eyes from mine.

"Tell me," I beg, "is it you?"

She remains shielded and silent. I reach over and take her chin in my hand to turn her face toward me.

"Let me see your face."

She shakes her head no, but I can see her tears cascading like jewels under her veil.

"How long did you think you could hide from me?" I scold gently.

She tries to turn her head away again, but I hold on tight. "Did you really think I wouldn't see you?"

She shakes her head, mute in response to my probing.

"Do you have any idea how much I've suffered without you?" I choke, anger slipping into my voice. "Do you know how often I thought life wasn't worth living without you? What if I had killed myself?"

Her hand slides out from underneath the burqa and she tries to put her fingers to my lips to quiet me, but I pull my head away and continue to talk.

"Did you think I was going to go away and forget about you? How could you think that? Didn't you know that burning in hell for eternity would be a better punishment than life without you?"

"Hush," she pleads.

"The fire that took you is still burning my heart."

"Please, stop," she whispers.

"No! Why should I? How can I?"

"I beg you, please, stop."

"Did they threaten your family? Was it Keivan? Did they threaten to take him away? Tell me the truth."

"Please, stop, please ..." She weeps, her words interrupted by ragged breaths. I stop and listen to her cries, and it feels as if someone is pulling my heart out of my chest. I'm filled with remorse, and I beg her to forgive me. I try to explain that a volcano has erupted inside me, and although I wish I could temper it, I am not in control.

She leans closer and wipes the tears from my cheeks with the palms of her hands, then quickly pulls back. I explain that I could never really picture my future without her, that it would have been like a vast, barren wasteland, waking each morning and not caring if it was sunny or rainy, hot or cold, early or late, winter or summer. I prayed to God to take me away, to put an end to a life that didn't matter anymore.

She quickly bites the skin between her thumb and index finger and says, "Don't say that!" then breaks into bitter weeping.

"Oh, God! What am I doing?" I say. "What you've gone through, my darling, is a hundred times worse than what I've endured. Forgive me for being so selfish."

"No, no, no! Please, stop saying these things!"

"Your walk, the way you move, your eyes, the way you scratched your head a minute ago, everything tells me that you are my Zari."

"You must stop."

"Let me hold you, let me feel the weight of your body against mine. Tell me that nothing will ever separate us again."

"Oh, God, forgive me," she whimpers. "I should never have let things go this far."

"All I want is for you to promise that you will never do anything like that again!"

"Oh, God, help me. Please, help me!"

"What are you afraid of?"

"Please, God, I'm sorry."

"Why are you sorry?" I say, starting to listen.

"This is going to break his heart—"

"I don't care what you look like," I interrupt. "Your appearance doesn't matter to me. I love you."

"God help me, I should never have let it go this far."

She gently pushes me back when I reach out to embrace her, and in the unbearable silence that follows I stare into her eyes, desperately searching for the answer to a question I don't have the courage to ask. She tries to say something a couple of times but her sobs get in the way.

"What are you trying to say?" I ask.

A long pause follows. My heart pounds, her heart pounds. I can hear both.

"I'm not her!" she cries.

I don't say anything because I'm afraid I'm hearing her right.

"I'm not her," she whispers, shaking her head and whimpering. "Don't you understand? I'm not her. I wish I were, I really do."

"Don't," I beseech, my voice falling away with my hope.

"I knew it would come to this," she weeps. "I foresaw all of this the morning you came home from the hospital. I knew that eventually you'd look for your angel under my veil, but I am not her. She loved you so much, I don't think she would've had the strength to hide behind this mask, no matter what she looked like after that cursed day." She sobs, and her body shakes violently.

I feel as if someone has injected me with ice water. A bitterness blooms in my mouth, rushes through my veins, and burns my skin.

If I had a horse, I would ride it.
If I had a heart, I would hide it.

"I should never have let it go this far, I know that now," she says. "Yes, I watched you every night from this spot—because I was curious about you. I knew you were watching me, and I knew that somewhere in the back of your mind, you were associating me with her. I knew that you saw me through the window while my back was to you, but I let you do it because I liked the way your gaze felt on me. I should've stopped you. I hope you can forgive me for that."

If I knew a rhyme, I would chant it.
If I knew a song, I would sing it.

I feel myself drifting away. Her voice buzzes in my ears, but I don't hear the words. I see her head moving, her body shifting from left to right, her large blue eyes bright in the moonlight, the tears sliding down her cheeks just barely visible beneath her mask. I close my eyes, pull my neck down between my shoulders, lick my lips, and pray to God for this moment to end.

I don't know how long I stay in that state, but when I open my eyes the Masked Angel is still sitting next to me—motionless, quiet, those eyes begging for forgiveness. I stare at the ground for a long time before asking, "Why?"

"I don't know."

I don't say anything because I have nothing to say.

"Maybe I wished I were her," she says. "They call me the Masked Angel, but even an angel can't resist the temptation of desiring love."

I don't respond.

"I wish I had made it clear to you from the start that I wasn't her. Please forgive me for not doing that. Can you forgive me?"

I'm as silent and weary as the stone on Doctor's grave.

"I don't blame you if you can't. Hate me, but please leave as you had planned. It's best for all of us. If she were with us, she would want you to go."

"No, she wouldn't," I say, bitterly.

"Okay," she admits, "you're right, she wouldn't want you to go away."

"No, she wouldn't," I repeat like a difficult child.

"Okay," she says again submissively, "you're right, she wouldn't want you to go away. I remember how sad she was about it. She worried that you'd go away and forget her; that you'd come back with a beautiful, educated wife who would be a million times more desirable than her."

"That would have never happened," I say forcefully.

"I know that now, but I didn't then," she says, "so I couldn't say anything to the contrary. You know, she loved the poetry you used to read to her. She always talked about how you read every verse as if you were the poet."

As she talks, I turn my head away. Her whispering voice makes me angry, and I wish she would stop, but she continues.

"She wouldn't want you to have bitter memories of her," the Masked Angel says quietly. "If she could be here for one minute—just one minute—she would use every second of that time to ask you to move on. She would ask you to do it for her because it would be the only way she could have peace."

She stops for a few seconds.

"She never told anyone about you, except me. I'm the only one who knows how much she loved you. Please trust me when I say that I know she would want you to move on. How could she rest in peace if you ruin your life because of her?"

She stops again and wipes the tears from her face. Then, as if she suddenly remembers something that needs to be said, she asks, "Do you remember her pointing to the biggest star in the sky and saying it was you?"

"Yes."

She leans over and tries to look me in the eye. "You have to go away and never look back. You need to leave the pain here, where it belongs. I know this is what she would want me to ask you. I knew her better than anyone else in the world. She was my cousin, and my best friend. You must trust me."

I scrub at my face with my fists and nod to let her know that I trust her. She cries for a little while, then apologizes again for leading me on and says that she needs to go back inside the house because her aunt and uncle might worry about her. But she doesn't leave; she keeps on talking. She says that she understands now why Zari thought that I had the largest star in the sky, that I have *That*. Zari was a good judge of character, and her assessment of me was right on. She will make sure to learn of my progress in life through our neighbors and my family, and she will pray for me every night for the rest of her life. She assures me that she is going to take care of Zari's parents because they are now her number-one priority. She will be a devoted servant and a lifelong companion to the family.

She stands up and extends her hand to shake, which I do, reluctantly. Her hand is cold, but her grip is warm. I squeeze her hand gently, and she squeezes back. I look down at her long fingers, and her fingernails that look and feel just like Zari's. I look back up and stare into those shining turquoise eyes.

I remember my last night with Zari, when I told her about the conversation I had overheard between her and the Masked Angel. Zari had said that was the last time she had talked to Soraya. The Masked Angel could not know about the night Zari and I spent together in her room, when she pointed to the skies and told me that mine was the biggest star. The next day, she set herself on fire.

"It's you, isn't it?" I whisper.

She starts to quake under her burqa.

"Those are my Zari's eyes," I say.

Her eyes close tight against my gaze.

"Is it you?" I ask again, desperate.

"Yes," she whimpers, "it's me."

Her knees buckle, and she collapses in my arms. I hold her up, pressing her to me as we slowly descend to the floor in each other's arms. I kiss the crown of her head, her forehead, and each closed eye through the fabric of the burqa. Her hands stroke my face, fingers gliding through my hair and meeting to clasp around my neck.

"I love you," I murmur.

"I love you, too," she murmurs back.

"I missed you," I complain.

"I missed you more."

I cradle the back of her head in my palms and pull her forward until our foreheads touch.

"I couldn't have made it without you."

"I'm so sorry."

"Could you hear me talking to you in my dreams?" I ask, rocking her gently.

"Every word," she says, "but I couldn't answer. I hoped you would go away and pursue your dreams, move on and let me fade away."

"What dream is worth pursuing without you?"

"Don't say that!" she cries, stiffening. "You can't stay. You have to promise me that you will go away, just as you've planned."

"No, never," I say, squeezing her tighter.

"But you must, for your sake and for mine, for everyone's safety," she pleads. "Oh, God, I remember you running after me. Your desperate cries of *Ya Ali, Ya Ali* will stay with me forever. I was so sorry for you. I don't know why I took you along to see that horrible scene. Maybe unconsciously I was hoping that your being there would change my mind. I'm so sorry. I'm so sorry, darling."

Zari reaches under her burqa to wipe away her tears. I press her against me to calm her down.

"The pain I felt for you was by far more hurtful than my burn marks. I remember the siren, the paramedics working on me, and the hospital. I could tolerate my own pain if I knew you were okay. No one talked to me about anything except the care I was to receive. My shoulders, neck, and parts of my face were burned, not too badly though. It looked a lot worse than it really was. I knew that my hair had been shorn, and that I had bandages on my head. I wanted to ask about Ahmed, Faheemeh, and you, but I couldn't because I didn't want to associate any of you with myself. Late at night, however, I secretly prayed for you all. Sometimes I repeated the same prayer hundreds of times, reasoning with myself that the more I recited the prayer, the greater the probability that God would take my requests seriously.

"A man visited me in the hospital every day: the same man who had punched Doctor in the face, the man with the radio. He watched me for hours from behind a large window, talked to the doctors and nurses, and took notes. He looked at me with a strange, sad gaze. He seemed to feel sorry for me. Once, I woke up in the middle of the night and found him standing by my bed, staring at me with that look on his face. I wanted to say something, but he left right away.

"I was brutally tormented by my separation from you, and that's how I knew that I truly loved you. I cursed myself for asking you to go along. What could you possibly gain from the experience of watching me set myself on fire, except a lifetime of torment and agony? I'm so sorry, darling, so sorry. And then, to make matters worse, I was alive and no one knew it. I wanted to die. I wished I had died. The pain I had caused you, Faheemeh, and Ahmed, and, of course, my parents. That was all unbearable to me. And now, my parents have to live the rest of their lives in exile for what I did. I wish I had died. I'm so sorry."

"I understand." I nod, while thanking God for keeping her alive.

"For my own sake, I never regretted my action," Zari says, "but I deeply apologize for involving the rest of you. I had to do what I did. Someone had to. Someone had to make a statement, in public, loudly and defiantly. Doctor used to say that the regime doesn't understand that killing people doesn't scare the activists and that death is a small price to pay for freedom."

Zari stops and collects her breath; she is trembling under her burqa.

"For every one they kill in private, ten people should do what I did in public, so the regime can see that killing only makes their crimes more visible."

Zari takes another short break.

"When my skin began to heal, they moved me to a different floor and a different room, where I had a window view into a yard that seemed to be always filled with people. The ambiguity around my fate had begun to wear me down. I used to sit by the window and wonder if you were okay, if you had gone to the United States, if Ahmed and Faheemeh were free and still together."

"I did the same in my room," I say. "Except I wondered if you could see me, if you could hear me. I cried and I kept asking why."

"And I would talk to you every night," she says. "I would hold you in my arms, caress your face, your hair. I would kiss your lips. I would have died if something had happened to you. The pain would have killed me."

Her breathing becomes irregular as if she is hyperventilating. "Are you okay?" I ask, extremely concerned.

She nods before continuing. "I had no communication with anyone; no television, no radio, and no newspaper. I didn't know what time it was, what day it was, or even what month. I had no idea what was going on in the world, except that the Shah was still in power because the man with the radio still visited me every day. Many nights I dreamed of our summer days by the *hose* under the cherry tree, and when I woke up I felt as if someone had placed a ton of bricks on my chest. I would try to remember what your face looked like, but I couldn't. For some reason, the more desperately I missed you, the harder it was for me to picture your face in my mind.

"One night I woke up in the middle of the night and realized that a pencil and some papers had been placed next to my bed. I immediately began to draw a picture of you. It was astounding how the eyes of my mind couldn't see your face, but my hands had no trouble tracing your every feature on the paper." Zari reaches over and touches my face lovingly. I can see through the holes in the burqa that her eyes are closed.

"When I finished the picture, I placed it on the nightstand by my bed and fell asleep. The next morning when I woke, the picture, the pencil, and the papers were gone.

"Later that day, I saw the man with the radio outside my window, and realized that the paper and the pencil had been placed by my bed to trick me into writing or drawing something that would give the agent a clue to the identity of my cohorts. The thought of you being hunted by that evil man threw me into a frenzy. I yelled, screamed, and beat myself in despair, cursing the Shah, his family, and all his supporters. The nurses rushed into the room, tied me to the bed, and gave me an injection that made me fall asleep.

"When I woke up, the man with the radio was in my room. He was standing close to the door, and he held my drawing in his hands. We stared at each other silently for a long time before he told me that he wasn't there to hurt me. He wanted me to relax and calm down. The soft tone in his voice eased my nerves. I asked what he was there for and he walked up to me and put my drawing on the bed. I picked it up, and pressed it to my heart. He whispered to me that he was not going to hurt the young man in the picture. They had been investigating all of us for a long time and were completely sure that we had nothing to do with Doctor's actions. 'Not affiliated with his group,' as he put it. Then he told me that I was going home, and that my parents had already been contacted. Since my father was an Olympic champion, the government had decided not to punish me, despite my stupid behavior on his majesty's birthday. However, my whole family was to be exiled to Bandar Abbas, where we would live the rest of our lives by the Persian Gulf, away from the rest of our relatives. He pointed to the drawing in my hands, and said that it would be best if I had no contact with the person in the picture. It was also made very clear to me that I shouldn't talk to Ahmed and Faheemeh. It was then that the idea of me masquerading as the Masked Angel was discussed. He suggested it and I thought it was a good idea. This was the only way I could still be around for a while. I wanted to see you desperately, and I wanted to be with my parents."

Zari stops, and I tighten my grip on her. "I love you," I whisper. "I love you."

"I love you, too," she whispers back.

I want to say that I'm surprised her parents agreed to this arrangement, but then I realize how Mr. and Mrs. Naderi must have suffered thinking that they had lost Zari. Pretending that she was dead to keep her alive was a small price they would have paid gladly.

I can tell from the way Zari leans against me that she's exhausted. I'm moved by her strength and courage. She never once complained of her personal pain, the unfairness of her fate, or her burned skin.

She grabs my chin, pushes my face up, and looks into my eyes. "Now you see why you have to leave. I can't be with you, and I can't go back."

I hold her tight. "But they cleared us," I whisper in despair.

"No, they cleared you and Ahmed. I still have to pay for what I did."

I press her harder against my chest.

"A lot can happen in a few years," she says. "Things will change—they always do—and then it might be safe for us to be together."

"How badly were you hurt?" I ask.

She shakes her head. I take hold of her face and start kissing her over the burqa.

"The thought of you being in so much pain kills me," I whisper.

"It wasn't bad," she says softly. "It really wasn't that bad. Maybe someday they can make the scars go away with plastic surgery. Who knows? The world is changing so rapidly. That's another reason you need to leave. You can find the best doctors in the U.S., and then you can send for me. When I get there, they can clean up my face and my body, and I can be pretty again. Then you can marry me and we'll have little babies." Her voice breaks. "I need you to go away."

I stay silent, hoping that if I don't speak, I won't have to agree.

"Trust me, it isn't easy for me to let you go. I'm miserable without you. There hasn't been a moment since last summer that I haven't thought about you. We need to make this small sacrifice now to ensure that we are together in the future. And between now and then I will dream every night about the day people start calling us Pasha and Zari Shahed."

"Mr. and Mrs. Shahed," I say.

"I love the sound of that."

"I love you." I squeeze her to me, and for the first time in months, the iron band around my chest is gone. The lump that had blocked my throat seems to have suddenly melted.

"I am yours," I whisper. "Do what you will with me."

"Then I'm sending you away."

We hold each other through the rest of the night, and soon the sun starts to rise in the east and the darkness gradually falls away. We sit there, her head on my chest, fingers entwined, her legs draped over mine, and watch the world come to life. I close my eyes and shut out all distractions, so that I can memorize every detail.

"Come to my room, I want you to have something," she says, stretching to rise. I follow her to her room, where everything is packed in boxes and ready to be carried away. She gives me the picture she had drawn of me in the alley. This time, however, my mystery woman has a face. Her face.

"Don't forget me," she says.

I think of her in a desert of loneliness while I'm abroad, and an idea forms. "If you feel lost," I say, pulling her close once more, "look to the sky and you'll see us there, together."

"I know your star, but which one's mine?" she asks, letting her weight sink into me for just a moment.

"The biggest, brightest one."

"That's you," she corrects.

"That's us," I whisper. "We share the same star."

Dear Reader:

I'm thrilled to welcome you to the world of *Rooftops of Tehran*.

I discovered the gift of reading when I was ten years old, sitting on my own rooftop in Tehran and losing myself in a Farsi translation of Jack London's *White Fang*. I was blown away by the power of words to take me to a place I hardly knew and make me feel as if I'd lived there all my life. It was an experience that never left me. Much later, I began to write stories of my own and quickly realized that writing was more satisfying than anything else I'd ever done. I'd start early in the evening and pause at dawn, exhausted, elated and barely aware that the night had passed.

In writing *Rooftops of Tehran*, I wanted to acquaint readers with Iran, and bring to life a small part of the centuries-old Persian culture. At a time when the country of my birth is often portrayed in the news media as "the enemy," I chose to tell a story about friendship and humor, love and hope, universal experiences valued by people in all times and places. I wanted to show a side of Iran that's usually hidden from view—its warm, funny, generous people. Perhaps as you read the novel—as you meet Pasha's friends Ahmed, Faheemeh, Doctor, Iraj and Zari; as you accompany Pasha down the alleys of his neighborhood; as you spend a night on his roof, peek into his neighbor's window, and fall in love with the girl next door—you'll understand my affection for Iran and its people. And you will see why the flame of hope for Iran still burns so fiercely in my heart, and in the hearts of so many Iranians at home and abroad.

Since I first lost myself in *White Fang* so many years ago, I've read hundreds of books, and often wished afterward that I could share my thoughts and feelings directly with the author. So I invite you to contact me. If you'd like to express a comment about *Rooftops of Tehran*, or if your book club would like to arrange a visit via speakerphone, just send a note to Mahbod@ rooftopsoftehran.com. I'd be delighted to discuss my novel, and share my story.

Best!
Mahbod Seraji

Rooftops of Tehran

❧

Mahbod Seraji

A CONVERSATION
WITH MAHBOD SERAJI

Q. You've lived in the United States for thirty-two years, since you arrived at the age of nineteen. What inspired you to write your first novel at this point in your life, and how much is it based on actual events?
A. Thank you for letting everyone know that I'm an old man!

Q. Old? I don't see how that's possible since I'm several years your senior, and I'm in the prime of life!
A. Ah, but it's well known that editors remain forever young. Anyway, getting back to your question, I've wanted to write ever since I was ten years old when I read my first book, Jack London's *White Fang*, a translation into Persian from the original English, on the same rooftop that's depicted in this novel. But life always got in the way of my writing. Then, a few years ago, I lost my job, and that was the best thing that ever happened to me. I started writing and haven't stopped since.

As for the novel, some of it is based on actual events, but not all of it. So it's important to point out that this is *not* an autobiography. It's also important to note that I fictionalized Golesorkhi's trial by changing the date and some of the words he used defending himself in court.

Q. You came to this country speaking very little English, but have obviously mastered the language. How did you accomplish that, and

what was it like to face the formidable challenge of learning a for-
eign language, in a strange new land, without the support of family
nearby?

A. I wish I could say that I've mastered the English language.
There's always more to learn! Learning a new language is a challenge faced by millions of people living in countries other than
their homelands, and learning English is hard. One of the hardest
things I've ever done. When I first came to the United States, I
ate Big Mac, Small Fries, Small Coke for six weeks because that's
all I knew how to order. I'm sure the McDonald's Corporation's
revenue skyrocketed that quarter! The trick to learning any foreign language lies in assimilating yourself into the culture of your
host country, mingling with the native speakers, watching lots
of television, and—the one factor that unfortunately many people ignore—reading as much as you can. The first non-textbook
English-language book I read was Erich Fromm's *Art of Loving*.
And for me that translated into the Art of Loving to Read. Since
then, I've been reading religiously. Some of my favorite authors
are named in *Rooftops of Tehran*: Emile Zola, Fyodor Dostoyevsky,
Maxim Gorky, Jack London, John Steinbeck, Bernard Shaw, Noam
Chomsky, and many others.

Q. In the novel, you convey the love-hate relationship that Persians
had with the United States in the 1970s—and some very funny mis-
conceptions. The U.S. was the power behind the oppressive Shah,
and thus their hated enemy, yet also a place whose freedoms and op-
portunities beckoned to them—what an emotional tug-of-war that
contradiction must have created! What surprised you about Ameri-
can society when you arrived here, and what misconceptions about
Iran do you still encounter among Americans?

A. I don't want to generalize or offend anyone in either country,
so please forgive me if I do. Americans are wonderful people:
kind, accepting, honest. They tend to do as they say and act in

fair-minded, balanced ways. This country's higher education system is excellent, both in terms of quality and accessibility. Here anybody can go to college. Many countries simply can't accommodate many students. And by the way, most people who came here in the seventies came to get an education. They didn't wake up one morning and say, "I'm going to America to be free." They said, "I'll go there to get an education." That's an important distinction. It was only after they were here for a while that they fully appreciated the freedoms we enjoy here.

What surprised me when I first arrived was how, despite the abundance of information available, only a small number of people knew about, or had any interest in knowing about, what was happening in the rest of the world. To a large extent, that's also true today. I was shocked, for example, to learn how little most people I met knew about Iran. I remember once during a class discussion, while attending college in the '70s, I mentioned the CIA's successful 1953 overthrow of Mosaddegh, the only democratically elected prime minister in the history of Iran, and half of the class accused me of lying because "the American government just doesn't do bad things like that." Even the teacher said I had my facts wrong.

Some Americans have a blind faith in their government. I mean, think about it. Institutional democracies such as America's must not support, in fact should oppose, undemocratic actions, movements, or forces anywhere in the world, at least in theory, right? But that's not always true in practice, and that's what some Americans have a hard time believing or even comprehending. Consider the situation in Iraq today, the summer before the U.S. presidential election. There are still people who are looking under rocks for weapons of mass destruction. They genuinely can't fathom that their government deceived them.

Iranians and Americans are on the opposite ends of the spectrum on this issue. It might take an act of God to convince some Americans that parts of their government are corrupt, but at the same time, you cannot, under any circumstances, persuade an Iranian that his government is *not* corrupt! Fascinating, isn't it?

As for current Americans' misconceptions about Iran, I see a lot of misrepresentation in the media. Because the governments of Iran and the U.S. don't get along, we tend to mischaracterize the people of Iran as evil. The media immediately conveys images and information that dehumanizes the Iranian people. Likewise, we're encouraged to forget that our so-called enemies have feelings and are capable of love and friendship. We see them as so dissimilar, we can't imagine that we may actually have a lot in common. It's really sad for me to see how far apart these two great nations have fallen.

Q. Americans know very little about Persian history. I was especially interested to learn of the long periods of occupation and oppression by foreign invaders that Persians have endured over the centuries. Are there obvious ways in which that history continues to shape Persian culture and society?

A. Iran is one of the oldest civilizations in the world, with an interesting, tumultuous history. Three massive invasions have left indelible marks on our culture, psychology, literature, and arts. These invasions included that of Alexander the Great, called in Iran "the cursed Alexander"; the Arabs; and Genghis Khan. Millions of Iranians lost their lives in those invasions, and were subjected to unimaginable violence, and modern-day Persians have not forgotten. In between those invasions our people suffered grim atrocities committed by our own homegrown despots. Each nation's history, and the way in which its people respond to it, help define the culture of that country. So because of our history, we tend to have a grim and fatalistic outlook on life. We suffer from pessimism. We're suspicious of authority figures, always feel victimized, and unwaveringly believe in the existence of unseen forces that control events from behind the curtains. We see strings where there are no puppets. At the same time, it's important to note that we are a resilient people and we can survive almost anything; nothing can break the passionate Persian spirit. We love to argue—not discuss, but argue politics. Family is very important to us. Our friendships are legendary. We are a generous nation, kind and extremely hospitable. Even now, many Americans who visit Iran talk about being overwhelmed by the warmth and hospitality of the Iranians they meet in public places. You hear stories of cabdrivers not taking money from their American passengers, restaurant owners not charging Americans for food, regular people going out of their way to help Americans. I know some readers may find this hard to believe, but it's true.

Q. Do you still visit Iran? How has it changed since you were growing up there?
A. I do go back for visits. My father still lives in Iran. I can't find my way around Tehran anymore—it's grown so much! And people are different. There is a feeling of melancholy in the air that you sense immediately upon your arrival. But, amazingly enough, as you get back into the daily routine of life, you rediscover that indomitable Persian spirit, that "we'll survive anything" attitude!

Q. I think of Iran as a rocky, barren, hot desert country. Yet when you sent me some pictures of Tehran, I was surprised to see that it's quite green, with full-sized trees, and that it snows there. Can you give us some idea of the size and geographical diversity of the country? And how much of a middle class does Iran have, compared to those who live in poverty?
A. Contrary to popular belief, Iran is one of the most mountainous countries on the planet. It's actually a pretty large country, sixteenth in the world in terms of its size, about one-fifth the size

of the USA, with a diverse population of over 70 million people consisting of such ethnic groups as the Azaris, Baluchs, Kurds, Lurs, Assyrians, Armenians, and many more. There are two large mountain ranges, Zagros and Alborz. The highest peak, the volcanic but thankfully dormant Mount Damavand, is 5,678 meters (or 18,628 feet) high. It's an easy-to-remember number and used to be a favorite geography quiz question, when I was in high school in Iran. There are two great salt deserts in the eastern part of Iran, mostly uninhabited. The climate varies from region to region. Winters can be bitterly cold with heavy snowfalls in the northwest. Spring and fall are absolutely gorgeous regardless of where you are. And summers can be hot and dry in some areas, and very humid in others, particularly in the north by the Caspian Sea and in the south near the Persian Gulf. In terms of wealth, the United Nations considers Iran a semi-developed country; its GDP is ranked fifteenth in the world. So Iran is not one big desert wasteland like many people think. Because of the type of work I do, I've traveled widely throughout the world, and the area by the Caspian Sea is one of the most lush and beautiful I've seen anywhere. In terms of standard of living, according to the figures I've seen on the Internet for 2007, approximately 18 percent of the population in Iran lives below the poverty line (compared to 12 percent in the U.S.). And of the almost 30 million people who make up the workforce, 15 percent to 20 percent, depending on whose statistics you believe, are unemployed. So there is a middle class in Iran, but I believe it's shrinking.

Q. Now that you've answered some of my many questions about Iran, let's get back to the book! One of the reasons I was originally drawn to the novel is because the love story between Pasha and Zari is so romantic. Are you in particular a romantic, or is that a Persian quality?
A. My friends will tease me for the rest of my life if I even hint at having a single drop of romantic blood in me! My wife may go into

shock. So let's be careful with this one! I think readers will connect with Zari and Pasha because everyone remembers the first time they fell in love. Zari's and Pasha's youth puts them in an impossible situation to begin with, and if you add their restrictive social conventions and Doctor's state of affairs, their situation becomes hopeless. And by the way, that is the dictionary definition of "romantic" in Persian literature. The beauty in romance lies in its inevitable tragic ending. What's worth giving your life for is what you can't have. For those who are interested in learning more about this topic, *Iranian Culture—A Persianist View* by Dr. Michael Hillmann (University Press of America, 1991) is a great source.

Q. In the novel's original version, the narrator was never given a name. Why was that your first choice and why did you change your mind and call him Pasha?
A. Well, the narrator is me, and those who know me will immediately recognize him as me. But I didn't want to give him my name. So I left him nameless, and I was getting away with it until you, my wonderful editor, convinced me that it's time for him and me to decouple, to go our separate ways, and to live separate lives. Then I couldn't find a name for him. Eventually I chose Pasha Shahed. Pasha would have been my first name if Mahbod wasn't chosen, and Shahed is my father's pseudonym, and also my mother's maiden name. My father is a Sufi poet who has published three books of poetry in Iran.

Q. In so many ways, the characters and events of the novel remind me of what is universal in the human experience—the essential support offered by caring friends and family, the power of humor to see us through tough times, the clever and not-so-clever ways in which people submit to, and resist, political repression, the desire to love and be loved. Yet Zari's horrific choice, and the characters' extravagant response to grief, may both seem very foreign to Western readers. Can you help put those acts in a context for us that might help us to understand them?

A. Yes, love, hate, humor, friendships are universal qualities shared by people of all nations. You're also right in that our cultures influence the ways in which we may respond to situations. In my non-writing life, I teach a course called "Understanding Personal and Cultural Differences." Persians, and Middle Easterners in general, live in what the experts call "Affective" cultures. These are cultures in which people freely show their emotions, especially in times of mourning. Americans, the British, and the Germans live in "Neutral" cultures. In these cultures people don't demonstrate their feelings; they keep them tightly under control. So, for example, the experience of attending a funeral in the U.S. would be very different from attending one in Iran. The Neutral people would come across as cold and unfeeling to the people in the Affective cultures, and conversely the Neutral people would see the Affective people as too emotional and overly expressive.

As for Zari's "horrific choice," I'd rather not give too much of the story away by commenting on it, except to say that what she does is not a common practice in Iran. It does occur, but rarely. She deliberately chooses such an extreme act to make a powerful statement.

Q. Do you plan to write another novel? Do you know yet what it will be about?

A. I'm already halfway through the second book. It's about a man who has four wives but feels he has been deprived of love all his life! I don't have a title for it yet. And someday, I'm not at all sure when, I will certainly write a sequel to *Rooftops*. I just need some time away from it for now.

QUESTIONS
FOR DISCUSSION

1. What's your general reaction to the novel? Did the author make the characters come alive for you? Did you care about them? Were you fully engaged? Did you laugh and cry?

2. Does Pasha's love for Zari remind you of the first time you fell in love? How is it similar? How is it different?

3. Ahmed, Faheemeh, Iraj, Doctor, Zari, and Pasha are young people in the Iran of the 1970s. How universal are the challenges they face? How common are their thoughts and feelings, discussions and interactions, reactions to authority, methods of going after what they want? Compare the young adults in the novel to ones you know in the U.S. today.

4. Do you agree with Doctor that time is the most precious human commodity?

5. What do you think about the open, unguarded nature of the male relationships in this novel, especially between Pasha and Ahmed? How would such a close male friendship in the U.S. be likely to differ?

6. Discuss the relationship between Pasha and his father. How is it similar to, or different from, the father–teenage son relationships you know?

7. Discuss the lives of the women in the novel. What surprises you about them and what doesn't?

8. The concept of *That* is discussed a number of times. What does this concept mean to you? Is there a Western equivalent?

9. What do you think motivates Zari's bold and tragic action during the parade? Do you see her choice as honorable or delusional, or something in between? How might a Western woman in a similar predicament react?

10. What aspects of Persian culture most intrigue you? Did the novel change or challenge any of your notions about Iran and Iranians? What did you learn?

11. The narrator discusses the unique way in which people in Iran react to grief, and the author dramatizes many scenes of mourning. What surprised you about those scenes? How do the characters mourn differently from the way people do in the U.S.?

12. Discuss how characters in the novel perceive the U.S., both accurately and inaccurately. What factors might be limiting or distorting their understanding? What distortions might be shaping your own understanding of Iran and Iranians?

13. What do you think happens to Pasha after the book ends? To the other characters?

RECOMMENDED READING

History and Culture

A History of Modern Iran by Ervand Abrahamian (Cambridge University Press, 2008)

Iran Between Two Revolutions by Ervand Abrahamian (Princeton University Press, 1982)

Targeting Iran by Noam Chomsky, Ervand Abrahamian, Nahid Mozaffari (City Lights Bookstore, 2007)

All the Shah's Men by Stephen Kinzer (John Wiley and Sons, Inc., 2008)

Iranian Culture by Michael Hillmann (United Press of America, 1990)

The Soul of Iran: A Nation's Journey to Freedom by Afshin Molavi (W. W. Norton, 2005)

The History of Iran by Elton Daniel (Greenwood Press, 2001)

Iran by Richard Frye (Mazda Publishers, 2005)

The Heritage of Persia by Richard Frye (Mazda Publishers, 1993)

Modern Iran: Roots and Results of Revolution by Nikki R. Keddie (Yale University Press, 2006)

The Iran Agenda by Ruse Erlich (Polipoint Press, 2007)

Memoirs, Novels, Poetry

Funny in Farsi by Firoozeh Dumas (Random House, 2004)

Reading Lolita in Tehran by Azar Nafisi (Random House, 2004)

House of Sand and Fog by Andre Dubus III (Vintage Books, 1990)

My Uncle Napoleon by Iraj Pezeshkzad, translated by Dick Davis (Mage Publishers, 2004)

Epic and Sedition: The Case of Ferdowski Shahnameh by Dick Davis (Mage, 2006)

The Rubaiyat of Omar Khayyam by Omar Khayyam, translated by Edward Fitzgerald (Collier Books, 1962)

The Love Poems of Ahmad Shamlu by Firoozeh Papen-Martin (Ibex Publishers, 2005)

Strange Times, My Dear, edited by Nahid Mozaffari (Arcade Publishing, 2005)

Neither East Nor West by Christiane Bird (Washington Square Press, 2002)

Mahbod Seraji was born in Iran and moved to the United States in 1976 at the age of nineteen. He attended the University of Iowa, where he received an MA in film and broadcasting and a Ph.D. in instructional design and technology. He currently works as a management consultant, and lives in the San Francisco Bay Area.

Please visit him on the Web at mahbodseraji.com and rooftopsof tehran.com.